The Silver Chariot Killer

Also by Richard A. Lupoff

Edgar Rice Burroughs: Master of Adventure (1965)
The Case of the Doctor Who Had No Business, or The Adventure of the
    Second Anonymous Narrator (1966)
One Million Centuries (1967)
Sacred Locomotive Flies (1971)
Into the Aether (1974)
Edgar Rice Burroughs and the Martian Vision (1976)
The Triune Man (1976)
Sandworld (1976)
Lisa Kane (1976)
The Crack in the Sky (1976)
Sword of the Demon (1977)
The Return of Skull-Face (with Robert E. Howard) (1977)
Space War Blues (1978)
Nebogipfel at the End of Time (1979)
The Ova Hamlet Papers (1979)
Stroka Prospekt (1982)
Circumpolar! (1984)
Sun's End (1984)
The Digital Wristwatch of Philip K. Dick (1985)
Lovecraft's Book (1985)
Countersolar! (1986)
Galaxy's End (1988)
The Forever City (1988)
The Black Tower (1988)
The Comic Book Killer (1988)
The Final Battle (1990)
The Classic Car Killer (1992)
Night of the Living Gator (1992)
The Bessie Blue Killer (1994)
Hyperprism (1994)
The Sepia Siren Killer (1994)
The Cover Girl Killer (1995)
Before 12:01 . . . and After (1996)
The Radio Red Killer (Forthcoming)

RICHARD A. LUPOFF

The Silver Chariot Killer

A Hobart Lindsey Mystery

ST. MARTIN'S PRESS 🙠 NEW YORK

THE SILVER CHARIOT KILLER. Copyright © 1996 by Richard A. Lupoff. All rights reserved. Printed in the United States of America. No part of this book may be used or reproduced in any manner whatsoever without written permission except in the case of brief quotations embodied in critical articles or reviews. For information, address St. Martin's Press, 175 Fifth Avenue, New York, N.Y. 10010.

Introduction Copyright © 1996 by Steven Saylor.

Edited by Gordon Van Gelder

Library of Congress Cataloging-in-Publication Data

Lupoff, Richard A.
    The silver chariot killer : a Hobart Lindsey mystery / Richard A. Lupoff. —1st ed.
        p.   cm.
    ISBN 0–312–14736–8
    1. Lindsey, Hobart (Fictitious character)—Fiction.   I. Title.
PS3562.U6S5   1996
813'.54—dc20   96–20058
                                                           CIP

First Edition: October 1996

10   9   8   7   6   5   4   3   2   1

For Whitey, Congo, Mr. Jinx, Smokey, Lady, Pepper, Snoopy, Bonzo, Lucy, Magnum, Daisy, Ramona, and Mister Boris Peabody. Faithful friends, none of whom has ever read a word I wrote.

Introduction

by Steven Saylor

ONE OF THE treats of working in publishing is getting to read books before they're actually published—sometimes hot off the word processor, in fact. Last week I read two prepublished books. One was my own latest novel about ancient murder and mayhem, which I reread as typeset galleys (for work); the other was the book you hold in your hands, which I had the rare privilege of reading in manuscript (for pleasure).

At first glance, you might not think that Richard Lupoff's *The Silver Chariot Killer* (which takes place mostly in modern New York) and my own *A Murder on the Appian Way* (set in 52 B.C.) could have much in common, aside from the fact that both revolve around a murder and so come under the increasingly flexible genre classification of "mystery and suspense." Yes, both are whodunits—but they share something more than that, something very significant. Both draw a special energy and inspiration from a certain place, a city that is more than just a city, whose legendary name evokes a whole registry of ideas and emotions spanning hundreds of lifetimes.

Here's a clue: All roads are said to lead there.

And when you're there, you must do as the locals do.

And while you're there, if you throw a coin into a certain fountain, destiny will inevitably bring you boomeranging back.

And the place will definitely still be there when you return, because it's the Eternal City.

The place is so legendary, you see, that our epigrams about it have become clichés.

But clichés can be powerful. Just ask any politician—but especially one with a fascist bent, like Benito Mussolini, who played at being Caesar and updated Roman ideals of order and beauty into twentieth-century jackbooted kitsch. Or consider a modern-day, right-wing politician like Randolph Amoroso in *The Silver Chariot Killer*, who proudly speaks of establishing an American empire to rival Rome's. Crazy, you say? It could never happen here? Amoroso thinks it could—and believes his movement would become unstoppable if only he could lay his hands on a certain ancient artifact . . .

Ah, but I'm getting ahead of the story, and that wouldn't be fair to anyone about to plunge into *The Silver Chariot Killer*.

Besides a fascination with Rome, there's something else that Dick Lupoff and I have in common: a passion for obscure, vintage mysteries. It turns out we've both read a whodunit from 1935 called *The Julius Caesar Murder Case*, by Wallace Irwin. Irwin's conceit was to have guys like Caesar and Mark Antony talk (and behave) like gangsters in a Hammett novel. The device works better than you might think, because when you come right down to it, Caesar and company pretty much *were* gangsters. (To drive home the point, Irwin sardonically dedicated the novel to Mussolini and Hitler.) Ancient Rome hasn't been the only place where you couldn't tell the politicians and the gangsters apart. It's happened before and it'll happen again. That's one of the implicit themes in *The Silver Chariot Killer*: the way things get all twisted and screwy when rich, powerful men become indistinguishable from criminals—are, in fact, criminals, though careful never to be classified as such.

More immediate dangers confront Lupoff's dogged sleuth, Hobart Lindsey—like the threat of getting blown away in some dark, slushy New York alley for snooping into the details of a brutal murder best left unexplained. But when you're a crack insurance claims adjuster, and you work for a boss like the imperious Desmond Richelieu, and the victim was one of your own co-workers, you don't let the threat of getting blown away deter you—not if you're made of the same stuff as Hobart Lindsey.

But what, readers of the five previous books in the series will ask, of Marvia Plum? Marvia, who's taken part in all of Lindsey's past investigations, beginning with *The Comic Book Killer* (1988). Marvia, who made her exit from Lindsey's life last time out, in *The Cover Girl Killer* (1995), when she married someone else. Lindsey misses her sorely, and so do we. Will Marvia come back? Is Lindsey's life possible without her? My lips are sealed.

I *can* tell you that a fascinating new female enters Lindsey's life in *The Silver Chariot Killer*, though this relationship is more avuncular than romantic. The reader may well decide that, as with Rome, all roads lead to Anna Maria Berry, the black, Jewish, Italian-American computer whiz kid and history maven. Indeed, with her mixed heritage, her knowledge of the past, and her computer-age outlook, Anna Maria seems the culmination of three thousand years of history, all wrapped up in a single girl. You'll meet her soon.

I feel at home in Lupoff's New York, even if Denverite Hobart Lindsey doesn't. It's a long way from my usual stamping grounds in ancient Rome, but here in *The Silver Chariot Killer* are a pair of brothers named Cletus and Petrus, from a city called Pinopolis; here is the chill season of the midwinter holiday (called Christmas by Hobart Lindsey, but better known as Saturnalia to my sleuth, Gordianus the Finder); here is the stimulating mix of races, nationalities, sexualities, and religions that makes a city truly cosmopolitan, whether it be modern New York or ancient Rome; here are the rich and the poor, the powerful and the powerless, the wise and the superstitious, the greedy and the generous, hunters and hunted, killers and victims.

Of course, Lupoff strikes some notes that are strictly modern—such as the young woman with the pierced tongue, the ins and outs of the Internet, and the deft citations of cultural nostalgia that emerge from watching too much AMC on television. (Those making fleeting cameo appearances in Hobart Lindsey's nostalgia-ridden imagination this time out include Bela Lugosi in *White Zombie* and another shared Lupoff-Saylor taste, Edna May Oliver as the one-and-only Miss Hildegarde Withers.)

Best of all, there is the eponymous silver chariot itself, said to have been the plaything of Julius Caesar. Lupoff describes the fabulous provenance of this artifact in fascinating detail—but does such a chariot really exist? Is it the stuff of gauzy myth, or of harsh, murderous reality? A mere MacGuffin, as Hitchcock might say, or a near-mystical "Numinous Object," as Auden said of Tolkien's ring, resonant with psychological magic? Will Lindsey discover the truth—or will the silver chariot prove to be as elusive as that famous bird of Malta, always just out of reach?

You have only to turn the page to begin to find out . . .

Chapter One

Berry was dead, to begin with. There is no doubt whatever about that. The register of his burial was signed by the clergyman, the clerk, the undertaker, and the chief mourner. Richelieu signed it. And Richelieu's name was good upon the 'Net for anything he chose to put his hand to. Old Berry was dead as a doornail.

Lindsey closed the glossy in-flight magazine and slipped it into the pocket of the seat in front of him. Leave it to the airlines to revive Dickens for the Christmas issue. He leaned his forehead against the Plexiglas window and let his attention wander across the moonlit clouds beyond the big jetliner's wing.

Of course it wasn't Berry, it was Marley. And it wasn't Richelieu, it was Scrooge. And it wasn't the Internet, it was the London Stock Exchange.

But Cletus Berry was dead, dead if not yet buried, dead as a doornail. And Hobart Lindsey was flying to New York, probably in time for Berry's funeral and certainly in time to try and find out what had happened to his—to his what?

Berry had been his fellow employee of International Surety. They'd been roommates during the orientation seminar when both of them were selected for SPUDS, International Surety's Special Projects Unit, and Berry had helped Lindsey research a couple of tricky cases. Probably that made them friends, or as close to friends as their positions allowed them to be in the wonderful world of the modern corporation.

There was still a cup of airline coffee on Lindsey's tray. He picked it up and sipped. The coffee had been weak and stale to start with. Now it was cold as well. He reached under his seat and pulled out the carrying case with his company-issue laptop computer.

He looked around for someone to take the coffee away. The flight attendants were decked out in Santa Claus hats. These made a complement to their quasi-naval uniforms. But at the moment there were no flight attendants near Lindsey's row. The passenger to his left, a seriously overweight teenager wearing a Denver Nuggets cap with the bill pointing backward, had fallen asleep and was wheezing softly with each breath. He wore a sweat-stained T-shirt with a picture of a giant mistletoe on the chest and the motto KISS ME, IT'S CHRISTMAS! There was no climbing over him, and Lindsey didn't want to shake him awake and ask him to let him reach the aisle.

Finally Lindsey got rid of the coffee by swallowing it and put the empty cup carefully on the cabin floor. He booted up the computer and opened the file on the murder of his friend.

There wasn't much there. Lindsey had showed up at the Special Projects Unit of International Surety, in Denver, as usual that morning. The air was sparkling and the cold didn't bother him too much. As Mondays went, this one looked pretty good. Lindsey was starting to feel comfortable in his new assignment as Desmond Richelieu's deputy. Well, less uncomfortable, anyway, than he had been when he first agreed to take the job.

For once Mrs. Blomquist had motioned Lindsey straight into the director's office with no corporate bureaucratic shenanigans to delay him. And for once Richelieu hadn't been seated behind his desk, his pinstriped suit immaculate and his gold-rimmed glasses reflecting the Colorado sunlight.

Richelieu had been pacing, and his salt-and-pepper hair had been in disarray.

He shoved a paper at Lindsey, a print of the morning report from International Surety's New York regional headquarters, designated in the corporate plan as Manhattan East.

Special Projects Unit—SPUDS—acted like a private empire within International Surety, but every "detached" SPUDS operative kept up a liaison with the local offices of the company. International Surety was as procedure bound and paper heavy as any multinational, but SPUDS agents were freed from the usual corporate structure. They reported directly to Richelieu. The director ran SPUDS the way his onetime mentor, J. Edgar Hoover, had run the Federal Bureau of Investigation. The FBI was Hoover's private empire inside the Department of Justice, and SPUDS was Desmond "Ducky" Richelieu's private empire inside International Surety.

The toughest cases came to SPUDS, the weirdest cases, and the biggest cases. Hobart Lindsey had handled some of the best—or worst—of them, but now he was on his way to New York to take care of a matter that had rattled his boss's empire to its foundation.

Cletus Berry had been found in an alley in Hell's Kitchen, the old New York slum to the west of the theater district and Times Square. The word had come via KlameNet/Plus from Morris A. Zissler, assistant to the International Surety branch manager, Manhattan East.

Lindsey took the computer printout and hurried from Richelieu's imposing suite to his own modest office. He picked up a telephone and called Zissler. From Zissler he got a few details.

It had been a freezing December morning in New York. A sanitation worker—they used to be garbagemen, Lindsey thought—had entered the alley to pick up a load of trash. He found Berry. He called the cops. By the time they arrived at the scene, the body had lain in the freezing sleet long enough that the coroner's technicians had had to chip it out of the ice.

Not that Berry was alone. With him was one Frankie Fulton, familiarly known as "FF," in part because those were his initials, but mainly because he was a longtime petty criminal, unsuccessful gambler, and perennial gangster wannabe.

Early in his career, Frankie had tried to bluff his way to the biggest pot in the biggest poker game he'd ever been in. He was deep in the hole, betting on credit—itself a rarity in Frankie's circles—and put his all on one five-card hand. When it came time to show, Frankie triumphantly produced a king, nine, eight, and three of diamonds, with one corner of a red ten peeping out between the king and the nine.

Frankie reached for the pot with one hand and for his hat with the other, happily crowing, "Diamond flush."

Unfortunately for Frankie, another player had two pairs, one of which was the tens of clubs and diamonds.

Frankie escaped from that incident with his life, a very badly broken leg that eventually healed but left him with a marked limp, and the permanent nickname "FF." Frankie "Four Flusher" Fulton, too, had needed to be chipped out of the frozen slush.

The two men were equally dead.

"How did they buy it?" Lindsey demanded.

"Shot."

"How?"

Zissler hummed into the phone. "That's a little bit odd. Fulton was shot a lot." He paused and hummed.

"Come on," Lindsey urged, "you've got to help me."

"Well, knee-capped—shot in both knees—that must have hurt like hell. And he was shot in both hands, and in both arms, and finally through the heart."

"And no one noticed?"

"It was sleeting hard last night. And this is New York. People don't get involved."

"You mean nobody heard the shots?"

"Eleventh Avenue isn't a great neighborhood, Mr. Lindsey. I don't guess you know New York, do you?"

Lindsey could never get used to being called *mister*. "No, I don't."

"Well, even in good neighborhoods, people don't like to get involved. In Hell's Kitchen—well . . ." He stopped speaking. He hummed softly.

Lindsey wondered how much of Zissler's humming it would take to get on his nerves. "You're telling me all about this Fulton person. What's our interest in him? Did he have a policy with IS?"

"No, Mr. Lindsey, but when two bodies are found together, both of them shot—you see? And the cops knew Frankie Fulton. When they found the bodies and found Cletus Berry's ID, they called International Surety. I talked to a detective. She knew all about Frankie Fulton. She didn't know anything about Mr. Berry.

She wanted to know about him. I couldn't tell her much. I knew the guy. I met him a couple of times. That was all."

There was a lengthy silence.

Lindsey said, "You met him? Tell me about that."

"Mr. Berry had his own office—he didn't like to work out of Manhattan East, he just wanted us to pay his bills, get him office supplies. Typical SPUDS big shot. He rented this little place and put a computer and a futon and a microwave in it and made himself a little home-away-from-home. I was up there a couple of times to deliver documents. Arrogant, too good to hang out with us peons. Whoops—"

Zissler paused.

Lindsey waited.

"I didn't mean that you were, uh—"

Lindsey said, "Never mind. What about Berry?"

"Uh, just twice. I mean, he was just shot twice. Small-caliber rounds, the detective said. Did I tell you that? Police don't have a lab report yet but the detective told me the holes were small and there wasn't much bleeding, almost certainly .22s. That wouldn't be too noisy, either, not like a .45 or a nine-millimeter or even a Police Special."

Lindsey held the phone in his right hand and held his left hand in front of his face. It was shaking. "Where was Berry hit?"

"Not nice," Zissler said. "One gut-shot. That's really nasty. You shoot somebody like that when you want him to take a long time dying and to suffer a lot. The detective told me that, see? And the other was through the head. Made a hole in his forehead, must have stayed in his brain, no exit wound. The detective said that the bullet must have bounced around inside his skull, chopped his brain to pieces. Probably still in there. Probably the coroner will get it out. The detective told me that."

Lindsey told Zissler he was coming to New York—Mrs. Blomquist would set up the trip from Denver—and would Zissler please make arrangements for him in New York. He took Zissler's extension, got the name and number of the detective in charge of the case, and hung up. Lindsey had jotted notes on a yellow pad as Zissler spoke. He transferred the key information to his pocket organizer and slipped it into his jacket. He trotted back to Richelieu's office.

Richelieu had run a comb through his hair and was seated behind his desk; he was back to his usual imperial style. "You're going."

"Of course."

"It's IS business."

"It's SPUDS business."

Richelieu looked up at Lindsey. "You're after my job, aren't you?"

Lindsey said, "No way."

He went back to his own office and logged onto KlameNet/Plus. He used his SPUDS override code to get into Cletus Berry's personnel file. How well had he really known Berry? After that first training course in Denver they'd only met a couple more times, always at SPUDS refresher meetings and seminars.

Were they friends? Maybe. Colleagues, surely. Partners of a sort. But Lindsey had a feeling that if he left Cletus Berry's murder in the hands of the NYPD, odds were it would never be solved, and if he relied on Morris Zissler to handle the matter, the odds would be even worse.

He heard a humming sound. He shook his head and it went away. He wasn't going to let Morris Zissler haunt him. The man seemed earnest enough, just not too bright, and slightly on the smug side. Not a promising combination.

Lindsey shut down the laptop and slid it into its case.

The teenager in the Denver Nuggets cap and the KISS ME shirt had sagged against Lindsey. Trying to get out from under the teenager's weight, Lindsey squirmed. The kid twitched in his sleep, jumped, then climbed out of his seat and waddled up the aisle, toward the toilet. Halfway there he glanced back over his shoulder and gave Lindsey a dirty look.

Lindsey pulled the in-flight magazine out of the pocket in front of him again and flipped through the pages. The reprint of *A Christmas Carol* was illustrated in colorful scenes that made Dickens's London look a lot like the set of a Tim Burton movie. The publisher noted in tiny type that the story was abridged for the convenience of busy air travelers. The magazine was full of ads for tropical resorts, business suites in big-city hotels, and offers of free sample watches, computer software, and carry-on luggage. Everybody was running a Christmas special, even on free offers.

Lindsey sighed and gave up on the magazine. There was always the folder illustrating evacuation routes to study. It was a marvel of graphic communication, hardly a word in it. Perfect for getting a message to a multilingual audience.

Outside the 777's windows the December moon shone so brightly that it seemed to blaze. A cloud layer beneath the jet reflected the moonlight. Above the plane the black sky was dotted with stars. However, there was no sign of either Santa's sleigh or the Star of Bethlehem.

The captain's voice broke Lindsey's reverie. They would be landing at JFK in half an hour. The temperature was well below freezing and sleet was falling in New York.

Lindsey slipped his International Surety credit card into the slot in front of him and made an air-to-ground telephone call.

Morris Zissler had agreed to pick him up at the airport. At least the man was good for that. Lindsey wondered what Zissler looked like. Based on the man's voice he expected a heavyset, middle-aged man in a brown suit. Zissler would be wearing a rumpled white button-down shirt and a worn, striped tie.

Coming out of the jetway, Lindsey was engulfed in a maelstrom of travelers and the families and friends who had turned out to greet them. Half the greeters and half the travelers had brightly wrapped gifts in their hands. He spotted his seatmate, the massive teenager, waddling from the gate, a flight bag in his hand.

A spectacular blonde, as tall as the kid in the baseball cap but easily two hundred pounds lighter, flew into his arms, hugging him and planting kisses on his face. Lindsey blinked. Maybe the fat kid had something that Lindsey didn't know about. Maybe the spectacular blonde just liked them fat.

By the time the crowd had thinned Lindsey spotted the man he guessed was Morris Zissler. His expectation was not disappointed. He approached the man, said, "Zissler?"

"Yes, sir. Mr. Lindsey? Oh, I see you've got one of those little potato badges in your buttonhole, just like Mr. Berry. SPUDS, I get it. That's clever. Just call me Moe, Mr. Lindsey. Welcome to New York."

He helped Lindsey collect his baggage. Lindsey liked to travel light, but for once he had checked his flight bag and for once the bag had made its way from Denver to JFK without disappearing, getting bashed beyond recognition, or taking a side trip to York, England.

Zissler insisted on carrying the heavy flight bag from the claim area to the parking lot. The sleet was falling and Lindsey turned up the collar of his seldom-used overcoat. He didn't have a hat, and he could feel his hair starting to crust over with sleet. Maybe the kid in the Nuggets cap had more on the ball than met the eye.

With a grunt that interrupted his humming, Zissler hefted Lindsey's flight bag into the trunk of a new sedan. Lindsey was too tired and sore to notice what kind of sedan it was. He held onto the laptop. He thought he might get used to this VIP treatment in time. It wasn't really so bad.

"You picked a rough night to fly, Mr. Lindsey." Zissler actually held the door open for him.

"Cletus Berry picked a rough night to get murdered."

Zissler started the engine and put the sedan into gear. Lindsey noticed that the car was full of peppermint fumes. He leaned his elbow against the door and squeezed his eyes between forefinger and thumb.

Even at this hour of the morning, and even in miserable, freezing, wet December weather, the freeway leading into Manhattan was jammed.

No, Lindsey told himself, *they don't call them freeways here.*

Chapter Two

LINDSEY SCRUNCHED DOWN inside the futon, alternately cursing himself for not calling ahead for a hotel reservation and either Mrs. Blomquist or Corporate Travel for not thinking to ask if he needed one. No, it was his own fault for relying on Morris Zissler's judgment.

It was *cold*. Of course, this was an office building—why would the landlord provide heat late at night? Fortunately, Berry had brought in a space heater. It helped a little. Only a little.

In his years with International Surety, Lindsey had done plenty of traveling, and he'd always stayed in comfortable accommodations. But when Moe Zissler asked Lindsey where to drop him off, Lindsey had no answer.

Zissler had suggested his using Cletus Berry's pied-à-terre, and after a moment's hesitation, Lindsey had agreed. Zissler rattled a key to the place, and when he drove through the Queens Midtown Tunnel and through Manhattan's slushy streets, Lindsey got his first real look at New York.

He'd have to learn the city fast if he was going to do anything with this puzzle. It was the first time he'd taken a case for International Surety where the company had no financial stake. Normally, Desmond Richelieu would have squelched any effort like this one, but for all the director's faults, he was loyal to his troops and he wasn't going to let Cletus Berry's murder stand as just one more statistic in the most murderous country in the world.

Zissler drove uptown for a few blocks, then pulled to a stop in front of a nondescript commercial building on West Fifty-eighth Street. "This is it."

He raced around the car and opened the door for Lindsey. The heater had been on, and the flow of warm, stuffy air had lulled Lindsey into a half-doze. He climbed out of the car and drew cold air into his lungs. That woke him up.

Torrington Tower. That was the name of the building, engraved into the granite lintel above the thick glass and tarnished cast-iron doors. Lindsey craned his neck. The Torrington Tower might have been considered a tower when it was erected; now, it was dwarfed by its neighbors.

"How we going to get in?" Lindsey asked.

Zissler separated a pair of keys from a massive batch. "I had an extra set made when I heard you were coming to town, Mr. Lindsey. There's a guard in the lobby, but we've got keys to the lobby door and to Mr. Berry's office, both."

He hauled Lindsey's flight bag out of the sedan's trunk. Lindsey clung to his laptop computer in its carrying case. Zissler opened the lobby door and stood aside while Lindsey entered. The door locked itself behind them with a click.

The guard was behind the desk, as Zissler had promised. He stood up when Zissler and Lindsey entered. He'd been reading; now he laid his book down on his desk, spine upward. Lindsey read the title. *Principles of Modern Accounting for the Medium-Sized Business.* The guard was a tall Hispanic with rich wavy hair and a small mustache. He wore a name tag. It said R. BERMUDEZ.

R. Bermudez said, "Hello, Mr. Zissler. This gentleman with you?"

Zissler said, "This is Mr. Lindsey. Rodrigo Bermudez." Lindsey extended his hand.

The guard smiled and shook it. "Rigo. Please just call me Rigo."

Zissler led the way to a small elevator that creaked and wobbled its way up six stories. On the way up, Zissler said, "Rodrigo's twin brother works here, too. Can't tell 'em apart except by their schoolbooks. Rodrigo's studying accounting. Benjamino's out to be a lawyer."

Once they reached Cletus Berry's erstwhile home-away-from-home Zissler put Lindsey's flight bag on the carpet, then handed him the keys.

"Didn't the coroner put a seal on this place?" Lindsey asked. "Or the police?"

Zissler shook his head. "This is New York, Mr. Lindsey." Apparently he regarded that as a full explanation.

Maybe it was.

Lindsey reached for his pocket organizer. He opened it and said to Zissler, "I want to make sure I've got this right. The detective on the case is named Marcie Sokolov. You've met her?"

Zissler shook his head. "I spoke with her. By telephone."

Lindsey chewed his lower lip. This guy wasn't going to be much help, that was obvious. He was like a big, good-natured, not-very-bright dog. He wanted desperately to please, but unless you kept the instructions simple, really simple, he was more likely to mess up than to help out.

"What was your impression of this, ah, Detective Sokolov?"

"She was okay."

Lindsey looked around the office for a chair. The furnishings weren't quite as sparse as Zissler had indicated. There was a nondescript gray rug on the floor and a couple of cheap prints of Rome on the walls. In addition to the computer, the microwave, and the futon, there were a desk with a telephone on it, a couple of chairs, and a filing cabinet. One window offered a view that surprised Lindsey. Some quirk of architecture had left a narrow line of sight to the north. He recognized Central Park from a hundred movies and a thousand postcards. He imagined he could see Dick Haymes and Deanna Durbin riding through the park pursued by the dastardly Boss Tweed, played by Vincent Price, on an AMC revival of *Up in Central Park*.

There were three doors in the room. One, Lindsey and Zissler had come through. Lindsey opened the others. A bathroom complete with shower stall. Okay. And a closet. A rack of clothes, a lightweight, mini-, what the heck did they call it, dresserette maybe. A shelf with a few pairs of shoes and a little TV set. The TV was one of those compact models with a built-in VCR.

Huh.

Lindsey dropped to his hands and knees and scoped out the electrical connections under the desk. There was a power line for the computer, a fax/modem connection, and a TV cable outlet.

"She, um, Detective Sokolov asked me some questions," Zissler added to his statement.

Lindsey stood up and looked out the window. There were still a few lights on, farther uptown, but it was the park that held his attention. "What questions?"

"Well, like, did Mr. Berry have any enemies? Did he use drugs? Did he go to Atlantic City often? Bet with bookies? Was he in debt? Did he run around with women?"

"And what did you tell her?"

"I told her no."

"But you told me you hardly knew Berry. How did you know he didn't have gambling debts? Or a dozen girlfriends?"

"Well, that's right, I guess I didn't know him very well. But he didn't seem to have any enemies. Or—or the rest of it. Gambling, I mean. Or drugs."

"Women?"

"I never saw Mr. Berry with any women. I wouldn't know anything about that."

Lindsey knew that Berry was married and had a child. Berry had mentioned his wife once or twice, but Lindsey could not remember his saying anything about a child. Lindsey had learned about the child—a daughter—from Berry's personnel file.

Cletus Berry was a sweet guy. Had been a sweet guy. Had been a top worker, Lindsey could testify to that. He had a pleasant personality, he made good dinner-table conversation, and he had been an easygoing, unobtrusive roommate. But he seldom spoke about his private life. Lindsey should have known that was a danger sign, but somehow he'd failed to pick up on it with Berry. *Put the dunce cap on me*, Lindsey thought. *There's more here than meets the eye.*

"Did Sokolov say what the police were planning to do about the killings?"

"About Mr. Berry and that other fellow? Well, Detective Sokolov said they were going to investigate fully."

Lindsey held his head in his hands. Then he lowered his hands and looked at his watch. He'd readjusted his watch as the jet approached JFK so the watch was running on Eastern Time even though Lindsey's body still thought it was two hours earlier.

Zissler said, "I'd like to help out, Mr. Lindsey, but it's awfully late. I have to drive back out to Queens. And my wife always worries when I'm late."

Lindsey said, "Sure. I'll call you at Manhattan East if I need you."

As Zissler headed for the elevator, Lindsey could hear him humming. He thought, *If only he'd hum something with a melody.* But with a Moe Zissler, you took what you could get.

Now Lindsey scrunched down inside the futon.

This was the same Japanese bed that Cletus Berry had used. There were almost certainly a few of Berry's hairs in the bed, and microscopic sheddings of dead skin.

Why had Berry kept this place? He was entitled to office space at Manhattan East, but as a SPUDS agent he was authorized to set up a separate facility if he chose. Lindsey had been offered the same choice and had come close to moving out of the Northern California office where he'd worked before his move to Denver. It wasn't strange that Berry had preferred the privacy and independence of a separate office.

But why a bed and a microwave oven? Why a TV? Why a closet full of clothing? Had Berry been leading a double life?

Lindsey had unpacked his flight bag and hung his suits in the closet along with Berry's. If there were any clues in the office, Lindsey would have to find them. If the police hadn't bothered to seal it off, there was no way they were going to send a forensics squad in to look for evidence.

What was Cletus Berry doing on Eleventh Avenue in the middle of the night, in the company of a petty mobster?

It didn't make sense.

Lindsey closed his eyes and tried to get a feeling for the case. It was early on, he didn't have much to work with, but sometimes you walked into a puzzle like this and you got a feeling for it.

Not this time.

He had half a dream just as he was waking up. He was swimming in cold water. It was dirty and gray and he didn't like it and it kept getting deeper the more he struggled. Then something was holding his arms and legs so he couldn't swim and he started to get cold water in his nose and mouth.

Then he woke up fully and discovered that it wasn't the water but the sunlight that was cold and gray. He climbed out of the futon and pulled on a sweater and a pair of pants. He padded across the carpeted floor and looked outside. The thoroughfares were filled with traffic. The accumulated sleet had already been shoved to the sides of the street, making shin-high gray-black berms along the curbs.

He looked at his watch. It was seven o'clock. He'd had less than three hours' sleep. He cleaned up, using Cletus Berry's little shower stall. Berry had left behind a plastic bottle of shampoo, and a razor on the sink. The only thing Lindsey had to provide for himself was a toothbrush.

He dressed in a gray woollen suit and overcoat and left the office. He rode down in the elevator and passed a couple of businesspeople in the lobby and nodded. They ignored him.

A different guard sat at the battered wooden desk in the front lobby. He looked up at Lindsey and frowned, clearly disturbed to see a stranger coming out of the elevator and leaving the building so early in the morning.

Lindsey told the guard his name, told him he worked for International Surety and would be using the rented office for an indefinite time.

The guard looked more puzzled than ever. Like Rigo Bermudez, he wore a gray uniform with a Sam Browne belt. There was even a holster buckled to the belt; Lindsey wondered whether there was really a weapon in it, or if it was just for show. The guard was easily thirty years Bermudez's senior and his uniform sleeve showed blue sergeant's chevrons. The plastic name tag attached to his uniform jacket said HALTER. He wore half-glasses on the end of his nose and he'd been reading the *Daily News*. He had reddish, mottled skin and a bushy white mustache and white hair that stuck out from under his uniform cap. He looked a lot like Wilford Brimley.

The guard frowned. "Linsley, is it?"

"Lindsey."

"I know. That's what Mike Quill called the mayor. Linsley. Name was Lindsay. Did it just to irk him. Great man, he was."

"Mayor Lindsay? I've heard of him. I don't think we're related."

"Not Linsley. Mike Quill was the great man. Ran the transit union. Great man." He laid down the newspaper and said, "International Surety, hey? Who's that? Sounds like some kind of insurance outfit."

Lindsey said, "It is. Cletus Berry worked for us."

"Oh." Daylight broke across the old man's face. "Sure, Mr. Berry. Nice man. Pity, what happened. Pity."

Lindsey said, "How did you find out about it? Has anybody been here investigating?"

The guard laid his *Daily News* flat on his desk, turned it so Lindsey could see the front page. A huge headline announced, BLOOD AND ICE! Beneath it, in smaller type, SANTA RUBS OUT DUO IN WEST SIDE ALLEY.

A stark black-and-white photograph filled most of the lower half of the page. It showed two bodies lying on an icy sidewalk, a couple of corrugated metal garbage cans and some cardboard boxes behind them. The face of one corpse was thin, middle-aged, unshaven. The man wore what looked like a badly frayed, too-thin coat, and the splotches on it had to be blood.

The second corpse was better dressed, but the angle of the photo showed little of its face. That shortcoming was offset by a smaller photo, framed in an oval and inset in what would have been the right-hand third of the larger photo. It was the face of a black man. He wore a white shirt and a dark necktie. You could see the edge of his suit inside his overcoat. His eyes were open and staring; they had the filmed-over look of the grisly postmortem photos taken to celebrate nineteenth-century hangings.

There was a perfect black dot above and between the eyes. On a Hindu, it might have been a caste mark. But on Cletus Berry's dark, African-American face, Lindsey knew that the dot was a bullet hole. He knew that inside the cranium behind that small, neat hole, Cletus Berry's brain had been scrambled like a pan of eggs.

"So you're from the insurance company," the guard said. "You come to pay off on a policy?"

Lindsey said, "No. I'm here to find out who killed Cletus Berry."

The guard opened his newspaper again. He grinned up at Lindsey. Come to think of it, he looked more like Edmund Gwenn than Wilfred Brimley. He'd need to grow a beard, of course. Then he could play Santa Claus in the next remake of *Miracle on 34th Street*.

"So, you going to be using Mr. Berry's office now?" Halter asked.

Lindsey nodded. "For a while."

The guard said, "I hope you can do some good. Cops sure won't. Too busy with politics and graft. Same as ever."

Lindsey said, "Sergeant Halter—" He reached for his wallet. He had a discretionary fund, and this looked like a good time to be discreet. He extracted a couple of medium-large bills from his wallet. "Mr. Halter—"

"Just call me Lou." The bills disappeared. David Copperfield would have been proud. "Anything I can do to help."

"Isn't it a little bit unusual for a tenant to have his office furnished the way Cletus Berry's was?"

Halter frowned. "How's that?"

"Well, it looks as if he might have lived there sometimes."

"Never in there. I wouldn't know."

"But is it even legal?" Lindsey persisted.

Halter frowned, concentrating. "Building's zoned commercial, not residential. But I guess anybody can put a couch in his office, don't you think? And maybe a little kitchenette, and nuke a cup of soup if he feels like it? And if he's working late and he decides he wants to catch forty winks . . . I don't think it's nobody's business. Nobody's. Do you?"

"No."

The lobby behind Lindsey was getting busy. People were arriving, the elevator was humming. Clearly, there were more tenants than the elevator could handle, and the ones who had to wait shuffled their feet and watched the indicator as the car creaked up and back down.

It was Christmas, though, so at least the small talk was friendly. "I was wondering, Sergeant—ah, Lou."

Halter looked at Lindsey over the tops of his glasses.

"What goes on in this building? It isn't exactly, well, the latest in posh surroundings, is it?"

Halter grinned crookedly. "Sure ain't. Probably get pulled down one of these days. But for now, it's a great address and it don't cost no arm and a leg to rent a little office. So you got a lot of little guys trying to look big in this building. Couple of music publishers and theatrical agents, half a dozen loan companies and lawyers. Shylocks and Sherlocks, I call 'em. Got a few outfits call themselves consultants, I wouldn't know who consults 'em or for what."

Lindsey grunted a vague thank-you. It seemed unlikely that the killer was a fellow Torrington Tower renter, but you could never tell. Somebody who had it in for Berry might want to do his dirty work away from the building to keep the spotlight off himself.

Lou Halter had gone back to his newspaper.

Lindsey crossed the lobby. In seconds he was part of the crowd passing on the sidewalk. Yep, it was Christmas. Christmas, and NFL playoff time.

Lindsey walked along Fifty-eighth Street. The morning was still gray, but the sun was starting to fight its way through the clouds. Lindsey wasn't used to sidewalks this crowded, to people moving with the speed and seeming urgency that New Yorkers did.

Well, he'd adjust. He'd managed to speed up for Chicago, to slow down for New Orleans; he'd find the right pace for New York.

He stopped in a counter-joint, slid onto a stool, and reached for a menu. Before he could look at the menu a waitress poured a cup of coffee and shoved it at him and asked, "What'll you have?"

Lindsey took a breath.

The waitress didn't wait. "How 'bout the special? I'm busy. Scrambled eggs and a muffin."

Lindsey said, "No. No eggs." An image of Cletus Berry's scrambled brain presented itself and Lindsey blinked, hard. "Bring me a couple of pancakes."

"You got it." And she was gone.

Lindsey had never seen the likes of this place. Most of the men and women at the counter held newspapers or magazines in one hand and read while they shoveled food into their mouths with the other. A few of them talked to each other. More of them talked to themselves.

He found himself wolfing his food, tapping his finger impatiently while the waitress brought his check, slapping his money on the counter and striding rapidly to the door.

Why?

He didn't have an appointment. He had work to do, but his style was to take a steady, gradual approach to each case. He wasn't in any hurry.

No, he wasn't in any hurry. He was just finding his pace.

Chapter Three

HE WANTED TO talk with Berry's wife. He knew she would be in shock. It was only thirty-six hours since the discovery of her husband's body, give or take a few hours, and she would not even have begun to come to terms with his death. But sometimes that was a help. She wouldn't have edited her husband's life and death, she wouldn't have erected any barriers or sealed off any facts or memories that might have a bearing on the case.

Lindsey found a working pay phone and looked up Cletus Berry's home number in his pocket organizer. It was a good thing he had the number with him. Ducky Richelieu insisted on all SPUDS agents having unlisted home telephone numbers. Sometimes that was a convenience, sometimes a nuisance.

He dialed and a woman answered. She was crying. That was no surprise. Lindsey identified himself, told the woman he was a friend as well as a colleague of Berry's, asked if he could come and see her.

She agreed, but not so early in the day, please, could he come in the afternoon.

The woman spoke with a light Italian accent.

That was no surprise. From Berry's personnel file, Lindsey had learned that Berry's wife was the former Ester Lazarini, an Italian citizen. Berry had married her in 1979, when he was serving as a warrant officer in the U.S. Army, attached to a satellite NATO headquarters in Rome doing liaison work with the Italian Ministry of Defense.

Lindsey made his appointment with Mrs. Berry and hung up. He studied his wristwatch. It was a little after nine. He looked up another number in his pocket organizer, punched Detective Sokolov's number, and introduced himself.

Marcie Sokolov had a pleasant voice but spoke with the hard-driving intensity that Lindsey thought typical of New Yorkers. "You're with International Surety, interested in the Berry shooting."

Lindsey acknowledged that was so.

"I already talked to your"—she must be fumbling with papers on her desk—"Morris Zissler. Have you spoken with him?"

Lindsey said that he had, that Zissler had briefed him on the case, but that he was representing the company now in the matter of Berry's death.

"Zissler has the facts. This is a law enforcement matter."

"Still," Lindsey said, "if you could spare a few minutes of your time. I flew in from Denver and if I go back empty-handed . . ." He let it hang there.

Sokolov took the bait. "Okay. I'm at Midtown North. Where are you coming from? You know your way around New York? You taking a cab or the subway?"

"Uh—I'm on Fifty-eighth Street. Near Seventh Avenue."

She laughed. "Never mind. Welcome to our lovely city. You can walk here. Midtown North is on West Fifty-fourth between Eighth and Ninth. Enjoy your stroll."

He walked to the corner and stopped to buy a copy of *The New York Times*. He tucked it under his arm and started down Seventh Avenue.

The walk was invigorating. Detective Sokolov might have meant to be ironic, but Lindsey really did enjoy it. He'd never seen such varied people jammed onto a single strip of pavement. He passed a group of teenagers in a full gang regalia, watch caps and hooded sweatshirts. They glared at him, but they didn't do anything more than that. Maybe God was watching over Hobart Lindsey.

He reached Midtown North in a matter of minutes. The police were housed in an utterly characterless building that Lindsey quickly labeled as Postwar Functional. He gave his name to a bored civilian receptionist and sat down with his *New York Times* while he waited for Detective Sokolov.

National and world news were the same as they'd been a day ago in Denver, but the local stories were enticingly different. The most intriguing was a piece on the expected announcement of a race for the U.S. Senate by a congressman named Randolph Amoroso. The resignation of the incumbent senator in the face of charges of sexual malfeasance and financial hanky-panky had left a vacant seat. Even though the Christmas season was generally quiet politically—who wants to compete with the Christ Child for headlines, or with the Jolly Old Elf for campaign contributions?—would-be senators were scurrying to qualify for a special election slated for June.

Lindsey had heard of Amoroso—barely—but apparently he was hot news in New York. A big Amoroso rally was planned for noon in Times Square. Lindsey looked at his watch. If he didn't spend too long in Sokolov's office—if Sokolov ever got around to talking with him—he might take a look at the event. He wasn't sure where Times Square was, but he suspected that it was fairly nearby.

Amoroso's congressional district was Dutchess County, wherever that was, but he was expected in New York to accept the endorsement of a right-wing radio personality. The event would be broadcast live on national radio and TV. Lindsey tracked back through the story to make sure that he'd gotten it right. He had. Amoroso was not an announced senatorial candidate—not yet—but he was issuing campaign manifestos and lining up endorsements anyway.

Reading the article about Amoroso, Lindsey felt a chill. An opponent was quoted as accusing the congressman of fascist leanings, and Amoroso's comment was only, "I think I could make the trains run on time." The Sons of Italy had disowned Amoroso, but a splinter group that claimed affiliation with a neo-fascist party in Italy had proclaimed its enthusiastic support, and Amoroso had welcomed it.

"These are true Americans," the *Times* quoted him, "and true

Italian-Americans. These are the people who built our great land. In this age when welfare loafers, drug peddlers, and deviates of every sort are wrecking our cities and our nation, it is time for real Americans to stand up and speak loud and clear, to City Hall, to the Congress and the Senate, and to the White House itself."

Lindsey shook his head. The article went on like that, with periodical references to the greatness that once was Rome. A potential rival accused Amoroso of wanting to impose an imperial Pax Americana on the world and on the country. Congressman Amoroso's rival was the mayor of the upstate community of Newburgh Heights. The rival's name was Oliver Shea. If Lindsey had barely heard of Amoroso before coming to New York, he was positive he'd never heard of Oliver Shea.

Amoroso responded to Shea's charge by stating that a return to the age of the Pax Romana would mean the salvation of American civilization.

Lindsey laid the newspaper back on the hard composition bench. He watched a couple of uniformed cops drag a couple of women past. If these were hookers they were cut from a different cloth than Julia Roberts or the whores-with-hearts-of-gold who turned up so often on "Barney Miller" reruns. Lindsey opened the paper again and leafed through it searching for coverage of the dual murder of Cletus Berry and Frankie Fulton.

He found the killings mentioned in a roundup piece on crime in the city. The article quoted Marcie Sokolov to the effect that the death of Frankie Fulton was just one more gang-related execution. Sokolov didn't say as much, but Lindsey got the feeling that she was perfectly happy to see mobsters removing one another from circulation. Berry's death was more puzzling, but Sokolov implied that even as solid a citizen as Cletus Berry seemed to be could get mixed up with the wrong type and find himself in big trouble.

The civilian receptionist caught Lindsey's attention with a shrill whistle and a sharp, "Hey, you!" Lindsey dropped his newspaper. "Hey, help us keep this place tidy, willya?" the receptionist complained. "Upstairs, third floor, just ask for Sokolov. Here, don't forget to wear this visitor's badge."

Lindsey folded his *Times* neatly and left it on the bench.

Detective Sokolov's office wasn't an office at all, but a desk in a noisy bullpen. Marcie Sokolov was a petite woman with glossy black hair, an olive complexion, and sharp features. She was wearing a pale blue blouse and a patterned pullover sweater. Her detective's badge was pinned to the sweater; beside it, she wore a plastic Santa face. Instead of eyes, Santa possessed green microlights that flashed on and off at random.

Sokolov put down a heavy coffee cup and stood up when Lindsey approached her desk, and extended her hand. She had a hard grip, gave Lindsey's hand a single tug up and down, and released his hand.

"I suppose you have ID."

He nodded and showed Sokolov his driver's license and IS credentials.

"You related to the mayor?"

"No." He shook his head.

"What's wrong with Zissler? How come they sent you out here from Denver? Where is that, Colorado, right? I always wanted to see the Wild West, since I was a little kid and I watched those 'Gunsmoke' reruns and the rest of the Westerns."

Lindsey stood uncomfortably.

"Take a load off." Sokolov pointed to a hard chair.

Lindsey cleared his throat. "Mr. Zissler comes from our Manhattan East office. He has his other duties. I'm from SPUDS—Special Projects Unit/Detached Status. Cletus Berry was part of SPUDS. He was my friend. I wanted to do what I could do."

Sokolov held her face pointed downward, looked up at Lindsey with great dark eyes beneath jet-black eyebrows. "When a man's partner is killed he's supposed to do something about it," she said.

Lindsey said, "That's right." He recognized the line but didn't say anything else.

"I told you on the phone, Mr. Lindsey, this is a matter for law enforcement. We have something like sixteen thousand police officers in New York. Hundreds of detectives. Evidence technicians. Laboratory analysts. The DA's office. Prosecutors and courts and jails. This city spends a fortune on law enforcement."

Lindsey waited.

Sokolov frowned. "What makes you think you can do anything we can't do?"

"When a man's partner is killed . . ." Lindsey repeated Sokolov's line. "Doesn't Bogie say that?"

"*Maltese Falcon*, by Dashiell Hammett, Sam Spade speaking to Brigid O'Shaughnessy."

"The line is in the movie, too."

"I know that. And it's true. My partner is out on a bust. If anything happened"—she paused—"I'd do something about it, you can bet on that. But then it would be bye-bye, Roscoe, and I'd have to get myself another partner. Life is hard, cowboy." She picked up a folder and laid it down again. Lindsey was surprised to see that she had sharply pointed, scarlet-painted fingernails. Somehow he'd expected her to trim them short and avoid nail polish. Come to think of it, she was wearing lipstick, too, the same color as her nails.

"Okay," she said, "talk to me. What do you need to know? What can you give me that I don't have already?"

Lindsey heard a slight scuffle and looked up. A young man in an immaculate three-piece suit and what looked like a hundred-dollar haircut was approaching with a scruffy-looking older man in a torn sweatshirt and faded jeans. The scruffy man had a badge pinned to his sweatshirt. The younger man was handcuffed.

As they passed Detective Sokolov's desk, Sokolov grinned at them. The scruffy man said, "Yowza, Mama," and Sokolov said, "Cat's pajamas. Congratulations, Roscoe." To Lindsey she said, "Speak of the devil."

Lindsey said, "Moe Zissler put me up at Cletus Berry's place."

"His apartment? With his family?"

"No. His office. On Fifty-eighth Street. His little place. There's a futon there and a microwave."

"Yeah. In the old days it would have been an army cot and a hot plate. What else is different?"

"Well, don't you think there might be evidence there? I mean, the man is killed. You're supposed to be detectives down here. There wasn't even crime scene tape on the place."

"It wasn't a crime scene, now was it?" Sokolov spread her hands as if she couldn't understand Lindsey's needing to have this explained. "Berry was killed in Hell's Kitchen. Look, Mr. Colorado, I'll make a deal with you. I won't sell life insurance and you don't try and solve homicides."

"You don't get it," Lindsey said. "Somebody murdered Cletus Berry and—"

"For the last time, what do you think he was doing in an alleyway with Frankie Fulton—sneaking a little kiss?"

Lindsey made a small shrug.

"I don't know either," Sokolov furnished. "But you can bet it was nothing he'd want to tell his scoutmaster about. People who are clean don't get mixed up with the likes of Frankie Fulton. I'd like to know what it was all about, and I expect to find out. All in good time."

"Then how come you didn't—"

"Seal off Berry's little pad?" Sokolov grinned. Lindsey thought, *She has pretty teeth, dear.* She said, "We were in there by noon yesterday. I was there myself. We turned up nothing. *Nada. Nicht.*"

Lindsey said, "Oh."

"That's why there was no tape. We rifled his file cabinet. Nothing. We peeked in his computer. Looks like routine insurance matters to me. In fact, you might want to take a gander yourself and see if there's anything strikes you funny. Give me a call if there is."

She stood up.

"Wait a minute," Lindsey stopped her. "Did you have a search warrant? How did you get in there?"

Sokolov looked annoyed. "We didn't have a warrant and we didn't need a warrant. Your Mr. Zissler kindly informed us that your company pays the rent on Berry's little nest. Zissler has a key and he let us in. Is that okay with you?"

Lindsey felt the anger he'd been building for Sokolov drain from him. Reluctantly, he nodded.

"Now, if you don't mind," Sokolov said, "I have to go powder my nose."

When she stood up, Lindsey saw that she was wearing fresh new jeans to go with her blouse and sweater. She had a holster strapped to her belt and the grip of what looked like a revolver sticking out of it.

It was still too early to visit Cletus Berry's widow. Lindsey stood outside Midtown North watching the traffic, then asked a stranger for directions and learned how to get to Times Square. It wasn't far.

He started walking.

He heard the noise well before he got there. Band music was playing through a loudspeaker and he could hear voices but he couldn't make out what they were saying.

When he got closer he found himself on the edge of a mob. Brawny individuals in neat suits were striding around, eyeing people who approached. They might have been Secret Service men but Lindsey doubted that they were. There was something about them that made him uncomfortable.

They were wearing lapel pins. Lindsey had trouble making out the shape of the pins, but he passed a vendor selling buttons that seemed to have the same design. Each button was attached to a campaign pamphlet. He bought one and studied the design. It looked like a Roman chariot pulled by a team of horses. He slipped the button and pamphlet into his overcoat pocket.

If he'd seen Central Park in a hundred movies, he'd seen Times Square in a thousand. It must have taken amazing political clout to have this piece of New York shut down, even for a few minutes. Amazing clout to shut it down any time, but this was the middle of the day, on a business day, counting down to Christmas.

A few blobs of sleet were falling. Lindsey felt one on his cheek, then another. They felt like icy tears.

He moved into the mass of people. He didn't see any opening in the crowd, but somehow a limousine managed to move down Broadway, rolling through a narrow lane, and a number of people climbed out. One was the broadcaster who'd been mentioned in the morning newspaper. Lindsey recognized another, Congressman Randolph Amoroso, from his photo in the *Times*. A well-dressed woman was holding onto Amoroso's arm; even from this distance Lindsey could tell that she was gazing at the congressman adoringly. The perfect political wife. Fourth was a distinguished middle-aged fellow with silvery temples and silver-rimmed glasses, a dark blue suit and a wine-red tie.

TV lights glared.

Some functionaries ushered the party to a microphone on the steps of a monument. Behind the microphone, the doughboys who fought in the Great War were memorialized forever. They had caught three-quarters of a century of pigeon droppings for their trouble. A couple of other flunkies were setting up a covered display behind the congressman.

The radio personality took the microphone, gestured for the music to cut off, and started warming up the crowd with a series of jabs at the president, the president's political party, and Mr. Oliver Shea.

Finally he introduced Congressman Randolph Amoroso from the great city of Poughkeepsie in the great county of Dutchess.

Amoroso stepped to the microphone. Someone on his staff must have coordinated the event with the Weather Bureau because the sun popped through and brightened Amoroso like a spotlight. It reflected off his bulbous, bald skull like a halo. It glinted off a silvery pin in the congressman's lapel.

"Just an hour ago," Amoroso said, "on the steps of my home in the beautiful Hudson Valley, I formally announced a great crusade for the heart and soul of America. I announced my candidacy for the Senate of the United States. I've been informed that I will be opposed in my bid by a very decent man . . ."

He grinned as the crowd rustled. There were a few boo's.

". . . an intelligent man . . ."

There were a few more boo's. Amoroso's grin widened.

". . . and a well-intentioned man."

Some shrill whistles. Amoroso positively beamed.

"But my opponent is thoroughly out of touch with the times. He offers us the same old solutions that were tried and failed ten, twenty, thirty years ago. They failed back then. He wants us to try them again." Amoroso paused.

"And maybe he's right."

More shrill whistles.

"But I don't think so." There was a round of applause. "I say"—he paused and looked around at the crowd—"that anybody who sells dope to a kid should be shot."

There were cheers.

"Anybody who sells porn to a kid—or who sells kiddie porn to anybody—should be shot." More cheers. "And anybody who tries to foist a filthy, degraded lifestyle on a decent, God-fearing America . . ."

He held up his arms and grinned at the audience.

They responded in unison: *"Should be shot!"*

Amoroso chuckled. His voice boomed through the loudspeakers. "Right you are. Right you are, my friends. Right you are." He waited for another round of applause and cheers. Then: "My opponent—my decent, intelligent, well-intentioned opponent—and his tweed-jacketed cronies at the universities and on the talking-head shows accuse me of wanting to make America into a new Roman Empire."

He tilted his head. He grinned and the sunlight actually sparkled off his oversized teeth. The lapels of his suit jacket—no topcoat for Congressman Amoroso—were just a trifle too wide. The pattern on his necktie was a trifle too loud. He was the perfect populist.

"Well, an honest citizen could walk down the main street of Julius Caesar's Rome and not get mugged, my friends. Nobody tried to sell him a syringe full of poisonous dope. And nobody offered to sell him a magazine full of kiddie porn, either."

He shook his head ruefully.

"The new Roman Empire?" He paused for a beat. Another beat. "The new Roman Empire?" he repeated. "I think it's a *great* idea."

Behind him, a tarpaulin was pulled from a giant poster. The poster showed a Roman chariot pulled by a team of rearing horses.

The congressman beamed.

The congressman's wife gazed at him adoringly.

The broadcast personality clapped him on the shoulder and grabbed the microphone and started working the audience again.

The television lights in front of the doughboy monument winked off, one by one.

Randolph Amoroso, Mrs. Amoroso, and the rest of his entourage climbed into their limousine, made a U-turn, and sped away, going the wrong way up closed-off, one-way Broadway.

The crowd dispersed.

Lindsey checked the time, then headed for a subway entrance.

Chapter Four

ONE THING ABOUT Cletus Berry. He hadn't talked about his private life, but he talked about New York. He wasn't a native—he'd revealed that much—but he'd taken to the city like a native, and over drinks at SPUDS conferences he'd told stories about New York with obvious pride in his voice.

His favorite was the story of the Second Avenue Subway. The city had planned a whole new line to serve the East Side, got a referendum past the voters and floated a multi-billion-dollar bond issue to pay for it. They'd torn down the elevated rail line that served that part of the city, the famous Third Avenue El. They even broke ground for the new subway line, but when it came time to start serious work they looked at their bank account and discovered that billions of dollars had somehow disappeared.

"One thing about New York politicians," Berry had roared with laughter, "they may be crooks, but at least they're not petty crooks."

Cletus Berry had lived in an old red-brick high-rise—or what must once have passed as a high-rise—the East Seventies. The building might be a little past its prime; Lindsey didn't expect to see high-flying yuppies screeching up to the front door in their Porsches or sleekly turned-out movers and shakers climbing out of stretch limos. Instead, he got the impression of solid, upper-middle-class urbanites.

All right.

New York was not so daunting after all.

An awning over the sidewalk, a doorman in a modest dark blue uniform. A lobby with neutral-colored walls, a couple of gilt-framed mirrors, a flagstone floor. As Lindsey entered the lobby a broad-shouldered middle-aged black man emerged from the elevator and crossed the lobby to the street door. Lindsey was startled; in that fleeting moment, the man bore an uncanny resemblance to the dead Cletus Berry.

Lindsey blinked and the man was gone.

Lindsey entered an elevator operated by another blue-uniformed minion, a woman this time. She asked politely for Lindsey's floor, and whom he was planning to visit. He told her and she responded, "Oh, it was such a pity. Mr. Berry was such a nice man, it was such a tragedy." And a pause—it was a slow elevator—and, "Are you a friend of the family?"

And Lindsey said, "Mr. Berry was my partner."

And when Lindsey pushed the button beside the massive, maroon-painted door, a small dog started to yip inside the apartment. Lindsey did not hear the heavy elevator gate slide closed until the apartment door had opened and Lindsey identified himself to the black-swathed woman who answered the door and invited him inside.

The woman's gray hair was unkempt and her dress hung on her. This was no smart mourning outfit. This woman was no Auntie Mame. This was real grief. The woman offered her hand and Lindsey shook it, then dropped it.

The woman's eyes were a dark green and her skin was olive. Her features were soft. She was a classic Mediterranean type.

He asked, "Are you Mrs. Berry?"

She shook her head. She said, "I am her sister." She spoke with a heavier Italian accent than the woman who'd answered the phone earlier; that must have been Berry's wife. "She just came home. She wanted them to give her his body. They won't give her his body. She's with the baby now. Come in the house and sit down, you want to talk to her."

He followed her. He detected the odor of cooking in the house, and of coffee brewing, but he couldn't tell how fresh it was.

The yapping had come from a tiny dog with a glossy, black-and-gold coat. The dog was circling Lindsey and the woman, darting forward as if it intended to nip at Lindsey's trouser cuffs, then dancing back, its fore-end close to the hardwood floor, its hindquarters and stumpy tail elevated.

The woman said, "Ezio Pinza, shame, you don't be a bad boy. You go keep Anna Maria company."

The dog looked up at her. He gave one more yip. The woman gestured at him, as if she were brushing him away. "Go, you. She's crying, you go."

The dog ran down a narrow hallway and scratched on a wooden door. The door opened and the dog disappeared into another room.

"You come and sit down," the woman said to Lindsey. She led the way into the living room. A blue-patterned sofa and two easy chairs were grouped around a low table.

Lindsey followed instructions.

The woman said, "I am Zaffira Fornari. I am going to be with my sister. You wait. She know you are coming here, so she sees you."

She walked along the hallway the little dog had scampered down and rapped softly on the door. If there was a reply, Lindsey didn't hear it. She opened the door and disappeared behind it. In a moment the door closed with a metallic click.

Lindsey looked around the room. A fireplace on one wall, two massive bookcases opposite. A large frame, obviously holding a picture or a mirror, but now there was no telling which because it was draped in heavy black cloth. A couple of windows overlooking the street.

The woman had introduced herself as Zaffira Fornari, the sister of Berry's wife. No, of his widow. Lindsey knew that Berry's wife was Ester Lazarini Berry; then her sister must be Zaffira Lazarini Fornari. Whoever Fornari was—obviously a husband.

The bookcases were jammed, and Lindsey's curiosity was just getting the better of him, pushing him to get up and scan the titles, when the bedroom door opened.

Ester Lazarini Berry emerged; her sister Zaffira remained behind.

Ester might have been beautiful once. She might have been beautiful yesterday, until she learned of her husband's death.

Now her face was drawn, her eyes were red from weeping, and her shoulders were rounded. She looked as if she was drawing in upon herself, racing to immerse herself in her thoughts and her memories and away from the world in which the body of her husband had to be chopped off the icy concrete in a garbage-strewn alley.

The sisters bore a strong mutual resemblance. Lindsey stood up when Ester Lazarini Berry entered the room. Like Zaffira, she was dressed in black. She walked toward Lindsey, almost steady on her feet.

He stood up and started to say something but she took his hand in hers—not the way one person shakes hands with another, but the way a child takes the hand of an adult.

She said, "You were his friend."

Lindsey said, "Yes."

She said, "I do not understand. Why did they kill him? I went there today, I had to look at him. Who would do that? They killed that other man, too, I did not know him, maybe he did something, maybe he needed to die. But Cletus needed to live. I need him, Anna Maria needs him."

She hadn't let go of Lindsey's hand, so he held her hand in both of his. She had graceful fingers and fine bones. She was trembling, gently, steadily.

"We need him," she repeated. "He has a baby. Ten years old. You know what it mean to a little girl, ten years old, they kill her father? Why did they have to kill him?"

Lindsey shook his head. "I came because—"

She pulled her hand away and said, "Sit. You like a cup of coffee? I make the best coffee on the East Side. I just made a pot. Cream? Honey? Sugar?"

He stammered a reply.

"Sit." She put her hands on his shoulders and pushed him down. He sat on the couch and watched her disappear into what must be the kitchen. He heard china and silver clattering. From the other room, the room from which Ester had emerged and into which Zaffira had disappeared, he heard soft sounds, sounds of voices and soft sobs.

He opened his pocket organizer and looked up half a dozen phone numbers that he already knew, including Detective Marcie Sokolov's. He wished that Sokolov had taken the case more seriously. She hadn't done much about it and Lindsey had the feeling that she wasn't going to do much about it.

Another murder, another corpse, another number.

The bedroom door opened and Ezio Pinza pranced out on the end of a leash. He gave a small yelp when he saw Lindsey. The girl holding his leash—she must be the ten-year-old, Anna Maria—looked at Lindsey, then looked away. Zaffira Fornari was close behind her.

Anna Maria was wearing a bright red and green mackinaw. Ezio Pinza wore a blue doggie sweater. Zaffira had put on a dark, shapeless coat and tied a black woolen scarf over her graying hair. They went to the front door, Ezio tugging at Anna Maria. Zaffira reached over the girl's shoulder to open the latch. Just before the door closed behind them, Zaffira Fornari looked back at Lindsey and said, "We go for a walk. Anna Maria's dog got to go for his walk."

Ester returned from the kitchen carrying a tray with a silver coffee service and cups. She poured a cup for Lindsey and pushed a silver creamer and a little silver cup of honey with a miniature ladle in it toward him. *She hadn't bothered to ask if I took decaf*, he thought. With an effort he refrained from smiling at the triviality.

But maybe, he thought, *that's how we keep from dwelling on painful things—we divert ourselves with trivialities. Maybe*, he thought, *that was why Zaffira and Anna Maria were walking Ezio around the block. And maybe that's why Ester has busied herself making coffee and playing the gracious hostess to this man she's never met before.*

"You came to offer condolences, Mr. Lindsey." Ester's English was better than her sister's, the accent barely discernible, the syntax perfect. "He told me about you, that he knew you from Denver. He told me about the case he helped you with, on Mosholu Parkway. He always thought the Bronx was an exotic land. Or another planet. He used to joke with me about going to

Mars. That was the Bronx. He called New Jersey Alpha Centauri, another galaxy."

She paused and asked if his coffee was all right.

He took a sip and said it was excellent.

She hadn't poured a cup for herself, but now she did, adding neither honey nor cream. Sweetener and whitener, the airline would have called them. The coffee had been scalding hot; even cooled with cream and honey, it pushed Lindsey to his limit. Ester took hers black. Pot to cup to lips. She squeezed her large eyes shut as she took a generous mouthful.

She swallowed.

"No more Mars. No more Alpha Centauri. I told him a thousand times, Alpha Centauri isn't another galaxy. It's our closest neighboring star. I studied astronomy as a girl, did you know that?"

Lindsey shook his head.

"I studied astronomy. Astronomy and history. I was going to be an astronomer or an historian, I hadn't made up my mind. But there wasn't much chance for me to do either of those in Italy. Maybe a schoolteacher, and teach history to schoolchildren. But then along came my handsome American and swept me off my feet. It was a scandal, my marrying Cletus, can you understand that?"

Lindsey could. He knew what it was like to be part of an interracial couple. He knew what it was like to be dumped, even though Marvia had said she still loved him. "It's the race thing, isn't it?" he'd asked, and she'd admitted that, Yes, it was, and that had been that and now she was married to a man with whom she could walk down the street without drawing stares.

"I think I can understand," Lindsey said.

"Pardon me, Mr. Lindsey, if I doubt that. I don't think you know who the Lazarinis are."

He held his coffee cup, taking microscopic sips from its edge. The cup was translucently thin, white china with a broad deckled maroon stripe and a gold rim. He'd seen this pattern before, paid out insurance benefits to a San Francisco homeowner whose beloved Wedgwood had been turned to a pile of worthless fragments by the Loma Prieta earthquake.

"Cletus was my good friend," Lindsey said. A little diplomatic exaggeration couldn't hurt. "But he was a private man, wasn't he?"

Ester Berry said, "He was a private man." Her smile was as rueful as it was faint.

"So, ah, we talked about our work, mainly. We were roommates, you know."

"Yes."

"And about nothing. Television. Football. Restaurants."

"Women?"

Lindsey blushed. "Not really."

"Do not be ashamed. We women talk about men. We do it all the times, all our lives. Little girls talk about their brothers and their fathers. Big girls talk about their boyfriends. Grown women talk about their husbands. Mothers talk about their sons."

Lindsey didn't have an answer.

"Widows," Ester said. She drank more coffee, then put her cup down carefully on the shining saucer. It clattered just once. "Widows," she said again. "Now I will learn what widows say about dead men."

Outside the apartment windows—they were behind Ester, covered with transparent, floor-length draperies—Lindsey could see another apartment building across the street. It was identical to this one, and from the architecture he would date them to the late 1920s. From his place on the couch he couldn't see the sky over New York, but the daylight was fading outside.

If walls could talk, he quoted to himself, *and windows tell what they have seen* . . . Who the hell had said that?

Ester Lazarini Berry started to stand up, then sat down again, running her fingers along her cheekbones and then clasping them in her lap.

"My mother used to say that we were the first Jews in Rome. We were there before Joshua ben Joseph was born. Do you know that, Mr. Lindsey? Do you believe me?"

Lindsey was startled. The woman was vehement. Or maybe just

nervous. Who could blame her for being nervous? "I don't really know. I didn't know you were, ah, I didn't know you were Jewish, Mrs. Berry. I didn't even know there were Jewish people in, ah, Jewish people in Italy. I mean, it's such a Catholic country."

Ester Berry asked, "Are you Catholic, Mr. Lindsey?"

Lindsey shook his head, then said, "No, I'm—" He didn't want to say that he was nothing. He'd been raised without religion, with a careful, politically correct omission of ethnicity. Sometimes he wished he could be a Cherokee or a Jehovah's Witness or a member of the International Flat Earth Society. Anything that would give him a sense of who he was. "No," he repeated, "I'm not Catholic."

"You were never in a Jewish house of mourning? We don't sit shiva, not the way we should. But we cover the mirrors, the pictures. And how can we stay home? The dog has to go out, does he understand the law? And the baby, she has to take the dog, and her aunt has to protect the baby. Even in this neighborhood."

She sighed, brought herself back on track. "They think that Italy is their country, the Catholics. Even the ones who hate their Church. But there were Hebrews in Rome in Caesar's day. Did you know that? There were free Hebrew traders and there were Jewish slaves in Caesar's own household. There were Hebrew prayers at Caesar's funeral, did you know that? No, I didn't think so. The Lazarinis trace their blood to those times. My first ancestor came to Rome from Athens with trade goods and gifts. Do you believe that?"

Lindsey didn't know what to say, so he kept his mouth shut.

"He settled in Rome and studied silversmithing. That became his trade, he was tired of traveling and he wanted to settle down. He found a nice Jewish girl and married her and there have been Lazarinis in Rome for two thousand years. More."

Lindsey heard the sound of a key in the heavy front door of the apartment, and the sounds of Ester Lazarini Berry's sister Zaffira and Ester's daughter Anna Maria and the little dog Ezio Pinza arriving from their walk.

Lindsey swiveled on the couch to watch Zaffira and Anna

Maria and the dog. They had a few snowflakes on them, and the woman brushed the girl, then the girl brushed the dog, before they came down the hall.

Behind himself, Lindsey could hear Ester's voice. She must have had too much momentum to stop. She got out another few sentences.

"There were Jews in the Roman Senate, did you know that? Two thousand years ago. And there were Jewish soldiers, officers, generals, yes, in King Umberto's army in the First World War. Commanders. Medal winners. They were Lazarinis."

The older woman and the girl came into the living room. They had left their coats in the front hallway. Even Ezio Pinza had left his doggie sweater in the hallway and stood in his short, glossy, black-and-gold coat, hiding behind Anna Maria's feet, peering around her at Lindsey. His eyes were black and shiny. He looked like an intelligent dog.

Anna Maria stood beside her mother's chair. Ester put her arms around the girl and said, "Mr. Lindsey, this is my daughter. Anna Maria Berry. Cletus is her father."

She hadn't gotten used to referring to her husband in past tense. That wasn't surprising; he'd only been dead since yesterday. And the police hadn't released his body to the widow for burial. Sure, they'd need an autopsy, they'd need a coroner's report. What was the cause of death? Oh, this little bullet hole in his forehead, yes, that's a definite clue. And what did he have for dinner the night he was killed? Oh, how nice. And did he have traces of any drugs in his bloodstream?

"Anna, Mr. Lindsey was your father's friend. He's come to help us."

Lindsey studied the girl's face. Her skin was darker than her mother's, but Ester's Mediterranean olive and Cletus Berry's African-American black had blended well. Her hair was glossy black and thick. She wore it in pigtails. Not yet switching to teenage sophistication. She was slim, almost wispy. She wore a plaid shirt and new-looking jeans and tennis shoes.

He felt a sudden pang, then realized its source. Anna Maria's skin was hardly lighter than Jamie Wilkerson's. Jamie Wilkerson,

Marvia Plum's son by her first husband. He had almost been Lindsey's stepson. He was Anna Maria's age, and if things had gone differently in California, Jamie and Marvia might have been in New York now, and Jamie and Anna Maria might have become friends.

Lindsey blinked himself out of his reverie and back to the moment.

Why had Cletus never mentioned his daughter? *If she were mine*, Lindsey thought, *she'd be the apple of my eye*. But the more he thought of Berry's friendly manner, his amusing conversation, his little history lessons and anecdotes, the more he realized that he'd learned nothing about Berry's personal life from their time together.

What do you say to a child whose father was just murdered?

"It's a pleasure to meet you, Anna Maria." The girl had extended her hand halfway to Lindsey. Ezio Pinza had crept around her ankles and watched Lindsey suspiciously. Lindsey shook the girl's hand. It was warm and pleasant to the touch. *If she were mine*, he thought, *I'd protect her from the world that killed her father. I'd—* He blinked and released her hand. He realized that she had been tugging it away. He felt embarrassed.

To her mother, the girl said, "Can I go to my room? I want to talk to Mosé."

Ester shook her head. "He doesn't know yet, Anna darling. I should call Abramo and Sara."

Zaffira, standing behind Lindsey, said, "I'll do it, Sister. It's too much, you don't have to do that."

"I already told him," Anna Maria said.

"You what?" Ester sat bolt upright.

"Last night. I couldn't sleep. I just sat in bed with Ezio and tried to read a book but I couldn't so I logged on and talked to Mosé. I know he told his parents. They'll probably phone you today."

Ester nodded. "All right, Anna. Go ahead." Then, before the child could leave, Ester stopped her. "You haven't said a word to Mr. Lindsey, Anna."

The girl looked angrily at Lindsey. "Mother says you're going to help us. How are you going to help us? My father is dead!" She burst into tears, then turned her back on Lindsey. Her shoulders shook.

Lindsey held his hand out before Ester could apologize. "I will help you. I met Detective Sokolov."

"So did I. She came here yesterday and talked to us. She isn't doing anything and I don't think you can do anything either." She whirled, snatched up her dog, and ran to her room.

Zaffira had followed Anna Maria Berry to her room. Before long she returned and took the second easy chair facing Lindsey, alongside her sister.

"What did you think?" Lindsey asked.

Ester was calmer than she had been.

"I think Detective Sokolov was trying to be kind to us. To Anna Maria and me. I think she thinks Cletus was some kind of scumbag, that was why he was with a scumbag when they were both shot. Excuse my language."

Lindsey said, "And I think you're right. Which means that the NYPD isn't going to devote too much effort to trying to solve this crime. They're busier frying other fish."

"Protecting Randolph Amoroso and his gang of fascists," Zaffira put in. "He makes me ashamed I am Italian."

Lindsey shook his head. He looked down and realized that he still had half a cup of coffee. He picked it up and drank. It was cold but it was still the best coffee he'd had since leaving Denver.

He said, "I think Sokolov is doing her best, but I think she has the wrong idea. I don't think Cletus Berry was that kind of man, and I don't think he deserved to die like that kind of man. I'm here to find out what really happened."

But he wasn't sure he was right.

Chapter Five

LINDSEY SHOVELED THE remains of his Hearty Man frozen dinner back into the grocery bag and shoved it in the corner of the bathroom. He didn't know if Berry's deal with the building included trash service; if not, he'd dispose of the detritus himself. He'd overestimated his appetite and underestimated his fatigue. You were supposed to get jet lag when you traveled east-to-west, not west-to-east, but somehow his body was still confused and he ached all over.

He sat in Cletus Berry's swivel chair and watched a few soft flakes falling outside the office window. He wasn't sure that staying in Berry's secret little home-away-from-home was such a good idea, but it would do for the time being.

Had he learned anything useful from his visit to Ester Lazarini Berry? A lecture on the history of the Jews of Rome. Well, he hadn't known that Berry's wife was Jewish. He'd inferred that she was white—there couldn't be that many black Italians—but he'd expected her to be Christian.

But did her background have anything to do with her husband's murder? It was a fact, but did it have any bearing? He didn't know, and he'd learned precious little else from his interview.

After Zaffira and Anna Maria returned from walking the little dog, Lindsey had thought it was time to leave. He'd intruded on their grief long enough. Ester had asked him to stay for dinner, but that was obviously a bad idea. The household was in a state of disarray. The family needed to renew their mutual bonds; friends and family might help, but the presence of an outsider—really a stranger—would only add to their stress.

So he'd left, intending to eat his dinner at a restaurant, but instead he'd stopped at a mom-and-pop grocery and bought a few supplies and taken a cab back to West Fifty-eighth Street.

The Torrington Tower was officially closed for the day when he got back. The street entrance was locked and one of the Bermudez brothers was guarding the lobby. He was reading *Civil Procedure of the State of New York, Revised*. Right. This had to be Benjamino, then, the Clarence Darrow of tomorrow.

Lindsey put his few groceries away, then set up Cletus Berry's TV and turned on the local news while he nuked the frozen dinner. There was controversy over Randolph Amoroso's rally in Times Square. The congressman's opponent in the race for Senate, the previously obscure Oliver Shea, got screen time to accuse the mayor of the City of New York of playing politics with the taxpayers' money and at the taxpayers' inconvenience.

Shea was a squatty, jowly man who favored a broad-brimmed black hat and a rumpled manner. "How dare the mayor shut down Times Square to stage a partisan political rally?" he demanded. "How many police officers were diverted from the vital job of fighting crime and protecting our good citizens to act as ushers for this sleazy playlet? As the mayor of a city myself, I can tell you that it cost a pretty penny. I demand that hizzonner the mayor provide an accounting, down to the last copper penny, and bill my opponent's campaign for the full amount!"

The camera cut from Shea to a spokesperson for the major. All the while the mayor's representative was speaking, Lindsey kept wondering who Shea reminded him of. Finally, he realized— Fiorello La Guardia, the onetime mayor of New York, famous for reading the Sunday funnies over the radio during a long-ago newspaper strike. Lindsey had seen ancient newsreels of the event, and Cletus Berry had told the story with relish, even though he couldn't possibly have remembered it.

Lindsey had almost missed the official response to Oliver Shea's blast, but he caught the tail end. The mayor and his family, it turned out, were conveniently out of town, attending a concert of sacred music composed by the late Duke Ellington, in the

National Cathedral in Washington, D.C. Following the concert they expected to fly to Puerto Rico for a brief holiday.

No, the spokesperson explained, there was nothing political about the mayor's absence and nothing political about his choice of Puerto Rico for his vacation. And if there was anything irregular about the Amoroso rally in Times Square, the spokesperson was certain that hizzonner the mayor would look into it as soon as he returned to his desk in the New Year, and hizzonner took this opportunity to wish all New Yorkers a healthy, happy, and prosperous holiday season and blah-blah-blah and . . .

Lindsey jerked awake. He'd set the timer and dozed off. Now the microwave signal was sounding. His dinner was ready, and he was too sleepy to do more than pick at it.

Once he'd disposed of the tray and the uneaten food, he washed up and climbed into Cletus Berry's futon. There were times when Lindsey had done some of his best thinking lying in bed at night, staring at the ceiling and reviewing the day's events. There were other times when he'd found comfort in the presence of Marvia Plum.

But tonight Marvia was almost three thousand miles away, and there was no comfort for Lindsey in that.

And as for thinking—he fell asleep thinking about thinking.

Not an idea, not an image or a hint of a dream. Just the watery December sunlight waking him again. He put on a pair of socks to keep his feet warm, even though Berry had furnished the office with a carpet. He made himself a cup of instant coffee in the nuker and sat at Cletus Berry's desk to drink it.

After he'd taken a few sips he got up and shuffled to the closet, warming his feet with the friction. He pulled the button and pamphlet that he'd bought at the Amoroso rally the day before from his overcoat pocket. He returned to the desk and laid them in front of Berry's computer, swallowed another sip of coffee, and opened the pamphlet.

The coffee was drinkable—barely—but grocery store instant was a far cry from the Jamaican Blue that Marvia Plum used to brew. For a moment he tried to imagine himself facing Marvia across a breakfast table in a cozy apartment, maybe with Jamie in colorful pajamas sitting in another chair, then shook away the image. That was not to be.

He focused on the pamphlet.

The front page featured a photo of Congressman Amoroso in what might have been a vaguely imperial pose, the familiar horse-and-chariot logo ghosted in behind him. The headline read AMERICA NEEDS AMOROSO and the body type—actually pretty minimal—touched on a series of hot buttons. Apparently Amoroso was a reformer. In fact, his solution to every problem seemed simple and emphatic. One word. *Reform.*

TAX REFORM!
BUDGET REFORM!
WELFARE REFORM!
EDUCATION REFORM!
IMMIGRATION REFORM!
LAW ENFORCEMENT REFORM!

The centerfold of the pamphlet consisted of a review of Amoroso's brilliant career and endorsement statements from leading citizens, all superimposed on that ghostly chariot image.

Lindsey picked up the shiny button. Yep, there it was again, in glossy silver ink on an imperial purple background, and the word AMOROSO in glaring yellow letters.

Back to the pamphlet. Lindsey shook his head. He was learning more about Randolph Amoroso than he really cared to know . . . and next to nothing about Cletus Berry. Even so, it was all information, and he'd been surprised more than once when seemingly unconnected facts had suddenly fallen into place to clarify a previously puzzling picture.

Back to the pamphlet.

The last page was topped by the chariot image, not ghosted this time, and a couple of paragraphs about its history, connecting it with the great men of history including Julius Caesar and the greatness that was Rome.

Lindsey shoved the pamphlet and button into a coat pocket; he was ready to forget about the Amoroso rally and the whole senatorial race. It had nothing to do with Cletus Berry, he kept telling himself. The trouble was, so far nothing had to do with Berry.

He phoned Marcie Sokolov at Midtown North. She was not happy to take his call and she had nothing new to tell him. She made it clear that she was a very busy police officer and that she didn't have time to chat with every amateur sleuth and detective wannabe who happened to take an interest in a strictly routine murder.

After that rebuff Lindsey climbed into a sweater and woolen slacks, pulled on a warm coat, and rode down in the elevator. Traffic in the lobby was light. Lou Halter sat at his desk wearing his gray guard's uniform, blue sergeant's stripes on the sleeve, his pistol strapped to his hip, coffee cup and *Daily News* in front of him. He looked up and nodded to Lindsey.

"Lou," Lindsey said, "if you don't mind—how many hours do you work? Is there a guard here around the clock?"

Halter said, "Regular eight-hour shift. Me and the Bermudez boys. Rodrigo and Benjamino. We swing through weekends, double shifts, so we can get a day off. Boss brings in temps for days like Christmas and Easter. I'd take the extra shift myself—it's golden time—but he won't go for it."

He folded his newspaper carefully and stifled a yawn. "The work isn't really too hard, see. I'm on Social Security, got nothin' else to do, this gives me a place to go, keeps me out of trouble—heh—and I get some nice pocket money. Send it to my kids and grandkids. I don't need it. Nope. Rigo an' Mino, they're a couple of go-getters. Came here, studyin' hard, the two of 'em. They're going places, believe you me."

Lindsey gestured at the tabloid and asked if there was anything new on the Berry case.

Halter turned to a black headline on an inside page. "Just finished reading about that, Mr. Lindsey. Not a peep about Mr. Berry. But they've got some stuff here on Frankie the Four Flusher."

He tapped a photo with one blunt fingernail. "See that? I guess he knew his way around a little." He turned the paper so Lindsey could see the photo.

It was a file shot. Lindsey recognized Frankie Fulton from the corpse photo in the previous morning's *News*. This picture showed Fulton in better days, posing with a prosperous-looking older man and a lightly clad showgirl. The scene was apparently a nightclub, and the clothing and hairstyles looked like something ten or fifteen years out of date.

The cutline identified Fulton as a "onetime mob enforcer and café society habitué." As for the showgirl with him—she was spectacular, there was no denying that, and she did not make any effort to conceal her charms. The cutline identified her as Millicent Martin, "photographed shortly before her still unsolved gangland-style slaying."

The older man was identified as "Prominent antiques dealer Alcide Castellini."

Lindsey blinked. He was not surprised to recognize Fulton. But the second man—the older man—looked oddly familiar, too. Who was he? Lindsey tried to visualize him in living color instead of static monochrome.

And then he had it. The man in the photo was younger, a little thinner, and his hair was darker. His eyeglasses were different—they had black plastic rims, and the ones he'd worn when Lindsey saw him were silver-rimmed. But he was the same man. He was the last man to climb from Congressman Randolph Amoroso's limousine at the Times Square rally.

Lindsey looked up from the newspaper. "You mind if I clip this?" he asked Halter.

The guard pulled open a drawer in his desk and came up with a pair of scissors. "From my sewing kit," he explained. "Never know when a button's gonna come loose or—something." He handed the scissors to Lindsey. Lindsey snipped out the photo and the accompanying story and put them in his pocket. He'd scanned the story itself. It added nothing to what he already knew.

But the photo had added two fresh players to the drama. Millicent Martin—probably a stage name, but it was a start—and Alcide Castellini. Martin had been murdered, "gangland style." And Castellini was an antiques dealer.

What could either of them—in fact, what could any of the three—have to do with Cletus Berry?

There was no way that Millicent Martin was going to tell Lindsey anything. She was dead.

Ditto Frankie Fulton.

But Alcide Castellini . . .

Lindsey found a working pay phone in a kiosk and punched for directory assistance. Apparently the vandals who had attacked pay phones for decades had finally lost interest and moved on to bigger prey, but there wasn't a telephone book to be found.

There was no listing for Alcide Castellini.

Lindsey walked to a drugstore with an indoor phone booth. A clerk loaned him a classified directory; now that condoms were on display beside candy bars, telephone books were kept behind the counter. There were antiques dealers galore, and the closest concentration seemed to be on Fifty-seventh Street.

He walked the few blocks, turned the corner at the old Carnegie Hall—he'd seen that building in a thousand movies—and found a row of antique stores.

He picked one at random and walked in. The store—he hadn't bothered to note its name—was filled with ornate gilt furniture and elaborately framed paintings of elegant French ladies. A woman in a gray woolen suit was waiting on a customer in an identical suit. The woman who was *not* the customer had a name tag on her jacket and the customer had a tiny hat pinned to her big coiffure; that was how Lindsey could tell them apart.

They appeared to be discussing a huge wall mirror framed in endlessly elaborated golden swirls. It was hard to tell whether a sale was actually taking place, but somehow the transaction reached its conclusion. The two women in gray suits exchanged a little hug and kissed the air beside each other's cheeks. The one who was not a customer found the customer's wrap and gloves and walked her to the street door, their arms around each other's waists, their heads bobbing and little breathless words escaping as if reluctant to leave the warm air of the shop for the cold, damp, gray Manhattan day.

The door whispered shut behind the customer. Through the front window of the shop Lindsey saw a yellow cab swing to the curb and swoop away with the woman inside. Wonder Woman's invisible airplane couldn't have responded more obediently to her telepathic summons.

The gray-suited woman with the badge on her blouse turned back and strode up to Lindsey. The expression on her face had changed. Lindsey wasn't certain, but he thought she hissed, "Bitch!" before she turned her smile back on for him.

Then something happened. Maybe it was the oncoming Christmas holiday. Maybe it was something about Lindsey, the loneliness he had known since Marvia Plum's abrupt departure from his life.

"Would you believe that woman has been dickering over that mirror for six months? Six *months!* And you know what she just told me? *Well, Howard and I have decided that we're going to have the wonderful new muralist, oh, what in the world is his name, oh, dear, I just can't remember it, well anyway, we've decided to commission him to do a whole wall in the drawing room, aren't you just so excited for me, I'm so terribly excited, but of course then we won't have anyplace to hang a Louis XIV mirror, don't you see, so I'm afraid you'll just have to sell it to somebody else.* And off she goes! I'm so mad I could just—"

She seemed to notice Lindsey.

"I'm so sorry." She took a deep breath. Her face had turned bright red during her outburst. It was returning to normal. Her name tag said *Cele Johnston.* She turned on her smile still again—it hadn't lasted long once her diatribe got rolling. "What may I show you, sir?"

Lindsey handed her an International Surety business card.

She read it and looked puzzled. "I don't understand. I didn't think we'd entered an insurance claim of any sort. And—why Denver?"

"No, I'm just looking for some information. This involves a death claim. A death under difficult circumstances. I'm just trying to clear up some questions about the decedent. We know that he was acquainted with an antiques dealer, and I thought you might be acquainted with him."

She raised an eyebrow.

"The antiques dealer's name is Castellini."

"I know him."

"If you could put me in touch? A telephone number or address? Does he have a shop?"

Cele Johnston looked up at Lindsey. He wasn't a very tall man, and she didn't have to look very far. She had gray eyes and blonde hair that was starting to streak with gray. She narrowed her eyes as if she could focus them on Lindsey's and peer directly into his brain.

"Come with me."

She led the way past satin-covered sofas and delicate, polished, scroll-like chairs. She opened a door and said, "Joseph, don't let any of the stock wander out. Browsers come in, be nice. If you get a live customer, call me."

Chapter Six

CELE JOHNSTON DIDN'T just give her customers coffee, she offered them espresso. She sat behind a mahogany desk, tiny cup in one hand and matching saucer in the other. Lindsey sat opposite her in what Sam Spade would have called a client's chair. Cele Johnston called it a Chippendale. His overcoat hung on a coat tree that could have stood in the palace at Versailles—if they had coat trees in the palace at Versailles.

"Mr. Lindsey, why are you looking for Castellini? Was he the beneficiary of a policy your company carried?"

Lindsey shook his head. "Nothing like that."

"Well?"

She'd poured for him. The cups were tiny but the coffee was dense and strong; a demitasse would be more than enough. "Ms. Johnston, have you ever heard of Cletus Berry?"

"No."

"He was one of our employees. He was murdered two nights ago."

"And—? Isn't that a matter for the police?"

"The police say it is." Lindsey grinned wryly. "But they don't seem to be taking the case very seriously. Berry was found in an alley in Hell's Kitchen. He was shot, execution style, and there was another body with his, a small-time gangster named Frankie Fulton."

Cele Johnston placed her cup carefully on its saucer and set them both on her desk. "Mr. Lindsey, I'm really very sympathetic, but your story just isn't interesting. I'm sorry if this man, this friend of yours—was he your friend, or are you just following company procedure?—oh, he was your friend," in response to Lindsey's nod. "I'm sorry that your friend was killed, but in all honesty, this sounds to me like a classic case of wrong place, wrong time. What was your friend doing in that neighborhood, in that kind of company?"

Lindsey put down his own cup and saucer. He spread his hands. "That's what I'm trying to find out."

"But what does Mr. Castellini have to do with it?"

"The *Daily News*—"

"I'm sorry, I don't read the *Daily News*."

Lindsey would have been surprised if she had. "—ran a file photo. It showed three people. Frankie Fulton, a showgirl named Millicent Martin, and Alcide Castellini. Fulton is the link to Cletus Berry. They were murdered together. Millicent Martin is dead. The paper says that she was also murdered. That leaves only Castellini."

Cele Johnston stood up and carried her cup and saucer to the baroque espresso machine. Over her shoulder she asked, "Another?" When Lindsey said no she poured for herself and sat down again behind her desk.

She opened a drawer and laid a business card on top of her desk. From an elegant brass-and-marble holder she lifted a pen and wrote something on the card. She slipped the card back into the drawer and slid it shut.

"Before I give this to you, I'm going to tell you a couple of things. But before I do that, I have to ask you a few questions."

She looked at Lindsey, waiting for him to accept her plan. He said, "Okay."

"People think that the antiques business is all tony society folk and the love of elegant objects."

Lindsey grinned. "I'm an insurance adjuster, Ms. Johnston."

"Cele."

Now Lindsey's eyebrows rose. "Bart," he said.

"That's right," she nodded, "I imagine you do know better than that. But you see, antiques can't be manufactured. Or at least they shouldn't be. There are plenty of counterfeiters around. But as long as we play by the rules— Well, I suppose the ultimate collectible would be a Stradivarius."

"Right up there," Lindsey agreed. "Musical instruments aren't my field, but I get the point."

"Well, the principle would be the same if we were talking about a Michelangelo sculpture or a Shakespeare First Folio or an Erté necklace. There are just so many in the world, and there can never be another. Antonio Stradivarius died in 1737, and his secret of violin-making died with him. But even if we could rediscover his secret, even if a violin maker today could re-create a Stradivarius down to the last detail, one that would look and feel exactly like a Strad, that would have the glorious sound of a Strad—it still wouldn't be a Strad, do you see?"

"Of course."

"I'm afraid I'm leading you the long way 'round on this." She clasped her hands oddly. The way, Lindsey realized, Bela Lugosi had clasped his hands to control his victims in *White Zombie*. "Look, antiques may seem to be a very genteel, very hoity-toity business, Bart, but in fact it's a tough, competitive racket. There's a lot of competition for merchandise, and there is just so much merchandise to be had. Just so many Strads, just so many Chippendales. Sometimes people play rough. Sometimes they play dirty."

"You're talking about Castellini."

"Alcide Palmiro Castellini. I didn't tell you anything about him. In fact, I don't know you."

She slid the drawer open once more and handed him the card.

All that it had on it was a seven-digit number.

I'm not a detective. Not a cop. Not a private eye. I'm just an insurance man, trying to do my job, trying to get a few answers so I can settle a claim.

Lindsey had used that line plenty of times, as often on himself as on anyone else, keeping himself focused on the task at hand, staying on course when a case tried to wander off in all directions. But if he wasn't a detective, he'd spent plenty of time working with them. With Dorothy Yamura in Berkeley, with poor Celia Varela who had gone undercover on a case and wound up garroted in the back room of a San Pablo Avenue saloon, with Lieutenant "Doc" High of the Oakland Police Department.

And one thing that they'd told him, again and again, was never to overlook the obvious in searching for information.

He walked back to Seventh Avenue and bought a subway token. It was about time to learn some more about the fabulous New York City subway system. He rode a BMT train to Times Square. It was the middle of the day, and the cars were only half full. Many of the passengers were carrying Christmas packages.

Lindsey climbed back into the pallid sunlight and chilly air and walked across Forty-second Street to the New York Public Library.

Everywhere he went in this teeming city, every sight he took in, seemed more like a visit to a soundstage than a real place. He'd had the same experience watching tourists gape at the colorful variety of Berkeley's Telegraph Avenue or climb merrily aboard the cable cars on Powell Street in San Francisco. To the tourists these were quaint and colorful sights. To the people who lived and worked in those cities, they were everyday realities.

He found his way to the newspaper room and picked up an index to *The New York Times.* He found a vacant chair at a long wooden table and opened the index. He found three listings for *Martin, Millicent.* He noted the dates and pages, then returned the index to a clerk and requested microfilm copies of the *Times* for the dates of Millicent Martin's three appointments with destiny.

The first article was a review of an off-off-Broadway experimental performance piece, bylined by Victor Hopkins. ("Not quite a play," Hopkins commented on the performance, "nor dance, nor concert. *The Princess from Planet P.* is an event all its own, with its own rules and its own values. As such, I can't say that I have ever heard such an uninterrupted stream of filth, beheld such a successful attempt to offend, disgust, and repel an audience. Whether the material, the production, or the small cast takes the prize as most execrable aspect of this disgrace to the theater, deponent sayeth not. A single ray of light shines in the person of Millicent Martin, a young actor/singer/dancer who displayed a well-trained voice, fluid movements, and a compelling stage presence that deserve far better than the beating she takes in her brief role as the much-victimized Countess Specula.")

The second item was dated six months after the first. It carried no byline. Millicent Martin, age twenty-six, had apparently been awakened in the middle of the night in her basement apartment on East Fifth Street. Neighbors reported nothing unusual but police responded to an anonymous telephone tip and found her bound hand and foot, duct tape over her mouth and nose. Unable to free herself and remove the tape, she had suffocated.

There was no sign of robbery or sexual assault, and no evidence of forceful entry. Police theorized that the victim was acquainted with her killer, and might have submitted voluntarily to the restraints as part of a sexual "game."

The third item was dated a month later. Martin was mentioned in it in passing, included in a list of "unsolved, unthinkable, unforgivable atrocities" enumerated in a speech by Congressman Randolph Amoroso.

Lindsey made prints of the three items, then rewound the microfilm and returned it to the desk. He folded the fresh copies of the newspaper clippings and slipped them into his pocket. He asked a librarian where he could find a reverse telephone directory and looked up the number on the card that Cele Johnston had given him. The number was written in a precise, feminine hand, in dark green ink.

Of course, Lindsey could just drop a coin in the telephone and try the number on Cele Johnston's card. But what would he say to Castellini? What if Castellini simply refused to take his call? At that point, Lindsey would be up against a stone wall. Better to bide his time, try to learn more about the ominous antiques dealer, and make his move when he was in a stronger position than he was right now.

Just for the hell of it he tried a normal Manhattan directory and searched its pages for Victor Hopkins. There was no listing for him. But in itself that meant little. Hopkins might live in one of the other boroughs, or even in New Jersey or Connecticut, or he might have an unlisted number like Alcide Castellini, or . . . there was no point in enumerating possibilities.

He telephoned *The New York Times* from a pay phone in the library and struggled with a voice mail system until he was ready to commit a crime himself. Finally a real live human being identified herself as "Arts. Amy Baines here." Lindsey asked for Victor Hopkins. The woman—she couldn't be as young as she sounded—said that Hopkins didn't work for the *Times* and never had. He was a freelance who occasionally picked up an assignment when the paper needed an extra reviewer, especially for more esoteric events.

Lindsey asked if the woman knew Hopkins's telephone number or address. She said it was against policy to give out that information. Lindsey explained that he was working on a case that involved Millicent Martin, the showgirl.

Now the woman responded. "Victor really thought Millie was hot shit."

Lindsey felt himself blushing. He was still not used to women using rough language. He seldom used it himself.

"He dated her a couple of times. I didn't think they were a serious item, but you should have seen him when she got snuffed. For a while there I didn't think he was going to navigate."

She paused.

Lindsey waited. This was where the game got tricky.

"You have some information about Martin?" Amy Baines said. "The cops never got anywhere. You're no cop, that's a slam dunk."

"No." Lindsey felt his pulse kick up a couple of beats. He was getting somewhere. "I'm just an insurance man. But I'm investigating my partner's murder."

"And when a man's partner is killed he's supposed to do something about it."

Thank you, young lady. Thank you, Humphrey Bogart, and thank you, Dashiell Hammett, wherever you are. Lindsey said, "That's exactly right."

Now the woman paused, and Lindsey paused, and finally she

said, "Give me your number. I'll call Victor. If he wants to talk to you, he'll call you. That's the best I can do."

Lindsey said, "I'm at a pay phone."

She said, "Give me that number and wait there. I can always reach Victor."

Lindsey complied.

New York City. Beeper City.

Somebody the size of the teenager in the Denver Nuggets cap but considerably older and with a definite attitude was waiting to use the telephone. Lindsey started to explain that he was waiting for a call to come in. It took him about six seconds to realize that sweet reason was useless at this time.

He took a deep breath and started spewing at the huge man every word he could think of that he would never have used in the presence of his mother. He could feel his face getting red. He was really getting into it. Library users walking past swerved away from him. He got to the end of his store of epithets and started over, arranging them in new and imaginative combinations.

The huge individual took two steps backward, made a couple of circles in the air with his hands, turned around, and tottered away, looking back over his shoulder and frowning.

Lindsey let go a last blast. He couldn't restrain himself. He had to add ". . . and your little dog, too!"

The huge individual disappeared.

The telephone rang.

Lindsey paused to catch his breath before he lifted the receiver. *When in Rome . . .*

The voice on the other end was clearly male, and almost as certainly young.

Lindsey identified himself.

The voice said, "This is Victor Hopkins. You want to talk to me?"

"About Millicent Martin."

"Where are you?"

Lindsey told him.

"Walk over to Third Avenue and head downtown. I'll meet

you in half an hour at the White Rose. You know the White Rose?"

"No." All Lindsey could think of was the Black Dahlia.

"Saloon and hofbrau."

"How will I know you?"

Hopkins said, "Never mind. You just describe yourself. And you'd better give me a piece of ID."

"You mean, a business card?"

"No. Look, Mr. Lindsey, I don't want to seem melodramatic, but I'm taking a chance even meeting you. Where are you from?"

"Uh—Denver. California originally, but I work in Denver now."

"That's a long commute. Okay. Good enough. What do you look like? What are you wearing?"

Lindsey told him.

"Okay. I'll try and get to the White Rose first. If I don't, you go ahead and order a drink. I'll find you. I'll say, 'I heard it's snowing in Boston today,' and you answer, 'It was sunny in Denver.' You got that?"

"Sounds silly. I mean, it sounds like a spy movie."

"You want to talk to me, Mr. Lindsey? White Rose, half an hour, remember the script."

Lindsey walked down the steps on the Fifth Avenue side of the library, walked up to Forty-second Street, waited for the lights to change, and headed east. There were Christmas decorations in most of the store windows and he passed more shoppers carrying shopping bags full of colorfully wrapped packages.

It was snowing steadily. A few pedestrians carried umbrellas to keep the snow off their heads; most relied on hats or scarves or simply let the flakes land on their hair.

Lindsey ducked into a hat store and bought a fedora. It was dark gray. It would look good with his overcoat and his suit. If he pulled down the brim of the hat and turned up the collar of his coat, he'd look like a real spy.

That was all he needed.

On a clear day, he thought, the cityscape ahead of him might be impressive, maybe even beautiful. But today the snowflakes filling the air turned everything to a soft white cushion after a few hundred feet.

He turned on Third Avenue as Hopkins had instructed him and looked for the White Rose. He should have asked which side of the street it would be on, and how far downtown, but it was too late now. He'd just keep his eyes open.

It didn't take long to find it.

He pushed through the swinging doors. The steam and the odors hit him even before the sight of the crowded room. With a start he realized that he hadn't eaten today. He was ravenous.

He pushed his way to the pitted wooden counter and ordered a corned beef sandwich and a cup of coffee. He looked around, wondering if there was any way he could spot Victor Hopkins before Hopkins spotted him. Lindsey had always thought of himself as average looking, but he'd told Hopkins his height and tried to give him an idea of what his face looked like. He even described his ordinary-looking overcoat.

Hopkins had told Lindsey nothing about himself, so Lindsey scanned the room. His job had taken him to big cities and small towns across the country, but he was still amazed at the variety of faces and styles that he saw in New York. Was that dapper, thin-faced man in the three-piece suit Victor Hopkins? The burly, red-faced bruiser in the stained gray sweatshirt? The towering, needle-thin African-American with the shaved skull and the quilted jacket?

"Here ya go."

Lindsey turned back to the counter. The sandwich looked delicious and the coffee was perfect for a day like this.

Behind the counter a mirrored wall had been decorated with paintings of Santa Claus and his reindeer. A Christmas tree stood at the end of the counter, covered with decorations and cards. A Hanukkah menorah—he'd learned about Hanukkah from his friend and sometime lawyer Eric Coffman—stood on the shelf in front of the mirror.

Lindsey picked up the sandwich and took a bite. The taste said

"Welcome home." He chewed and swallowed, took a sip of the strong coffee. A TV set in the corner seemed to be running an old reel of New York Knicks basketball highlights. In the mirror behind the counter he caught a look at himself and his neighbors. On one side of him an old man was reading a copy of the *New York Post*. The headline had something to do with a threatened strike.

Lindsey's other neighbor was a woman with a craggy face and orange hair. She wore a tan tweed coat. She was holding a martini glass in one hand, staring at the olive as if she could make eye contact with it. She looked up and caught Lindsey's eye in the mirror. She frowned and resumed communion with the olive.

". . . snowing in Boston today."

Lindsey couldn't hear the beginning of the sentence over the rumble of conversation in the room and the announcer's voice on the TV, but he got the important part. He was seated on a wooden bar stool. He started to swivel but the voice said, "Nope."

Instead of turning, then, he peered into the mirror. He wasn't sure which person behind him had spoken, but he had a pretty good guess.

"It was sunny in Denver."

The woman with the martini gave him a puzzled look and shifted away from him, as far as she could without leaving the crowded counter.

The voice behind Lindsey said, "Go ahead and eat your sandwich."

Lindsey took another bite and washed it down with coffee. He dropped a bill on the counter and slid backward off his stool. This time Victor Hopkins—it had to be Victor Hopkins—didn't stop him.

"That good?"

"It was."

"Let's get out of here."

Hopkins led the way out of the White Rose. Lindsey wasn't very good at pegging ages, but Hopkins had to be in his late twenties or early thirties. He was taller than Lindsey but he weighed easily twenty pounds less. He wore dark-rimmed glasses that framed startling blue eyes, a small blond beard and mustache and a knitted skiing hat over blond hair. Red and green snowflakes were worked into the wool of his dark blue sweater.

As they pushed their way out of the White Rose, Hopkins removed a tan down vest from a wooden peg and slipped it over his sweater. On the sidewalk he halted and faced Lindsey.

"Tell me who you are and what you want," he said. He sounded earnest enough. He reminded Lindsey of himself as he'd been fifteen or twenty years ago—or as he might have been if he'd broken the bonds of safe, conservative suburbia and seized the opportunities that he hadn't even realized were there to be seized. He felt a rush of envy for the younger man.

Lindsey said, "I'm trying to find out who killed Cletus Berry."

"Never heard of him. Amy said you were investigating Millicent Martin's death."

"I am."

"You're not making sense. Look, I'm taking a chance talking to you at all. You'd better talk turkey to me or I'm gone. Vanished. Vamoosed."

"No, look." Lindsey reached out, then pulled his hand back before he took Hopkins's arm. "Berry was my friend. He was shot. They found him in an alley a few days ago."

Hopkins's eyebrows bounced up and back. "Oh, okay. I didn't get his name. I saw the picture, though. I get it now. Your pal was that overdressed black dude who got killed with Frankie Fulton."

"That's right."

"You're not a cop."

"Not at all." Lindsey handed him an International Surety business card.

Hopkins said, "Looks real enough." He turned the card over, shoved it in his pocket. "Of course, anybody could make one of these with a laser printer nowadays. Or have a job shop print 'em up if you didn't have the know-how yourself."

"What do I have to do? Do I have to prove I'm me? You want to see a driver's license? Birth certificate? Get real, Mr. Hopkins. What would I be up to, if I'm not bona fide?"

Hopkins pursed his lips. "Okay. Let's go find a place to sit."

The traffic was rumbling down Third Avenue despite the steadily falling snow. The street had been clear earlier in the day, or at least Lindsey thought it had. Now the snow was beginning to accumulate, packed down by vehicles. From somewhere uptown a siren whooped and howled. The traffic edged toward the curb and a fire chief's car careened past followed by a hook-and-ladder truck.

In seconds the traffic was back to normal. No sign remained that anything out of the ordinary had happened.

Hopkins led Lindsey to a Christian Science reading room. They found two chairs in a corner and sat facing each other. Hopkins picked up a copy of *The Christian Science Monitor* mounted on a wooden rod and spread it across his lap. He leaned back. He said, "Fill me in."

Lindsey told him the story, as much of it as he knew. When he finished, Hopkins said, "All right. Frankly, I don't really care that much about your pal Berry."

Lindsey had heard the same blasé line from Cele Johnston and come away with at least a telephone number. Now he waited for Hopkins to continue.

"But I do care about Millie."

"You and she were an item?"

Hopkins grinned. There was something bitter in the grin, but a touch of amusement as well.

"You really have been talking to Amy Baines. She's the only person I know who still uses that expression. *An item.* I guess you could say we were an item."

"And when she was killed, the police weren't interested, were they?"

"Not very."

"Is that the way it is in New York? I mean—I've heard that New Yorkers are jaded, people don't even bother to report burglaries and the like."

"True enough."

"But—murder?"

Hopkins shook his head. He had a gesture that he made every

so often, of taking his spade-shaped beard in his hand and squeezing. It looked as if he were wringing it out.

He said, "They pay attention to serious crimes if they think there's anything they can do. Or if the victim is rich or famous. Or if the crime is particularly gruesome. High profile stuff. *Daily News* or *Post* screamer stuff. Evening news footage on Channel Two."

"The *Daily News* described Millicent Martin as a showgirl. But your review of her in the *Times* made her seem like . . ." Lindsey didn't know what the review had made her seem like.

Hopkins snorted. "Seem like what? I didn't know myself. She was talented. She was a sweet little Italian girl from a town in Pennsylvania where everybody else was Polish. The Martinellis, with the Krystowskis on one side and the Wajowiczes on the other. You know the story, Lindsey."

Lindsey said nothing.

"She went to Mass every Sunday. The priest wanted her to become a nun, her parents wanted her to find a nice Italian boy and get married and make babies. She couldn't wait to get out of there and come to New York and get famous. She did all the standard stuff—class plays, homecoming queen, the works. She got to New York and she went a little crazy."

Hopkins wrung out his beard.

"How long did you know her?" Lindsey asked.

"Only a year. I saw her in that God-awful performance piece. *Princess of Planet P.* You know, it was really pee. It was all about this planet—this spaceship lands from earth and the world is made entirely of piss, and there are piss-mermaids, they welcome the astronauts. You wouldn't believe what a pile of crap can get produced in this town."

He dropped the newspaper, picked it up and set it back on the rack it had come from.

"But you said that she was good. In your *Times* review."

"I did. And she was. Talented. Beautiful." He shook his head. "A real Italian beauty. Blue-black hair, skin like— Look at me, Lindsey." He held his chin up, putting himself on display. "Mister WASP, right? Native New Yorker. Nothing can surprise me, nothing I can't handle. And I fall in love with this wonderful little Italian Catholic girl and she gets murdered."

He locked eyes with Lindsey. "She was going to move into my place. She got into a real mess but she cleaned up her act, she was doing okay. But they caught up with her, they wouldn't let her go. So—"

He spread his hands, a helpless gesture.

Lindsey leaned forward. He was going to ask Hopkins another question, but Hopkins beat him to the punch.

"I don't want to talk any more."

"But we're just starting."

"I can't."

"But I need to talk to you. What was Millicent's connection to Fulton? To Castellini? We haven't scratched—"

"Maybe another time."

"How can I reach you? I can't just call the *Times*."

Hopkins stood up. Lindsey followed suit. He saw a tremor in Hopkins's hands. Hopkins started toward the street.

Lindsey said, "Come on, Victor. You can't just leave me hanging."

Hopkins stopped. "All right. Give me your number. I'll call you when I'm ready to talk again. Promise me you won't bother Amy Baines. I'm going to tell her not to forward messages from you. I'll call you when I'm ready; that's the most I can offer."

Lindsey put on his new hat. He found an International Surety card and wrote the number of Berry's answering machine at the Fifty-eighth Street apartment on it. He handed it to Hopkins.

Hopkins looked at it, shoved it into his pocket, and pushed his way into Third Avenue.

Lindsey followed closely. "Are you sure you won't—"

Before he got any farther, Hopkins had disappeared into the crowd of pedestrians. Lindsey craned his neck, tried dodging left and right to keep Hopkins in sight. He thought he caught a glimpse of Hopkins's skiing cap half a block ahead, moving rapidly downtown. Then he saw no more of him.

Chapter Seven

No point in chasing Victor Hopkins, he was younger and more athletic than Lindsey. And besides, he was a native New Yorker. There was no way Lindsey was going to catch him. He'd just have to hope that the skittish young man would contact him.

In the meanwhile, he would keep working on the case.

He phoned Berry's East Side apartment and spoke with Zaffira Fornari. He told her he'd like to talk with Ester Berry once more.

Zaffira asked, "Did you not get your answers before when you were here?"

Lindsey said, "There are just a few more questions, if that wouldn't be too much trouble." Christ, straight out of a "Columbo" rerun.

"We got the autopsy report today. My sister is very upset."

Lindsey frowned. "Was there something—?"

"No, no. It's just—she's crying some more." There was a pause, then Lindsey heard Zaffira sigh. "Well, you come ahead. Maybe to talk will help her. You are coming now?"

Lindsey said yes, he was coming now.

Zaffira Fornari said, "Okay, you come now."

Lindsey was getting the hang of this town. He climbed aboard a Third Avenue bus, paid his fare, and actually found a seat.

A couple of kids were running a three-card monte game in the back of the bus. One of them was dealing, another was playing the part of the gambler and winning every time. Exclaiming, *This is easy, this is taking candy from a baby*. A third kid—they couldn't be more than twelve years old—was running up and down the aisle, inviting passengers to win easy money.

The pitchman must have spotted Lindsey for an out-of-towner. He jabbed a thumb at the dealer and the shill and said, *How 'bout it, how 'bout it, can't lose, everybody wins.*

Lindsey said, "Scram."

The kid looked hurt, shrugged his shoulders, moved on to another prospective sucker.

Lindsey reached for his pocket organizer and discovered that he still had the pamphlet and button that he'd gotten at yesterday's Amoroso for Senate rally. He studied the button, then slipped it back in his pocket. He turned the pages of the pamphlet idly. Who was the scholar they quoted about the fabled chariot? William Van Huysen, Ph.D., Yale University. Huh. Nothing if not classy. The bus was stuffy and getting crowded.

He looked over his shoulder at the passing street scene. Here, farther uptown, Third Avenue was lined with posh shops and restaurants. He couldn't see the sky, but the afternoon was growing dark. The snow was continuing to fall.

Enough.

Before he slipped the pamphlet back into his pocket he read Professor Van Huysen's little essay again. It was only three paragraphs long.

> The Silver Chariot of Caesar—actually a silver chariot drawn by a brace of horses sculpted of finest marble—has a long history. Its origins are shrouded in mystery. Legend has it that King David ordered it crafted as a plaything for his son Solomon. In later years it made its way to ancient Hellas, where Philip of Macedonia taught the youthful Alexander to use it in planning his later conquests.
>
> Carried to Rome by an itinerant Greek, it was presented to Julius Caesar when Caesar was but a child. The chariot brought him good fortune in war and in politics, but was lost to history shortly before Caesar's assassination. Some scholars believe that Charlemagne played with the toy chariot before becoming Holy Roman Emperor in the year 800.
>
> For over a thousand years the chariot was reported in

different parts of the world, only to disappear again and again. It was last exhibited in the Italian Pavilion at the New York World's Fair of 1939. In 1940 the chariot was supposed to be returned to Italy, but it never arrived there and has not been seen since.

Lindsey dropped the pamphlet back into his pocket. *Bogie*, he muttered, *where are you now that we need you?*

A woman sitting opposite Lindsey frowned at him, then buried herself in a copy of the *Post*.

The bus stopped at Seventy-second Street and Lindsey walked another block, turned right for half a block, and entered the Berrys' apartment building.

The elevator operator nodded to Lindsey. "Here for the Berrys again?"

Lindsey nodded.

When they reached the Berrys' floor the elevator operator didn't wait for Lindsey to be admitted before she returned to the lobby.

"Mr. Lindsey."

Ester Berry extended her hand and Lindsey shook it again. He'd been ushered to the couch once more. Today Zaffira Fornari served tea and joined her sister and Lindsey. Anna Maria, she explained, had taken Ezio to visit her friend Shoshana across the street. It was better. Today the autopsy report. Tomorrow the funeral. A child had to be protected, but how could you protect a child when her father was murdered?

Lindsey left his organizer in his pocket. He opened a little notepad and turned the barrel of his gold International Surety pencil. He'd been proud of that pencil once, had seen it as a kind of emblem of his own importance and his standing with the great corporate entity that had given it to him.

He looked at it now, and it was just a pencil.

"Mrs. Berry, I know this must be hard, but if you wouldn't mind . . ."

Ester Berry sighed. "You have to be better than that Sokolov woman. She called me this morning. She told me the results of the autopsy. She said she was sending a copy but she didn't want to keep me waiting."

She squeezed her eyes shut and shook her head.

"I don't mind waiting. What do I care if she calls me today or she calls me tomorrow? I don't care."

Lindsey said, "Mrs. Fornari said there was nothing—"

"No, nothing." She shook her head again and managed a ghastly suggestion of a smile. "You want to know what Detective Sokolov told me?"

"I think . . ." Lindsey wanted to indicate that the more information he had, the better chance that the pattern would become visible. The pattern that would point to the reason for Cletus Berry's murder. And once you knew *why* a murder was committed, there was a good chance you'd figure out who committed it.

"I think—if you don't mind," Lindsey repeated.

"She told me that my husband had fettuccine Alfredo for dinner before he was killed. And a salad, too. And maybe some rich dessert. I know. He used to eat tiramisu every chance. He didn't eat soul food. He ate Italian food. He loved Italy. I know that. She couldn't surprise me. She told me he had some alcohol in his blood, but just a little, he was not drunk. She told me he had no heroin, cocaine, or marijuana in his blood. She told me he was killed between eleven at night and two o'clock in the morning. She told me the bullet in his belly went right through him and out his back. They found it in the alley. The bullet in his head, it was still in his head when they opened him—"

Ester Lazarini Berry's face turned green. She lurched to her feet.

Zaffira Fornari was faster than Lindsey. He dropped his pencil and started to stand but she vaulted upright. She caught her sister by the arms and led her away.

From another room Lindsey heard the sound of a woman retching and moaning. Lindsey didn't know what to do. Should he follow the sisters? No, he rejected that idea. Let them have their privacy. He walked to the window and looked down into the quiet street. The snow had accumulated deeply enough to cover the blacktop. Darkness had fallen and streetlights had come on. The snow looked clean, almost blue, and peaceful.

A car turned into the street from the east, its headlights making twin cones of yellow-white through the falling flakes. Somewhere in the building someone must have turned on a stereo; he heard an orchestra playing a Christmas carol.

"Mr. Lindsey."

The two sisters had reappeared. They both wore black, as they had the previous day.

Lindsey said, "Maybe I should go. I mean, you're upset. Maybe I should come back another day. After, ah . . ." He swallowed and tried again. "I mean, after—"

"The funeral?" Zaffira guided her sister back to her easy chair. She poured tea and handed Ester the cup. Ester held the cup, stared at it as if she didn't know what it was, then sipped and put the cup back down.

She said, "Stay, Mr. Lindsey. What can I tell you? What can I give you that will help you? I know you are helping us; how can we help you?" Without asking if he wanted it, she poured a cup of tea for him.

Lindsey picked up his notebook and pencil. He didn't have any questions written out, but he wanted to make notes. Sometimes it gave an interview a kind of shape to write things down.

"Mrs. Berry—if you don't mind my asking—you told me that your family disapproved of your marrying Cletus. But how did you know him? How did you meet him?"

Ester smiled again, this time a real smile despite the load of grief attached to it.

"I'll tell you too much," she said. "I don't know where to start, what to tell you."

"Anywhere."

"I had a very protected childhood, you understand? I was born—I come from a good family. A very old family. My family thought they were real Italians, they were in Rome for thousands of years. Can you understand thousands of years? In this new country, this new America? I remember the fuss, the bicentennial they called it, in 1976. I was still in Italy then, I was a schoolgirl, eighteen years old. I remember, we saw on the television, all the carrying on in America."

She exchanged a look with her older sister.

"We laughed about it. This big baby of a country, America, two hundred years old. And making so much fuss." She tilted her head to left and right, rocking with remembered amusement. "Of course, you make birthday parties for children. Not so much for grown-ups, eh?"

"About your childhood," Lindsey prompted.

"Oh, yes. I told you, I'm not so good at—what—condensing. Editing. I wouldn't make such a good editor."

She lifted her cup and took another sip of tea. There was a dish of little cookies on the silver tray beside the teapot and the sugar and lemon. Lindsey took a cookie and nibbled at the edge. He put it down on his saucer beside his cup.

"How did you and Cletus meet?" he asked once more.

"He was a soldier. An officer. What they call a warrant officer, you know that, what that is?"

Lindsey nodded.

"He was part of NATO. They had their big headquarters in Belgium, they had headquarters in other countries, too. We were supposed to be afraid the Russians were coming in their big tanks to crush us, like they did in Prague. That I remember. Yes, Sister?"

"I remember," Zaffira agreed. "We are little girls then but we remember that."

"We didn't understand, you see?" Ester resumed. "Seven years old, eight years old, we were like two babies. My daughter is ten years old, I look at her and I see what a baby she is still. So smart, she can do anything she wants in this country but such a baby should have her father with her."

Lindsey nodded. "But you say you met Cletus in 1975?"

"Oh, no, no." She waved her hands in front of her, waving away the mistake. "I was telling you about the bicentennial, that's all. I was seventeen when I met him. I was in the museum. With my sister, you remember, Sister?"

Zaffira said, "I remember."

"We were looking at paintings. We always loved the paintings. I thought that the history of the world was best recorded in its art. Paintings, statues, tapestries. We were in the Pinacoteca Capitolina of the Palazzo dei Conservatori. I remember, I was standing in front of a Tintoretto virgin. You remember, Sister?"

"No, Sister. It was *The Fortune Teller* by Caravaggio. I remember it very clearly."

"No, Sister. This is something I would never forget. Never. It was the Tintoretto."

"The Tintoretto," Zaffira conceded.

"Wearing schoolgirl clothing, you understand. A uniform. Very modest. You understand, Mr. Lindsey? Nothing provocative."

"I understand."

"And I saw this American soldier. He was wearing his uniform. I knew the insignia, I knew all the uniforms. We used to see British, Dutch, all the uniforms. Of course we knew the Italian uniforms. But I knew the American. And this soldier, this warrant officer, came over and spoke to me in Italian. He spoke Italian very well. He asked if I knew anything about Tintoretto and I was so frightened of him that I tried to hide behind Zaffira. Do you remember, Sister?"

"I remember."

"I didn't say a word to him. I just hid my face from him, I was so embarrassed. I was terrified. Remember, Sister?"

Outside the apartment a car horn sounded in the street. The Christmas carols in the next apartment—or was it the apartment upstairs?—gave way to a symphony that Lindsey didn't recognize.

"Did he follow you home?" Lindsey asked.

"No, nothing as trite as that. I saw him again at a museum. You weren't there, Zaffira. I was there with my friend Veronica Scaletti. You remember Veronica? Of course."

This time she really smiled as she relived the event.

"We went to the Galleria Spada. Were you ever there, Zaffira? On the Piazza Capo di Ferro? I remember, Veronica and I, we were standing in front of *Saint Cecilia Playing a Lute*. I always loved that painting because the artist was a woman, did you know that? Artemisia Gentileschi. Women were thought to be good only for bearing children and cooking in those days. Some men still think that. But Artemisia proved her mettle."

She paused and sipped at her tea. Then she resumed.

"Veronica and I were talking about Artemisia, when he appeared again. He came over to us. He was very polite. He said he was surprised to see me. He asked if he could buy us an espresso. He loved espresso, you know?"

"That I know," Lindsey said.

"Ester!" Zaffira gasped.

Ester giggled. "You never knew that story, Sister? You're scandalized, aren't you?"

"A man you didn't even know. A man you'd never been introduced to." She shook her head.

"Mr. Lindsey, Cletus was very proper. He took us both for espresso and biscotti. He knew Rome very well, you know."

Lindsey said, "No, I didn't know. I didn't even know he'd been in the army. There's so much that Cletus never talked about."

"When he came to my house the first time, the whole street buzzed. There were no gentiles on our street. The Piazzetta del Pancotto has been a Jewish street for centuries. Even when the Nazis came, my mother told us, the Jews stayed. Some of them, anyway. Others hid, others the Nazis took. The Lazarinis have owned their house in the Piazzetta del Pancotto for so many generations, nobody knows when we first got it."

Zaffira rose and went to the window behind Ester. She looked into the street.

Ester said, "Sister, stop worrying."

"I worry."

"I know. She's all right."

"She has to cross the street."

"She goes to school herself every day. Sister, she's ten years old. What were ten-year-old Jews doing in our parents' day? You and I, Zaffira, we were raised in a sheltered world."

"My husband was not sheltered. Your husband was not sheltered. Let the child be protected."

She rubbed at the inside of the windowpane. "There, I see her coming now. With her dog."

Lindsey said, "Should I leave, then?"

Ester held out a hand toward him, not touching him. "Stay," she said. "Take supper with us. We're not having much tonight. If you—"

"I don't want to intrude. I mean—"

"You were Cletus's friend. Stay."

Lindsey headed for the table. The telephone rang and Zaffira scurried to answer it. He heard her speak in Italian, then call her sister. Ester spoke for a while, then hung up the phone.

She drew a deep breath, pulled her shoulders back, and went into the kitchen.

"Relatives," Zaffira said. "Cousins. Aunts and uncles. Our family. My husband, may he rest, his family. They call every hour. They bring food and sit. I guess they try and help. I know they try. But who can help?"

The meal was plain, chicken soup with vegetables and noodles. There was no separate dining room in the apartment, merely an ell off the living room, with the kitchen door just beyond.

Anna Maria had gone to her room to wash and change her clothes for dinner. She returned wearing a white T-shirt and jeans. Her hair was thick and black and drawn behind her head with a ribbon.

Ezio Pinza sat in a corner, watching them eat. Lindsey thought, *He's suspicious of me.* Then he thought, *Am I sitting in Cletus's chair? If I am, I don't blame him for being suspicious.*

Zaffira brought the food from the kitchen.

Before anyone touched it, Ester said a prayer in Hebrew. Lindsey had shared evenings with Eric Coffman and his wife, Miriam, and their daughters. Consequently, the little ceremony did not catch him totally off guard.

He knew that Cletus Berry's funeral was scheduled for the next morning. He expected to be there. It was International Surety policy. It was also his friend's burial. He thought that Berry's widow and her sister and daughter might prefer to be alone tonight, to prepare themselves for the ordeal. But the two women seemed to be trying to make the evening seem remotely like a normal one, probably for Anna Maria's sake.

"What did you do at Shoshana's house?" Ester asked.

"She has some new software she showed me. Some history software. We looked up Italy and Africa and Israel. We both have to do papers for school. Then we surfed the 'Net for a while. We met some interesting kids and talked about basketball. There were a couple of Sonics fans and a Utah Jazz fan. Lame. And one kid who wanted to talk about cooking. Shoshana told him about her dad and that shut him up for good."

"Fine." Zaffira ran her hand over her niece's hair. To Lindsey she said, "Shoshana's father is a chef. A place they call it Pete's Tavern. Downtown. Good food. He calls it Italian. Not so Italian, but good."

Anna Maria looked at Lindsey. He'd never seen eyes like this child's. Huge and liquid. A dark brown shade. The mixture of genes she'd inherited had harmonized to perfection. He thought, If things had worked out differently, if he and Marvia Plum had ever given Jamie a half-brother or -sister, would she be this beautiful and this vibrant?

"Mr. Lindsey?"

He swallowed a spoonful of the soup, then nodded encouragingly at Anna Maria.

"Were you really my father's friend?" she asked.

"Yes, I was."

"Did you know him well?"

"I'd have liked to know him better than I did. What can I tell you, Anna Maria? Or, what can you tell me?"

"Maybe some things," she said. She turned her attention to her plate and speared a bright orange piece of carrot with her fork. She cut it in two, ate the first piece, then the second.

Ester said, "Anna Maria is the family historian now. She took that over from her mother. I was the historian. I went to school with the great Carlo Pacinelli. You don't know him in America, but in Italy he is a great man now. But in school he was my friend.

When I was younger I was the family historian, but my daughter is now."

Anna Maria turned her head away.

"Just like you," Zaffira said. "Just like her mother."

"Can I show Mr. Lindsey my computer?" Anna Maria asked eagerly.

"Finish your meal first."

"After, then."

Lindsey said, "I don't think I should stay late. Tomorrow is— I mean, I thought you might want to—" He let the rest of the thought trail away. How could he say that they would need a good night's rest before burying their dead?

"Maybe we should be together. Thank you, Mr. Lindsey."

Zaffira retired to the kitchen, returned with coffee for the adults, a glass of milk for Anna Maria.

"We don't keep kosher," Ester explained. "We don't sit shiva and we don't keep kosher. Another scandal. My sister couldn't believe it when she came here. I told her, When in America, do as the Americans do."

"I have enough on my mind when I come to America," Zaffira said.

Lindsey wiped his lips on his linen napkin. "Another time." He smiled at Anna Maria. "Another time, I'd like to see your computer."

She said, "My dad bought it for me. It was a present for my last birthday."

Lindsey rode down in the elevator, struck by the stray question: What had happened to Zaffira Fornari's husband?

Chapter Eight

BACK AT THE Torrington Tower apartment, Lindsey hung his suit carefully along with Cletus Berry's. He washed up and pulled on a set of sweats and athletic socks and slippers.

He checked his watch. Even allowing for time zones, it was after normal office hours in Denver, but Desmond Richelieu was in the habit of working late. If nothing else, Lindsey could leave a message on Richelieu's voice mail, or send him an E-message from his laptop.

Or from Cletus Berry's desktop.

The police had checked the contents of Berry's computer, Sokolov had told Lindsey, and found nothing out of the ordinary. But they didn't know Berry even as well as Lindsey did. And more to the point, they didn't know International Surety procedure in general or SPUDS in particular. They didn't know SPUDS at all.

This was something that Lindsey would look into.

But first he picked up Berry's telephone and punched in the number of Desmond Richelieu's private line.

Richelieu picked up on the first ring. He recognized Lindsey's voice at once. He wasn't hostile, but he minced no words. "What have you got for me?"

"I'm not sure. I'm trying to put this together."

"You haven't filed a report."

"I'm not ready."

"Lindsey, this isn't just a claim. It isn't just dollars. Somebody scragged one of my boys, and I'm damned if I let it slide."

"I understand, Mr. Richelieu."

"I'd do the same for you. I'd do the same for some minimum-wage office slavey."

Lindsey could see Richelieu communing with the autographed portrait of J. Edgar Hoover that hung behind his desk in Denver. "I've been collecting pieces," Lindsey said. "They don't make a picture yet. I'm not sure if I'm missing some important piece or if I don't understand what I have."

"I know you, Lindsey. I know your work. You keep on collecting pieces. I know you'll put it together. What time is the funeral?" He shifted gears without pausing for breath.

"Tomorrow at eleven."

"I spoke with Morris Zissler, Lindsey. He ordered flowers. Per the manual. He'll pick you up. Where are you staying?"

Lindsey told him.

There was a long pause. Lindsey envisioned the sun setting in Colorado. From his apartment in Denver he could see the sun set most evenings behind the Rockies to the west of the city. It was seldom a lingering, rosy sight. The mountains were silhouetted, the sun a brilliant disk, and then it was gone and it was night. As if a god had died.

"You think that's a good idea?" Richelieu asked. "We'll spring for a hotel room, Lindsey. What kind of cheapskate outfit do you think we are?"

"It isn't that," Lindsey demurred. "I'm— Look, Mr. Richelieu, you know I'm no mystic or anything like that."

Richelieu snorted. "You can say that again."

Lindsey resumed, "I just feel as if I might get something, some idea, pick up some clue by staying here. I mean, Cletus's belongings, his files. I think I just might get something."

"Okay, Lindsey. You stay with it. Look"—another shift of the gears—"what kind of cooperation are you getting from the police there?"

Lindsey told Richelieu of his visit to Midtown North and his meeting with Marcie Sokolov.

"Not so good, eh?"

"No, not so good."

"All right, Lindsey. I don't want you just going through the motions on this thing. I know you won't do that, that's why I gave you this job."

"He was my friend, Mr. Richelieu."

"Keep at it. You're my best agent. You're a damned thorn in my side half the time, too. But you're still my best."

Lindsey heard the line go dead. That was Richelieu's style. He didn't say good-bye and he didn't slam down the receiver. He just cut the connection when he'd heard what he had to hear and said what he had to say.

Okay.

Lindsey laid down the telephone and swung around in Cletus Berry's swivel chair. He thought of booting up his laptop computer, even got as far as laying his hand on top of its smooth black lid, then turned instead to Berry's desktop computer and hit the power switch.

The machine was standard International Surety issue; unless Berry had gimmicked the software Lindsey should be able to work with Berry's computer as easily as he did with his own. Even if Berry had protected his files with passwords, Lindsey had access to SPUDS override coding that should get him through the barriers. Such were the prerogatives of standing near the flagpole.

Time was when Lindsey was a computer illiterate, threatened at the thought of a machine that understood him better than he understood it. That was back in his pre-SPUDS days, when he'd worked out of International Surety's branch office in Walnut Creek, a few miles to the east of Oakland, California.

That was Lindsey's first brush with an authentic, bona fide, no-doubt-about-it genius, M. Martin Saxon. Saxon had turned a start-up computer company into a major industry player, sold out and moved to a farm in Vermont to tinker with circuits and invent software. He'd invited Lindsey to look him up, and Lindsey had agreed to and put Saxon's Vermont address into his pocket organizer and never looked at it again.

Berry's files were pretty conventional. One thing that Berry had done was set up a name-and-address file—no Rolodex for him. Lindsey scrolled through it, hoping to find an entry for Alcide

Castellini, but there was none. Well, that was probably too much to hope for. If there was something fishy going on with Castellini, Berry would either have encrypted the entry or simply committed it to memory. If it was encrypted—or simply listed under a phony name—the odds against turning it up were pretty bad.

Still, Lindsey gave it a shot. Try a word search for Castellini. No luck. Try one for Alcide. Nothing.

He tried again, using the telephone number that Cele Johnston had given him. Nada.

Nor was there an entry for Cele Johnston—a long shot—or for Frankie Fulton or for Millicent Martin/Martinelli.

In fact, scrolling through Berry's address file, Lindsey found few surprises, if any. He found himself in the file, Desmond Richelieu, Aurora Delano, half a dozen other SPUDS stalwarts. Moe Zissler at Manhattan East. That was no surprise. And plenty of others that rang no bell with Lindsey. Some of the addresses indicated business connections. Others might be friends; Berry was personable enough to have a huge Christmas card list. And how in the world was Lindsey going to check out every Epstein, O'Hara, and d'Agostino in the file?

He was on the edge of giving up when a name caught his attention.

Harry Scott.

A familiar name; Lindsey could almost identify it. Leaving Berry's address file open, he toggled into KlameNet/Plus and dialed up the SPUDS master directory. There was Harry Scott, SPUDS Regional, Southern Europe.

It might mean something that Cletus Berry had Scott's addresses—E-mail, snail mail, fax—as well as a Rome telephone number in his personal look-up. If it did, though, precisely what it meant was a mystery. The man might simply be an old buddy from Berry's army days.

Lindsey closed the file and took a look at Berry's directory. The biggest part of his records was given over to case files, sequenced by IS policy number.

Outside the windows of Cletus Berry's pied-à-terre and secret hideaway, streetlights illuminated the tops of cars and the surface of the street itself. There was little vehicular traffic on this street at this time of night, and even less pedestrian activity. The flakes had ceased to fall, but the wind had apparently sprung up, and swirls of snow were swept off the roofs of buildings and spun and danced through the glow of the streetlights in pure white, miniature tornadoes.

After a few snowstorms in Denver, Lindsey knew that the pale beauty of the cityscape would turn dark and ugly within a few days. In fact, in New York the transformation would probably take only a matter of hours. But the sight of the city covered with fresh snow seized his heart all the more because of its fleeting nature.

Beauty and happiness did not endure. He pictured Marvia Plum, remembered her smile. He leaned his forehead against the cold glass, blinked his eyes, and went back to Cletus Berry's chair. What did he have to complain about? Think of Ester Lazarini Berry. Think of Anna Maria Berry.

He started through Berry's personal case files.

Most of the cases were routine—or as close to routine as SPUDS cases ever got. Some of them were peculiar; some were even funny. He came across an entry for one of his own cases, the MacReedy death claim on which Berry had ferreted out a sixty-year-old copy of the *Mosholu Parkway Jewish Community Center Bulletin* and relayed its contents to Lindsey. That investigation hadn't saved the company any money—International Surety's financial stake in the case had been minimal—but the information had helped Lindsey to unravel a bizarre and complicated puzzle.

But aside from the MacReedy case, and a few others that Lindsey had had a fleeting connection with, or about which Berry had told them at one of the periodic SPUDS conferences they both attended, nothing looked familiar and everything looked kosher.

Except . . .

Except for one oddity.

The case numbers were eight digits long. If you knew the coding—it wasn't really arcane—you could easily tell whether the claim had been filed against International Surety or one of the predecessor companies that had amalgamated decades ago to form IS.

And you could tell the year the policy was issued, the year the claim was filed, the status of the claim and year it was paid out of it had been paid.

Most of Berry's cases came on IS files. That was no surprise. And while the policy issue dates in some cases stretched back into the 1950s or even further, the claims had been filed no earlier than 1981.

Even the MacReedy case. The policy had been issued by Global National Guarantee Life, one of IS's smaller predecessor companies. Issue date was 1931. Claim date was 1994.

Everything fit together properly.

But here was another peculiar one. Issuing company was the New York Amalgamated Guarantee Insurance Company. Lindsey had seen occasional references to the company. Global National and New York Amalgamated had been affiliated long before they disappeared into International Surety. They even had nicknames. *Gingle* and *Nyagic*. They rhymed with single and tragic. But this case had a seven-digit number.

The MacReedy case had involved a Gingle policy.

And the Nyagic case that Lindsey had found in Berry's records had an issue date of 1938. A claim had been filed against the policy in 1940. And the claim had been paid and the case marked closed in 1951.

Why had it taken eleven years to pay the claim?

And why did Cletus Berry have a copy of the file on his hard disk when he hadn't joined IS until 1981?

Lindsey hit the familiar sequence of keys that would open the case file for him, and nothing happened. He tried again, in case he'd made a mistake. He was very careful this time. Access was denied.

Curiouser and curiouser.

Lindsey logged onto Klamenet/Plus, International Surety's master data system. It was easy enough to navigate KNP if you stayed in your own work area. If you wanted to go outside, it was tough—deliberately so. Corporate management didn't want every little branch office or claims agent peeking into sensitive areas.

But Lindsey's top-level SPUDS clearance should get him anything he wanted, outside of top-level, personal-and-confidential corporate files. He keyed in the odd, seven-digit policy number and drew a blank. It just wasn't in the International Surety master file.

His clearance got him into an ancient New York Amalgamated Guarantee directory. Talk about disturbing the bones of the dead! He keyed in the file number for the 1938 policy, but again he drew a blank.

He walked around the problem, poking his electronic finger at it from every angle he could think of. And still drew a blank.

He bailed out of KNP and scooted Cletus Berry's swivel chair over to the closet, fished his pocket organizer out of his suit jacket, and looked up M. Martin Saxon. There he was, snugged away in the bosom of Bellows Falls, Vermont. And—mirabile dictu!—he'd given Lindsey both a telephone number and an on-line address, as well as his mailing address.

If only they were still valid . . . It had been half a decade; in the electronic world, that was more like half a millennium.

Lindsey composed an E-mail and zapped it off to Saxon.

He put some cocoa powder into a cup of milk and nuked it in Cletus Berry's microwave. By the time he sat down with it there was a reply from Saxon. At first Lindsey thought he'd scored a lucky hit, catching Saxon online. Then he realized that Saxon must spend a lot of time online. Bellows Falls, Vermont, after all. Bellows Falls, Vermont.

Nice to hear from you. Wondered whatever became of you and those comic books. What are you up to?

Lindsey scratched his head. What *was* he up to? He sketched out his problem with the New York Amalgamated policy. When Saxon's reply appeared on the monitor screen, Lindsey could almost hear the laughter.

You corporate types and your security coding. I guess you'll never learn that there's no lock without a key. Even if you can't open the file, see if you can unload it and zap it to me.

Huh. Showing IS policies to outsiders—and even though this was a Nyagic policy, the merger had made it an International Surety policy, de facto—was a breach of confidentiality. Unless the policyholder gave permission . . . But in this case, there was no way to get that permission without first reading the file to find out who the policyholder was.

Somewhere, Joseph Heller was laughing up his sleeve.

Lindsey explained the problem to Saxon.

A message came back.

Pay me one dollar. Hire me as a consultant. I'll sign a confidential disclosure agreement.

A couple more messages and they'd settled. It was only a virtual dollar, of course, but then it was only a virtual signature. Lindsey figured they were equally real.

He uploaded the Nyagic file and zapped it to Saxon.

Saxon sent a message back.

Go walk around the block. Enjoy Nature. This is going to take a little while.

Lindsey wasn't going to walk around this section of Manhattan, alone, in the middle of the night. He sipped his cocoa, reviewed the case, finally phoned Moe Zissler.

Yes, Zissler had ordered flowers for Cletus Berry's funeral, and he was planning to attend the service and the burial, per company policy. Of course he'd pick Lindsey up at Fifty-eighth Street and they could ride together.

Lindsey lay down on top of the futon, comfortable in his sweats. He was half-dozing when Berry's computer sounded a chime. He went to the sink and threw some cold water on his face, wiped it dry, and sat down in front of the monitor.

Piece of cake. I only read the heading on the file to make sure I'd cracked it. Then I wiped it. Your secrets are safe with me. Attached coding will do the trick for you. First line will tell you how to install it. Call me anytime. That buck will come in handy.

Lindsey downloaded the code and followed Saxon's instructions for installing it on Berry's desktop. Then he crossed his fingers and hit the Nyagic file with Saxon's code. It opened with a pop he could almost hear.

The first thing Lindsey looked for was the name of the policyholder. The policy had been issued in the name of His Majesty Victor Emmanuel III, King of Italy and Sardinia.

He clicked Berry's laser printer into life. Lindsey preferred working with hard copy to reading lengthy files on the monitor screen. But before he could start printing the Nyagic file, the printer flashed a low-toner alert. Grumbling, Lindsey searched for a cartridge.

No luck. Either Berry was simply out of toner, or he relied on somebody else to handle that for him. Knowing Berry as a handy, self-reliant person, Lindsey assumed the former. In any case, he'd just have to read the file on the monitor and jot down any salient points that he needed at his fingertips.

He flipped the switch on Cletus Berry's space heater to high. He logged onto KlameNet/Plus and put the Nyagic file back into International Surety's database. He didn't know who had erased it, although Cletus Berry had to be a prime candidate for that little caper.

Feeling like a good corporate citizen, he logged off KNP, brought the file back up, and leaned back in his chair. At least Berry had a good big monitor with nice bright phosphors. Always look at the sunny side.

Still, it was going to be a long night.

Chapter Nine

LINDSEY HATED FUNERALS.

He hated the service at the funeral home on the Upper West Side. He stood between Moe Zissler and the grieving women, listening to the sound of crying. Zissler wore a dark suit, a white shirt, a dark, striped tie, and a yarmulke.

Lindsey wore a similar suit but he'd brought a black tie with him from Denver. He knew when he left home that he'd be attending Cletus Berry's funeral, and he brought the tie as a symbol of—

Something.

A symbol of something.

Ester Berry and Zaffira Fornari and Anna Maria Berry were a mass of blackness. The two women kept the little girl between them, as if the presence of their bodies, one to either side, could protect her from the reality of the event.

Lindsey recognized the broad-shouldered man he had seen leaving the Seventy-third Street building the first time he'd visited the Berry apartment. He was standing with Ester and Zaffira and Anna Maria, touching the women's shoulders, murmuring to them, stroking the child's hair as if he were petting a nervous colt. Anna Maria took his hand between hers and held his palm over her eyes.

Lindsey caught a glimpse of skin on Ester's shoulder. He peered at her, then at Zaffira and at Anna Maria. Each of them had opened a seam at the shoulder of her dress. The broad-shouldered man wore a small black ribbon, pinned to his lapel. It had been cut partway through, and the lower half hung at a crooked angle.

More Eric Coffman data. The opened seams were symbolic of the mourners rending their clothing in anguish. The sliced black ribbon represented a heart torn by grief.

The crying that Lindsey heard had been Anna Maria's.

She'd kept up a good front the times he'd seen her at Seventy-third Street, but now she was dealing with her father's death. If the service at the funeral home was bad, he feared that the graveside service and burial would be worse.

The service was Jewish. Berry had never mentioned religion to Lindsey, and Lindsey had gotten the impression that Berry was indifferent to the subject. He wondered if Berry had discussed the subject of funerals with his wife, if this had been agreed to in advance, or if it was just Ester's last-minute decision.

Whatever got the mourners through the ordeal, Lindsey thought. Cletus Berry didn't care.

The congregation was mixed—half white and half black. No one talked much except the rabbi. He referred to *the deceased*. Not Mr. Berry, not Cletus. The deceased. And the bereaved wife of the deceased, dear Ester, and the bereaved daughter of the deceased, dear Anna Maria, and the bereaved brother of the deceased, dear Petrus.

Dear Petrus.

At least Lindsey knew who the broad-shouldered black man was—and why he'd looked so familiar. Lindsey had never known that Cletus Berry had a brother. That was one of the many things he had never known about his dead friend.

The rabbi delivered a eulogy. Probably it was a very good eulogy, but Lindsey had trained his ears to tune out platitudes and there was little else to hear. Platitudes. Platitudes and the sound of weeping.

He detected a strong minty odor and saw Moe Zissler pocketing an enameled tin. Lindsey and Zissler made eye contact and Zissler telepathically offered Lindsey a mint and Lindsey telepathically refused it.

When the service ended and they filed out of the funeral home for the ride to the cemetery, Lindsey spotted another familiar figure: Marcie Sokolov. She nodded to him, then slipped out the door.

They rode across one of the city's bridges to Queens, and to the cemetery. Lindsey finally noticed what kind of car Zissler drove. It was a new—or at least newish—Buick Somerset. Once in the car, its heater on high to fight the cold, damp morning, Zissler asked Lindsey how he liked New York.

Lindsey shrugged.

He let his gaze wander. The city looked gray and dingy; the day was cold and bleak.

Lindsey said, "Maybe it's more fun in the spring."

Zissler grunted. "You don't mind if I turn on the radio?"

Lindsey shook his head, then said, "Go ahead."

Zissler punched a preset and pulled in a sports-talk call-in show. A caller with a high-pitched, irritating voice was speculating on various NFL playoff scenarios, trying to work out the likely Superbowl teams. The host reminded him that the studio guest was a member of the New York Knicks basketball team.

"But if the NFC wild-card team makes it past the Central Division winner while the AFC East champs beat the AFC West champs, then when they get to the conference finals—"

"Did you hear me?" the host asked.

"Then when they get to the finals, if you still have a wild-card team with a realistic shot at the Superbowl, this will be the first time since nineteen—"

"Sir, the topic is basketball."

"Yeah, I know, but listen—with two weeks left in the regular season, think back on this now, with more than half the teams in the NFL still in the mathematical running, if—"

"Good-bye, sir. Call again. Never. Listen, I'm sorry about that idiot; he calls every week and I can never get rid of him. I even tried using caller-ID and blocking his calls, but he uses a different pay phone every week."

Moe Zissler guffawed. The Buick was filled with a blossoming cloud of peppermint.

Lindsey said, "I guess I've changed my mind. Would you mind if we didn't have the radio on?"

Zissler said, "Okay." He killed the voices and started to hum.

At the cemetery they gathered around the grave. Lindsey shuddered. His skin tingled and his ears rang. It was hard to accept the reality of the scene. Everything was cliché—the mourners, their breath rising in columns of steam, the murmured conversations, the sobs.

Ester and Zaffira had made a shelter of themselves for Anna Maria.

Marcie Sokolov stood a few yards away, her eyes darting from person to person.

The hearse arrived last, preceded by the rabbi's car.

There were a few folding chairs. A funeral director led Ester and Zaffira and Anna Maria to them and urged them to be seated. The metal must be freezing. Could they feel the cold through their layers of black clothing? Lindsey wondered.

The cars of the funeral party stood on a gravel road twenty or thirty yards from the grave.

The cemetery was an old one, with stone mausolea and upright markers. Not like the modern practice of low, flat markers that would lie flush with the earth and facilitate the passage of riding mowers in the summer.

The mourners ranged themselves near the grave, save for one who stood near a limousine. Lindsey got one clear glimpse of the man. Silver hair, distinguished handsome face, stocky build, fifty-ish.

It was Alcide Castellini.

The rabbi was praying in Hebrew. The kaddish, Lindsey remembered. Some of the mourners followed, also in Hebrew. Ester and Zaffira mixed sobs with words Lindsey didn't understand; the little girl only cried.

Lindsey watched Petrus Berry advance and put his arms around the three of them, dipping his head to the level of the women's faces. Lindsey could see the two women nodding. The man reached between them to take Anna Maria away from the graveside, but she dug her heels into the frozen earth, refusing to go. The man stopped tugging and remained with the family.

The casket was lowered, the ceremonial handfuls of dirt were thrown onto it, the three shrouded females walked to the limousine, Petrus Berry with them, managing somehow to keep them encircled in his arms.

A driver opened the limousine door. Before he could close it the rabbi made his way to the limousine, spoke briefly with the family of the dear deceased, then turned away.

The driver closed the passenger door, climbed into the driver's seat, and slammed his own door.

The procession began to move from the cemetery, the tires of the vehicles crunching on the gravel-covered blacktop. Lindsey blew a cloud of breath into the air, feeling like an extra in a Hammer horror film, save for the icy fist clutching his heart.

Lindsey looked around for Alcide Castellini. He was gone.

Lindsey spotted Moe Zissler. He heaved a sigh and headed for Zissler, ready to return to Manhattan, but he was halted by a hand clutching his biceps. He turned and saw Marcie Sokolov.

"We've got something."

"That's—" For a moment Lindsey was stymied. Everything he'd heard from Sokolov had told him that she was just going through the motions, that her caseload was overwhelming, and that to her the Berry-Fulton slayings were just two more statistics, Cletus Berry and Frankie Fulton just two more bad actors who would never be missed.

"You can come over to the shop this afternoon if you feel like it. Phone first, so I won't be out. But I think I can show you something good."

That was all he could get out of her.

He rode back to Fifty-eighth Street with Zissler. Halfway there he listened to Zissler's humming. When he couldn't take any more he reached down and turned on the radio himself. He hit Zissler's presets one after another, then tried the seek button and managed to find an oldies station playing "Time of the Season." He'd never liked the song but it was the best he could do this time, so he sweltered in the Buick heater's stale hot air, Moe Zissler's peppermint fumes, and the Zombies' lugubrious lyrics.

As the Buick curved down an off-ramp, Zissler asked, "Do you want to come up and look around Manhattan East?"

Lindsey rolled his window down and pulled a load of what passed in New York for fresh air into his aching lungs. "No thanks, Moe. No thanks. Just drop me at Seventh Avenue and I'll, ah, I'll go on from there."

"Okay." Zissler popped his lips, exhaling a fresh cloud of peppermint fumes. "It's your funeral."

Perfect, Lindsey thought, *that's just perfect, Moe.* But he held his tongue until Zissler pulled the Buick to the curb and Lindsey opened the door and got out. Then he said, "Thanks, Moe."

He stopped for a salad and a cup of tea and walked the cold city sidewalks back to the Torrington Tower. He waved to Lou Halter, back on duty and sitting like a fixture at the desk in his gray guard's uniform, then rode up in the elevator and entered Cletus Berry's private digs.

He laid Congressman Amoroso's campaign brochure on the desk beside Cletus Berry's computer. Then he pulled the Nyagic file up and displayed it on the monitor once more. He scrolled through the file, then checked the credit-line on the brochure, picked up Berry's telephone, and dialed directory assistance. A few minutes later he heard the buzzing of a telephone ringing in New Haven, Connecticut. He hoped that William Van Huysen was home, and that he'd be willing to talk with him.

A child answered the phone and Lindsey asked if Dr. Van Huysen was there. The child summoned Van Huysen. It was winter break at Yale University, and Lindsey offered up a breath of thanks that Van Huysen had not left town when the students did.

"I just read your little essay in Congressman Amoroso's campaign brochure," Lindsey began.

Van Huysen stopped him right there. "I'm sorry about that. I thought Amoroso was getting up a little educational pamphlet. I didn't know it was for a piece of campaign literature. I am not a political person and I don't want to get involved with politics."

Lindsey said, "No, I'm not political either. I'm—"

"A journalist?"

"No, sir. I'm in the insurance business. I was up all last night, studying an old case file and—"

"What did you say your name was?"

"Lindsey. Hobart Lindsey. I'm associated with International Surety. Perhaps you've heard of us."

Van Huysen had not heard of International Surety, he told Lindsey, but that didn't mean very much; he was sure there were a great many insurance companies he'd never heard of.

Lindsey admitted that was true.

"What was that about an old case?" Van Huysen spoke in a bland, droning voice. Perfect for a professor of classics. Lindsey didn't want to alienate the man.

"Your essay about the silver chariot, Dr. Van Huysen."

"Yes. Caesar's chariot."

"Was it really? Caesar's, I mean."

"I don't know." Van Huysen heaved a sigh. "Mr.—Lindsey, was it?—I've got a journal article to write over this holiday break, and a doctoral student I'm advising who is absolutely hopeless, hopeless, and— What is it, precisely, that you want from me?"

"Well, your essay about the chariot says that it disappeared in 1940. Can you tell me about that? In any more detail, I mean."

"Mr. Lindsey, you'd better tell me what this is all about. Before I answer any more questions for you, I need to know, precisely, what it is that you have in mind."

"It's rather complicated, Professor."

"Well, frankly, I don't like dealing over the telephone. Is this something that your company needs to know? Are you trying to settle a claim, or what?"

"Not really. It's— One of our employees was murdered, you see. He was also a friend of mine, you see, so I really have both a personal and an official interest in justice. The police have the case, but I'm not really confident that they're handling it effectively. So I'm trying to gather some information myself."

There was a long silence. Lindsey thought he heard a baroque quartet playing softly in the background and a fire crackling on a New England hearth. *Christmas in Connecticut*, Barbara Stanwyck, Dennis Morgan, the great Sydney Greenstreet. A far cry from his role as Kasper Gutman. Lindsey could never see Greenstreet without a bottle of Johnnie Walker whiskey and a Corona del Ritz cigar in his hand.

"I'll tell you what," Van Huysen said, interrupting Lindsey's brief reverie. Just as well, Lindsey thought. The music and the fire were probably in his imagination. Sydney Greenstreet surely was.

Lindsey waited for Van Huysen to tell him what.

"If your corporation wants to pick my brain, they can hire me as a consultant. Pay my fee, you come on up here to New Haven, and I'll be happy to answer your questions." He paused. "Although you could just go to the library, you know."

"I'm sure we can arrange that," Lindsey consented. "How about tomorrow?"

Tomorrow it was. Van Huysen named a fee and Lindsey agreed. It was nice having the authority to commit International Surety to an expenditure without fighting the corporate bureaucracy.

He telephoned Marcie Sokolov and made an appointment to visit her at Midtown North later that afternoon. He put on his overcoat and locked up Cletus Berry's office and left the building.

The city's lovely covering of snow had turned to filthy slush; it hadn't taken long for that to happen. A scrawny Santa had set up his station on the sidewalk and was ringing his bell dispiritedly. A few pedestrians put money in Santa's kettle. Lindsey folded up a five-dollar bill and slipped it into the slot.

Santa said angrily, "You could just of handed it to me, son of a bitch."

Lindsey reached the corner and turned downtown. He wondered how long International Surety would pay for the space. There would have to be another SPUDS agent sent to New York; there was no way the company was going to leave so important a territory unfilled.

Another Santa was ringing his bell outside Midtown North, and a few yards away some Black Muslims—Lindsey guessed they were Black Muslims—had set up a folding table and were selling almanacs and road atlases two years out of date.

Inside the lobby Lindsey picked up a visitor's badge and made his way to Detective Sokolov's station.

Sokolov looked up at Lindsey. She had dressed quietly, elegantly for Cletus Berry's funeral. Lindsey had been surprised when he first saw her in high heels and a dark suit, but he realized that she'd fitted in with the mourners that way.

But now she had changed back to her jeans and blouse. She looked up at Lindsey and smiled. "You're still pushing on this, aren't you?"

"Not quitting, no."

Sokolov nodded to a hard chair and Lindsey lowered himself into it. He said, "I guess I have a different view of this murder than you do, Detective. You've made your position pretty clear to me, and I'm not satisfied with the wrong-place wrong-time theory. I think Berry was killed for a reason, and I think I'm starting to get a handle on that reason."

"Really?" She rested her elbows on her desk, laced her fingers under her chin, and gave him a *tell-me-all-about-it* look.

"I think Cletus knew Frankie Fulton."

"So do I."

"And I've been following a chain that led from Frankie Fulton to a dead showgirl named Millicent Martin."

"I see you like alliteration."

Lindsey ignored the jibe. "And from Millicent Martin to an antiques dealer named Alcide Castellini."

Sokolov lifted her chin off her laced fingers and leaned back in her chair. "Really, Mr. Lindsey. And what is the connection between all these people, and why would Alcide Castellini want to kill Cletus Berry?"

Lindsey shook his head. "I didn't say Castellini killed Berry. I just said that the chain led to him. Link by link. I don't know whether it ends with Castellini or whether there are more links. But I'm going to find out, even if the NYPD isn't interested."

Sokolov smiled broadly. "So the determined amateur is going to show up the professionals again, is he? I submit, sir, that you've been watching too much series TV. Or have you been reading those novels about that Philadelphia schoolmarm who keeps stumbling across corpses every time she goes to the teachers' washroom and finds the murderer while the cops stand around eating sandwiches?"

"Neither, I—"

"Never mind." Lindsey watched as Sokolov stood up and carried a manila folder from her desk to a copier. She ran a couple of sheets of paper through the machine and handed a copy of one to Lindsey.

She was wearing high-top sneakers.

"Take a look, Mr. Lindsey. That's a composite sketch by our best artist. Look familiar to you?"

Lindsey studied the artist's rendering of an Asian man wearing a knitted watch cap. The man looked fairly young—maybe twenty-five, certainly no more than thirty. His face was thin, his skin stretched tight over protruding cheekbones. He had a large wart on one side of his jaw.

"I don't know him. Doesn't look even remotely like anybody I can think of."

"No luck, eh? You'd be surprised; our sketch artists are pretty amazing sometimes. Want to take another look?"

Lindsey focused obediently on the drawing, then looked up at Sokolov. She was back behind her desk, leaning forward eagerly. "I'm sorry. Nothing."

"All right. Look at this." She handed him a second sheet of paper. This one was apparently a photocopy of a regular photographic print. The quality left a lot to be desired, but it was obviously a photo of the man in the sketch.

"Gotcha, right?" Sokolov was gleeful. "You can play amateur sleuth to your heart's content, but it's the professionals who break the cases, trust me."

Lindsey asked, "Who is this?"

"Low budget hit man named Johnny Thieu Ng. Parents were boat people. Johnny was born here, grew up in Vietnamese gangs, graduated into the mainstream after a couple of shoot-outs between Asian and Anglo mobs. If you can't beat 'em, hire 'em."

Lindsey raised a picture in each hand, looking from one to the other. "You think this man killed Berry and Fulton?"

"We've got an eyewitness."

There was a long silence. Finally Lindsey yielded. "Who is it?"

"I don't think you'd know him, and I wouldn't tell you anyway. He's a good source. He's helped us on a number of cases. If we let his identity out he'd lose his usefulness to us." She snorted. "And probably to himself."

"But how did—" Lindsey left his question hanging there.

"He saw the killing. He's— It won't be saying too much to tell you our source isn't exactly a leading citizen. Right down there in the gutter with Frankie, in fact. He says he was out for a walk—"

"A walk at—what was it, midnight, one in the morning? In December, on a freezing cold night?"

Sokolov's grin exposed rows of perfect teeth. Either she took good care of them or she spent a lot of money on dentists. "That's his story and he's sticking with it, Mr. Amateur. He was out for a walk, he heard a quarrel, he thought a citizen might be getting mugged so he raced to the rescue. And his time line jibes with the coroner's estimated time of death. Right smack in the middle, in fact."

"Oh, please." Lindsey shook his head.

"Alas, our stroller arrived too late to play the hero. He heard a series of shots, ran to assist the victims. If he couldn't prevent the tragedy, perhaps he could render emergency first aid. As he entered the alley he saw a man run out with a pistol in his hand. He bent over the victims but saw that they had both expired. What to do? He turned and pursued the perpetrator but he slipped on a patch of icy sidewalk. He fell and hit his head. He was stunned. He lost his memory of what he'd just seen, but when he heard a broadcast offering a reward—"

She smiled again.

"You knew we'd offered a reward for information leading to the shooter, didn't you? No? Well, we did. Good heavens, Mr. Lindsey, it was all over TV."

"I haven't been watching much TV."

"Well." She spread her hands on her desk. "Our good citizen was jolted into remembering, and came right in, and told us what he'd seen, and asked for his usual finder's fee plus the reward money. Isn't that wonderful, Mr. Lindsey? So now maybe you'll just go back to Aspen—"

"Denver."

"—and let us do our jobs."

Lindsey looked at the sketch and the photograph. "You matched the drawing to a mug shot?"

"In a flash."

"And you've picked up Ng?"

"We've put out an order."

"And you think that's the end of the case?"

"What do you think?"

"I think it's the biggest pile of baloney I've ever heard."

"Pile of baloney?" Sokolov chuckled. "I like that. What preschool did you pick that up from, Mr. Lindsey?"

Lindsey asked if he could keep the pictures.

Sokolov said he could.

Lindsey remembered to leave his visitor's badge behind when he left the building.

Chapter Ten

THE GLORY DAYS of the New York, New Haven & Hartford were clearly long gone, but there were just too many commuters and too little room on the highways to do without rail service in and out of Manhattan.

Walking into Grand Central had been like walking into still another movie. Lindsey expected to see Cary Grant or Myrna Loy appear at any moment. He bought his round-trip ticket to New Haven, drank a cup of coffee while he waited for the gate to open, and climbed aboard a coach.

He was traveling against the rush, so he had no trouble finding a window seat and settling in. He opened his laptop and booted up the Nyagic file. He knew what he wanted to ask Professor Van Huysen but he wanted to review the case once more before they met.

He looked around and discovered that the passengers were divided almost evenly between those working with laptops and those wearing earphones, sitting with their eyes closed, zoned out listening to whatever people listened to on those gadgets.

The policy was written in the name of the King of Italy and Sardinia, but that was obviously a matter of form. The real policy-holder was the Italian government. In 1938 that would have been Benito Mussolini's fascist gang.

Why would New York Amalgamated have sold a policy to that outfit? Lindsey had wondered when he first read the file. The answer was obvious, and it was no different now than it had been six decades ago. But what was insured?

Lindsey probed deeper into the documentation. Ah! The policy actually covered the Italian Pavilion at the New York World's

Fair of 1939. The building itself, furniture and equipment, the staff, exhibits, possible injuries to visitors . . .

It all looked pretty routine.

There was an appendix, also standard in such policies. It was an inventory of furnishings and exhibits. Desks, chairs, office machines—and the items on exhibit. Industrial machinery and munitions, symbols of the might of Il Duce's New Rome.

The New Rome. A vision like Randolph Amoroso's.

But there was a bow to the Old Rome as well, and to the Italy of the Renaissance and the risorgimento. Paintings by Correggio and Titian, Giotto and Raphael, even a da Vinci. Sculptures by Cellini, Donatello, Michelangelo Buonarroti. And a separate category for toys, or rather, for a single toy.

Chariot, silver and ironwood, drawn by two horses, one of black marble and one of white marble. Craftsman unknown. Date of manufacture unknown. Dimensions approx. .7 metre length × .2 metre width × .3 metre height. Mounted on black marble base. Weight approx. 10.5 kilogrammes.

Alleged to have been childhood plaything of Julius Caesar.

Value $5 million (US).

Julius Caesar's silver chariot.

The Italian Pavilion at the fair had been inventoried by the Nyagic agent and everything in the inventory was in place. The agent had even hired a couple of authorities in the field to accompany him and authenticate the antiquities and art treasures. *Non c'è problema.*

The first season of the fair had been a success. Lindsey knew that. He'd seen a PBS documentary about it. But the Second World War broke out in September of that year, and by the time the fair reopened for its 1940 season, half the exhibiting nations were either at war or already defeated by Hitler's armies. Their pavilions remained closed. Whatever could be transported back to Europe was loaded onto ships and sent home. The rest was sold for salvage or simply scrapped.

The Italians had packed everything carefully in padded crates, loaded their treasures onboard the *Fior de Rimini*, and sent them back to the museums of Rome and Florence.

Did Nyagic care?

You bet it did!

And when every statue and painting and suit of Roman armor and ancient coin and medieval manuscript was unpacked and safely signed for, a sigh of relief must have gone up that Lindsey could still hear, echoing across the decades.

Every statue and every painting and every suit of Roman armor.

But not Julius Caesar's silver chariot with its two marble horses.

The chariot had been the centerpiece of Il Duce's exhibit, and it had taken a packing crate the size and shape of an elaborate coffin to protect it. Even then, the file indicated, the *Fior di Rimini* had carried a staff of curators whose sole duty aboard ship was to monitor the artworks and antiquities and make sure that nothing happened to any of them.

But something had happened.

When the returning crates were inventoried on the dock at La Spezia, prior to transshipment to Rome, everything seemed to be in order. Not so with the curators. One of them, Dottore Massimo di Verolini of the University of Rome, could not be accounted for.

The fascist authorities panicked. A bureaucrat named Salvatore Castellini was sent up from Rome to sniff around. Literally. One of the crates drew his attention because a very peculiar odor was coming from it. Castellini wasn't a professional curator; he was a fascist party hack who had worn a black shirt and marched on Rome with Mussolini and clubbed Communists and Socialists and liberals and everybody else who got in Il Duce's path. He ordered the crates opened, and . . .

And when the crates were opened, every painting and every medieval manuscript, every ancient coin and every elaborately worked goblet, was safe and unscathed.

Except for Caesar's chariot.

The coffin-sized and coffin-shaped packing crate that was supposed to yield up the beautiful silver-and-marble miniature contained instead the remains of Dottore di Verolini. The dottore had been dead for several days, the hold of *Fior di Rimini* was warm and unventilated, and the remains were ripening very nicely.

But the body was not so far gone that a hastily organized autopsy failed to determine the cause of death. Dottore di Verolini had been attacked from the rear; that was obvious. His skull had been crushed with the proverbial heavy instrument. But this time it was not blunt. It had had a sharp corner. The victim had apparently died at once.

When and where had the crime been committed?

It was impossible to tell. Possibly in New York, before the *Fior di Rimini* had even set sail. Or possibly while the ship was en route from New York to the port of La Spezia. In any case, the victim's body was returned to his family and buried with all due dispatch.

What heavy, non-blunt instrument had been used?

The chariot, complete with horses and base, had weighed 10.5 kilograms—well over 20 pounds. The base had probably had sharp edges. It would make a somewhat clumsy murder weapon, but obviously an effective one.

The chariot was missing, of course. It was never seen again.

Lindsey looked up from the laptop computer screen and blinked. A grim winter landscape whizzed past the car's grimy windows. He closed the laptop and walked the length of the car, carrying the computer with him. Suddenly the world was not to be trusted. He felt stale, his legs were stiff and wobbly, and there was a faint ringing in his ears.

He stood on the platform between passenger coaches, watching the Connecticut landscape roll by and wondering if there was any connection between Salvatore Castellini the fascist party hack and Alcide Castellini the silver-haired antiques dealer. Was the name Castellini the Italian equivalent of Smith or Jones? Was this another of life's peculiar little coincidences?

That was hard to believe.

Lindsey blinked at the wintry New England view. This was no Grandma Moses fantasy, no greeting card image of nature's white beauty. Patches of gray snow alternated with patches of bare, gray dirt. Grim red-brick factory buildings, most of them looking dead and abandoned, alternated with peeling wooden tenements and clotheslines with shirts and blankets frozen in place.

It didn't take long for Lindsey to feel better. A little exercise to get the circulation going again, a few deep breaths to get some oxygen into his lungs, and he was ready to return to his job.

He reopened the Nyagic file. He was starting to get a headache from reading the file on the laptop screen. If only Berry had had the consideration to keep his printer primed with toner. Well, think no ill of the dead. Lindsey closed his eyes and massaged his temples with his fingertips. Soon he was ready to get back to work.

The King of Italy had filed two claims against New York Amalgamated: one for the death of Massimo di Verolini, one for the loss of the silver chariot.

The di Verolini claim was in the amount of $15,000—a sizable sum in 1940. The claim for the lost chariot was, yes, in the amount of $5,000,000.

Apparently a check had gone out to the King of Italy for $15,000. Lindsey could only hope that it had somehow reached Dottore di Verolini's *vedova e bambini*—assuming that he had left a *vedova e bambini*—and not into the coffers of Benito Mussolini's fascist war machine.

But fifteen grand—even fifteen grand in 1940 dollars—was chicken feed compared to the claim for the missing chariot. And it looked as if Uncle Sam had stepped in and done a little arm-twisting at New York Amalgamated to get the company to stall that payment.

The file was conspicuously vague about that. Maybe something had been lost in transition from paper to microfilm to Mylar-coated disk, or maybe someone had gone in and sanitized the record somewhere along the way. But it looked as if the government had encouraged Nyagic to route the claim through a corporate maze, lose a few papers and ask the claimant to refile them, send documents back for clarification or notarization or whatever it took to keep from shelling out.

And Lindsey knew well that insurance companies could find reasons to delay shelling out large payments.

Before the money moved, the U.S. was in World War II, Italy was an enemy nation, and the silver chariot claim was in limbo.

When the war ended, Italy was an occupied country with a provisional government. Mussolini was dead, Victor Emmanuel was still on the throne, and a referendum was in the works.

The chariot had never turned up, but Italy was in a shambles, as was most of Europe. Nazi *Gauleiters* had stolen hundreds of millions of dollars worth of art treasures in occupied countries, including Italy after the fall of Mussolini and the surrender of his successors to the Allies.

Victor Emmanuel lost the referendum.

Italy became a republic.

The new government reinstated the claim against New York Amalgamated—only to learn that that company had become part of International Surety. And to discover that the 1940 claim filed by the King of Italy and Sardinia was still on file.

If the $5,000,000 was to be paid out, to whom would it be paid? The new government of the Republic of Italy, or the king, now the ex-king, living in comfortable exile with a flock of other royal has-beens, never-weres, and hoped-to-be's on the Riviera?

Lindsey looked up again. The conductor had announced that the train was approaching New Haven. Outside the window the ramshackle tenements and decrepit industrial buildings that lined the tracks were growing more dense.

There was just time to finish reading the file. The official Nyagic and IS documents were straightforward enough, but somebody— bless the anonymous somebody!—had added an historical commentary that set the events in context.

An Italian politician named Alcide de Gasperi had served in the provisional government under the occupation, and when the republic got on its feet, he became premier. Initially, de Gasperi's government was a coalition that included the Italian Communist party, headed by Palmiro Togliatti.

The Communists were beholden to Moscow. They made no secret of their intention of taking full control of the government and swinging Italy into the Soviet orbit. The Cold War was in its early stages and the U.S. government was beside itself at the prospect of a Communist Italy.

In 1947, with American encouragement and support, de Gasperi broke with Togliatti, throwing the Communists out of his coalition.

But the Communists were the largest single party in Italy, and without them in his coalition, de Gasperi's government collapsed. He had no choice but to call for elections, and at that point, Uncle Sam gave International Surety a gentle nudge.

International Surety had run into some tax problems as the result of its takeover of Global International and New York Amalgamated. And Uncle Sam dropped a none-too-subtle hint that things would go a lot better for International Surety if the old silver chariot claim was paid out—with interest—to the de Gasperi government.

And it had been.

And de Gasperi had won the election, using International Surety's millions for campaign funds.

And the world had been saved for free enterprise and democracy.

And fifty years later the silver chariot file had mysteriously disappeared from International Surety's database and turned up under electronic lock and key in Cletus Berry's desktop computer.

And Cletus Berry had served in the United States Army in Italy in the 1970s.

And now Cletus Berry was dead.

Curiouser . . . and curiouser . . . and curiouser.

William Van Huysen met Lindsey at the railroad station near downtown New Haven. The station was a cavernous, echoing revenant of an earlier age, and New Haven in mid-December was no showplace at best.

At Van Huysen's suggestion, they climbed into Van Huysen's Jaguar XJ-6. From the exterior the car looked like a piece of modern sculpture; inside, it was like a luxurious living room.

Van Huysen said, "So you want to know about my little essay for Congressman Amoroso, is that it? You looking for some dirt on Randolph? I'm afraid you've wasted a trip if that's what you're after."

"Not exactly. I'm not interested in Amoroso. I'm interested in the chariot."

"In the chariot itself?"

"That's right."

Van Huysen grunted. He eased the Jaguar to a stop behind a huge, mud-splattered delivery truck. "Say, have you eaten lunch yet? I don't imagine they gave you much on that train."

Lindsey realized that he'd had only microwaved instant coffee for breakfast and nothing since. "Nothing."

"How about a cozy campus hangout?"

"Whatever."

Van Huysen maneuvered the Jaguar through openings in traffic like a fencer driving a foil through an opponent's defense. The conversation lapsed and Van Huysen turned on a CD player. Lindsey recognized some of the tunes but not their source.

"Elizabeth Schwarzkopf and Erich Kunz. *Die Lustige Witwe.*" He shot Lindsey a glance. "*The Merry Widow.*"

Lindsey said, "Oh."

Van Huysen's notion of a campus hangout surprised Lindsey. He'd expected to be taken to a stuffy faculty club in one of the Gothic granite buildings on the Yale campus, but Van Huysen's choice turned out to be off campus, a bustling bar and restaurant decorated with an eclectic mix of sports memorabilia and Irish patriotic symbols. The front window was fogged from the inside and rimed from the outside; green letters edged in gold identified it as Kelly's Chop House and Saloon.

They wound up in a wooden booth under a photo-mural of the 1949 Yale-Princeton football game. A beefy waitress in a peasant blouse asked if they'd like a drink and Van Huysen ordered an Irish whiskey, neat.

Lindsey blinked and asked for his with caffeine.

The waitress laughed and slapped him on the shoulder. She wore a little name tag on her blouse. It said *Brigid*. Lindsey thought—*naah*. To Van Huysen she said, "I like your friend,

William. You ought to bring him around more often." She went off to fetch their drinks.

The place wasn't overly illuminated, and the natural light that crept in from outside didn't help much, but still Lindsey got his first good look at William Van Huysen.

The man could be anywhere between forty and fifty. His hair was a metallic gray, beautifully trimmed. His face looked as if he visited a tanning salon regularly. His eyes were the same color as his hair, and his face was long and muscular rather than fleshy. He wore a gray tweed jacket, a blue button-down shirt, a striped tie.

But of course.

Brigid the waitress brought their drinks and Van Huysen said, "We'll order our food in a little while," and she went away.

Van Huysen lifted his shot glass to eye level. "Live well."

Lindsey touched his glass to Van Huysen's and touched rims. They drank.

Van Huysen said, "The meter is running, Lindsey. If your company wants to pay me fee plus expenses while we keep warm on a chilly day, I'm perfectly content. But maybe you'd like to ask me some questions. It's up to you."

Lindsey laid out his story for Van Huysen. He'd already touched on Berry's death and his own interest in the case during their telephone conversation. Now he gave Van Huysen a fuller version. A fuller version, but one that was slightly edited. Van Huysen wasn't entitled to know everything that Lindsey did, and Lindsey wasn't going to tell him more than he thought Van Huysen needed.

In a nutshell, Lindsey had taken over the caseload of an IS colleague who had recently died. Most of the inherited files were strictly routine, but one of them involved an old claim arising from the loss of the silver chariot as it was being shipped back to Italy from the New York World's Fair. Could Van Huysen give Lindsey some more background on the chariot, so he could figure out just what the odd case was all about?

When Lindsey finished, Van Huysen signaled to Brigid. "Another round. And a green salad for me. Lindsey?"

Lindsey ordered a bowl of chowder.

Chapter Eleven

VAN HUYSEN HAD downed his first whiskey fast. The second, he nursed. When his green salad arrived he picked at it, carefully nibbling at the shiny leaves.

Between mouthfuls he told the story.

First of all—Lindsey hadn't asked, but Van Huysen offered the information anyway—the chariot was real. It existed, or at least had existed, as recently as 1940. Lindsey's information about its place in the Italian Pavilion was accurate, and there was ample documentation to support that.

On the other hand, if the chariot had indeed been returned to Italy on the *Fior di Rimini* it might have been destroyed in the carnage of the next five years.

Or—Van Huysen had a habit of holding his hands just above the tabletop, palms flat as if weighing opposing ideas and tilting his head like the balance of a scale—or, the chariot might never have been loaded on the *Fior di Rimini* and might still be somewhere in the United States. Somewhere in some second- or fifth- or ninth-rate museum out in the farm belt. Or, more likely, carefully locked away in some private collector's personal treasure trove.

Collectors were odd ducks, and some of them were fanatics.

That, Lindsey already knew. All too well.

But what about the earlier story of the chariot? How old was it? Who made it? What paths had it wandered in its odd career?

"The origins of the silver chariot are lost in antiquity," Van Huysen told Lindsey. "Nobody knows how old it is, or who made it."

Lindsey shook his head. "Can't they tell by the style of carving? Or—what, carbon dating?"

"You can't carbon-date silver, Lindsey. Or marble."

"The wood, then. The description in our insurance file says that it's made partly of ironwood."

Van Huysen snorted. "First of all, there's no such thing as ironwood, or an ironwood tree. That's just a term for any kind of hardwood. My guess would be that the wooden parts of the chariot—probably the axle and wheel spokes—are made of olive wood. But they could be cedar or pine, although pine is a notoriously soft wood. And it would be a desecration of the chariot to take even a shaving of the wood to test."

He signaled the waitress, asked Lindsey with a gesture if he wanted another beverage, relayed the information, and continued his lecture. "That's all moot anyway, isn't it? There's no chariot to test."

"But there are pictures. There's one on the Amoroso pamphlet. There's one on his campaign button."

"And probably quite accurate."

"You're sure of that?"

"Epstein knows more about pictures than I do."

Lindsey winced. "Who's Epstein?"

"Oh, Epstein. He's an archaeologist."

"So—come on, help me with this."

Van Huysen sighed, a man exasperated. "Congressman Amoroso's people came to Epstein first for help. He's the outstanding man in the field, but he's an archaeologist."

He said the last word as if its very syllables might soil his tongue.

"An archaeologist would deal with artifacts. I'm a classicist. My work is mainly in texts. Original texts. Greek, Latin, Hebrew, Aramaic. But Epstein wouldn't touch it. Told Amoroso's representative to get a classicist. Or an historian."

He said, "Or an historian" as if he were saying "Or a blithering moron."

"Finally," Van Huysen went on, "Epstein gave them my name and the arrangement was made."

Lindsey nodded. All right, back to the main topic. "Didn't, ah, the design of chariots change? Sometimes you can tell what century a ship is from, or a piece of clothing, or even a painting. We learn more about mechanics. I mean, look at a wood-and-fabric biplane from 1917 and an all-metal fighter from World War II and a modern jet. You can tell."

Van Huysen accepted another whiskey from Brigid.

Lindsey laced his fingers around a fresh Irish coffee. He knew what cold was, but in Colorado the cold was dry; here on the Atlantic it was heavy with moisture, ready to condense on your face and hands.

"You can indeed," Van Huysen agreed. "But the chariot may have been modified. In fact, there are some old pictures—we can't be sure that they are pictures of *this* chariot, but we think they are—and it looks rather different. These are not photographs, you understand. A toy chariot turns up in an old drawing or painting. It's the artist's vision of the chariot. Was it the same toy? We have to consider how the artist viewed the object as well as what the object actually looked like."

Lindsey unlaced his fingers. His chowder bowl was almost empty but Brigid had brought a basket of rolls and he tore one in half and used it to get the last of the chowder. It wasn't elegant but it was delicious.

Van Huysen did not comment. He'd pushed aside his almost-empty salad dish and it had disappeared from the table.

"Now, why would the chariot look different at different times?" Van Huysen asked, "assuming that the difference was not merely one of perception? Do you know the story of the Roman trireme?"

Lindsey shook his head.

"It's a logic puzzle, Lindsey. A Roman merchant owned a trireme. Every time the ship was outfitted for a sea voyage the merchant had the hull and the decks and oars and all the other parts checked, and anything that was showing signs of wear or rot was replaced. Eventually every part of the ship had been replaced."

He looked at Lindsey with a cheerful grin on his face.

"Question: Was it the same ship or a different one?"

"Of course it was the same ship. Just because the merchant replaced some planks—"

"Not *some* planks, Lindsey. *All* the planks. The rudder. The rowers' benches and their oars. The anchor and the lines. Everything. There was not one nail or shred or splinter left from the original ship. How could it be the same ship?"

"But—" Lindsey inhaled. "But it's the same *ship*."

Van Huysen leveled his hands and tipped his head, first left, then right. "Not to quarrel. I was just making a point. We don't know if parts of the chariot have been replaced over the years. It *was* a toy, don't you see. One generation's cheap toy, the next generation's valuable antique, another age's priceless art treasure."

"All right." Lindsey paused. "In a couple of thousand years do you think one of Chelsea Clinton's dolls will be as valuable as the chariot is now?"

"That's easy." Van Huysen leaned forward, resting his leather-patched elbows on the wooden table. "If Chelsea becomes as important as Julius Caesar, yes. Otherwise, no."

"Touché."

"My point, Lindsey, is that the chariot may actually have changed over the ages. Suppose someone dropped it and a marble horse lost its head and a new horse was substituted. Or the chariot itself was damaged and a silversmith reworked a part. Anything could happen."

Lindsey shook his head. "You're telling me you don't know how old this chariot is or who made it or—or anything about it. How could you write that pamphlet?"

"Do you have a copy of my little essay, Lindsey?"

Lindsey produced the pamphlet.

Van Huysen quoted himself. " 'Its origins are shrouded in mystery. Legend has it that King David ordered it created as a plaything for his son Solomon.' I should think that is clear enough. *Shrouded in mystery . . . legend has it . . .* No responsible scholar could say more than that. Maybe the chariot was made in Atlantis. Maybe it was left behind by visiting Martians. We can speculate, but we should try to keep our speculations within reason. And we should label them clearly for what they are. I assure you, I was well aware of that when I wrote the essay for Congressman Amoroso."

Lindsey asked, "Did he pay you?"

Van Huysen laughed. "No man but a blockhead, Mr. Lindsey."

Lindsey leaned his forehead against his hand.

"All right. I guess what I need to know is—huh, let me think. All right. First, give me the history of the chariot as best you can, speculation or no, legend or no. All right? Second, tell me where you think it is now. To the best of your ability. And third, why is it important? Why would my colleague have had the file on it in a collection of cases that otherwise are all either current or recent? It doesn't make sense to me."

"Very well. As long as you understand that most of this is a mixture of folklore and speculation."

Someone in the bar must have turned on a tape. Lindsey hadn't seen a jukebox and Kelly's Chop House and Saloon didn't seem the kind of place to have one. Lindsey would have expected an Irish tenor singing "Danny Boy," but instead he heard a Louis Armstrong trumpet piece. It made him think of Marvia Plum.

". . . David and Solomon was admittedly stretching a bit," Van Huysen was saying. "But the Hebrew letters *chet yod* appear to have been worked into the silver. At least they appear on some images of the chariot. They are the eighth and tenth letters of the alphabet and total eighteen, a very important number in Hebrew tradition. Together they spell *chai*, or life. To say that they mean good luck would be an oversimplification, but they might appear on such a gift from a father to a son."

Lindsey said, "I didn't know that Hebrew letters and numbers meant so much."

Van Huysen leaned back in the booth and smiled. "Very clever people, the Hebrews. Some of the world's great minds. But there's a streak of primitive superstition, too. They have a prayer or blessing of God, the *chalel*, that they say eighteen times a year. They light candles eighteen minutes before sundown. They have to put their matzos in the oven no more than eighteen minutes after they mix the flour and water. They believe in thirty-six secret saints—double eighteen. The most powerful name of God has seventy-two letters—quadruple eighteen. Heh! Superstition isn't the word for it."

The Louis Armstrong piece ended and was replaced by another trumpet performance. Lindsey didn't recognize the artist but he had heard the tune before; Marvia had several versions of it in her collection. It was "Easy Living."

"After David's time," Van Huysen continued, "the chariot disappears, then reappears—I emphasize, this is legend—in the court of Philip of Macedon. Again it is a plaything for a royal prince, this time, Alexander the Great. After Alexander's death the chariot disappears for more than two hundred years, turning up in the household of Senator Gaius Caesar and his dear wife Aurelia and their three darling children, Julia Prima, Julius, and Julia Secunda. The Romans did not display great imagination in naming their children." He chuckled at his witticism.

Lindsey admitted that he had never heard of Julius Caesar's two sisters.

"Alas," Van Huysen sighed, "so few have. At any rate," and he signaled Brigid again, "the Caesars were a pretty old and pretty successful family in Rome, but their fortunes had been declining gently for a century or so by the time of little Julius's childhood. But the family was still quite influential, and in Rome, politics was all. Gaius Caesar still had some worthwhile clients, and the chariot may have made another appearance in the sack of Corinth in the year 146 before the Common Era."

He looked up, accepted a full whiskey glass, said, "Maybe this is more detail than you really need, Lindsey. But if the chariot had been in Corinth since Alexander's time, somehow it made its way to Rome. It may have come with the doctor who delivered little Julius. Caesarean sections are not so called for nothing. The best Roman doctors were Greeks, and a disproportionate number of them were Hebrews. I think—no, I have to admit, I only guess—that the chariot had fallen on hard times. Some Roman scavenger or junk dealer got his hands on it, saw the *chet yod*, gave it or more likely sold it to a Jewish doctor, and the rest, as they say, is history."

William Van Huysen pushed himself erect and made his way unsteadily to the rest room.

Lindsey thought that wasn't really a bad idea at all, but he decided to wait. As soon as Van Huysen was out of earshot Lindsey signaled Brigid and asked if it would be safe for Van Huysen to drive home. She assured Lindsey that Van Huysen was a valued regular at Kelly's and she would drive him home. Not for the first time.

Van Huysen managed to finish his story with just a few slurred words.

After Caesar's assassination, the toy disappeared again, this time for almost eight hundred years, turning up as a gift—source not known—to the infant Charlemagne.

And then, Van Huysen told Lindsey, the story really got crazy. "Did Ivan the Great play with the toy? Did Suleiman the Magnificent? The Emperor Joseph of Austria? Nobody knows. From what I've seen of the chariot—twentieth-century photographs— the great Benvenuto Cellini may have refurbished the metalwork. That would be in the sixteenth century. But who knows? Cellini left an autobiography; there are some ambivalent references to minor projects. What Cellini considered minor projects." He shook his head. His iron-gray hair actually wobbled. Could it be— no, it couldn't possibly be a toupee.

"All we know is that Mussolini set great store by the chariot. He almost refused to let the chariot be sent to the World's Fair in 1939. He finally decided that the glory of the New Rome would shine across the world. You know, he came to power in 1922. He was Adolf's senior partner, at first. Then Hitler started to outshine Il Duce, and Mussolini wanted to get the spotlight back."

Lindsey nodded. "And that's very nearly the end of story, I suppose."

"Very nearly. The chariot was at the fair. The chariot was supposed to return to Italy. It disappeared. And you know what happened to Mussolini. He shouldn't have let it out of his sight. Oh, well."

He looked at his wristwatch. The loudspeakers, wherever they were, were giving forth a female voice singing "Guess I'll Hang My Tears Out to Dry."

Lindsey said, "I guess that's about all I need."

Brigid conferred briefly with the bartender, then returned and rumpled Van Huysen's iron-gray hair with her fingers. Huh, must be real after all. She nodded to Lindsey and said, "Help me with William, will you?"

They got Van Huysen to his feet and started him toward the door, Brigid on one side and Lindsey on the other. Nobody had paid for the meal or the drinks, but Van Huysen must have a tab at Kelly's. He'd get the bill, Lindsey expected, and in due course International Surety would see it. What would Ducky Richelieu think of his right-hand man getting Yale professors drunk in Irish pubs?

Brigid retrieved the car keys from Van Huysen's trousers pocket. Together she and Lindsey poured Van Huysen into the Jaguar. Brigid said, "Where can I drop you, sir, before I take poor William home?"

Lindsey checked his wristwatch. If he caught the first available train he could get back to Fifty-eighth Street at a reasonable hour. He didn't see any reason to spend the night in New Haven. He asked Brigid to take him to the railroad station.

In the front seat beside Brigid, William Van Huysen began to sing in German. Lindsey studied rows of old tenements and struggling businesses as the Jaguar moved through icy streets. Van Huysen had slumped in the Jaguar's front passenger seat. Now he swung around and peered bleakly at Lindsey. "Come on, Lindsey, sing along. It's a duet. *'Zauber der Hauslichkeit.'* Sing."

Lindsey shook his head. "I don't know the words."

Van Huysen slung his arm over Brigid's shoulder. "Imagine that. A savage from the wild West. Doesn't even know *Die Lustige Witwe.* Well, well, home, Jane."

Brigid patted him on the thigh. "Have to drop your guest first. Then we'll go home."

Van Huysen said, "You'll receive my bill in the morning, my good man. My very good man. Say, you are satisfied with services rendered, Lindsey, are you not?"

"Very."

"Well, if you're not, say, you might try Dr. Selvatica."

Lindsey couldn't repress a smile. "Who's that?"

"Colleague of mine. I think. Never could quite find out."

Lindsey caught Brigid's eye in the driver's rearview mirror. She raised an eyebrow, shrugged her shoulders, and kept driving.

"You say, Dr. Selvatica?" Lindsey persisted.

"Yes indeed. Doesn't know beans about classics or ancient history, but she's really great on modern Italy. I guess she's a she. First name is Mora. Mora Selvatica. Don't think there's any such person. Probably Pearson at Columbia. Maybe Mayhew at Fordham. Hah, probably Pearson or maybe Mayhew. Maybe Pearson or probably Mayhew. Who knows? Look 'em up, give 'em my regards, have a lovely trip back to the big city. Merry Xmas, Lindsey."

They had reached the railroad station and Brigid pulled the Jaguar up to the curb. She said, "I'm sorry about that. He just hasn't been the same since— well, I'll get him home. I'll put him to bed and cook supper for his little one. It's going to be a slow night at Kelly's anyway, with the students all out of town."

Lindsey climbed from the Jaguar. He hefted his laptop. He said, "Thanks, Brigid. Thank Professor Van Huysen for me, too."

She waved and pulled away from the curb.

Waiting in the cold, cavernous station, Lindsey whispered to himself, *He actually did say Merry Ex-Muss.* He shook his head and tried to understand William Van Huysen. He didn't expect to succeed.

Chapter Twelve

LINDSEY TOOK A cab from Grand Central to Seventh Avenue and ducked into the Stage Delicatessen for a sandwich and a cup of coffee. He didn't worry about coffee keeping him awake. One thing he'd seldom had to worry about was sleeping. He ordered a hot pastrami and watched the flow of customers while he waited for his food.

Clearly, he had stumbled into a late-night dress rehearsal for a revival of *Guys and Dolls*. At one table, Nathan Detroit was attacking a plate of turkey and mashed potatoes while the long-suffering Adelaide sniffled into her handkerchief. Nearby, Nicely-Nicely Johnston worked his way through a giant slab of cheesecake, washing down the morsels with noisy slurps of cream soda. An elegantly overdressed Sky Masterson looked on disapprovingly.

Where, Lindsey wondered, was Sister Sarah?

Lindsey's order arrived. He took one look, wondered how he could even make a dent in the mountainous sandwich, and then surprised himself by finishing it off. He'd been hungrier than he realized.

He paid his check and walked the short distance to his temporary home. He kept his computer at his side, the way a Western gunfighter kept his shootin' iron at the ready. He checked his watch as he made his way through the frozen streets. It was a little after 11:00 P.M. Nine-something in Denver. He didn't think Richelieu would be at his desk. He could leave a voice-mail message, or send him an E-mail via KNP, or wait for morning.

Eight-something in California. He wished he could phone Marvia Plum just to hear her voice, but she was married to Willie Fergus now and living in Nevada. He didn't even know their phone number. And if he did, what would be the point of calling?

Willie would answer the phone. Lindsey would ask for Marvia. She would pretend to be happy to hear from him, but she'd just be uncomfortable.

And what would he have to say to her anyway?

That was a bad idea, *b-a-d*.

He could call his mother and her new husband, or his friend Eric Coffman, or . . .

There was an ambulance in front of the building, and a police car with flashing roof-lights. What in the world?

Lindsey's laptop thumped against his leg. He maneuvered over the slush and across the sidewalk, avoiding the patches of ice that had somehow managed to sneak back despite the day's salting and sanding.

A uniformed cop stood outside the lobby door. Beyond him, Lindsey could see a couple of white-coated paramedics, another uniformed officer, and several figures in civvies.

The cop nearest Lindsey said, "Please no rubbernecking, sir. Just move along."

Lindsey said, "Is that Detective Sokolov?"

The cop looked over his shoulder as if he didn't know who was inside the building. "You know Detective Sokolov?"

"Yes. I live in the building. I—"

"You *live* here?"

"Well, I mean, I live in Denver. But I'm here for a few days and—"

"Maybe you better step inside, buddy."

The uniformed cop swung the door open.

Lindsey stepped past him.

The door swung shut behind him.

The lobby was brightly lighted and bustling with activity. The uniformed cop was trying to look important. A couple of technicians were scouring the lobby, dusting for fingerprints, picking up paper clips and matchsticks and putting them in Baggies.

The paramedics were working over a bloody figure lying beside the battered wooden desk that Lou Halter shared with the Bermudez brothers. Lindsey got a look at the figure on the floor. He was lying in a blood slick, his arms outstretched.

There was no question, he was one of the Bermudez brothers. Lindsey couldn't see his badge from here. He'd met both brothers by now. He knew they weren't twins, but they were close in age and similar in appearance; he didn't know them well enough to tell which one he was looking at.

But a copy of *Civil Procedure of the State of New York, Revised*, lay just beyond Bermudez's fingers, its pages soaked with his blood.

Lindsey knew then that he was looking at Benjamino.

He felt a hand on his arm. The touch was not gentle.

"Mr. Lindsey, what are you doing here?"

He whirled and locked eyes with Marcie Sokolov. He felt a heave in his stomach and managed to turn his face away from Sokolov, so the contents of his stomach—bits of pastrami and pickle from the Stage Deli floating in the rich chowder he had consumed at Kelly's Chop House and Saloon—splattered onto the grimy terrazzo floor.

He gasped for breath, wiping his mouth with a pocket handkerchief. He realized that he was still clutching his laptop computer in its black canvas carrying case. He felt light-headed. Marcie Sokolov took him by the elbow and guided him to the old swivel chair that the lobby guards used.

"Sit down. It's already been dusted."

He collapsed into the chair and looked up at her gratefully.

"You never see a stiff before?" Sokolov asked.

Lindsey had, as many as a man his age typically did. For the most part they were cleaned up and neatly dressed and laid out for burial, ready to meet their Maker in their Sunday-go-to-meetin' best.

But he'd seen fresh corpses. The freshest he'd ever seen was that of Nathan ben Zinowicz, who had pointed a revolver at Lindsey and announced his intention of killing him, then reversed both his decision and the barrel of the revolver and blown away his own face and the back of his own head.

Lindsey still had nightmares about that.

"I've seen bodies," he managed to tell Sokolov. Through his light-headedness he took in odd details of his surroundings. He realized that Marcie Sokolov was wearing thin surgical gloves. Everybody in the room was wearing them except Lindsey. He blinked and stared at Sokolov's hands. Was she protecting the crime scene from contamination, or herself from whatever monsters dwelt in Mino Bermudez's spilled blood?

She said, "You know this fellow?" She jerked a thumb toward the body on the terrazzo.

"I know him. Knew. He's a security guard. Works—worked— in the building."

She nodded agreeably. "Figured as much. Considering that he's wearing a security guard's uniform and all. I'm not a detective for nothing, you know." She rubbed the back of one hand against the tip of her nose. She was wearing a dark brown tweed jacket over a pale tan shirt. She displayed her badge on the jacket. The Santa head was pinned beside it, as it had been on Sokolov's sweater at Lindsey's first meeting with her. The eyes still winked, green and green, on and off. The jacket was unbuttoned and swung open when Sokolov moved. She was wearing her gun on her hip.

"Who is he?"

"Uh—Benjamino Bermudez." He pronounced the *j* properly, the way a Spanish-speaker would pronounce it. "He's a security guard here. He—"

He realized he was repeating himself. He stopped.

Sokolov nodded. "Funny coincidence. His name tag says Bermudez, too. How do you know him? And what are you doing here at this hour of the night?"

"I work here."

"I thought you were from the West."

"I'm— Cletus Berry had a place here."

"I know that."

"I'm using it while I'm in New York."

"At this hour?"

"I, ah, I've been staying here, too. Cletus had it set up so he could stay over once in a while. I'm using it as an apartment for a few days. I guess it isn't quite legal."

She snorted. "I won't read you your rights over that. And I know all about this place. Remember? What I'm interested in is, how come Mr. Bermudez caught a couple of bullets tonight, minding his own business, sitting in the lobby studying away at his law book? You have any idea, Mr. Lindsey?"

Lindsey turned slowly, surveying the body, the paramedics, the evidence technicians. He shook his head. "I—I'm still trying to figure out what happened."

Sokolov smiled. "So am I. It's hard to be certain, but I'll tell you what I think happened. Somebody came a-knock-knock-knocking at the door over there. Mr. Bermudez was sitting here, looked up, and recognized the person at the door. He let him in and the visitor popped him."

"How do you know he knew him?" Lindsey frowned.

"Look at his book."

"Okay."

"Think about it. If the visitor had been a stranger, Bermudez would have waved him away. Late evening, building closed, go away, come again another day. You got that?"

Lindsey got it.

"Suppose the visitor had persisted. Rapping at the glass with a key. Maybe pointing a weapon. What would Bermudez do then?"

"He had a gun of his own. At least, I think he did. He wore a holster."

"That's right. And his weapon is still in it. What's he do?"

"Let's see. I think he'd duck under his desk, try to get away."

"Maybe. Maybe. Or maybe he'd go over to the door and let the visitor in. If the visitor was pointing a big scary cannon at him, he would, don't you think?"

"Wouldn't he draw his own weapon, defend himself?"

"You mean, play Quick-draw McGraw? Not smart. In fact, I'm kind of surprised these bozos wear iron anyhow. Usually does more harm than good. But Mr. Bermudez did neither, see? Didn't dive for cover. Didn't slap leather. He was between the desk and the front door when he was shot. We can be pretty sure of that.

No blood anywhere else in the lobby. No sign of a struggle. But look at the law book. He had it with him when he went to the door. Why would he do that?"

Lindsey waited.

"If the visitor was somebody he knew, somebody he felt confident with—he'd put his finger at his place in the book, carry the book with him, open the door with one hand, and then return to the desk. Except he never returned to the desk."

Lindsey nodded.

One of the evidence technicians pointed at Lindsey and said, "Hey, Detective, you want this guy's puke?"

"No." Sokolov shook her head. "It wasn't part of the crime scene when we got here. Leave it for the sweeper."

To Sokolov, Lindsey said, "Why would somebody do that? Why kill Mino Bermudez?"

Again, the grin. "You tell me, Mr. Amateur Sleuth."

"I can't tell you. But one thing I learned from murders I've worked on is that coincidences are very, very unusual. It's true, they happen. But they make me nervous." He made a mental note to thank Lieutenant Dorothy Yamura, Berkeley Police Department, for the use of her line.

Sokolov put her hands on her hips. For a moment she looked like an angry schoolgirl, then she reverted to being a tough homicide dick. She said, "Thanks for the philosophy. Next time I see Immanuel Kant I'll pass it along. Now tell me what the hell you meant by that crack."

"Okay," Lindsey snapped. "What I meant was, Berry rented space in this building. A few days ago he was murdered. The cops don't seem to be doing much about the case, but a towhead boy from Colorado turns up and starts digging into the case and actually moves into—what did you call it over at Midtown North?— Berry's little nest. And somebody gets into the building after hours and offs poor Mino Bermudez. What kind of sense does that make to you?"

This time it was Sokolov's turn to admit that she didn't know.

"What's your New York bet, Detective? Dollars to doughnuts? I'll bet you dollars to doughnuts that whoever killed Bermudez rode up to the sixth floor and inspected Berry's nest. Which is now my nest, of course."

Sokolov said, "Let's take a look." She signaled a uniformed policeman to join them and they climbed aboard the elevator.

Chapter Thirteen

THE OLD ELEVATOR creaked and wobbled its way upward. As it approached the sixth floor Sokolov jabbed Lindsey in the ribs. "Okay, cowboy, who had keys to the nest?"

"I don't know. Zissler. Me. Were there keys on Berry's body?"

"Yep. They're evidence now."

"That's all I know of," Lindsey said. "But the landlord must have one, and—who else, I couldn't even guess."

They stood outside Lindsey's door. Sokolov put her ear to the wood panel, then shook her head.

She motioned Lindsey and the uniform out of the way, set herself against the wall beside the door, and knocked. "Police. Open up. Police!"

No response.

She gestured to Lindsey. Made a hand motion that said, clearly as words, *Give me the keys.* With her other hand she drew the revolver from her holster.

He managed to dig the keys from his trousers pocket and hand them to her without their rattling.

She unlocked the door and pushed it open. She crouched and ducked into the room, weapon at the ready.

Nothing happened.

Lindsey heard her grunt as she hit the light switch. The room was flooded with light. Sokolov said, "Come on, then." She motioned Lindsey inside, signaled the uniform to stay in the hallway.

"Just stand there, Mr. Lindsey. Turn slowly. Tell me of anything looks different to you. We'll have some technicians in here to dust for prints, but you eyeball the scene right now and tell me if anything is missing or added or moved around."

Lindsey did as she instructed. He realized that he still had his laptop in his hand. He knew that it weighed less than five pounds, but suddenly it seemed a crippling weight. He laid it on the futon.

"There's nothing missing. Nothing moved."

"Look in the closet. Look in the bathroom."

"Nothing. Nothing touched." He rubbed his forehead, standing over Cletus Berry's computer. Had the keyboard been moved? He couldn't be sure. He frowned. "I wonder . . ."

"What?"

"If somebody was here—would he know about the Nyagic policy?"

Sokolov shook her head. "Help me, Mr. Lindsey. I need more than that. What are you talking about?"

"Uh—Nyagic—" He explained the term, the oddity of finding the old policy file on Berry's hard disk, the problem he'd had cracking the shell of protective software that surrounded it.

"And you'd printed this policy out?"

"No. I was going to but the printer is out of toner so I copied the file into my laptop and took it with me." He indicated the computer lying on the futon.

"Took it with you? Took it with you where?"

Lindsey hesitated. "Yale."

"Yale, as in, the tables down at Mory's? Yale, as in New Haven?"

"That's right."

Sokolov frowned. "I hope you'll tell me about that. But not now. Unless you think there's some connection with your visitor. If you had one."

Lindsey shook his head. "I don't know. I think there might be."

Sokolov pursed her lips. "Okay. Spill. I want the *Reader's Digest* condensed-books version."

"I had a meeting with a professor up at Yale. It's their holiday break, you know."

"Thank you."

"But he was still in town. I took the train up there, we had a long conversation about the missing chariot—"

"You're losing me again. What chariot are we talking about?"

"It's really just a toy. But it's very old, very valuable. I had to talk to Professor Van Huysen about it. Anyway, I wanted to study the Nyagic file on the train and I couldn't print it out, so I copied it onto my laptop and—well, you see?"

Sokolov nodded. "So you think this file was the reason for the break-in? You think somebody did break in here, do you, and took it?"

Lindsey nodded. "I don't think that. I *know* it."

Sokolov said, "I envy you."

Lindsey said, "I want to try something. I want to boot up Cletus Berry's computer and take a look at something."

"And what is that?"

"Just let me try it, okay?"

Sokolov let out a hissing breath. "All right, hold on." She leaned her head out the door. "Officer, go downstairs and send up a print tech. I want this computer dusted before Mr. Lindsey plays a tune."

The technician was fast, and there were plenty of fingerprints on the keyboard and a few more elsewhere on the computer. Sokolov told Lindsey that most of them would probably be his own, or Cletus Berry's. But if the intruder had touched the machine, they might pick up a fresh print.

"But anyway, you can use it now. Let's see you make it sing 'On a Bicycle Built for Two.' And while you're at it, here, put on these gloves. Just to stay on the safe side."

She pulled an extra pair of white surgical gloves from her pocket and handed them to Lindsey.

He tugged the gloves over his hands and sat down at the computer. He couldn't resist holding his hands up and wriggling his fingers just once, like Liberace.

He called up the directory of Cletus Berry's case files.

He whirled around in the swivel chair and told Sokolov that the Nyagic file was missing.

She peered at the screen. "Give me that again?"

Lindsey pressed a latex fingertip to the screen. "See those case numbers?"

Sokolov grunted.

"If you can read the coding you can tell which company issued the policy, and when, and a few other things. Without looking at the file itself. Just the code number."

"And you can tell which is this Nyagic policy you're so hipped on?"

This time Lindsey was the one who gave the wolfish smile. "What I can tell you is which of them *isn't* the Nyagic policy. *None* of them is the Nyagic policy. It's gone. Erased."

Sokolov shook her head. "I don't know if this is a crime scene or not. Breaking and entering—no sign of breaking. If somebody got in here he was either one hell of a Raffles or he had a key to the joint. I could sure use a cup of joe. Mr. Lindsey, do you have the makings? Could I prevail on you to nuke me a cupful?"

Lindsey smiled and spooned instant coffee into a couple of cups and nuked it for Sokolov and himself. As they took their first sips he realized that this was the closest he'd come to any social life since arriving from Denver. True, there had been dinner with the Berry family at their Seventy-third Street apartment, but that was a combination investigative visit and condolence call. And there was the mostly liquid lunch with William Van Huysen at Kelly's in New Haven, but that was business, too.

He smiled at Sokolov across the rim of his cup. "Raffles?"

He thought he detected a wink in return. "Ronald Colman, 1930."

"David Niven, 1940."

"John Barrymore, 1917."

Lindsey said, "You win."

Sokolov said, "Jesus, Lindsey, I didn't even play my ace. House Peters, 1925."

Sokolov was showing an astonishing human side. And, more important, maybe she was coming around to Lindsey's belief that Cletus Berry's murder—and those of Frankie Fulton and Benjamino Bermudez and maybe even those of Millicent Martin and

the long-dead Massimo di Verolini—were more than unconnected, random tragedies.

Sokolov put her cup carefully on the floor beside the desk.
"That's a whole lot better. Now, what's so special about this file,
and how could the mysterious stranger know how to—what did
you say he did? Steal it? Destroy it?"

Lindsey shook his head. He gave Sokolov a summary of the silver chariot story.

"Damn!" She looked out the window, toward Central Park.
"Sounds like the Maltese Falcon to me. Who are we looking for?
Kasper Gutman? Wilmer the gunsel? If Cletus Berry is Miles
Archer and you're Sam Spade, who the hell does that make me?
Brigid O'Shaughnessy or Effie Perrine?" She turned back and
looked at Lindsey. "Never mind. I'm just being silly. What hap-
pened to the Nyagic file, then?"

Lindsey felt an urge to reach for Marcie Sokolov's hand. He'd
been alone too long, and suddenly he was bantering classic movie
trivia with a woman. With, he realized, an attractive woman. He
looked at his own hand, then at Sokolov's.

When latex meets latex . . .

Don't be an idiot, Lindsey.

"Whoever was here wiped the file from Berry's hard disk. If
he's as computer savvy as he seems to be, he downloaded the file
first and carried it away on a floppy. I can log onto International
Surety's master data bank and find out whether he knew enough
to erase it there, too. I don't know if there's a backup anywhere
in IS, but it doesn't matter because I've got the file in my laptop."
He tilted his head toward the black canvas bag on the futon.

"Could you make a copy for me?" Sokolov asked.

"A breeze. I can copy it back onto Berry's machine and back
into the big database. This is the second time it's been deleted and
I've had to put it back. I'm sorry I can't print it out for you, but
I'll download it onto a floppy and you can have that."

He stopped. "There is a confidentiality problem."

"Mr. Lindsey, I can get a court order. Don't make me."

From fantasy romance to by-the-book cop in thirty easy seconds. Lindsey took a deep breath. Everybody and his brother had

had his fingers into this case, from Benito Mussolini to the mysterious file thief. He made an executive decision. He'd clear it with Desmond Richelieu when he got around to it.

He downloaded the file and handed it to Sokolov. She slipped it into her pocket.

They left their empty cups in the little kitchen and rode down in the elevator. In the slow-moving car, Sokolov suggested that Lindsey move to a hotel.

"Why should I do that? You're not going to get on the zoning thing, are you?"

She shook her head. "Don't be silly. Look here, whoever killed that guard in the lobby and got into your little fortress of solitude up there—"

"I was wondering about that." Lindsey watched the lights on the floor indicator blink slowly. *Five. Four. Three* . . . "If he had a key, he was probably up there before. Wouldn't the guard know him? Wouldn't Benjamino just say, 'Hello there, Mr. Smith, cold enough for you tonight?' We already know that Mino knew the visitor. That whole business with the textbook. So why did the visitor kill Mino?"

Sokolov frowned. "Okay, Mister Amateur, you tell me."

Two.

"Because," Lindsey said, "if Benjamino Bermudez knew that the visitor was up there so soon after Berry's death, he'd see a connection. The visitor would figure that Bermudez was smart enough to put two and two together and blow the whistle. No way the visitor was going to leave a witness to his visiting Berry's nest late at night, so soon after Berry's death."

Lindsey continued, "But he had to go there to delete the Nyagic file. He didn't know that I'd already found that file. And he certainly couldn't know that I'd have an old acquaintance who happened to be a software genius and could help me crack the lock on it. And he didn't know that I had a copy of the file in my laptop."

One.

"So the visitor thinks he's covered his trail now."

"I think so."

"I don't know." Sokolov sounded worried. "You could be next."

Lindsey said, "I'll be careful. I don't think he'll come back here. And I'm sure the building will tighten up their security. And I suppose I should have the lock changed on my door. I'll have International Surety pay for that."

The elevator door rolled back.

In the terrazzo-floored lobby the technicians had removed Benjamino Bermudez's body and cleaned up the pool of blood in which it had lain. Lindsey sneaked a cautious peek and saw that his own vomit was gone as well.

A harried-looking man in a badly outmoded brown suit was fidgeting nervously. When he caught sight of Marcie Sokolov's gold detective's badge he introduced himself as the building manager. Lindsey had never seen him before. The manager seemed uncertain of what line to take: distraught, apologetic, angry.

A uniformed cop approached Sokolov and said that the building had been checked out. The manager had provided keys to the offices. There was no sign of an intruder hiding anywhere.

Sokolov and Lindsey traded glances. If the building manager had a key to every door in the building, the gates were wide open.

Sokolov said to Lindsey, "I think we've done all we can do tonight. You want, you can come down to the shop tomorrow and we'll work on this some more."

The building manager said, "What am I going to do for a guard? Benjy was a good man." He pronounced the *j* the way you'd pronounce the *g* in magic.

Lindsey said, "Who comes on in the morning, Benjamino's brother, or Lou Halter?" He pronounced *Benjamino* properly.

The manager furrowed his brow. His thin hair was disarrayed. "I'd better call Rodrigo anyway. But Lou Halter's due. I guess I could call him now and start him early. Damn, that's going to put him into overtime." He tilted his head and peered at Lindsey. "How do you know my guards?

"I was a friend of Cletus Berry's. I work for International Surety. I guess I'm your new tenant."

The building manager squinted at Lindsey. Lindsey wasn't a

very tall man, but the manager seemed almost to crouch so he had to tilt his head back and peer up into Lindsey's face. He studied Lindsey for a few seconds, nodded, and reached into his pocket for a cell phone. He punched in a precoded number. After half a minute he said, "Rodrigo? Listen, Rodrigo, there's some bad news here for you."

He wandered to the rear of the lobby, crouched even lower into himself, and dropped his voice so Lindsey could no longer hear him.

By the time Lindsey rode upstairs again he was exhausted. It had been a long day and it had ended in blood and vomit. He undressed and climbed into heavy pajamas, then brushed his teeth and washed his mouth out and climbed into Cletus Berry's futon. He put down his head and closed his eyes, then opened them again.

Something was blinking at him. It was the light on the answering machine.

For a moment he lay there watching the red light wink on and off, on and off, like Santa's green eyes on Marcie Sokolov's Christmas pin. The call must have come in while he and Sokolov were in the lobby the second time. Romance with Marcie Sokolov? What a fool he was being. What a hormone-crazed schoolboy. Lindsey wanted to go to sleep. He could check his message in the morning.

Fat chance.

He'd never get any rest with the message light blinking and its secret preying on his mind. He crawled out of the futon and hit the playback button.

"Thought I'd find you at home, chum. You want to chat some more, meet me at the Bird & Trane on Perry in the Village. I'll be there tomorrow night. Don't look for me, I'll look for you."

The voice paused. Lindsey could hear some noise in the background. It was a piercing screech, almost an inhuman scream.

"Gotta make my train," the voice resumed. "Tomorrow. Ten-ish."

The message ended with a click.

The voice had been that of Victor Hopkins.

Chapter Fourteen

THE TELEPHONE WAS ringing and Lindsey woke up utterly lost. This wasn't his room in the stucco house on Laurel Drive, the house in Walnut Creek where he'd lived most of his life. Nor was it his sterile, modern bedroom in the sterile, modern Denver high-rise where he'd lived since his promotion to deputy director of SPUDS. It was—

The morning light was filtering through the window that looked northward across Fifty-eighth Street.

He was in New York, in Cletus Berry's live/work space, and the telephone was ringing.

He crawled out of the futon and picked up the handset.

"Mr. Lindsey?"

He admitted it.

"Mr. Lindsey, this is Petrus Berry phoning. We've never met but I saw you at my brother's"—a momentary pause—"obsequies yesterday. Maybe you saw me at the funeral home or at the cemetery." His voice was both deeper than Cletus's had been and dryer, as if he'd been crying a lot lately.

"I saw you, yes."

"Mr. Lindsey, my brother spoke very well of you. He told me about rooming with you in Denver, and about a case he helped with. Something up in the Bronx."

"Cletus was a fine man," Lindsey said. "I wish I'd known him better. I'm very sorry for what happened. I'm—I'm just sorry."

There was a pause. Petrus Berry was having a hard time navigating his way across the chasm between polite small talk and whatever it was he really wanted to say to Lindsey.

Finally he made it. "Mr. Lindsey, Ester tells me that you're not satisfied with the police work on this case."

"That's true. Was true. I've talked with Detective Sokolov and I think she's taking it more seriously now. I think she may do some good work."

"You're satisfied, then? You think the NYPD is going to right this outrage?"

Lindsey drew a deep breath and let it out slowly. "No, sir. I think they're trying harder than they were. Detective Sokolov is. But frankly I'm not at all confident about it. I intend to keep working on the case."

"Mr. Lindsey, I think I know a little bit about you, sir. From Cletus. You have a way of getting your teeth into a case and not letting go. You shake and shake and shake until something comes loose."

"Cletus told you that about me?"

"He did."

"Well." Lindsey didn't know what to say. "I guess—that's quite a compliment."

"I didn't say it to flatter you, Mr. Lindsey. Look here, I'm a retired police officer myself. I was ten years older than Cletus. I grew up in Pinopolis, South Carolina. It isn't much of a town, but my parents saw to it that I got a pretty good education. I was in the army for a while, then I went to college, and by then things had started changing in the South and I got a job on the local police force and I put in my years and now I've got my pension."

He paused, then resumed.

"My brother, though, he came along later. He went off to see the world. Studied art history. Got himself a good job, earned his way to warrant officer in the army."

"Ester told me that," Lindsey said.

"Well, then after Cletus finished his military service, why, he'd seen Paris and Athens and Rome. There was nothing for him in Pinopolis. Especially not with an Italian wife. A white Italian wife, if you understand. He never brought her to Pinopolis. That was wise, I think. They just settled down up here in New York, and I guess they would have lived happily ever after if it hadn't been for—well, the perpetrator."

Lindsey checked the time. It was a little before nine o'clock. A few patches of blue were visible in the sky this morning. Not many, but they made a pleasant break in the unremitting gray.

"Mr. Berry."

"Yes."

"Let's work together on this."

"That's what I wanted to ask you to do."

"That's what I thought. When can we get together? And where?"

Petrus Berry told Lindsey that Zaffira Fornari had given him the use of her apartment guest room while he was in town. It was near her sister's home on Seventy-third Street. Zaffira had moved in with Ester and Anna Maria for the time being anyway, and the smaller apartment would have stood empty if Cletus didn't use it.

Lindsey said, "Even so, why don't we meet at Ester's. She has a right to know what we're doing. And she may have some information we can use."

"Later," Berry said. "I think we should talk first, Mr. Lindsey, just you and I, before we go up there."

Lindsey agreed.

Cletus Berry suggested that they meet at a restaurant on Second Avenue, just around the corner from Ester's apartment. They would have lunch, talk, and then head up to Ester's.

But before Lindsey got out of his nest, Marcie Sokolov phoned. "You'd better get over to Midtown North."

Lindsey hadn't phoned in to Ducky Richelieu's office in Denver yet. He asked, "Is it urgent, Detective?"

She said, "It's urgent."

Richelieu would have to wait. But still, before he got moving he placed a brief call to Manhattan East. He arranged to have the lock changed on his temporary digs. And to get a couple of toner cartridges for the printer.

On his way out of the building, he noticed a new lobby guard.

He stopped and introduced himself. The guard's name was Hassan Muhammad. Lindsey blinked. He couldn't be sure, but he thought he'd seen Hassan Muhammad selling obsolete road atlases on the street near Times Square. Lindsey explained that he sometimes worked very late hours. Hassan Muhammad said, "I am only here the few hours."

"Yes, fine. Well, if you see me again, you'll know me." He scribbled Cletus Berry's suite number on an International Surety business card and handed it to Hassan Muhammad. "There may be some other people around from my company."

Detective Sokolov must have pinned her Christmas brooch to her jacket before leaving home and turned on the flashing lights before she got the news this morning. Unlike the Santa pin, this one was shaped like a forest-green holiday wreath, and the miniature decorations on it flashed red, white, green in sequence. The dark green actually went very nicely with her dark brown jacket.

But there was no Christmas cheer in her face.

"Sit down, Lindsey. I'm glad to see you here."

"Why wouldn't I be here? You asked me to come in."

"Right. You want a cup of coffee?"

"Does this town run on caffeine? Sure."

She filled a heavy mug for him. It had a Vassar College crest on the side, in gold. She was already drinking from a matching mug.

"You remember I told you we had an eyewitness to the Fulton-Berry murders, Lindsey? And that we ID'd the shooter? Sure I did."

"I remember. Johnny Thieu Ng."

"The good news is, we found him. The bad news is, he's dead."

Lindsey had taken a sip of cop coffee. This early in the day it was fresh and hot even if you couldn't say anything else in its favor. When Sokolov told him that Ng was dead he was barely able to hold the hot coffee in his mouth. He put his mug down on her desk with a thump.

"The worse news is, the source who ID'd him for us was with him. I don't suppose there's any harm in telling you his name now. Not that it would mean a lot. Bilbo Sax." She raised an eyebrow. "Ring a bell?"

Lindsey shook his head.

"Apparently Bilbo died at home. He lived on Amsterdam Avenue. Little basement apartment, pretty minimal, bare pipes on the ceiling, bare lightbulbs, that kind of place. He lived alone there, just ol' Bilbo and a few rats. Neighborhood kids were playing spy. Too young to earn money as lookouts for the local drug dealers, they were pretending. Good training; when they get a little older they'll be experienced. Nice, hey?"

Lindsey waited.

"Well, they saw these two figures in the room. Not too much light there, and the windows were pretty grimy, of course, so the kids couldn't be certain. But they thought they saw the two of them, Johnny Thieu Ng and Bilbo Sax, naked. Kids actually managed to find a grown-up who'd listen to them. Somebody's mom, most likely. She came and took a look and went home and phoned nine-one-one. Didn't leave her name, of course."

Lindsey was trying to catch up. "They were naked? Just sitting around naked? So what?"

"They weren't sitting around. They were hanging. Both of them had leather belts around their necks, and they were hanging from the water pipes."

Lindsey's hands went cold. He laced his fingers around the Vassar College mug, drawing the warmth of the porcelain into his hands. "Suicide? Murder?"

"I think it was meant to look like accidental suicide. There were skin books strewn around. Lots of naked bodies, lots of people doing interesting things to themselves and each other."

Lindsey said, "I don't see the connection."

"Of course not. Out there in God's country, the only sex you have is missionary position, right?"

Lindsey reddened. "Not quite."

"Well, it's supposed to get you off better. You buckle a belt around your neck so your breathing is cut off and then you jerk off or you get a friend to do it for you and— I'm sorry, Mr. Lindsey, am I upsetting you?"

Lindsey shook his head.

"It's supposed to be the maximum male orgasm. I wouldn't know about that. But there have been cases where guys try this. See, you're supposed to come just as you black out. And your partner opens the belt then, and you come to. Sorry, no pun intended."

She took a sip of coffee.

"Dangerous to play around with if you don't have somebody there to make sure you don't suffocate. And Johnny and Bilbo— I think the idea was—I think we were supposed to figure that they were playing together with their skin books and they both got carried away. Neither one would wait for the other to finish up first. They were going to try it together. And it didn't work. Or it worked too well, depending on how you look at it."

She set her coffee mug on her desk and leaned forward on her elbows. Her little Christmas wreath went wink, wink, wink.

"Do you buy it, Mr. Lindsey? No? Neither do I. Tell me, what bothers you about the story?"

Lindsey stood up. "I don't know, Detective. I mean—if Sax turned in Johnny Thieu Ng—if they had that kind of relationship—he wouldn't—or he wouldn't go back—or—" He stopped, feeling queasy. He sat down again.

"That's pretty good. But there's something else I didn't tell you. Johnny and Bilbo had both been beaten before they were hanged. There were fresh bruises on their faces. And on their arms. As if they were trying to defend themselves."

She inhaled sharply. She looked down, noticed the tiny flashing wreath on her jacket, and reached for it. Then she stopped. "Ah, what the fuck. I'm not gonna turn this thing off. I need all the cheer I can get." She dropped her hands into her lap. "We'll see what the coroner has to say, but right now it looks as if they were beaten unconscious, then strangled and strung up so it would look like a double sex-strangulation."

Lindsey shook his head. "Who did it? I mean—who do you think did it? And why?"

"Good questions. Very good questions. I wish I had the answers. I don't. But I'll tell you this: the more bodies that turn up, and the more strands we can tie between them, the more certain

I am that we'll find a nice spiderweb with some fat son-of-a-bitch spider sitting in the middle of it. Sooner or later, that web is going to come together. And when it does, we'll have our killer."

Lindsey felt his stomach heave, but this time he was able to clamp his throat shut and hold down the bile. It tasted hot and sour in the back of his mouth.

"Who's dead so far?"

Together, they made the list, in order of death.

> Millicent Martin
> Frankie Fulton
> Cletus Berry
> Benjamino Bermudez
> Johnny Thieu Ng
> Bilbo Sax

Detective Sokolov said, "Have we left anyone out?"

Lindsey said, "Massimo di Verolini."

Sokolov tilted her head. "Massimo who?"

Lindsey repeated the name.

"Who in hell is that?"

Lindsey told her about the *Fior di Rimini* and the body found in the crate that should have contained the silver chariot when that ship unloaded in Italy in 1940.

"Do you really think there's a connection, Lindsey? Do you mind if I drop the *mister*? And you can call me Sokolov. Only my closest friends have that privilege. Do you really think this di Verolini who's been dead for almost sixty years is connected to the others?"

"Sokolov. Sure. I thought you already had." Maybe last night's odd little mating dance of latex gloves and Hollywood trivia had never taken place. Lindsey studied the wall clock behind the detective. He had plenty of time to meet Petrus Berry. "It's going to take two more names to make that web of yours appear, Sokolov, but I think it's going to happen, and I think di Verolini is going to be part of it."

Sokolov arched an eyebrow at Lindsey. "Two more corpses?

We've got six corpses already. Seven if you count what's-his-name, Massimo di Verolini."

"Two more names," Lindsey corrected, "not necessarily dead ones."

The scruffy-looking detective who had passed Sokolov's desk during Lindsey's first meeting with her walked past again. This time he was directing Santa Claus by one elbow. Santa was perfect. Red cheeks, white beard, round belly. He was handcuffed.

Sokolov smiled at the scruffy detective. "Say, you're really cleaning your plate, Roscoe baby."

The scruffy detective grinned. "Year-end stats, mama, year-end stats."

Sokolov said, "This is Mr. Lindsey. He was a friend of Berry's. You know, that Hell's Kitchen case."

"Oh, yeah. Nothing like chipping 'em out of the ice. How ja do, Lindsey. Handle's Roscoe. Roland Roscoe, dick, NYPD."

Lindsey shook his hand.

"And this here is Santa Claus." Roscoe showed his teeth.

"Motherfucker just book me so I can make my bail, I got an appointment I gotta keep," Santa Claus growled.

"Okay, Santa," Roscoe told him. "Just keep your reindeer dry. We'll get this over with as fast as we can. Can't keep jolly old Saint Nick locked up when the little kiddies are all waiting to see him."

When Detective Roscoe and Santa Claus were gone, Marcie Sokolov said, "We were playmates, Roscoe and I. Grew up together. Smoked weed in sixth grade. I got the sap's cherry, too. Man, that was a long time ago. Ever wish you were a kid again, Lindsey? Never mind, tell me those other two names. Make this make sense for me."

"Randolph Amoroso," Lindsey said.

Sokolov's eyes widened but she said nothing.

"And Alcide Castellini."

"Holy shit! What are you talking about?" Sokolov reached across her desk and grasped the curved edge nearest to Lindsey. She leaned forward, her torso almost parallel to the surface of her desk. She hissed the words. "Do you know what the fuck you are talking about?"

"Listen." Lindsey lowered his voice. "The first I knew about this was when I heard that my friend had been murdered. Then I found out he'd been murdered with Frankie Fulton. Then the *Daily News* published a file photo of Fulton together with Alcide Castellini and a showgirl named Millicent Martin. She had also been murdered in a nasty, sexually suggestive way."

They locked eyes.

"Are you with me?" he asked.

She said, "Go on."

"I saw Castellini buddying it up with Congressman Amoroso at his rally in Times Square the other day. And I picked up an Amoroso-for-Senate brochure, and there he is using the silver chariot as a campaign logo."

Sokolov frowned. "I've seen it."

"Okay. The silver chariot—the real silver chariot—was on display in the Italian Pavilion at the 1939 World's Fair. When it was shipped back to Italy in 1940, it mysteriously disappeared and Massimo di Verolini's corpse turned up in its place."

Sokolov was looking very sour but Lindsey kept on going.

"Somebody breaks into Cletus Berry's pad in the Torrington Tower and wipes the Nyagic file from Berry's computer. That's the file on the chariot, you see? Wipes it, and maybe swipes it. And deletes the file from the International Surety data bank. Not knowing that I've got a copy."

Sokolov was rapping her knuckles softly on the top of her desk, nodding her head in time with her wrist action.

"And," Lindsey wound up, "Bilbo Sax rats on Johnny Thieu Ng for the Hell's Kitchen killings, and Bilbo and Johnny die together in a faked accidental suicide that you yourself tell me was really another double murder."

There was a long silence. It lasted until Santa Claus came swaggering back past Marcie Sokolov's desk. He stopped and sneered at them. "Fuck you, sister. And you too, Elmer Fudd. You can both go to hell."

He left.

Marcie Sokolov grinned. "Nice fella. He'll be back."

Lindsey said, "What do you think?"

Sokolov said, "I don't see any reason for it all. You've tried to pull all these killings together, but I don't see a motive. I don't see what they mean. You gotta show me a motive."

"The chariot."

Sokolov picked up her long-forgotten coffee mug. She tilted the mug, dipped her tongue into the cold coffee, and made a sour face.

"What about the chariot?"

"That's what I was doing in New Haven yesterday. Talking with this classics professor at Yale. William Van Huysen. He even wrote part of Amoroso's brochure, the part about the chariot. Trying to get a line on the chariot."

"And?"

"And it's a symbol of Roman power. One of those legends, you know, like the Holy Chalice or a fragment of the True Cross. *Down through the centuries* . . . That kind of thing. Randolph Amoroso—"

"Oh, I'm glad you finally got around to the congressman."

"—is running his campaign on *America, the New Rome*, right? Every politician who's owned the chariot goes on to greatness. Maybe even King Solomon—if you believe Van Huysen. Alexander the Great. Julius Caesar. Charlemagne. Mussolini. When each of them lost the chariot, he lost his empire, or he died young, or the thing came apart on him. The chariot vanished in 1940 and it was all downhill for Mussolini after that. And the chariot has never resurfaced."

"Do you have any idea where the chariot is now, Lindsey?"

"I don't. But I think Cletus Berry did. And I think Alcide Castellini—éminence grise of New York antiques dealers, or so I've been told—"

"That's putting it very kindly."

"I think Alcide Castellini is after the chariot, doing acquisition work for Randolph Amoroso. I figure we can follow Castellini, and if he finds the chariot the whole thing will fall into place. Including the murders. Or better yet, if we can beat Castellini to the chariot, he will come to us."

Chapter Fifteen

LINDSEY WARMED UP on a crosstown bus ride, then froze walking up Second Avenue looking for the restaurant Petrus Berry had suggested. He stopped at a candy store and picked up a copy of the *Post*. There was nothing on the murders of Johnny Thieu Ng and Bilbo Sax. They must be too ordinary for New York. Or maybe nobody had got any good photos of the corpses dangling from the water pipes, and without the pictures, the editor had decided that nobody would bother to read the story.

After another half block Lindsey spotted the restaurant. It was a dark, cavernous place with a wooden sign outside announcing its name as the Bear Garden. The temperature outside was close to zero; inside the Bear Garden a massive log blazed in a stone fireplace.

Lindsey recognized Petrus Berry almost at once. He was settled at a wooden table. Even indoors, beside the fire, he wore a heavy sweater.

Anna Maria Berry sat opposite him. A bowl of chili stood in front of each of them. Anna Maria was eating her chili. Petrus Berry sat quietly watching over the girl. Before Lindsey made eye contact with Berry, the older man lifted a glass of red wine and sipped.

Lindsey crossed the room. It was late for lunch, and the place was nearly empty. At one table a college-age couple held hands and drank cappuccinos; at another, a pair of young parents ignored their food while they gazed admiringly at their baby, dazed with joy.

Petrus Berry lowered his glass to the rude wooden tabletop and stood up. He shook hands with Lindsey. Even though they'd spoken on the phone, they exchanged names. Petrus Berry said, "You know my niece, Anna Maria?"

Lindsey nodded. He took an empty chair.

"Mr. Lindsey, Ester and Zaffira tell me that you've been doing a lot of work. I wish you'd tell me what you know. Are you getting anywhere?"

Lindsey grunted. Before he could answer Berry's question a waiter appeared and asked what he'd like. Lindsey looked at the chili and nodded. "One of those, please. And a cappuccino."

Then he addressed the child. "Is this going to upset you, Anna Maria?"

She'd laid her spoon on the table. She looked into Lindsey's eyes. Her shoulders were narrow, Lindsey noticed; there wasn't much flesh on her bones and she was, if anything, small for her age. But the look in her eyes was not the look of a ten-year-old.

"I want to know who killed my dad. I want him caught and punished. You go ahead."

Petrus put his hand on his niece's hand. He nodded to Lindsey. "Go ahead."

Lindsey repeated the facts and the partial theory he'd worked out with Marcie Sokolov. He held his hands up and ticked off the list of murders on his fingers. When he finished he didn't wait for Petrus Berry to comment or to ask him any further questions. Instead he said, "There's a connection, and I think it's the chariot. What I need to know is, what was Cletus doing in Italy back in the seventies?"

"That's when he met Ester," Petrus supplied.

"I know that. What was he doing for the army? He was part of NATO, right?"

Petrus nodded.

"But still—what were his duties? And what were his off-duty connections? Could he have had something to do with the chariot?"

Petrus shook his head. "I'm ten years older, Lindsey. I was in the army, too, but I was in and back out again before Cletus ever put on khaki. I was military police. They sent me from Fort Gordon, Georgia, to Okinawa. What a bore. You know what we did for excitement? We sat in the dayroom and played chess. Had a really bright boy there, real chess wizard. Hated me at first because—because he didn't like people like me. But he was desperate for a decent opponent. First he taught me the rules, then he taught me some strategy. Then one day I actually won a game. And the more we played—I started winning as many games as I was losing."

He smiled. "After a while, he forgot that he hated me. We became chess buddies. Black against white, white against black."

He paused. Then, "I guess that was how I got into cop work when I got back home. From playing traffic cop on an army base. You want some thirty-year-old reminiscences of the bars and strip joints in Naha, I can give 'em to you. I don't know anything about Italy."

Anna Maria said, "I do."

Lindsey tilted his head. "What do you know? What you study in school?"

The question elicited a rare smile from the child. Lindsey couldn't blame her for her sadness. He'd grown up without a father; Joseph Lindsey had been a promising cartoonist before the Korean War, before he'd died on the deck of a destroyer in the Sea of Japan when a MiG had crashed headlong into the destroyer. This had been no World War II–style kamikaze attack. The pilot had wanted to live just as much as Joey Lindsey had wanted to live.

They died together.

Back in California, Hobart Lindsey was born six weeks later.

Which was worse: Never to have known a father, or to have one and lose him before the end of your childhood?

"We don't learn much about Italy at Beth Israel." She looked up at Lindsey.

What eyes! Dark Italian eyes. Dark Hebrew eyes. Dark African eyes.

"But I want to learn about my heritage. I have a rich heritage. I'm everything."

She was the future, Lindsey thought.

"I want to learn about my Jewish roots and my Italian roots and my African roots. I talk about it with my cousin all the time. Mosé Lazarini."

"Your cousin." Lindsey's food had arrived, and his cappuccino. He spread a linen napkin on his lap; he was surprised that such an informal place used linen napkins. He took one taste of the chili, lowered his spoon, and sipped at the rich coffee. This chili could start a conflagration.

"My cousin Mosé lives in Rome. He's my first cousin on my mother's side. I met him in a history chat group. It was wonderful, finding a cousin I didn't even know about."

Lindsey shook his head. "What kind of chat group? Were you in Italy?"

She shook her head. "A computer chat group. On the 'Net. I was looking for something about Italian Jews. There's nothing in my schoolbooks. My mom says we were in Italy for thousands of years."

"I know. She told me. I didn't know that."

"We were in Rome before the Christians were. Before there were any Christians. My mom told me about it, but I wanted to know some more, so I was just browsing around, looking in on discussion groups, and here was somebody talking about Jews in Italy and I introduced myself and we went off to a private room—"

"Wait a minute. Private room?"

Petrus Berry was watching, a bemused expression on his face. He caught Lindsey's eye and nodded. Out of the depths of their grief . . .

"When you're in a group on the 'Net, you can set up a private room and talk to each other."

"Like E-mail."

"A lot like E-mail. Only in real time. Like chatting. But it's in private."

Lindsey spooned another sample of chili into his mouth, more cautiously. There was a bowl of crackers on the table, and he'd crumbled some into his chili this time, before he burned out the inside of his mouth.

"Tell me," Lindsey said, "what have you learned from your cousin?"

She started to answer, but before she had a chance Lindsey said, "And, ah, Anna Maria, Petrus—I went up to New Haven yesterday, talked to a Professor Van Huysen. He—"

"I know William." Anna Maria grinned.

"You've been to Yale?"

"No, he's in our chat group. He's a little stodgy, but he is fairly knowledgeable."

Fairly knowledgeable. Ten years old. Professor Van Huysen was fairly knowledgeable. Lindsey restrained a laugh. But it kept trying to come out, and he let it. Why not? "That's funny," he managed, "he didn't mention you."

Anna Maria grinned. "Maybe he did."

"No." Lindsey ate some more chili, drank some more cappuccino. "I was careful, I noted everything he told me. I'd remember. I would have noticed."

Anna Maria looked at Petrus Berry. "Uncle Pete, should I tell him? It's a secret, Mosé's and my secret."

"You told me, darling. Mr. Lindsey is here to help us."

"Maybe I should ask Mosé first."

Petrus turned to Lindsey. "Would you make a confidential disclosure pledge?"

Lindsey agreed.

"My cousin and I—once we got to know each other—we made up another screen persona."

"Screen persona." Lindsey waited.

Petrus grinned, proud of his brother's child.

"A fictitious identity. You know, I learned about them when I was in a flirt group."

"A flirt group." Lindsey felt like a straight man in a black-and-white sitcom from his own childhood. All he had to do was keep feeding setup lines back to the top banana and she'd keep getting the audience reaction.

"You know, it's a chat group where kids go to flirt. I thought it was pretty exciting at first. Boys would ask you to describe yourself, and how old are you, and did you ever—well . . ."

She blushed.

Lindsey covered his mouth with his hand.

"Anyway, the way some of them described themselves. It couldn't be. Then I talked to my friend Shoshana. She's older than I am. Seven months and eleven days. She told me that kids make up screen personas and just make up stories and flirt. She told me that sometimes adults sneak into flirt groups. Some of them are real scumbags. There was one man in Ohio, he pretended he was a teenager and he made a date with a girl he met in a flirt group, I knew her from the group, she lives in Cleveland, and he came to pick her up at her house and the girl's father shot him. He deserved it, the piece of shit."

Lindsey caught Petrus Berry's eye. Telepathy worked even faster than the 'Net.

Gently, Lindsey said, "You were telling me about Professor Van Huysen."

"Oh, yeah. Uncle Pete, could I have a cocoa? I love cocoa in winter."

Petrus signaled to the waiter.

"See, the history group isn't just kids. Sometimes people talk about who they are. There are teachers and professors. There's one woman who wrote a book about pre-Columbian civilizations in Chile and Colombia. And a lot of college students and high-school students. I think Mosé and I are the youngest members. Nobody knows how young we are. Mosé is my age. He wants to visit me. He thinks it's cool that I'm half African. He thinks it's cool being Italian and Jewish, but he's never seen an Italian-African-American Jew. I sent him my picture by snail mail and he sent me his, but he wants to meet me someday. If I had a scanner I could have zapped my picture, but I don't have one yet."

Anna Maria's cocoa arrived. It came in a huge mug. Marcie Sokolov would have been envious. The mug's handle was shaped like a bear. There was a heap of whipped cream on top of the cocoa. Anna Maria took a sip. When she lowered the mug she had a whipped-cream mustache. Lindsey almost choked with his yearning for a family.

"Mosé and I made up a persona, a history professor who travels back and forth between America and Italy. Her name is Mora Selvatica."

Lindsey dropped his spoon. "*You* are Mora Selvatica?"

"Did William say we were friends?"

"Uh—not exactly. He was, well, actually kind of drunk."

"I know he drinks. We've had some chats. In chat rooms. He has a little boy. William is divorced, and he has a little boy and he asks Dr. Selvatica for advice, and we tell him we need to think about it a little and we ask our parents, Mosé and I do."

She stopped and grabbed her napkin and rubbed her eyes.

Petrus Berry pulled her onto his lap and stroked the back of her head and her shoulders.

Lindsey said, "I'm sorry, Anna Maria. Maybe we should stop. Do you want to go home? Do you think your mother is home yet?"

Petrus Berry shook his head at Lindsey. "Ester went to the lawyer's. Zaffira's with her. Anna Maria and I are spending the day together." He pulled an oversized bandanna from his pocket and held it to Anna Maria's nose until she blew into it. He returned it to his pocket as if it was something precious. Maybe it was.

Anna Maria put her mouth to Petrus Berry's ear. Lindsey waited while she delivered some confidence. Petrus nodded assent. Anna Maria jumped from his lap and headed deeper into the Bear Garden.

Petrus said, "Pit stop. Through it all, when nature calls, we answer." He smiled a rueful smile and exhaled.

"Do you have a family of your own?" Lindsey asked.

Petrus Berry shook his head. "Never met the right woman. Always thought I'd get married. Always thought the next woman I met would be the right one. I had plenty of time. Woke up one morning and looked in the mirror and my hair was gray and I went to work and they were throwing a retirement party for me."

He nodded in the direction Anna Maria had taken. "I never thought a little Italian-Jewish girl would be the only thing I care about in this world, but she is."

"You love her?" Lindsey asked.

"You wouldn't believe how much," Petrus said.

"Yes, I would."

Petrus Berry leaned across the table. "Listen, you're staying in Cletus's pad, are you?"

"Right."

"I'd get out of there if I were you."

"Yes. I got that same suggestion from Marcie Sokolov. But look, whoever was up there and deleted the Nyagic file doesn't know that I broke the lock and copied the file. He thinks he's safe. It would be more suspicious if I moved out than if I stayed, don't you see?"

Petrus Berry tilted his head and squinted. "What Nyagic file?"

Lindsey explained.

"Okay." Berry picked up a napkin and touched it to his lips. He dropped it on the table. "I see. But I still don't think you're safe there. Did Sokolov offer to put you in a police safe house?"

"We didn't get that far."

"Well, you might want to move to a hotel."

Lindsey looked into his bowl of cooling chili. He'd had enough. He moved the bowl to a vacant table. He still had his cappuccino, but one sip finished that and he put the empty cup beside the chili bowl.

He looked at Petrus Berry and shook his head.

"Well then—tell you what. Zaffira has her own place. She's given it to me while I'm in town, and she's staying with Ester. I think she'd have done that anyway. Better for Ester to have her sister with her. Better for Anna Maria, too, probably." He made a sound, something like *huh*. Then he said, "If you don't want to move into a hotel, you could move in with me. Into Zaffira's place."

Lindsey considered. He didn't need access to Cletus Berry's paper files; everything was in International Surety's databank and he could get at anything he needed through KlameNet/Plus. Besides, the key item was the Nyagic file, and that was in Lindsey's laptop.

He spotted Anna Maria returning from the ladies' room. Before she reached the table he said, "Okay, Petrus. I think you're right."

He found a pay phone and located Moe Zissler at Manhattan East. He told Zissler he was moving out of Cletus Berry's nest. He would come by for his belongings. Zissler was to remove Berry's computer and all other IS property and return them to Manhattan East. And pack up Berry's clothing and personal effects and wait for word from Berry's widow as to disposal.

Petrus patted Anna Maria on the shoulder. "Mr. Lindsey's going to stay at Aunt Zaffira's with me. We're going to move his things now. You want to come along with us?"

She agreed. They took a cab to Fifty-eighth and Seventh. Santa Claus was still ringing his bell. This time Lindsey didn't give him any money.

Lou Halter was on duty in the lobby. He looked up as Lindsey entered along with Anna Maria and Petrus Berry. He gasped and reached toward his holster, then stopped and held his hand out. It was trembling. His face was ashen. To Lindsey he suddenly looked more like eighty than sixty-five.

Halter said, "He gave me a start." He jerked his head toward Petrus Berry. "He looks like Mr. Berry. You know about Mino Bermudez. I'm getting out of here. I'm turning in my gun. I don't want any part of this. I didn't want a gun to start with, but the agency pays a bonus if you'll carry a gun. But I don't want this job anymore anyhow. I'll take my Social Security and sit in my little house and do the crossword puzzles. I don't ask much and I don't need much and I don't need this, I'll tell you that for sure."

Lindsey said, "He's Mr. Berry's brother." He walked Petrus and Anna Maria past Halter to the elevator.

When they entered the rooms upstairs Anna Maria said, "Daddy brought me here. He showed me his other office, it was on Lex. Lexington and Fifty-third. I wasn't supposed to let on that I knew about his other office."

Lindsey packed his belongings.

"Once Daddy brought me up here to help him with his computer. He wasn't really very good at it. He had this old insurance file on his disk, he told me he downloaded it from the company database, and he couldn't open it. I took a look at it and figured it out. It was easy. I showed him how to do it and he said that he'd just keep the lock on it except when he wanted to use the file."

So much for security, Lindsey thought.

Downstairs they caught another cab. Lindsey let the cabbie stow his flight bag in the trunk. He held on to his laptop.

Zaffira's apartment was a block north of Ester's, on Seventy-fourth Street east of Second Avenue. The building was an old brownstone. Zaffira's apartment was on the third story, in the rear. Anna Maria helped her uncle heft Lindsey's flight bag up the stairs. Petrus had insisted on carrying the bag, and Lindsey had toted his laptop.

Petrus Berry's key opened both the street door and the front door of the apartment. He followed Lindsey and Anna Maria inside. "Have to get another key for you," he grunted.

Lindsey asked where the telephone was. Petrus Berry pointed it out. Lindsey said, "I need to check in with my boss. International Surety will pay."

Petrus Berry grinned. He said, "Come on," to Anna Maria, "let's give Mr. Lindsey some privacy." To Lindsey, "We'll go and browse that candy store down near the Bear Garden."

Anna Maria said, "Sure, they always have good comic books and computer magazines."

Lindsey punched in Desmond Richelieu's private number. When Richelieu answered, Lindsey brought him up to date on the case.

Richelieu listened until Lindsey finished. Then he said, "I've been checking with Legal. You know, we paid out that old claim back in forty-something."

"I know it."

"You think this chariot really exists, Lindsey? Did it ever, or is it just a myth? And does it exist now?"

Lindsey sat in an overstuffed chair and looked out the window. He saw a high-rise on the other side of Seventy-fourth Street. The late afternoon sky had clouded over again; the patches of morning blue had proved a false promise. He'd been raised in a private house and he could never get used to the idea of occupying one six-sided cell in a giant honeycomb, not even in his apartment in Denver.

"Lindsey?" Ah, the new mellow Richelieu was reverting to his classic self. "You sleeping on company time? I asked you a question."

Lindsey told him that he was pretty sure that the chariot was real, that it was very old, and that it had actually existed as recently as 1940.

Richelieu snapped, "I wouldn't call 1940 very recent."

Lindsey didn't rise to the bait. "Whatever. That was the last time—I'm relying on Van Huysen now—that was the last time we're pretty sure it was around. It was in New York. It was supposed to be aboard the *Fior di Rimini*. It wasn't in the packing case when it was opened in La Spezia."

It was the mysterious Salvatore Castellini who had both discovered the loss of the chariot and the body of Massimo di Verolini. And it was Alcide Castellini who seemed to lurk behind every brutal event in Lindsey's investigation.

"Let me approach this from another angle, *bubbe*. Let me ask you this. What do you think that chariot is worth, if it still exists and if you could turn it up?"

"Van Huysen would know that better than I would. But it would be priceless. I mean, it's an art treasure. It's an historical artifact. There's no way you can put a price on it."

"Well, here's what Legal says, Lindsey. I think you've been hanging out with those artsy types too much lately. You're an insurance man, remember? Not some wine-swilling, Brie-munching interleck-chul. International Surety forked out five million bucks to save some Italian lollapalooza's political ass fifty years ago. Five million at five percent compound interest for fifty years—I'm rounding, *bubbe*, don't interrupt—is now worth on the order of $57,336,949."

Lindsey gulped.

"Did you hear me, *bubbe?* That's fifty-seven million simoleons plus some pocket change."

Lindsey said, "Uh."

Richelieu said, "I want you to find out who killed Cletus Berry.

I want to string the bastard up as high as I can reach. That's because I take care of my kiddies. I couldn't do less. J. Edgar would never let me do less. But, Lindsey, you'd better hope that little chariot still exists. And you'd better find it. If you do, International Surety returns it to the grateful government of the Republic of Italy. Along with a claim for the return of the five million we paid them back in Harry Truman's day. With interest."

Lindsey said, "Uh."

Richelieu said, "Get on it, *bubbe*." Then he hung up.

Chapter Sixteen

THE BIRD & TRANE was dark, noisy, and crowded. To Lindsey it looked as if every college student in the eastern half of the country had descended on the club, along with a healthy sprinkling of yuppies, a smattering of cyberpunks, and a handful of revenants of the Jack Kerouac generation.

He'd paid a door charge and squeezed into the place. There was an ornate wooden bar. The long mirror behind it was decorated with Christmas wreaths, Santas, and Rudolphs. The walls had been painted a flat black. Couples huddled over flickering candles in red jars on tiny round tables.

A drum kit and a set of microphones and speakers stood on a low bandstand at the far end of the room, but no musicians were in sight. Instead, recorded jazz squirmed its way into the room, to be battered and crushed by the sound of conversation.

Lindsey looked around for Victor Hopkins. Unsurprisingly, there was no sign of the young man.

With an effort, Lindsey managed to work his way up to the bar. There were no unoccupied stools so he slithered his way between a massive, curly-haired individual in a torn black sweatshirt and a pallid female who looked as if she'd had her last meal during the Vietnam peace conference. Her only visible decoration was a metal hoop in her pierced lower lip.

When the bartender condescended to notice him, Lindsey ordered a bottle of beer.

Anything that came sealed was probably safest.

The pallid female to Lindsey's left turned and ran her eyes up and down him. She looked amused. "You lose someone, grand-dad?" she asked.

Lindsey said, "Matter of fact, I'm supposed to meet somebody here."

The pallid female grinned. "Good luck." She snickered and turned away. She leaned over her drink and sipped through a short, opaque plastic straw. Her drink had been served in a martini glass, but it was a vicious green color.

She straightened up. There was a drop of liquid on her lower lip. She ran her tongue over her lip. She wore a smaller metal ring through the tip of her tongue. When the two rings met they made a little sound, *ching*, like tiny finger-cymbals.

Lindsey lifted his bottle—no glass—and wiped the rim with his hand. He tasted the beer. At least it was cold.

The club had been dark when Lindsey arrived, or so he thought, but now it grew darker.

A crimson spotlight picked out a woman on the bandstand. Lindsey suspected that her skin was death-white like his neighbor's, but in the spotlight it was a lurid red against her black costume.

Perfect for Christmas.

She detached one of the microphones from its metallic stand and announced the band. Lindsey had never heard of them, but that proved nothing.

They trooped onto the stage and began to play.

Someone had him by the elbow. He turned and saw Victor Hopkins. Lindsey said, "Do you have to be so damned melodramatic, Victor?"

Hopkins said something.

Lindsey flapped his free hand. "I can't hear you."

Hopkins tugged him toward the entrance.

Outside the Bird & Trane, Perry Street was surprisingly busy. The population was a mixture of the well-dressed and the grungy. Taxis dropped off mixed and unmixed couples who disappeared into bars and apartment buildings.

Hopkins pulled Lindsey against a brick wall. He said, "I've got some more information for you."

"About Millicent Martin?"

In the cold air their breath condensed visibly.

The cloud cover had cleared and a bright moon had risen over the city's buildings. Its light reflected off the dirty snow, restoring a fraction of its lost beauty.

"About Millicent Martin and Alcide Castellini."

"That I want to hear."

Hopkins looked around. Lindsey thought, He could have been a character in some silly spy movie. Then he thought of two bodies in the ice in an alley in Hell's Kitchen, and of two more in a basement apartment in Harlem. Maybe Hopkins wasn't so silly.

"Come on." Hopkins tugged at Lindsey's elbow again. "I don't want to stay in one place too long."

They walked along Perry Street. When they reached a corner Hopkins tugged Lindsey around it. Lindsey looked up at the sign and read *West 4th Street*. There weren't as many commercial establishments here, and most of the residential windows were dark, but streetlights on both sides of West Fourth Street illuminated the sidewalks.

"You know that photo of Millie with Fulton and Castellini."

Lindsey grunted agreement. "Castellini keeps turning up. There are too many corpses in this tangle, and Castellini always seems to be around the edges."

"Millie worked for him."

"Doing what?"

They circled a patch of ice in the middle of the sidewalk.

"Castellini brought antiques into the U.S. Artworks and antiques. Some of them had—well, questionable provenances. You know what I mean?"

Lindsey said he did.

"Customs had a line on Castellini. They try and keep an eye on the likes of him. So he uses mules. He hires solid citizens—semi-solid, anyway. Go to France, go to Italy, go to an address and pick up a package and bring it back with you."

"Uh-huh." A hulking shape wrapped in what looked like layers of stained blankets lurched toward them, hand out, mumbling.

They swerved around the hulk. "I know that dodge. They still need to come through customs."

"Right. That's the whole point of using mules. If somebody like Castellini came through customs with a Luini painting or a panel from a Fabriano altarpiece—I mean, he'd never get away with a Michelangelo or a da Vinci, that would be too much—but a really good item by some second- or third-rank genius—can you dig the concept, a third-rank genius? Somebody like the sculptor Sansovino?"

Lindsey waited to see where Hopkins was going.

"Look, Millie comes through customs with a minor masterpiece and a bill of sale that says it's a *reproduction*, see, a fucking *copy* worth fifty bucks or a hundred bucks. Castellini puts the whole thing together. He travels back and forth to Europe every couple of months making deals. But he never actually brings anything back with him except a little paperwork. Or ships anything back at all. They're too smart; they're onto him, they'd nail him in a second."

A streetlight had burned out on West Fourth Street. Something huddled against the stoop of a brownstone . . . shifted. It might have been another derelict, one who had settled down for the night cheered by the layers of a sleeping bag and the contents of a bottle of wine.

Lindsey and Hopkins gave the shadow a wide berth.

"But some office slavey or some housewife from Omaha jets in from Europe and proudly declares a genuine reproduction of a panel by Coimo Tura. She bought it in a shop in the Piazza Santa Maria for ninety bucks U.S. and she has a receipt to prove it. She gets waved through customs and a week later Alcide Castellini is supplying a *genuine* Tura panel to some Fifth Avenue collector. This dude knows the real from the phony and what he buys is no phony. There's even a legitimate bill of sale. That's what Castellini carried home in his briefcase, while the mule was waving the phony bill of sale at the customs inspectors."

The stoop of another brownstone loomed ahead of them, jutting onto the sidewalk. Something rose from the blackness beside it. A vaguely human shape raised its arm and pointed at Lindsey and Hopkins. Blond hair so pale it was almost luminous swung around the head. An errant ray of light—from the moon, from a streetlight, from a window—glinted off metal.

From behind them a voice shouted, "G'down!"

Lindsey felt Victor Hopkins shove him to the sidewalk, felt Hopkins crash on top of him. He heard two firearms discharge. A single shot came from behind him, from the direction of the Bird & Trane. A fusillade sounded from ahead of him, and sparks flew from buildings where stray shots struck.

He felt Victor Hopkins jerk once and heard him grunt with the impact of a bullet.

Someone ran toward Lindsey. He felt Victor Hopkins lifted off him. Lindsey's own face was pressed to a filthy berm of frozen slush at the edge of the curb. Someone grabbed his shoulder and turned him over. He looked up and blinked at the worried face of Cletus Berry—

—of Cletus Berry—

—of *Petrus* Berry peering into his own.

Berry lowered him to the cold cement and trotted away. Lindsey struggled to his feet. He peered after Petrus Berry and saw that Berry was hotfooting it along West Fourth Street. He knelt and tried to get a proper look at Victor Hopkins. Blood was bubbling from Hopkins's mouth, and gushing from a hole the size of a baseball in Hopkins's throat.

There was no question about Victor Hopkins.

Lights were springing up in windows along West Fourth Street. Lindsey tried to catch a glimpse of Berry. He didn't see any sign of him, but he ran in the direction Berry had run and picked up a trail of blood.

He followed the trail, running a few yards, pulling up short of breath, then staggering on. West Fourth Street crossed Charles, then West Tenth. For a moment Lindsey was disoriented; then he ran on. He saw a broad-shouldered figure crouched ahead of him.

When he got there he recognized Petrus Berry. He clutched a revolver in one hand. He raised his eyes from the figure lying on the sidewalk and shook his head.

Lindsey said, "Hopkins is dead."

Petrus Berry said, "So is this one." He pointed at the figure on the sidewalk. The face was utterly generic. It showed no discernible gender or race. Even the age was hard to judge. The body could belong to someone who had died after fifteen years of abuse or twice that many of a less damaging lifestyle. The flowing, platinum hair was done in a long-out-of-style pageboy bob. Even so, it could have been blond and glamorous or simply white with age. In the harsh light, the hair spread around the dead face on the cold gray sidewalk, it was impossible to be certain.

"You recognize this person?" Petrus Berry asked.

Lindsey shook his head. "Not a clue."

The body had a single hole in its chest. Either Petrus Berry was the world's finest sharpshooter or the world's luckiest shot. He had fired a single round and put it straight through the slim individual's chest, dead center, through the heart.

Berry said, "The police should be here any minute. Listen—you hear sirens?"

The whooping and wailing was coming closer. Lindsey said, "Maybe one of us should go back and stay with Hopkins. Show the cops the way when they get there."

"Not a chance. I don't want us separated and I don't want to leave this body unguarded. You can bet it'll get up and walk away if we don't keep watch."

A police cruiser came wailing past, its roof-lights flashing. Petrus Berry waved at the car. He still had his revolver in his hand.

The cruiser screeched to a halt. A uniformed cop jumped out, pointing a weapon at Berry and Lindsey. Without waiting for orders, Lindsey raised his hands in the air. Berry held his hands away from his body, slowly placed his revolver on the sidewalk, and took two steps away from it.

The uniformed officer moved toward them. "Get away from the gun and get down on the ground."

They didn't argue.

Petrus Berry was an old cop himself, and Lindsey had worked with police too often to do anything stupid.

Feeling the cold cement against his cheek, he wondered if Berry had a permit to carry his revolver. It didn't seem likely that he did. Not a New York permit.

That was okay. That would get sorted out.

Victor Hopkins was not okay, and neither was the strange being who had killed him.

Lindsey felt handcuffs snapped around his wrists, heard another set go onto Petrus Berry. He said, "I'm sorry I got you into this mess, Petrus. I never thought anything like this would happen to us."

Berry said, "I followed you, Lindsey. You didn't drag me along."

The cop said, "Shut up. Can you sit up? Good. Scrunch along, scrunch over to the wall there. Sit with your backs to the wall."

When Berry and Lindsey had complied, the cop said, "Jesus, Joseph, and Mary. What the hell happened here? We got a call from somebody over by Waverly."

Berry said, "There's a body there. This fella"—he nodded toward the dead gunslinger—"this one did it. Used an Uzi or a Tek, I think. I killed him. That's my .38 on the ground." He gestured again with his head.

The cop stood over Berry and Lindsey, looking down, shaking his head. "You're pretty cool, mister. You're in big trouble and you're pretty cool."

Berry looked up at the cop and smiled. Lindsey watched them, thinking that Berry could have been the cop's father, even his grandfather. Berry said, "I'm a retired police officer. You'll find my ID and my concealed weapon permit in my wallet."

The cop nodded. "That's good."

"The permit is from Pinopolis, South Carolina," Berry added.

"That's bad," the cop said.

Chapter Seventeen

It took a long time and a lot of persuasion to get them to call Marcie Sokolov. Once they did it took her a while to arrive at the crime scene. Yellow ribbons were up, coroner's technicians and forensics squads were on-site, and Lindsey and Petrus Berry were out of their handcuffs but in a kind of informal custody that suggested they'd better stick around or they'd be in formal custody.

Not that Marcie Sokolov was exactly thrilled to be wakened from a sound sleep (or so she claimed) and summoned long after her normal duty hours were over for the day.

The detective in charge of the scene was a Lieutenant MacArthur, no, no relation, thanks for asking. He conferred briefly with Sokolov. They were out of earshot of Lindsey. After a little while MacArthur gestured to Petrus Berry and Berry joined the group.

Lindsey watched the tension dissipate among the three of them, to be replaced by the camaraderie of cops being cops together. MacArthur had already taken Lindsey's and Berry's stories. Lindsey saw a handshake exchanged between Sokolov and Berry. He could follow the bobbing heads and read the body language. First they were talking about the newest shooting. Then they were talking about the death of Cletus Berry and Sokolov was offering her condolences to Petrus. She must have seen him at the cemetery, but then Sokolov had been an observer at the funeral; now she was a friend in need.

Sokolov crooked a finger at Lindsey.

He joined the group.

MacArthur said, "Your story checks out, sir. You don't know what a lucky stiff you are. Chief Berry here—"

Lindsey exclaimed, "Chief? You didn't tell me."

Berry said, "Pinopolis is just a tiny town. Only a handful of officers on the whole force."

"Chief Berry," MacArthur went on, "was worried about you, Mr. Lindsey. If he hadn't taken it upon himself to appoint himself bodyguard, you'd be back there with your friend on Waverly Place."

He had a pad and a silver pen in his hand. He used the pen to indicate Marcie Sokolov. "Detective Sokolov is going to handle this matter. I'm just as happy, I've got plenty of scrapple on my plate already. I'm just going to make sure that the boys and girls do their job right. Once the scene is cleared I'll do my paperwork and then I'm delighted to place it in your capable hands, Detective Sokolov. May you catch all the bad guys and never miss a clue."

He made a mock-military salute. "Lady and gentlemen, I leave you to your affairs."

Sokolov said, "Thanks, Lieutenant, sir."

"*No hay de que.*"

Sokolov looked from Berry to Lindsey. Obviously she had dragged a comb across her head but had not done much more. She wore a thick brown cable-knit sweater and a quilted vest and jeans tucked into heavy boots. She wore her badge on her vest, and she'd left her supply of Christmas ornaments at home.

"I wish you'd checked in with me sooner, Chief."

Berry said, "Sorry. I didn't really expect to get so involved. Thought I'd pay a courtesy call and then head home."

"You're not going to now, are you? Head home, I mean."

"I'm here for the duration, Detective."

"Glad to have you." She blew a long plume of white breath from her mouth. She had unusually distinct features, Lindsey realized. The police had set up portable lighting that made both the streetlights and the moonlight irrelevant. Sokolov's nose and brow were chiseled sharply and cast dark shadows against her cheeks.

"I want to walk down and have a look at the bodies," Sokolov said. "Chief, you'd better recover your weapon there or somebody will buy it in a pawnshop in a few hours. Good. Now, MacArthur knew the shooter and he tells me that you knew the fellow with the beard, Lindsey. Is that true?"

"His name was Victor Hopkins." Lindsey filled her in on his connection with Hopkins, about Hopkins's connection with Millicent Martin and Hopkins's theory about her being a mule for Alcide Castellini.

Sokolov nodded. "That's no surprise about Castellini."

"Then why?" Lindsey demanded.

"Whuh?"

"Why haven't you gone after him? Everywhere I turn I come up against Alcide Castellini. If you know, why don't you get on his case?"

Sokolov smiled bitterly. "Get on his case is right. We are on his case. Have been for months. You know what happens when we go after some thug with deep pockets. First of all, Castellini is smart enough to cover his tracks, so we haven't been able to build a case against him for anything bigger than dropping a slug in the parking meter."

"He did that?"

"Hyperbole, mountain man, did you ever hear of hyperbole?" She took a deep breath. "And if we ever did put him in a courtroom, what do you think would happen? Do you read the newspapers? Do you watch TV? He'd bring in a squad of overpriced mouthpieces and tie us up for a million years."

"You get one, once in a while. Didn't you finally get John Gotti?"

Her brittle smile softened a little. "Once in a while, that's right. Once in a while we actually get to put somebody away who's bigger than the street-corner dope dealer or the gutter-grade enforcer. Just once in a while. It does give me hope."

She swung her arms vigorously, hugging herself. "Come on, *boychiks*, let's go look at the stiffs."

She walked them past the yellow tape and they bent to peer at the mortal remains of the shooter. The body lay in the middle of a chalked outline and a V-shaped piece of cardboard with a number on it had been placed on the dead shooter's chest alongside the hole where Berry's .38 slug had entered.

Sokolov looked at Lindsey, then at Berry. "You did this, Chief? First shot?"

"I learned as a boy. Got a lot of practice in the army. Figured I ought to keep up my skills once I got on the force."

Sokolov whistled. "Either of you gentlemen recognize this here-now cadaver?"

Lindsey bent farther. He'd already had a fair look at the shooter, but he wanted to make sure. The platinum hair still framed the dead face. Lindsey straightened. "No idea in the world."

"Chief?"

Berry shook his head. "Total stranger. I don't keep up too well with wanted posters, though."

Sokolov snorted. "You wouldn't have seen one on this fella. Merle Oates. Male Caucasian, age twenty. I guess you caught him out of season. His favorite trick is to dress up like a hot whore when he's on a hit. You'd be surprised how often it works. I guess it's too cold for that tonight, but he's got his favorite wig on, anyway. Sometimes he's a redhead and sometimes he's a brunette."

She leaned over the body. "Bye-bye, Merle." She straightened. She called out to an evidence technician who was working nearby. "Hey fella. Where's his piece?"

The technician looked at her. "Who, me? I didn't see any piece."

Sokolov bit her lip. "Did anybody?"

"I don't think so."

"All right." Sokolov sighed. "Chief Berry, you say he was using a streetsweeper?"

"I didn't get a clear look at his piece, but it sure sounded like one. And those muzzle flashes had to come from an automatic. Nobody's finger is that fast."

"Right. They found some casings and a couple of slugs. I'm sure you're right. We'll keep looking for the piece. What's the chance it went down a sewer grating? It's amazing how often they do that."

"You don't think maybe a little elf made off with it, do you?" Berry asked.

She gave him another of those cop-to-cop looks. Then she said, "Let's take a peep at the other cadaver."

They walked back to Victor Hopkins's body, ducking under another strand of yellow tape to reach it. There was more flashing of badges and vouching for outsiders and then Lindsey was standing over the body. His stomach lurched, but he didn't lose any food.

"What do you think, Lindsey? Was Merle after you or was he after Victor here? What's your professional amateur judgment?"

"I don't know." Lindsey was perplexed. "Hopkins has been in hiding. I thought he was acting paranoid about meeting me, sending messages through the *Times*—"

"What about the *Times?*" Sokolov asked sharply.

Lindsey explained about Amy Baines and about Hopkins's unwillingness to give Lindsey his address or phone number.

"Huh!" Sokolov turned her face upward, as if she might find a message written on the moon.

Maybe the Bat Signal.

"Here's what I'm gonna do," Sokolov said. "I'm gonna bend the rules. You know what a good bureaucrat does. She never breaks the rules, but she always finds a way to get what she wants without breaking the rules."

She stared at her toes, looking for inspiration in her boots. They looked expensive. They must have been handsome boots when she left home in them. Now they were marred with slush and ice.

She said, "Chief Berry, when one of our officers discharges a firearm in public we have to take away his piece and put him on desk duty or administrative leave until there's a hearing on the incident."

"Sure," Berry replied. "Even down in Pinopolis we have procedures like that." He pursed his lips. "You want my piece, Detective?"

"Please."

She held out her hand. He placed his revolver on her palm. She slipped it into a pocket of her heavy winter coat.

"Thanks."

Sokolov kicked a ridge of ice with the pointy toe of one boot. A chunk of ice broke off and skittered from the sidewalk into the street. Sokolov walked over to a group of uniforms and dragged one of them back with her. She got the officer's name.

"Okay," she said again, "Gulbenkian, George H. What happened, your parents run out of G names and move on to the next letter of the alphabet? Never mind. Officer Gulbenkian, I'm Detective Sokolov, you know me, right?"

"Yes, ma'am."

"Good. Meet Chief Berry and Mr. Lindsey."

Officer Gulbenkian nodded twice.

"Here we go," Sokolov said. "I'm convening a special emergency hearing into the shootings of Victor Hopkins and Merle Oates, with particular attention to the conduct of Retired Chief of Police Petrus Berry, Pinopolis, South Carolina, PD. You got that, Officer?"

Gulbenkian asked, "You want me to take notes, Detective Sokolov?"

"Please."

He opened a notebook and stood with ballpoint poised.

Sokolov said, "It is the finding of this hearing that Victor Hopkins was shot by Merle Oates, a person known to this court to be of bad character and lengthy criminal background. It is the finding of this hearing that Merle Oates was shot by Petrus Berry, Retired Chief, Pinopolis, South Carolina, PD, while in the act of illegally and without provocation discharging a firearm at the aforesaid Victor Hopkins and Mr. Hobart Lindsey."

A cold wind swept along West Fourth Street, bringing with it a horizontal spray of sleet particles. They stung Lindsey's face and made him blink.

"It is the ruling of this hearing," Sokolov went on, "that Chief

Berry acted justifiably and correctly in discharging his firearm at the aforesaid Merle Oates."

She looked at Patrolman Gulbenkian.

Lindsey looked at them both. Sokolov was poker-faced. Gulbenkian looked as if he'd been poleaxed.

Sokolov said, "Have that typed up and ready for my signature ASAP, Officer. At Midtown North. Thank you."

She reached into her pocket and pulled out Berry's revolver and handed it back to him.

Berry checked it carefully, then slipped it into a shoulder holster.

Lindsey hadn't seen Berry draw the revolver. He didn't know that Berry wore a shoulder holster.

Sokolov said, "Listen, fellas, it's colder than a eunuch's kiss out here. Let's head uptown. I'll get us a nice warm conference room and we can talk about this. That okay with you?"

She got them a ride in a cruiser. Officer Gulbenkian, of all the cops in the City of New York, drove them. When they got there they stripped off their outer clothing and settled down around a pot of coffee.

One thing Lindsey could say for New York—its police department served the best coffee he'd ever had in a station house.

Sokolov opened the conference by asking Petrus Berry for a suggestion. Lindsey felt miffed. It was his case; Cletus Berry had been his partner and he had been sent to New York to unravel the circumstances surrounding Berry's death. Well, but Petrus had a blood interest in the case. And there was the bond of professionalism between him and Sokolov.

"—this fellow Castellini," Berry was saying.

"But we can't show any direct involvement," Sokolov countered. "Even if we take Bilbo Sax's word that Johnny Thieu Ng killed your brother and Frankie Fulton, Chief—which I doubt we could make stand up, even as a dying declaration—we know he was just an errand boy."

"An errand boy with a gun," Lindsey put in.

The others gave him a withering look.

"Please," Sokolov said, "the Chief and I are professionals. Okay?"

Lindsey frowned, she waited, he nodded.

"And we have Lindsey's statement that Victor Hopkins told him that Castellini runs mules to and from Europe to move art treasures. That right, Lindsey?"

"Yes."

"How useful is that?" Petrus Berry asked. "You don't even have Hopkins's dying declaration, you only have Lindsey's statement of what Hopkins told him. Weak tea. Not even good hearsay." He patted Lindsey on the arm. "Nothing personal. Just the way it works."

Lindsey tilted his head. "So you're saying we don't have anything? I mean, anything we can use against Castellini?"

Berry deferred to Sokolov.

Sokolov said, "That's exactly what I'm saying." There was a long pause, then she added, "Plus, Castellini nestles comfortably under the wing of Randolph Amoroso, our distinguished congressman from up in Dutchess County."

Lindsey pushed his chair back from the table. He was angry. "You're telling me you're going to run around picking up corpses and as long as they're scum like Frankie Fulton or Johnny Ng or Sax or Oates it's okay. I guess it's okay that Millicent Martin is dead because she was a mule for Castellini. Maybe. And what about Hopkins? And what about Cletus Berry? Is it okay they're dead because they were involved, somehow, with the little bad guys, but we don't dare touch the big bad guys? Is that what you're telling me?"

Sokolov said, "Lindsey, I swear to you on my parents' graves, I will hang Alcide Castellini from Cleopatra's Needle in Central Park if I get a chance. But I'm the New York Police Department, not the X-Men, okay? You want a vigilante, you can find one in the Yellow Pages. But I'm not it. I bent the rules like a pretzel tonight to keep Chief Berry out of trouble and to let him keep his gun. I did it because he's one of the good guys and I know he would have come out clean anyhow, in the long run. So I found a wormhole to scoot us both through."

She was breathing hard and there was color in her face that was not put there by the cold night air. Not inside Midtown North.

"But I tell you and I want you to hear me: I cannot touch Alcide Castellini right now. If and when I can, I will. But right now, I cannot raise a finger against the man."

Chapter Eighteen

PETRUS BERRY PACED restlessly. Lindsey sprawled on a sofa, tracing the gold and orange floral pattern in the upholstery. The third-floor living room of Zaffira Lazarini Fornari's flat over-looked a small garden in the rear of the brownstone. A set of French doors and a tiny balcony overhung the open area. A pair of trees stood in the garden; they had lost their leaves and stood stretching skeletal fingers into the night sky. Lower shrubs were coated with snow and the snow-covered ground reflected the moonlight, creating a spectral image.

"Look at that, will you?"

"At what?" Lindsey sat up straight.

"Never mind." Berry raised his head. "I thought I saw a little bird in the tree. It's too late in the year. A robin. They've all flown south by now. Maybe this one got left behind, but it's gone now anyway."

An antique—or antique reproduction—clock stood on the mantel; its filigreed hands showed three o'clock. Marcie Sokolov had sent them home from Midtown North in an unmarked car. "I don't want to scare you guys—" she had started to explain.

Lindsey interrupted. "What's to be scared of, just because that little creep Merle Oates tried to kill me?"

"I don't think he was trying to kill you, Lindsey. You're just asking questions. If they kill you, somebody else will come along and ask even more questions. But Victor Hopkins was giving you answers. That's what they didn't want."

She grinned and snorted. "Of course, Merle wasn't trying *not* to kill you. As long as he got Hopkins, killing you would have been a little extra something for nothing."

She tapped a fingernail against her upper teeth. Lindsey hadn't noticed earlier that she had large front teeth; they looked unusually white under the pallid fluorescents of the conference room.

"But in any case, I'm glad that you're out of the Torrington Tower and I'm double glad that you'll be bunking in with Chief Berry here. But just in case somebody's watching, I don't want to send you home in a cruiser. We'll send you fellas out through the garage in an unmarked car. I seem to have inherited Gorgeous George Gulbenkian there, at least for the rest of the shift. He did a good job driving us up from the Village. He'll make sure there's no tail before he drops you off at your digs."

Gulbenkian had cruised up the West Side, through the Central Park transverse, and across town to Second Avenue. If anybody had followed them, it must have been Wonder Woman making a return visit in her invisible airplane.

Petrus Berry and Lindsey had agreed without discussion that neither of them was ready for sleep. Berry had located Zaffira Fornari's stash of CDs and put one on the player. Lindsey had heard this music before. It was a Schubert piano trio. One more thing to thank Marvia Plum for; one more thing to regret.

Berry stood at the French doors, staring down into the white garden. From the floral sofa, Lindsey watched him. The Schubert piece was a surprising choice for a retired cop from Pinopolis, South Carolina, but maybe it was all that Zaffira Fornari had.

Or maybe there was more to Petrus Berry than met Lindsey's eye.

Berry and Lindsey each held a snifter of brandy. Zaffira Fornari had impeccable taste.

"I never thought I'd see my brother dead," Petrus Berry said. The words rebounded off the glass panes of the French doors. "I'm ten years older. Our parents are gone, I have nobody of my own. He should have buried me." He shook his head sadly. "It isn't fair and it isn't right. All the years I was a cop—"

He'd unstrapped his shoulder holster and laid it, the revolver in it still, on Zaffira's dining table.

"All the years I was a cop, you know how many times I got shot at, and how many times I shot at anybody else?" Lindsey didn't answer and Berry didn't wait. "Once. Once and never, to answer both questions. Couple of good ol' boys got tanked up on cheap whiskey and decided they didn't like the idea of people like me wearing badges and carrying guns, so they lay in wait one night and tried to run me off the road. I was in a cruiser; they were in a rusty pickup with mud on the license plate. Sounds like a bad movie, doesn't it?"

Lindsey waited.

"I got around 'em. Took a shotgun blast in my rear window. I kept rolling and they kept after me and I called in for backup and led 'em straight into a trap. We had another cruiser waiting, blocked the road, another one came up behind 'em and they were boxed in. They had to choose between shooting it out and giving it up and they kept on shooting and the guys on our side kept on shooting."

Lindsey said, "You didn't fire back, yourself?"

Petrus Berry shook his head. "Nope. I was bleeding too badly. I took a few shotgun pellets in the back of my neck but it was the glass slivers that gave me the trouble. Almost severed my spine. I was bleeding like a stuck pig. By the time we wrapped it all up, I was closer to dead than to alive. Couple of shotgun loads came through my front windshield, too. I was under the dashboard by then or I wouldn't be here today. God bless those other cops. They saved my life."

He nodded and made an inarticulate sound, agreeing with himself.

"Of course, those other cops might have been aiming at me. No way to know, is there?"

"They wouldn't have done that, would—" Lindsey stopped even before the question was fully asked, but Berry answered it anyway.

"Maybe they would and maybe they wouldn't. We'll never know now, will we?"

"A jury convict those good ol' boys?" Lindsey asked.

"They did. Everybody was astonished. My mama and papa, they said they thought they'd never live to see the day, but they saw it. Saw one son a police officer—they didn't live to see me chief, but they saw me with a badge and a gun and a uniform. Saw the other son a warrant officer in the United States Army." He paused and peered into his brandy snifter. Watching him, Lindsey took a sip from his own snifter.

"At least they didn't have to bury their sons. Cletus is with them now. I believe that." He looked up, looked across the room at Lindsey. "Do you believe that, Lindsey?"

Lindsey said, "I don't know. I wish I did." He set his snifter down and rose to his feet. There was no fire in the fireplace and he didn't feel like starting one this late at night—or this early in the morning. He was bone weary but his nerves were twitching. Overtired, Marvia Plum had called that state, when a pleasant drowsiness dissolves, unfulfilled, and leaves behind only an almost painful sense of fatigue.

He said, "Petrus, I think Cletus's army service is the key to this whole thing. That damned chariot keeps popping up—well, no, it doesn't really. It's just out there somewhere in the mist, isn't it?" He waved his hand vaguely, as if the chariot were floating through the air, or maybe flying over the snow-covered garden like Santa's sleigh.

"Didn't he ever tell you anything about Italy? About what he did there? About—anything—any—" Lindsey rubbed his hand across his face and tried again. "Did he ever say anything that might have tied in with his death?" he asked. "And all the others?"

"You have any brothers, Lindsey?"

Lindsey said, "No."

"Sisters?"

"No."

"Ten years is a long time between children. When Cletus was born, I could hardly believe it. I was starting to think about growing up by then. Ten years old. Nineteen forty-nine. They had us ducking under our desks at school, convinced that Joe

Stalin was going to drop an atom bomb on us. He stole the recipe from us and he was out to conquer the world, and America was his main target. That was the story we had pounded into us every day."

He was standing, turned sideways, the French doors to his right, Lindsey to his left. He turned his head, now looking down into the snow-covered garden, now looking back into the room at Lindsey.

"Why, along comes this little brother and I'm frightened for him. You know what I was frightened of? I was afraid the Ruskies were going to come and conquer America and take my little brother back to Moscow or Siberia or someplace and raise him up to be a Communist and hate his own country and I wouldn't have my brother anymore."

He paced, then asked, "What do you think of that, Lindsey?"

Lindsey shrugged. "I wasn't born until '53. I wouldn't know."

"You wouldn't."

"My father was killed in Korea. In the navy. In the Sea of Japan."

"Do you know why?"

"Politics."

"All politics is shit," Berry said. He advanced until he was standing in front of Lindsey. "So that little weasel Johnny Thieu Ng killed my brother, and Merle Oates, whatever he was, killed Victor Hopkins, and all the other corpses that are lying around this city, and you think Alcide Castellini is behind the whole thing."

"I do. And I think your brother's involvement started when he was in the army."

Petrus Berry shrugged. He looked at Zaffira Fornari's antique clock. "Quarter to five. Almost dawn. I'm going to hit the hay. I suggest you do the same. I'll set the alarm. We'll get up and tackle this when our heads are clear."

He jerked a thumb toward a dark wood door. "Linen closet." He gestured again. "Bathroom."

Lindsey said, "Got it."

Berry said, "Eight o'clock okay?"

Lindsey blinked. "Sure."

"We'll consult the official family historian. Anna Maria. See what she has to say." Berry disappeared into the bedroom and closed the door behind him.

"I wouldn't call myself a hacker." Anna Maria shook her head. She wore her hair in pigtails today, with bright red ribbons at the end of each. It was good to see her out of black. Lindsey wondered if she was commenting on pickaninny styles. If the word was even in her vocabulary.

She was amazingly bright, and this soon after her father's funeral, fairly cheerful. She didn't wear the mourning weeds that her mother and aunt did. Ezio Pinza sat on her lap, turning his head frequently to take in the conversation.

"I wouldn't call myself a hacker, not compared to some of the people I've met online. But I can do a few tricks. You want to know about my father?" When she wasn't clattering away at the keyboard, she stroked Ezio Pinza's shiny black-and-gold coat.

"He was my brother," Petrus Berry said.

"And you are Professor Blackberry," Lindsey said. "Mora Selvatica."

"Mosé and I together. I'm not Professor Blackberry and neither is Mosé. We're both Mora Selvatica. Neither one of us is Professor Blackberry, we both are."

She had admitted them to her room. She proudly showed off her up-to-date computer. Lindsey wouldn't have tried to gain admittance to Anna Maria's room, not with just himself and Anna Maria present. But Petrus Berry, Anna Maria's Uncle Pete, was there as well.

"I hacked into the Pentagon," she admitted. "That was so easy, it hardly even counts. They have all these software locks, but anybody who knows anything can open one in a minute."

I ought to introduce her to Marty Saxon, Lindsey thought. *They're birds of a feather.*

"Do you want to see my dad's service record?"

"Very much so," Lindsey said.

Anna Maria turned to make eye contact with her uncle. As Lindsey watched, Petrus Berry nodded silently. Anna Maria said, "All right, then. You'll have to give me a few minutes."

Lindsey studied the contents of her room—the visible contents—while she clattered away at the keyboard of her computer. She had posters on her walls and a row of Barbie dolls, one or two of them white, the rest dark brown. A long bookshelf ran from the closet door to the edge of her window.

Half the shelf was filled with computer manuals. The rest of her collection seemed to be composed of history books and biographies. Benjamin Bannecker, Sojourner Truth, Golda Meir, Giuseppe Garibaldi, Shirley Chisholm, Albert Einstein, Italo Balbo.

"Here it is," Anna Maria said. "I have a copy on my hard disk, but I thought you'd rather see the actual Pentagon 201 file."

Lindsey exchanged a look with Petrus Berry.

"What's a 201 file?" Lindsey asked.

"Military personnel record," Berry furnished.

They settled behind the girl.

When Lindsey and Petrus Berry had arrived at the apartment, Zaffira Fornari took her sister out for a walk and a snack. International Surety's benefits package included a company-paid death benefit and a fat life insurance policy. The double-indemnity clause would apply since Cletus Berry had been murdered. His family would not go hungry.

Except for his presence.

Anna Maria said, "I can print this out if you want. I never did because I don't want to have any paper here that somebody could see and cop to what I'm doing."

She sounded too grown-up for a child of ten. Lindsey found himself wondering if anybody had a childhood like the childhood his generation had enjoyed. Then he wondered if his generation had enjoyed that at all; were his memories real or were they the product of the golden glow of hindsight combined with reruns of "Leave it to Beaver?"

"Actually a floppy would be good," Lindsey said, "and a hard copy, too. If you don't mind."

Anna Maria said, "Sure."

Cletus Berry had gone to the infantry school at Fort Benning, Georgia, then to the Army Finance School in Indiana, and finally to the Army War College in Pennsylvania.

That seemed odd, for a warrant officer. Lindsey didn't know much military protocol, but he had the impression that a warrant officer was a pretty small character in the army's scheme of things. Why did Berry have these qualifications?

He'd been assigned to NATO headquarters in Brussels, then sent to Southern Command, assigned to Rome, with frequent visits to the NATO office at the Italian naval base at La Spezia.

Why did La Spezia ring a bell? Lindsey wracked his brain. It didn't take long to put that together. La Spezia was the port where the *Fior di Rimini* had docked in 1940. The port where a cargo inventory had discovered the body of Massimo di Verolini in the crate that should have contained the missing silver chariot. And the port where the investigation was taken over by a fascist official swiftly dispatched from Rome—Salvatore Castellini.

There was something else peculiar about Cletus Berry's service record. Lindsey might not have noticed it, but Petrus Berry did. He made an odd sound, and when Lindsey turned to look at him Petrus had a peculiar expression on his face.

"What's the matter?"

Berry frowned. "Look at that. Look at Cletus's discharge status."

Lindsey complied. "General discharge. What does that mean?"

"Huh, that's right, you were never in the service. It means that Cletus was discharged from the army, um, how did they put it, it's been so long . . . under honorable conditions. But it's not an honorable discharge."

"I don't understand that."

"Well, an honorable discharge means you served your country and your enlistment had expired or your draft time was up or whatever. They give you a gold watch and a handshake and send you home. No watch, not really, but everything else."

"And dishonorable?"

"Well, you punched out your CO or you stole a pistol from the armory and sold it off-post or—you see? You could be court-martialed for what you did, they could send you to jail or impose some other penalty, and then when they were finished punishing you they'd hand you a *dis*honorable discharge. You couldn't get a decent job in those days, with a DD. You didn't get any veteran's benefits. No GI bill. No VA hospital. Nothing."

"But look." Lindsey pointed at the screen. How much of this was Anna Maria taking in? How much should he and Petrus say? If Cletus Berry had feet of clay, did they need to reveal them to his daughter?

"He didn't get an honorable discharge *or* a dishonorable discharge. He got a general discharge. What does that mean?"

"What I told you. It means he was discharged under honorable conditions but he didn't get an honorable discharge. And it doesn't say why. Either somebody kept the reason out of his file or somebody cleaned it out later on. Anna Maria—"

He put both his hands on the child's thin shoulders.

"Did you show your dad how to get into this file?"

"No. I was afraid he'd take my computer away. I was afraid I'd get in trouble, so I never told anybody I could do this."

"Okay," Petrus Berry said. "He didn't do it himself. Either the reason was never there or somebody else cleaned it out."

A key grated in the front door lock and Ezio Pinza jumped off Anna Maria Berry's lap and ran from her room. His claws clattered on the hardwood floor as he sped to greet Ester and Zaffira.

Ester came into Anna Maria's room and embraced her daughter. She gave her brother-in-law a chaste kiss, shook Lindsey's hand. "What are you learning?" Her voice was hoarse, her English almost unaccented.

"Mrs. Berry—"

"Ester—"

Lindsey and Petrus Berry exchanged looks. Lindsey nodded, indicating that he deferred to Berry. Blood called to blood.

"Ester, we need to know more about what Cletus was doing in Italy."

"What do you mean, what was he doing? He was in the army. You know what you do when you're in the army. You go where they send you, you do what they tell you."

"Right. Yes. What was he doing in Rome?"

She shrugged angrily. "He was an officer. He did as he was told. It was a long time ago. Fifteen years ago. A lifetime ago. Look at me." She held out her hands. "I was a schoolgirl. Ask Zaffira. She's older. She knows more. Ester Lazarini is dead. I am in the grave with my husband."

Anna Maria started crying. "Mama, no." She clutched her mother, buried her face in her chest.

"What was he doing in La Spezia?" Petrus Berry persisted.

"Out." Ester Lazarini grasped her daughter with one hand, tore at her own hair with the other. "Out," she wailed. "Out."

Chapter Nineteen

"I BLEW IT, I'm sorry."

Petrus Berry and Lindsey walked westward on Seventy-third Street. A cold wind picked up and whipped their coats, stung their faces.

"Don't—" Lindsey was going to say, *Don't blame yourself*, but Berry cut him off.

"I'm still a cop. Sometimes being a cop and being a human being don't jibe at all. How could I do that to those two girls?"

Lindsey shook his head. "It's done. Over. Give Ester a chance to calm down. We have to talk to Anna Maria again. And her cousin in Italy. What time is it over there? What, halfway across the world, how do they talk to each other, Anna Maria and Mosé?"

"We'll ask. I'll ask. I screwed it up and I'll fix it up."

They crossed Fifth Avenue and turned downtown, skirting the low wall that set Central Park off from the broad sidewalk and the whole East Side.

"There's Anna Maria's school," Berry said. They'd reached Sixty-fifth Street. The sun had finally burst through the grayness of the past days. The sky was a brilliant blue. When a gust of wind swept a cloud of ice crystals off a rooftop the crystals fell to the street in a glowing rainbow.

"It's too soon to get back to them. Let them mourn. We'll try later."

They turned and walked across Fifty-eighth Street. As they passed the Torrington Tower, Lindsey spotted Hassan Muhammad seated behind the guard desk. Lindsey said, "Petrus, just hold on a minute. I have a hunch."

They entered the lobby.

Hassan Muhammad looked at Lindsey, uncertain of who he was. Lindsey reminded him and Muhammad said, "Yes, I have a letter for you." He handed Lindsey a business-size envelope. The International Surety crest was embossed above the return address, and in ballpoint ink someone had added the initials MAZ.

Morris A. Zissler.

Lindsey borrowed a letter opener from Hassan Muhammad and carefully slit the envelope. He scanned the contents, slipped the single sheet of paper back into the envelope, then tilted his head toward the lobby doors. "Petrus, take a look."

Petrus Berry reached for the envelope. Lindsey shook his head, held onto it until they were outside again, headed toward the corner. Then he handed it to Petrus Berry. Without breaking stride, Berry read the note and handed it back to Lindsey.

"Who's Moe Zissler? And who's Cele Johnston? What's her point?"

"Zissler's a small-timer in International Surety. Cele Johnston runs an antiques shop on Fifty-seventh Street. She must have phoned Manhattan East because I gave her my card and it only has the Denver number on it. She must have called there and they told her I was in New York. So she looked—"

"Got it, got it. Enough. This has something to do with the case, right?"

"Cele Johnston knows Alcide Castellini. The first time I talked with her—the only time—she started to open up about Castellini. Then she changed her mind and practically threw me out of her office. Now she wants to talk to me again."

"Right now? You think you ought to call ahead?"

"I don't think so. She got spooked the other time. Looks as if she keeps changing her mind. If she wanted to talk to me enough to phone International Surety, I don't want to give her a chance to change her mind again."

Cele Johnston gave Petrus Berry a suspicious up-and-down. Her eyes settled on the slight bulge under his left arm and she nodded, almost imperceptibly. Lindsey had introduced him by name, saying nothing about his relationship to the case. She offered Lindsey and Berry the use of a century-old coatrack and two cups of tea shimmering in translucent bone china.

She said, "You made the *Times*. Congratulations. Now all the best people will know about you." She nodded toward Petrus Berry.

Lindsey said, "I didn't see the paper today. Did you, Petrus?"

"Guess we're getting too wrapped up in our own doings. Dangerous."

Cele Johnston slid open a drawer of her desk and laid a morning newspaper on the desk, facing Lindsey and Berry. The newspaper was already opened to a story about the slaying of Victor Hopkins and Merle Oates. Lindsey scanned the copy. It ran a few paragraphs on an inside page. There was no photo. The story described the deaths of Oates and Hopkins, and went on to describe the unconventional hearing that exonerated Petrus Berry. How the *Times* reporter got that was a mystery all its own. Maybe Amy Baines knew the answer.

There was no mention of Hobart Lindsey, Cletus Berry, or International Surety.

Cele Johnston leaned forward and raised her eyebrows. "You're related to Cletus Berry, sir?"

"Brother."

"Mr. Lindsey, I think you're out of your mind." Cele Johnston snatched the newspaper from her desk and deposited it in a tooled leather wastebasket. "I think you should pack your bags and head back to Denver."

She shifted in her chair.

"Mr. Berry."

He raised his eyebrows.

"My condolences, Mr. Berry. On the death of your brother."

He sat like a statue.

"Your being here complicates this. I'd expected Mr. Lindsey to come here alone."

"Anything you have to tell me . . ." Lindsey said.

"I'm not so sure of that."

"Please."

She steepled her fingers in front of her face, the thumbs supporting her chin and the forefingers pressing against the sides of her nose. Finally she nodded.

"All right. Alcide Castellini wants to see you. Wants to see Hobart Lindsey. He didn't say anything—indicate any wish to see you, Mr. Berry. I don't think you would be welcome. I really don't."

Petrus Berry nodded.

Lindsey said, "When and where?"

Cele Johnston took a sheet of elegant notepaper in one hand and an equally elegant pen in the other and jotted a few lines. She folded the paper and laid it on the edge of the desk nearest herself.

"Mr. Castellini asks that you come alone. No companion. No weapon of any sort. No electronic devices of any sort. Do you understand what he's saying?"

"No wire." Lindsey had never worn a wire, never used a wire. The only person he'd ever known who did was Celia Varela. She'd worn a wire in Berkeley and wound up with a different kind of wire around her neck and her tongue purple and swollen and protruding from her mouth.

"Sounds like he's making himself safe from me."

"He is."

"How safe am I from him?"

"Mr. Lindsey, if he wanted you dead you'd be dead right now."

"Really." Lindsey stirred his tea with a delicate silver spoon. "What about last night?"

Before Cele Johnston answered, Petrus Berry said, "I'm not really happy, folks." Lindsey could see that Petrus had his right hand inside his suit coat. "I think maybe we should leave, Lindsey."

"No." Lindsey shook his head. "Ms. Johnston is right. If Castellini wanted us dead, we'd be dead." He turned toward Cele Johnston. "But you haven't answered my question. What about last night?" He nodded toward the hand-tooled leather wastebasket, toward the discarded copy of *The New York Times* with the Oates-Hopkins story in it.

Cele Johnston actually blushed. "That was a mistake."

What the hell *was* Cele Johnston? Lindsey wondered. At their first meeting she had seemed to despise Alcide Castellini, and also to fear him. She'd given Lindsey Castellini's telephone number—Lindsey had never used it—and hustled him out of her store, apparently in a state of near panic.

Now she was acting as if she was Alcide Castellini's right-hand woman.

Lindsey reached toward the folded sheet of notepaper. Toward it, not for it. A subtle game of manipulation was taking place. Even though Lindsey was one of the players, he only dimly understood the rules. If he reached for the note, he knew, Cele Johnston had the choice of snatching it away from his outstretched fingers or of letting him take it. Instead, by holding his hand a few inches above her desktop, he was forcing her to place the notepaper in his hand.

She did, and shot him a coldly venomous look.

She understood the game better than he. She realized that she had yielded a point.

But Lindsey wondered if he had needlessly made an enemy, and lost by winning.

They sat in a wooden booth over bowls of soup in a place on Broadway. Judging by the decor, the restaurant had been there since Fiorello La Guardia's day, if not Jimmy Walker's. Judging by the people inside, the customers and the staff had been there equally long. Lindsey didn't recognize more than a quarter of the dishes on the menu. This was a place that Eric Coffman would have loved. Lindsey would have to tell him about it if he ever got back to California.

Even though it was warm in the restaurant he shivered.

If he ever got back to California.

Lindsey reached across the table and handed the sheet of notepaper to Petrus Berry. He watched Berry's eyes track as he read the brief lines.

Berry handed the note back to Lindsey. "Very nice."

"You noticed it, too."

"No time. And no telephone number. Just an address." Berry tore the corner off a hard roll. He dropped it into his soup, fished it out with his spoon and ate it. "Not elegant," he commented. "Time was, I'd have staked my choppers against anything short of a hickory limb. Now—oh, well. Getting old beats the daylights out of the alternative."

"Cele Johnston doesn't strike me as a careless woman," Lindsey said. He slipped the note into his pocket organizer. Good old organizer. It had been with him through a lot of cases. But it was getting ragged, and it lacked electronics. Maybe it was time to retire it to a bureau drawer.

"Nor me," Berry agreed.

"Then why would she write the note that way? Did she expect me to rush right over there? Do you know that address?"

"I'm a stranger here myself."

"Last time I saw Cele Johnston, I was trying to track down Castellini. She gave me a card with his phone number on it. *A phone number.* I'd assume it was Castellini's, but maybe not."

He tucked into his own meal. Berry had ordered kreplach soup. Somehow it figured. Lindsey had ordered something called *schav*. When he tasted it his only reaction was puzzlement. Outside, the clouds had disappeared and the day was brilliant. But the cloud layer, now departed, had held whatever warmth there was, down in the city.

Today New York was colder than ever.

Berry asked, "Did you call the number?"

Lindsey shook his head.

"Why not? If you're convinced that Castellini is at the center of this case . . ."

"I didn't know enough. I didn't want to go up against him until I was stronger. Until I was ready."

"You're ready now?"

"I'm not sure. I've put together a lot of information."

Berry signaled a waitress and ordered a cup of coffee. He said, "Lindsey, look here. We've got different methods. I'm a small-town cop. You're a big-time corporation man. I'm a pretty simple man, but I'll tell you I had a good record down in Pinopolis.

And I guess you've got a record with International Surety. My brother never told me much about this SPUDS thing, but I know it's an elite outfit and you would never make it into SPUDS if you didn't have plenty on the ball."

Lindsey fidgeted.

"Or if you did," Berry continued, "and you didn't perform, you'd be out on your heinie in quick time. So look here—I'm not just buttering you up, I'm leveling with you."

His coffee had arrived and he added a drop of cream, no sugar, and stirred.

"What I'm saying is, asking I guess, What the hell do you have in mind?"

Lindsey's eyes widened. Before he could formulate an answer, Berry went on.

"You don't intend to make a cold call on Castellini, do you?"

"I don't think so."

"So you'll phone for an appointment, like a good little insurance man?"

Lindsey made a rolling gesture with one hand. And nodded.

"So let's plan this. You going in there alone?"

"Whatever." Lindsey ate soup.

"What are you going to say to the man? 'You killed my partner and I'm here to do something about it.' That it? He says, 'No, I didn't. Don't you read the newspapers? Johnny Thieu Ng killed your partner, and then the little freak-o checked out with a stroke book in one hand and his pecker in the other and a belt around his neck.' And you say, 'You killed Millie Martin.' And he says, 'Merle Oates did that, the little creep, and then he killed your pal Hopkins and then your other pal Pete Berry killed Oates and everything is nice and even-Steven, case closed.' And he laughs you out of there."

"What about the chariot? The mules? The Amoroso campaign?" The air in the restaurant was full of warm cooking odors and Lindsey was full of hot soup. Suddenly he was sweating.

"What do you have, man? What do you have?"

Lindsey's ears were ringing. "What are you saying, Petrus? That Castellini is all right? That I should just figure, okay, Ng killed Cletus and he got what he deserves, and all the rest of it is none of my business?"

"You might think about that."

Berry had finished his soup. He had amazing powers of non-verbal communication. Without breaking into his conversation with Lindsey he had ordered a slab of chocolate cheesecake. His soup bowl was gone, his coffee cup had been refilled, and he was slicing efficiently into the cheesecake.

Their check was tucked under the sugar bowl in the middle of the table.

Berry transported a triangle of cake to his mouth and raised his coffee cup and washed it down. He watched Lindsey over the rim of the cup.

Lindsey took a generous sip of ice water.

"My company has fifty million bucks riding on this case."

Berry lowered his coffee cup onto its saucer in time to avoid dropping it on the table. No fine china here; this joint used heavy tan cups and bowls with broad, dark brown stripes as their only decoration. It would take a jackhammer to chip one of these. Forget about breaking it.

"Fifty *million?*"

Lindsey explained the Nyagic policy and Desmond Richelieu's calculation of the rebate International Surety stood to collect if IS could recover the chariot and return it to the Italian government.

"Oh, my, my." Berry shook his head. "So that's what it's all about. Damn, I should have known as much."

Lindsey said, "No, that's not what it's all about. I wouldn't care if International Surety stood to make fifty cents instead of fifty million dollars. I'm in this for Cletus Berry. Period."

There was a silence, filled with the clatter of silverware and dishes and the buzz of conversation all around them.

Lindsey fumbled in his trousers pocket, found a folded handkerchief, and mopped his forehead. He'd been cold, then so hot he was sweating, then cold again. Not a good combination.

Berry said, "Thank you." Softly. He picked up the check, reached for his wallet, and started toward the cashier.

Lindsey said, "No need. This is on IS."

Berry snorted and handed him the check.

They started down Broadway. Holiday shoppers were taking advantage of the clear day and the sidewalk was crowded. Traffic swept noisily down the broad street like ice floes on the face of a river. A perfect setting for anonymous conversation.

"You don't think I should follow up with Castellini, then."

"I do. But I think you need more ammunition before you go face-to-face. And you need a plan, Lindsey, for heaven's sake, you need a plan. From everything I've heard and seen, Castellini is a chess player. He plans his game, he moves his pieces around, you see the pieces but you don't see him. He makes sacrifices. What do you think, Fulton, Ng, Sax, Merle Oates—they're all just pawns and he's lost them and so what? What does he care?"

A truck backfired and Berry's right hand leaped reflexively toward his left shoulder.

Lindsey froze for a fraction of a second, then grinned and continued walking.

Berry dropped his hand to his side. "Who are our pieces? We've lost Cletus. He was more than a pawn, Lindsey, he was a knight. We've lost Millie Martin and Victor Hopkins. Huh, and the poor fellow in the Torrington Tower, Bermudez." He studied the sidewalk, kept moving ahead. "And if your theory about Italy and the chariot is correct, I suppose even, what's his name, Massimo—"

"Massimo di Verolini."

"Right. Was the first piece to go. All the way back in 1940."

Lindsey said, "Okay. We're the good guys, Castellini's the bad guy; we've lost some pieces, he's lost some pieces. What now?"

"Now? Now I think we consider our options, Lindsey, we consider our options." He nodded. They were in the West Forties. They stood on a crowded corner. The light was against them and the crosstown street was packed solid with vehicles, mostly cabs, a few limos, some daredevil messengers on bicycles.

"And there's one more thing we do, Lindsey. We try to analyze our enemy's strengths and weaknesses and see if we can scope out *his* intentions. Question: What the f—pardon me—what the fuck is Castellini after?"

The lights changed and they maneuvered their way through a maze of halted vehicles, exhaust fumes billowing from their tailpipes, and so much for the Clean Air Act of nineteen-eighty-whatever-the-hell-year-it-was.

"That's easy," Lindsey furnished. "He's after the chariot."

"I think you're right."

They reached the opposite curb, like explorers who had forded a stream and reached the farther shore undevoured by giant lizards and unpoisoned by aquatic vipers.

"And why is he after the chariot?"

"I don't know if he knows about the old Nyagic policy and the chances of getting that money back for International Surety."

Berry frowned. "You can be sure he knows about it. If he was working with Cletus . . . he knew about Cletus's place in the Torrington . . . If Alcide Castellini is connected with our old friend—our very old friend—Salvatore Castellini . . . which seems to be very likely . . . you can be damned sure he knows about the insurance policy. But he's not International Surety. How the hell could he profit from finding the chariot and turning it over to International Surety or to the Italian government? What's in it for him? Some dinky finder's fee? Hardly. And we know this man is no altruist. What the heck is in it for him?"

Lindsey said, "Politics."

"What politics? You know how I hate politics. What does politics have to do with the chariot?"

"Randolph Amoroso. The New Rome. And Benito Mussolini and *his* version of the New Rome. Salvatore Castellini. Alcide de Gasperi and Palmiro Togliatti."

"You're losing me."

"That's okay," Lindsey said. His stride picked up. "I don't know much about this stuff either, but I know somebody who does." He dragged Petrus Berry along, cutting through the crowds like a punt returner, toward a subway entrance.

"Who are you talking about?" Berry demanded.

"I'm talking about Mora Selvatica. Professor Blackberry!"

Chapter Twenty

ANNA MARIA BERRY and Ezio Pinza were walking west on Seventy-third Street when Petrus Berry and Hobart Lindsey arrived, making their way from the IRT station at Lexington and Sixty-eighth. Anna Maria wore a knitted ski cap and a quilted jacket. Ezio Pinza wore a bright red dog-sweater.

"He's done everything," Anna Maria said. "We were ready to go home anyway." Her Uncle Petrus got a kiss. Lindsey got a handshake. Ezio Pinza looked up suspiciously between Anna Maria's ankles.

Lindsey said, "Anna Maria, I think we're making some progress on—" He stopped in midsentence. He wasn't good at talking to children about death.

"It's about your dad," Petrus supplied.

Lindsey thanked him silently. "You know the silver chariot you talked to Professor Van Huysen about, in your chat group?"

"Yes."

"Do you know how much that chariot is worth, Anna Maria? Do you know who would want it, and why?"

She shook her head. Her glossy black hair poked out under the edges of her ski cap. It swung against her cheeks when she shook her head.

"What I was thinking," Lindsey said, "was, if we could get in touch with your cousin Mosé, maybe we could learn something more about the chariot."

"It's just a history chat group," Anna Maria said. She paused. If she didn't want to help, there was little Lindsey could do. Appeal to her mother, perhaps, to talk her into it. But that seemed a poor idea. Ester Berry was too deep in her grief to be of much assistance. Her Aunt Zaffira? Her Uncle Petrus, Cletus's brother?

Maybe.

"Maybe Dottore Pacinelli would know."

Lindsey inhaled cold, clear air. They had reached Anna Maria's building. Ezio Pinza seemed eager to get inside where it was warmer, and where he might have a doggy treat awaiting.

Lindsey thought he'd heard the name before but he couldn't put anything with it. "Who is Dottore Pacinelli?"

"He's Mosé's teacher. He's his friend. He's a great scholar. He knows the whole history of the Jews in Italy, from ancient times to now."

That was where he'd heard the name before. Carlo Pacinelli, Ester Lazarini's childhood friend.

"Would Mosé ask il Dottore?"

"Better." Anna Maria managed a grin. She took Lindsey's breath away. "What time is it, Mr. Lindsey?"

He told her.

"Mosé should be online in a little while. His parents are friends with Dottore Pacinelli. He visits them a lot. He might even be there now, or Mosé could telephone and he'll come over."

She booted up and set up a chat with Mosé. Il dottore was visiting Mosé's parents, Abramo and Sara. Mosé told Anna Maria that they had shared their dinner. Mama had made *lokshen* kugel, Dottore Pacinelli's favorite, and they were lingering over espresso and poppy seed cake.

Ester Berry and Zaffira Fornari had insisted that Anna Maria drink a cup of hot cocoa and put on warm socks and shoes before she did anything else. Ezio Pinza had devoured a charcoal bone and was curled up on Anna Maria's bed with a bright yellow porcupine half his size. Anna Maria had hung her ski cap and jacket in the closet. She wore a blue Beth Israel Academy sweatshirt with the school mascot, a tough-looking honeybee, printed in white on the chest.

Why a bee? Lindsey wondered, but he didn't ask.

Anna Maria clattered away at the keyboard. Her message appeared in black letters on the monitor screen. Lindsey and Petrus Berry sat on kitchen chairs, one to either side of Anna Maria. She hit *Enter* and they waited for a response. It came in seconds.

Dottore Pacinelli here. So sorry about your father. I write to your mother. Did she get my letter?

Anna Maria told him she hadn't yet. But snail mail, after all . . .

Sì. Posta di chiocciola. Please, tell to her my condoglianza.

Anna Maria asked—Mosè? Il dottore?—what they could tell her about the silver chariot. She explained that her Zio Pietro and her father's friend Signore Lindsey thought it held the key to the murder.

Una leggenda. Un mito. There was no such thing.

But there was. Lindsey was prepared to prompt the girl, but she needed no prompting. She wasn't just Anna Maria Berry. She was Mora Selvatica, or half of Mora Selvatica, and her cousin Mosè Lazarini was the other half, and they knew the history of the chariot as well as anyone, including William Van Huysen, Ph.D.

But not—perhaps—as well as Dottore Carlo Pacinelli.

It took some coaxing. Lindsey was amazed at what a skillful coaxer Anna Maria Berry could be. But eventually il dottore gave a veiled history of the chariot, post-1940.

All of this was speculative, of course. No one knew for certain. He could not swear, he would not publish his findings, his reputation as a scholar, his standing in the community . . .

Anna Maria coaxed, and Carlo Pacinelli yielded.

It may have helped that Mosè Lazarini was his star pupil and Mosè Lazarini was at his side at the keyboard. It may have helped that he was the onetime schoolmate and friend of Ester Lazarini. The embers of youthful loves glow stubbornly.

Some good fascist crewman aboard the *Fior di Rimini* had bashed in the skull of Massimo di Verolini not long after the ship had cleared the harbor at New York, those five decades before (Dottore Pacinelli said). Who had given him his orders? No one could even guess. What had become of him? No one knew. Long dead, probably, fighting the Allied invaders at Anzio in 1943, or fighting the Nazi occupation in 1944 when German armies rolled into Italy after the surrender, or fighting Communist partisans in the streets of Rome or the countryside in 1945 when Italy lay in ruins and writhed, close to civil war.

And where was the chariot that should have been where instead was found the not-so-fresh remains of Massimo di Verolini?

Somewhere on the ship.

And when Salvatore Castellini, that good fascist functionary, hurried up to La Spezia from Rome and reported in horror that the sacred relic, the silver chariot, was nowhere to be found— what had really happened?

Chi sá? Lindsey could almost see the dottore's shrug.

But he might guess. Yes, he might offer a conjecture.

Signore Castellini, he was a good fascist. Or maybe he was not such a good fascist. *Forse*—maybe—he had some ideals that were not the same as the party's ideals. *Forse*—maybe—he had some personal ambitions that were not the same as Il Duce's ambitions.

It was not for sure, *non era possible sapere per certo*, but suppose Salvatore Castellini had been the employer of the crewman involved. Suppose his report to Rome had been false, a setup. Suppose he had received the small crate containing the chariot that had been intended to go in the large crate, and done—what?—with it?

If this story was true, this *nozzione*, this *teoria* . . . And if the chariot had survived the Allied bombings and the invasion from the south that followed, and the Nazi invasion from the north, and the turmoil and violence of the war . . .

It was just *possible* that the chariot was still hidden away somewhere in Italy.

And, Lindsey thought, Alcide Castellini was looking for it.

And Cletus Berry, who had been in Italy as early as 1972 and as late as 1979, who had left the army under unspecified other-than-honorable conditions, and who later found the Nyagic file and got his brilliant daughter Anna Maria to unlock it for him . . .

Might very well have found the chariot.

Lindsey buried his face in his hands.

Why would Alcide Castellini order Cletus Berry's murder?

Lindsey had thanked Mosé Lazarini and Carlo Pacinelli for their help. Before Anna Maria logged off he also got their telephone numbers. Voice communication might be going the way of handwritten letters, the day of keyboard-to-keyboard communication might be at hand, but Lindsey might want to talk with the Roman players in this game before everybody's vocal cords turned into vestigial organs.

To Anna Maria he said, "Don't forget, International Surety will reimburse you for the online charges."

Anna Maria smiled wanly. "Is that all? I think I want to play some games now."

Lindsey rubbed his temples with thumb and forefinger. "One more thing. If you don't mind."

She looked up at him, waiting.

"You got your dad's, what did you call it, 201 file."

"Pentagon's easy," Anna Maria said. "Beth Israel Academy's the tough one. None of us has been able to crack that. Even my friend Shoshana, and she's really good at this stuff."

"Could you get somebody else's 201 file?"

"Sure. What do you have for me to search on?"

"Will a name do?"

"It's something. But unless it's a really uncommon name, there are millions and millions of files there. A service number or a date of birth or anything else you could give me would be better."

Lindsey pondered. "Afraid I only have a name. Well, he'd probably be about your dad's age. Does that help?"

Anna Maria pursed her lips and blew. "Leaves out the Civil War, I guess. What's his name?"

"Harry Scott," Lindsey told her.

Anna Maria groaned. So did Petrus Berry.

It took an hour, disposing of deceased Harry Scotts and Harry Scotts who were too old to be the right one (World War II vets) and too young to be the right one (Gulf War vets) and Harry Scotts who were in veterans' hospitals in various parts of the country and Harry Scotts serving time in prison and Harry Scotts who were still in the military and a few hundred other Harry Scotts.

Then they found Harry Scott who had served from 1960 to 1980. Retired after twenty years' service. Spent his last three years on active duty at NATO Southern Command. Current address for pension checks, c/o International Surety, Rome, Italy.

Bingo!

"Can you go deeper into the files?" Lindsey asked.

Anna Maria tilted her head and looked at him over her shoulder. "What do you want?"

Lindsey thought about that. He was getting close to something vital. This he knew. But it was likely to reflect badly on Cletus Berry. How much did he want to upset Berry's daughter? Bright she was. Brilliant, in fact. But still, she was just ten years old. He didn't want to inflict more pain on her than she had already suffered.

"Could you just pull up everything you can, on Harry Scott, and give it to me on a floppy? He works for the company, and I need to find out about his background."

"*Schnecken*," Anna Maria said.

"What's that?"

"Yiddish for snails. But it's the name for a kind of sweet, sticky pastry. Means the same as a piece of cake."

That's it, Lindsey thought. That's what I miss in my life. Eric Coffman's girls could talk to Anna Maria Berry and they'd all know what *schnecken* was. Jamie Wilkerson wouldn't know at first but he'd pick it up. Ten-year-old Yiddish-speaking Mafiosi. World, watch out.

Lindsey lay on Zaffira Fornari's living room couch staring at the ceiling, trying to make pictures in his mind. Moonlight drifted through the French doors providing cold illumination to the room. Zaffira's antique clock ticked softly and if Lindsey listened carefully he thought he could hear Petrus Berry's occasional snore from the bedroom.

He projected a mind picture on the ceiling. It was shaped like a movie screen, and it was all in black and white.

Hildegarde Withers and Oscar Piper were there, horse-faced Edna May Oliver and dapper, mustached Jimmy Gleason, walking around a polished wooden table. A row of Barbie dolls lay on the table but they weren't really Barbies at all. They were Cletus

Berry and Frankie Fulton, crusted in blackened ice; Johnny Thieu Ng and Bilbo Sax grasping stiffened organs in their fists while leather straps tightened around their necks; Mino Bermudez with a law book in his hand; Victor Hopkins with the blood gushing from a hole in his neck . . .

Withers and Piper, Oliver and Gleason, were talking about the case, carefully circling the table, trying to figure out how all the pieces could fit together.

It just didn't work.

Finally Piper snarled. He threw his cigar through the French doors and it tumbled into the snowy garden; he jammed his battered fedora on his head and stalked out of the room. Withers snatched up her furled umbrella and caught his arm just in time to accompany him.

Two more individuals walked into the room. One was tall, austere, thin as a rail, immaculately turned out. The other was short, roly-poly, wore a double-breasted pinstriped suit that did nothing to diminish his rotundity. The taller man spoke in clipped, commanding, precise tones. The shorter one answered in a peculiar froglike croak.

Philo Vance. Sergeant Heath. Warren William and Eugene Palette.

Philo Vance leaned over the table, studying the Barbie dolls through a magnifying glass. He drew a pair of tweezers from the pocket of his elegant suit coat and began rearranging the dolls into two rows. Good guy, bad guy, good guy . . . But when he finished, even the great Philo Vance shrugged his shoulders in frustration, threw an arm around Sergeant Heath's beefy shoulders, and exited.

There was nothing he could do.

Nothing that any surrogate could do, no shadow summoned up from the vaults of 1930s Hollywood.

This was another world, and Hobart Lindsey had to face this one himself.

He'd booted up the floppy before he went to bed. Anna Maria had gotten everything. Uncle Sam's secrets were a joke. And Harry Scott had a commendation in his file for snooping out a ring of American military personnel who'd been engaged in art racketeering in the late 1970s under guise of NATO business.

The commendation didn't mention any of their names, but the dates were right, the geography was right, the facts were right. Everything fit. Everything came together and made a picture of an accusatory finger that pointed straight at Cletus Berry.

Sooner or later . . . and more likely sooner than later . . . Lindsey was going to have to talk with Harry Scott, SPUDS Regional, Rome.

He sat up, momentarily disoriented, then remembered where he was and wrapped the quilt that had covered him on the couch, around his shoulders. He padded across Zaffira Fornari's living room and looked down into the garden.

He felt a premonition of dread. There would be a small black shape lying motionless against the snow. It would be Petrus Berry's robin. It would have returned once more. Unable to find its way, unable to find its fellows, it would have returned to the only home it could remember. Even though it could no longer live there, still Zaffira's garden had been its home, it had built its nest in one of her trees and there it would die.

But there was no sign of the robin.

Lindsey looked at the antique clock on Zaffira Fornari's mantel. He did a quick computation, found the telephone, and put through a call to International Surety in Rome.

The line clicked and hummed and then he was speaking with a receptionist. Lindsey looked down into the motionless moonlit garden, imagining the receptionist looking out an office window in Rome at a busy, sunlit street.

He identified himself and asked to speak with Harry Scott, SPUDS.

The receptionist must be a local hire; she spoke English flawlessly, but with an Italian overtone that was nothing short of charming. Mr. Scott was out of the office.

This was SPUDS business, most urgent.

Mr. Scott was on holiday, on vacation.

When was he expected back?

In a few days.

This couldn't wait. Where could Mr. Scott be reached?

Mr. Scott didn't leave any address or telephone number.

Lindsey pondered. Maybe Scott had a laptop and a modem. Maybe he'd check his E-mail, even on vacation. Maybe—but he wasn't quite ready to give up with the receptionist.

"Do you know where he went on vacation? Did he ever go in past years and send a postcard to the gang at the office? Did he ever come back from vacation and show off his photos and his souvenirs?"

"No, he— Oh, wait. I do remember. He sent a picture postcard from Pisa. The tower. You know the Leaning Tower of Pisa?"

"Good. That's good. He was staying in Pisa? Did he visit any other cities?"

"Let me think. No, I'm sorry, I can't remember. I remember only Pisa, because he sent the postcard,"

After the call, Lindsey ransacked Zaffira Fornari's apartment until he found a world atlas. He found Pisa easily enough, and there was La Spezia, just a hop, skip, and a jump away.

Got you, Harry Scott.

In the morning, Petrus Berry brewed coffee and scrambled eggs and toasted rye bread. A copy of *The New York Times* was spread on the kitchen table. Zaffira Fornari was a faithful subscriber.

The day was bright again. Beneath Zaffira Fornari's French doors a robin sat on a tree limb looking confused. It was Petrus Berry's robin, and it was real after all.

Where in the world had all its friends gone?

Lindsey could sympathize.

Even as he watched, the robin hopped from the limb and flew away. Lindsey hoped that it knew where it was going, and that it would get there safely. Its friends could gather 'round and it would tell them what winter was really like.

A photo on the front page of the *Times* showed a smiling, shiny-domed Randolph Amoroso and his wife emerging from Mass at a church in Little Italy. Amoroso was handing a minia-ture reproduction of the silver chariot to a priest while Mrs. Amoroso stood by, providing the standard politician's wife's adoring smile. The caption referred to Amoroso stumping Little Italy in search of support for his senatorial bid. Apparently, he was getting plenty of it.

"You awake enough to make some decisions?" Berry asked.

Lindsey laid down the newspaper. "This thing is starting to come together," Lindsey said. "Anna Maria's contacts in Italy—"

"I think so, too." Berry shoveled eggs onto two plates and set them on the table. "You know the line about a little child."

Lindsey picked up a fork and sampled. "Delicious. My turn tomorrow, Petrus." He chewed on a piece of toast, then downed it with coffee. "What Pacinelli said—he was being cautious about committing himself but I think he's more certain of his facts than he lets on."

"Then you think the chariot is in Italy after all? It's been there since 1940?"

"And I think Cletus knew about it. I'm sorry, Petrus, I know you loved your brother—"

"Facts are facts." Berry sat down opposite Lindsey and methodically loaded his fork with scrambled eggs, ate the eggs and nodded approval. "Keep on going."

"Cletus got in some kind of trouble in Italy in 1979. We know that he made trips from Rome to La Spezia. We know he was studying Italian antiquities. That's how he first met Ester and Zaffira. And he kept running into them in museums and galleries."

"Okay. I know that." Petrus Berry tasted his coffee, grumbled "I'd forget my head if it wasn't screwed on," added a spoonful of sugar and stirred.

"Here's what I think." Lindsey pulled his upper and lower lips between his teeth and chewed on them. He didn't like this—he didn't want to say it—Cletus Berry had been his friend as well as Petrus's brother.

Berry said, "Go ahead."

"I think he was mixed up with the trade in art and antiquities. There's still a whole catalog's worth of art that's been missing since the Second World War. What's in Germany, what's in Russia, what's in private collections, what was destroyed—we'll never know the whole story. Twenty years ago, with the Cold

War still raging and everybody paranoid about Soviet spies or anti-Soviet spies or God knows what other kind of spies, things were far worse."

He paused and looked out the window. The robin was back. He got up and opened the window and yelled at it. "Shoo! They went thataway!"

The bird cocked its head. Obviously it understood every word. It nodded once and flew away.

Lindsey said, "I don't know if Cletus was mixed up with Castellini as long ago as 1979 or if they got together later. I don't know whether he knew about the Nyagic policy in '79 or if he just poked around the IS database after he got into SPUDS and stumbled across it by accident. More likely the latter. How would he know about Nyagic before he came to work for IS?"

The robin appeared again, swooped over the garden, and disappeared. "God bless you, little bird," Lindsey whispered. For some reason he was touched to the core. *If that bird makes it south then maybe there's hope for us all.* When he spoke again he had a lump in his throat.

"Cletus knew where the chariot was, or at least he had a damned good idea. He was trying to sell it to Castellini. What could Castellini do with it? He could smuggle it into the U.S. using his Omaha housewife dodge and sell it on the underground antiquities market. He could get a fortune for it. Or he could turn it over to Randolph Amoroso. That's what I think he was going to do."

He paused.

Berry looked up at him, coffee cup in hand. "Why?"

"I think Amoroso wants to be more than a senator. He's got crazy ambitions. He wants to set up some kind of pseudo-fascist government. Rally all the old Nixon and Reagan types, the Gordon Liddys and the Ollie Norths, maybe tie in with some of those wild talk-radio characters. It sounds crazy; it's outside the bounds of American politics."

Berry growled. "You know what I think."

"All right. But it could be a lot worse, Petrus, a whole lot worse."

Berry shook his head, glowering. "Are you saying that Amoroso is the bad guy, or Castellini?"

"I think Amoroso wants to be an American Il Duce. Good God, he's even imitating Mussolini's style and his posturing. But I think Castellini sees Amoroso as a puppet. Castellini knows all about using fronts. Think of Omaha. Amoroso isn't a good guy, but he's a lightweight. Castellini is the danger. And Harry Scott— there's a wild card for you—Harry Scott is our man in Rome and he's been snooping around La Spezia for years."

"All right." Berry heaved a sigh. He pushed himself away from the table. "You finished, Lindsey? I hate to waste food, Mama always told us it was a sin to waste food."

Lindsey picked up his plate and his fork and finished his portion of scrambled eggs. Then he finished his toast, finished his orange juice, and finished his coffee. Domesticity came in the oddest forms.

"I want to check in with Marcie Sokolov, but I don't think she's going to buy this. She's NYPD to the core; her feet are on the sidewalk, I don't think she'll buy my blue skies."

"What then?"

"I'm going to bring my boss up to date. Cletus ever tell you about Desmond Richelieu?"

"J. Edgar Hoover, Junior?"

"That's him. But inside there's more to Richelieu than that. I want to go talk to Castellini. Depending on how that comes out, I may have to go to Italy."

"You really think so."

"You want to go along? I'd appreciate it, Petrus. Really."

Berry shook his head. "You know what, Hobart? You come on like Caspar Milquetoast, but inside that mild-mannered exterior lurks one crazy operator. Cletus told me how you hated to ever let go of a case, but he never told me that you could be one wacko individual."

He stopped.

A beat.

Another beat.

"And one dangerous man," Berry concluded.

Lindsey said, "I'll get SPUDS to start pulling wires. You have a passport? No? Neither do I. What do you bet that Desmond Richelieu can call some old buddies in Washington and have a pair of them in our hands tomorrow?"

Berry said, "I don't bet."

Chapter Twenty-one

PETRUS BERRY DIDN'T insist on taking two cabs, but he did insist on their paying off the cabbie and sending him on his way a couple of blocks from their destination. Then they separated. Lindsey walked on to his destination. Berry refused to say where he was going or what he would be doing, but Lindsey suspected that Berry would be up to his old tricks again. Well, not so old, but still . . .

Lindsey had called the number Cele Johnston gave him at their first meeting. The voice that answered was neutral and so devoid of characteristics that Lindsey almost took it for a computer-generated signal. No gender, no age, no ethnicity, no emotion.

"A.P.C. Enterprises."

That was what it said. The ball was in Lindsey's court. He asked for Alcide Castellini. The voice said that Mr. Castellini was regrettably unavailable, but if he/she/it could be of assistance, perhaps the caller would care to express his needs.

Lindsey stared at the telephone. He told the voice that Cele Johnston had given him an address and suggested that he visit Mr. Castellini, and he was calling to make an appointment.

The voice said, "I see." There was a lengthy pause. Then the voice said, "If I may, please, ask your name, sir."

Lindsey identified himself.

The voice said, "Thank you. If you will hold for just a moment, sir; I do apologize for the inconvenience."

Lindsey waited. At least there was no sappy music to tolerate.

"Mr. Castellini will see you at four this afternoon. Please observe the terms of visitation."

And that was all. A soft click at the other end, and then silence. Lindsey knew enough not to phone again.

The day had been brilliant and the city seemed more alive than it had at any time since Lindsey's arrival from Denver. The crowds were upbeat, Christmas decorations were everywhere, the street-corner Santas were less hostile, and even the cabdriver grunted a grudging thanks for his tip.

He directed Lindsey to Gramercy Park in a strange language, but Lindsey found the house facing the charming little park, just off Irving Place. The cabby had referred to it as "Oiving's Place." It was exactly four o'clock.

As Lindsey was about to press the doorbell the door opened and Congressman Randolph Amoroso and his wife stepped out. Lindsey stared up at Amoroso. The congressman was struggling with his overcoat, trying to adjust a red-and-yellow plaid scarf. Lindsey took in Amoroso's trademark one-off clothing, his slightly out-of-fashion suit, his shirt collar just a trifle too long, his tie just the wrong shade and width.

Mrs. Amoroso smiled. She was not quite as far out of style, but her plain Republican cloth coat with its ratty fur collar could only offend a handful of antifur fanatics. If it was fake it was pretty convincing; even up close, Lindsey couldn't tell.

Before Lindsey could enter the house, the door swung shut. The Amorosos moved carefully down the short flight of stairs and away.

Lindsey pressed the doorbell. His pulse was racing and he could hear his own blood rushing and pounding in his ears. The house was surrounded by an iron fence, matching the fence that surrounded the park itself. The small lawn was covered with snow.

The door opened. A young woman in a severe outfit stood in the opening, looking businesslike and very much as if she was expecting something from Lindsey. Lindsey handed her a business card. Without a word she led him to a pair of tall, black-stained wooden doors fitted with gold appliances. The carpeting was richly patterned. The ceilings were tall and the architecture was ornate. If you pushed it any farther, Lindsey thought, it would be camp. But the architect had not pushed it that last bit.

The doors closed behind Lindsey. Before him a middle-aged man sat at a desk. The room looked more like a gentleman's study than a business office, but the middle-aged man said, "This is A.P.C. Enterprises. I am Mr. Campana. How may I serve you?"

Lindsey recognized the sterile voice. He identified himself. "I'm here to see Mr. Castellini."

Campana nodded. "You understand the terms. You have complied with them?"

"Yes." Lindsey was astonished that Campana would take his word. That he had come alone was obvious—although he knew that Petrus Berry was somewhere nearby. But—no weapons? No wire? Maybe he'd passed through a detection device without knowing it. Or maybe Alcide Palmiro Castellini was simply above such things. You wouldn't shake hands with Alcide Palmiro Castellini wearing a buzzer ring, or hand him a drink in a dribble glass.

Nobody needed to stop you. You just wouldn't do that.

Campana rose and led Lindsey to a second, grander pair of dark wooden doors. He knocked softly, waited, then opened the doors to let Lindsey through, and departed, pulling the doors closed behind him.

This was a new realm. Lindsey liked playing ball on his home field, or at least on one where he knew the layout, where the foul lines were and where the base paths were and where the batter's box was. Not today. Campana could have ushered him into the court of the last Empress of China or the final, ornate bedroom of the ancient man. But this was neither *The Last Emperor* nor *2001*; it was neither the doing of Bernardo Bertolucci nor Stanley Kubrick.

This was the headquarters of Alcide Palmiro Castellini.

Castellini himself stood beside an easy chair. He wore a dark blue, pinstriped suit that might have cost Lindsey a month's salary, a soft white shirt, and a solid maroon tie. His silvery hair had been razor-cut to perfection. He nodded formally.

Before Lindsey could say a word, Castellini motioned him to a chair similar to his own. A low table stood between them, and a third chair nearby. The walls were hung with paintings of the Italian Renaissance. Lindsey longed for a chance to study them. The little that he knew about art, he had learned from his insurance work.

He might not be able to identify the pieces, but he had seen a few authentic works of genius in his life, and he knew that such canvases glowed with a power as undeniable and as uneradicable as a radioactive isotope. Every canvas in this room glowed with that power.

"Would you like a drink, Mr. Lindsey? I would offer you a cigar, but my curator advises against smoke in this room. Or in the house, for that matter. It was designed by Stanford White. He himself lived here in Gramercy Park. A brilliant architect. Wild and self-indulgent. A sinner. Do you believe in sin, Mr. Lindsey? Hobart? May I call you Hobart? And you call me Alcide? Just not Al, please, I find that demeaning. If you'll grant me so much."

Who was the chess player, who the pawn?

Castellini eased himself into his chair and lifted a highball glass from the table. He said, "You are a remarkable man, Hobart. You astonish me." He spoke English with that slight, cultured Italian accent that Lindsey was growing accustomed to. It was aristocratic, almost musical. Nothing like J. Carroll Naish in "Life with Luigi." But then Alcide Castellini was no Luigi Bosco, nor Mr. Campana—if that was actually his name—a Pasquale.

But Luigi Bosco had been an antiques dealer in the old series. Life was imitating art once again.

"No drink, no thank you," Lindsey managed. He found himself fumbling for a prop. His laptop, his pocket organizer, his gold International Surety pencil. Determinedly, he folded his hands and placed them in his lap. Cele Johnston had been right. If Castellini wanted him dead he'd be dead by now. Consequently he need not worry about that.

At least, that was what he told himself.

Castellini held a square, textured highball glass. The glass itself was clear. It contained ice cubes and a pale liquid. If it was whiskey and, it was mostly *and* . . . Castellini lifted the glass and sipped. He placed it carefully on a coaster.

Lindsey looked around once more. The furnishings and art in the room were museum grade, no question.

Castellini said, "Congressman Amoroso was just here, Mr. Lindsey, with his lovely wife. You must have just missed them, what a pity."

Lindsey said, "I recognized him. We'd never met. Nor you and I. Mr. Castellini—"

"Alcide."

"In honor of Signore de Gasperi?"

Castellini grinned widely. "I didn't take you for so knowledgeable a man, but yes. And my middle name—Palmiro?"

"For Comrade Togliatti, I should think."

"Bravo! The doing of my father. He followed Mussolini. Don't think ill of him, Hobart, for that. Most Italians followed Mussolini, at least at first. But once Il Duce was gone, well, who was going to win? The Communists? The Christian Democrats? Who could tell? So my father named me for both, and whoever won, why, he was the namesake of Salvatore Castellini's son. What do you think of that, Hobart?"

"Opportunistic."

Castellini grinned at that, showing beautiful teeth. "I saw you at Cletus Berry's funeral, Hobart."

"And I you."

"Sì, sicuramente. He was my friend. A fine fellow. We went back together, many, many years. A tragedy. You're from his company, you've seen to his widow and his daughter? What a tragedy. I couldn't let them bury him without coming to show my respect. Very strange, a Jewish funeral, what do you make of that?"

"His wife is Jewish."

"Ah, yes. I'm getting forgetful. There are so few Hebrews in Italy, one forgets. Perhaps Cletus took her faith. Did he ever speak to you of God, Hobart? Of religion? Only close friends discuss those things, don't you think?"

Lindsey blinked. This was getting out of control. He'd come to—why had he come here? He'd been pursuing Castellini so long, and now they were face-to-face. When Lindsey started the search he would have known what to say, but now everything had become so complicated, and Castellini was going on like an old buddy.

"Did you kill him?"

Castellini looked distressed. Not angry, not surprised. It was as if a dear friend had accused you falsely of betrayal. You were saddened to think that someone of whom you thought so highly could think so ill of you.

"No." He shook his head. His silver hair seemed to have a life of its own, the light from the room's ornate torchères skittering through the beautiful coiffure. "No," he repeated, "Johnny Thieu Ng killed Cletus. Cletus and Frankie Fulton."

"You paid him."

Castellini shrank as if Lindsey had reached toward him with a handful of some repellent substance, but Lindsey hadn't moved.

Lindsey said, "What was your relationship with Millicent Martin?"

Castellini frowned in concentration, then brightened. "Oh, you must mean Millicent Martinelli. What a calamity. Why do you ask about poor Millicent? What do you know about her?"

"I saw the newspaper photo of her with you and Fulton."

"Ah, yes. I've learned to stay out of nightclubs."

Lindsey was getting annoyed. He'd come here, ready to play chess, but the game seemed more like one of cat and mouse, and he did not enjoy playing the mouse. "Was she your mule?"

"Who told you such a thing? She was—how to put this delicately? She was my protégé, yes?"

"You mean your mistress?"

"Protégé, mistress, there are other terms, euphemisms, some of them more polite than others. What do you prefer?"

"I didn't know her, I'm not involved."

"Of course not. Then what does it matter? We traveled together, she was charming, vivacious. I am not as young as I used to be, Hobart. Her companionship was a joy. I didn't hide her; we appeared in public many times, many places, here and abroad."

"Did you kill her, too?"

Castellini's face clouded. "I'm starting to get annoyed, Hobart.

Do you understand the seriousness of your charges? We're not talking about minor peculations. I could be very angry at what you're saying in private, and if you repeated these things in public you would be subject to a serious lawsuit."

Lindsey said nothing.

"I will say it one time and one time only," Castellini went on. "Your charges are absolutely absurd and I will not waste more time on them. Now either drop your slanders or get out. I did not invite you here to be maligned. Do you understand me?"

Lindsey leaned forward. The situation was at once menacing and absurd. Here he sat in the lion's den. He'd called Castellini a murderer and Castellini seemed only mildly annoyed. If Castellini really was a killer, if he was directly or indirectly responsible for all the deaths that seemed to swirl around him, he would hardly hesitate to add one more.

The old Hobart Lindsey—the pre–Marvia Plum Lindsey—would never have dared act this way. He would have avoided Castellini, or tried to finesse him, or caved in and apologized.

Instead he demanded, "Why did you invite me here?"

Castellini relaxed. "You've been looking for me."

"Who told you that?" It had to be Cele Johnston, Lindsey thought. Castellini had issued his invitation—or summons—through Johnston.

Castellini said nothing.

"All right, Alcide." He injected a microsecond of silence between the first syllable and the second, then instantly regretted it. It was a cheap shot.

Castellini didn't notice. No, there was an extremely fine distinction to be made. He had not taken notice.

"I have been looking for you. Cletus Berry was my friend. I'm not satisfied with the police attitude. They're ready to write off his death as part of urban life. I want to nail the son of a bitch who killed my friend."

"Mm, mm, mm." Castellini drained the last of his highball. He rose and went to a small, inconspicuous bar. Over his shoulder he said, "Hobart? Are you sure?"

Lindsey looked at his watch. What was the rule, Never before six? "All right."

Castellini poured Lindsey a Scotch on the rocks, refreshed his own, returned to his seat.

"Enough fencing. You may be trying to find Cletus Berry's killer. That's noble of you. You're also sniffing after Caesar's Chariot. *Il Cocchio di Cesare.* So am I."

He paused and looked up at a fresco mounted on one wall of the room. Lindsey followed Castellini's gaze. By an odd happenstance, as little as Lindsey knew of Italian art, he recognized the fresco, a portrait of Angelo Ambrogini Poliziano, a fifteenth-century academic and writer, posing with Lorenzo di Medici's son Piero.

Why did Lindsey know the work? Oh, yes—there had been a flap in SPUDS when International Surety paid out the policy on the fresco, which had disappeared mysteriously and almost impossibly from the Sasseti Chapel in Florence.

Lindsey grinned behind his highball glass. He got control of himself and said, "I don't have the chariot. I don't know where it is."

"Cletus Berry did."

"Then why did you kill him?"

Castellini glowered.

Lindsey rephrased his question. "Why was Berry killed?"

"You aren't wearing a wire, Hobart. I'll tell you something you maybe shouldn't know. Certainly your friend Detective Sokolov doesn't know this and doesn't need to know it."

Lindsey nodded, *I'm listening.*

"I worked with your friend Berry. I'm in the import business. I bring in goods from Europe, things of rarity and beauty, and sell them to those who will love and cherish them. I think of myself as one who facilitates the preservation of fragile treasures. Their protection for the enlightenment of posterity."

"Customs would have a different name for what you do."

"Customs." Castellini spat the word. "*Il Cocchio* has been missing since 1940. You know the story of *il Cocchio?*"

"William Van Huysen told it to me."

"Good. And you know about the World's Fair and the closing of the Italian Pavilion after the 1939 season."

Before Lindsey could respond, Castellini stood up and moved toward the doorway. Lindsey thought he had heard a soft, almost inaudible chime just before Castellini made his move. "*Scusi*, Hobart, a telephone call. Please indulge me." He left the room.

Lindsey set his glass on a coaster. He rubbed his hand across his face. For the first time he became aware that the room was windowless. He was in Alcide Castellini's world, in a manifestation of Alcide Castellini's mind. There was neither day nor night here. There was no snow-covered garden where a robin might have come to die.

Castellini returned. "Please, no more unpleasantness, Hobart. You deny knowledge of the whereabouts of *il Cocchio*. Maybe you are telling the truth, maybe not. How much do you know about Nyagic?"

Lindsey could tell the truth, he could lie, he could say nothing. He told the truth.

Castellini nodded. "You know more about Berry's work than anyone else. You understand his files. I think you can locate the chariot, even if you don't know now where it is. Find it. Give it to me. Not to your company. I will pay you—how much does your employer pay you in a year?"

Lindsey told him.

"At your present age, Hobart—you know the actuarial tables—with promotions, with economic changes, your lifetime earnings—what do you think they would be?" Castellini named a figure.

Lindsey said that sounded about right.

Castellini said, "I will pay ten times that amount. Cash, no taxes. I know how not to pay taxes." He smiled. "You resign from your job, you live out your life in the States or in Italy or in the country of your choice. You never lift a finger again unless you choose to."

Lindsey picked up his Scotch and water, took a substantial drink, then lowered the glass. He stared at Alcide Castellini. The man did not look like Sydney Greenstreet, but he looked exactly like Sydney Greenstreet.

Chapter Twenty-two

CREDIT DESMOND RICHELIEU'S old Washington connections for getting the passports as easily as phoning out for pizza, and Express Mail for delivering them faster than any pizza parlor chain that advertised on your local cable service.

More astonishingly, credit Moe Zissler of Manhattan East for booking Lindsey and Petrus Berry on a quick flight to Rome. Lindsey had expected a struggle with Corporate Travel, having to use SPUDS clout to get what he wanted, having to appeal at least to Richelieu himself and possibly higher in the corporate tower. He would have done so if he'd had to, to get Petrus Berry laid on as a short-term consultant at a dollar a day so he could fly with Lindsey on short notice and so International Surety would pick up the tab.

But Moe Zissler, stolid, not-very-bright, peppermint-breathed Morris Zissler, had come through for good old International Surety.

Lindsey and Berry were seated side by side on an Alitalia 747. JFK was behind them and it looked as if they might spend Christmas in Rome.

Lindsey didn't know if that was exactly what he wanted. Maybe Harry Scott would be back at his desk; Lindsey could enlist him as an ally, and the whole case would be wrapped up and he'd be back in Denver before the holiday arrived. Right, and maybe the pope would come out to Leonardo da Vinci in his popemobile and give them a ride back to their hotel.

Once the 747 left the ground, Petrus Berry managed to immerse himself in a paperback novel. Lindsey had no such luck, no such power of inner tranquillity. Maybe he would gain that someday, but for him that day had not yet come.

His mind kept circling around the case. He turned off the little light above his seat and closed his eyes. Faces floated into his consciousness as he tried to perceive connections and find meanings.

Cletus Berry, alive and vital as Lindsey had last seen him in Denver—and blank-eyed and lifeless as he appeared in the *Daily News* photo. Millicent Martin, smiling and provocative in another newspaper shot—and bound hand and foot, duct tape over her mouth as she suffocated. Johnny Thieu Ng and Bilbo Sax, hanging from a water pipe in a basement apartment. Cele Johnston sipping espresso behind her gorgeous Louis XIV desk. Victor Hopkins with a baseball-sized hole gouged from his throat. Randolph Amoroso and his wife emerging from the magnificent Stanford White house in Gramercy Park. Alcide Palmiro Castellini, surrounded by priceless art treasures, the room light glinting off his oh-so perfect teeth . . .

. . . and Harry Scott. The name without a face. Scott, who had served in NATO Southern Command with Cletus Berry. Scott, whose service record pointed straight to him as the whistle-blower who had ended Cletus Berry's army career.

But Scott was in Berry's electronic Rolodex. Had Berry never realized that Scott was his own personal Judas? Had Scott maintained a bogus friendship with Berry, all the years after betraying him to the army's criminal investigation division? And had Berry never seen through Scott?

Or had Berry realized, at some point, that Scott was his betrayer, and maintained the fiction of ignorance for purposes of his own? Were Scott's visits to La Spezia part of his quiet search for the silver chariot? And if they were, as seemed certain, was he acting on his own, or as Berry's stalking horse, or as Alcide Castellini's?

Kasper Gutman and Joel Cairo, Wilmer the gunsel and Brigid O'Shaughnessy and Effie Perrine and Iva Archer and the false Miss Wonderly, and Sam Spade and Miles Archer . . .

* * *

The pope didn't meet them at Leonardo da Vinci, but somebody did.

Lindsey had no idea they were going to be met at the airport. Rather than rent a car and attempt to drive on unfamiliar roads in a country where he didn't know the language, he planned to hire a car and an English-speaking driver. But there stood a middle-aged man, neatly dressed in houndstooth jacket and cloth cap, leather-gloved hands holding a neatly lettered sign on a piece of corrugated cardboard. *International Surety—Mr. Lindsey, Mr. Berry.* Lindsey and Berry headed for the man.

The man greeted them with, "*Benvenuti in Italia, signori. Benvenuto a Fiumicino.*"

Lindsey stammered, "*No parlare italiano.*" He knew his grammar was terrible, but surely this fellow would get the idea.

The man threw his arms around Lindsey and Berry. "Of course you don't speak Italian. Who could expect you to?" His English was perfect, American, with the flat twang of an Indiana farmer.

What in the world?

Lindsey said, "Who are you?"

A bellow of laughter. "Why, I'm Harry Scott. Got back into town last night. Found a stack of message slips on my desk this morning. *Call Hobart Lindsey. Call Hobart Lindsey, SPUDS.* Oh, you know, SPUDS get the kid-glove treatment. Whatever Ducky Richelieu wants, Ducky Richelieu gets. *Call Hobart Lindsey, SPUDS, urgent!* Oh, so I tried SPUDS in Denver and tracked you to Manhattan East and spoke with a fellow named Zipper—"

"Zissler?"

"That's the name, Moe Zissler. He said you were already on a jet, headed for Leonardo. Fumiano, the natives call it hereabouts. So I thought I'd just truck on down to the airport and pick you fellows up. Say, you don't look as jet-lagged as I thought you might. Feeling all right? Hungry? Thirsty? Need a hotel? Got a reservation? Harry Scott at your service."

Scott's perfect English wasn't totally Midwestern after all. There seemed to be a veneer of upper-middle-class Brit on top of the Indiana twang. Very odd.

He yanked his cap off his head and swept a low bow.

God bless Moe Zissler.

Lindsey said, "Zissler made reservations for us. We're at the"— he fumbled for his pocket organizer—"the Hotel Villa del Parco."

"Oh, wonderful, wonderful! I know it well, Via Nomentana, lovely old place. Nineteenth-century. Tiny establishment, couple of dozen rooms, *très intime*, gorgeous furnishings. You'll have a great time. How long you in town for, Zimmer didn't know. Or he wouldn't tell me, anyway. He's cagey, you know. He any relation to that baseball fellow, the one they used to call the Chipmunk?"

"Zissler," Lindsey said.

"Oh, right, the other fellow was Zimmer, not our Moe. You ever meet Zissler? Do I have it right, Zissler?"

Simultaneously, Lindsey said "Yes" and Berry said "No."

Scott had a hearty laugh. "Listen, there's no need to stand here in this drafty terminal. It is December, you know."

Lindsey looked around. The signs were in a variety of languages, most of them in Italian, and the buzz of conversations had a different sound to it than English. But otherwise, he could have been in Boston or Los Angeles or Detroit for all the difference he could find in the airport.

Scott drove a tan Alfa Romeo. Lindsey found himself sinking into the soft upholstery. Scott's taste in music was Italian. Lindsey wasn't sure but he thought he recognized something by Respighi. The roadway leading from the airport to the city was broad and smoothly paved, packed with shiny new cars intent on reaching their destinations at top speed and at any cost.

Before they reached the car, Lindsey and Berry had introduced themselves a little more formally to Scott. "You related to—?" Scott asked Petrus Berry.

"My brother."

"Shame. Tragedy. Tragedy and a crime. I learned about it over KlameNet/Plus. Must really have shaken SPUDS, pierced Ducky Richelieu to the quick. He's a tough cookie but he cares for his boys and girls. Uh, men and women."

A white Volvo limousine, windows tinted opaque, whizzed past them so fast that its slipstream shook the Alfa.

"Skillful driver," Harry Scott commented. "Can't say I admire his attitude, but I can't fault his skill." He shifted subjects without missing a beat. "What are you fellows doing in Rome? I know you're SPUDS, Lindsey, but what about you, Berry? You part of the team now?"

Berry said, "Temporarily."

"Well, welcome," Scott said, "even if it is temporary."

They entered the city as dusk was falling. Southern Europe was enduring a severe winter, and snowbanks lined the streets of Rome. The city was decorated for Christmas just as New York was. Under other circumstances, Lindsey would have loved to play tourist. If Marvia Plum and young Jamie Wilkerson were with him, it would have been the best Christmas of his life.

They weren't and it wasn't.

Harry Scott switched on the Alfa's headlights. "We're almost there, fellows. Say, I'll check you in and then I'd love to stay but I'm afraid I have an appointment. The wife, you know—mustn't keep her waiting first night back in town. But if you fellows need a recommendation for where to get some tolerable eats, maybe I can help out. Unless you're too jet-lagged for a meal?"

Petrus Berry said, "I'll sleep later. I'm too keyed up to think of turning in yet."

Lindsey had no quarrel with that. Instead, he asked Harry Scott how he had come to welcome them by speaking Italian.

"Married *una bella signorina*. Luckiest day of my life. You know the old saying, 'May you have an Italian sports car and a Chinese mistress.' Half true. Great cars in this country, but the women are even greater. Gorgeous, smashing! Came to Italy a confirmed bachelor, friend at the office introduced me to Giulia Pazzi, I knew it was all up. Married her first chance I got."

"So you learned Italian from your wife?"

"My darling *moglie, sì*. Italiano, even English. You know, I'm a farm boy. Little town in Indiana, you never heard of it."

Bingo!

"Pazzis are an old Italian family. Educated. Giulia learned her English at Cambridge, I'll have you know. Think I've picked up some of her mannerisms. Don't know what they'll make of me if

I ever get back to Connersville. But I know what they'll make of Giulia—what a knockout, that's all they'll have to say about my darling bride."

Scott pulled the Alfa to the curb in front of the Villa del Parco. The hotel lived up to his description. Lindsey and Berry shared a room overlooking the Via Nomentana. Full night had fallen by the time they unpacked their bags, and by that time Harry Scott had piled back into his Alfa and headed home to his gorgeous smashing knockout of a *moglie*.

Lindsey looked up a couple of telephone numbers in his pocket organizer. Before he reached for the telephone he said to Petrus Berry, "You hungry? You want to head out for food?"

Berry said, "Make your calls first."

Lindsey studied the Italian telephone. It wasn't too different from the American variety. He crossed his fingers and punched in a number.

"*Pronto?*"

Lindsey introduced himself, praying that there wouldn't be too much of a language problem. "Is Signore Lazarini there? Signore Abramo Lazarini? This is Hobart Lindsey, of International Surety.

"Sì, yes. I am Lazarini."

Lindsey breathed a sigh of relief. He told Lazarini that he was in Rome with Petrus Berry, the brother of Cletus Berry."

"I know, I know." Lazarini had a heavy accent but Lindsey could understand him well enough. "I know all about Cletus. You Americans, the crime in your country, so terrible. I try to get my sisters to come back to Italia, bring the little Anna Maria, they won't come. Now maybe they come."

Lindsey tried to explain his mission, what he and Petrus Berry were doing in Italy.

"I know, I know everything. Mosé learns everything from his cousin. The *ragazzi*, the children, they know everything *oggigiorno*."

Lindsey echoed the phrase. That one got past him.

"How do you say," Abramo Lazarini asked, "these the days, is that how?"

Lindsey puzzled over that. "Could it be *nowadays?*"

"Sì, the *ragazzi*, *i giovani*, know everything. What time, oh, you come here. Did you eat? No? Come, Lindsey and Petrus Berry."

Lindsey jotted down the address. He asked if it was anywhere near the home of Carlo Pacinelli.

"Pacinelli? Il professore? He is the neighbor. You want to speak with il professore? I invite him, too. You come ahead. Come now."

Lindsey set down the telephone. He grinned at Petrus Berry. "Talk about hospitality." He described his conversation with Abramo Lazarini.

"I got most of that," Berry replied. "From your half. What do you think? Friendship and hospitality, traditional Mediterranean warmth?"

Lindsey waited for him to go on.

Berry did. "I think there's more to it than that. Something that the signore maybe didn't want to talk about on the telephone."

Lindsey was in the bathroom by now, his shirt off and a towel draped around the upper half of his body. Fatigue hit him without warning and he leaned against the sink. When he regained his equilibrium he said, "I'm going to take a shower and put on fresh clothes."

"Good idea. Don't use all the hot water."

The concierge got them a taxi and the driver recognized the address that Lindsey gave him. He had some English. It seemed that everybody in Italy did. "'Via del Portico d'Ottavia, sì, you go to il ghetto *ebreo*. You try the *carciofi alla Giudea*. Most best food in Italia."

Lindsey wasn't sure whether the Roman cabbie was as reckless as the ones he'd ridden with in New York, or even wilder. But where the New York drivers seemed to regard their profession as a form of war, the Italians regarded it as a big happy game. How this driver avoided one accident after another was a mystery, but he delivered them to their destination without a scratch.

The Via del Portico d'Ottavia took a dogleg toward the Lungotevere de Cenci and the Tiber. The taxi dropped them at the house of the Lazarinis. It looked as if the family had indeed lived there for generations.

Before leaving the Villa del Parco Lindsey and Berry had discussed their agenda for the evening. In part the visit would be social, a sort of reverse condolence call in which Berry and the Lazarinis would discuss the tragic death of his brother, their brother-in-law.

But Berry suspected there was more to the matter. The Lazarinis' son and his friend il professore would play a role. Berry suspected that they could contribute something to their quest for the silver chariot.

Lindsey considered that. "What about Carlo Pacinelli?"

"What did Amoroso say about him?"

"He said, ah, 'Pacinelli is the neighbor. I invite him, too.' "

"Just like that, eh? Not Amoroso's idea at all, was it? Or was it yours? What do you bet, if you hadn't asked about him, il professore would have dropped in while we're visiting to return a borrowed frying pan, or something equally innocent?"

"Petrus, you have a devious mind."

"Ever know a cop who didn't?"

Abramo Lazarini welcomed Lindsey and Berry at the door of his home. Lindsey studied the man's face. There was something about the eyes, something about the cheekbones, that he had seen in the faces of Ester and Zaffira—and Anna Maria.

Lazarini ushered them into the living room. The furnishings were comfortable but they looked like something out of the 1920s. A plush sofa and overstuffed chairs, a Persian carpet on the floor, a few framed prints on the walls, a lovingly polished menorah on one table, surrounded by family portraits.

Here Lindsey and Berry met the Roman branch of the Lazarini family.

And il professore Carlo Pacinelli.

Lindsey took one look at Pacinelli and blinked. He was a dead ringer for the young Marcello Mastroianni. Not Mastroianni as the helpless, jaded journalist of *La Dolce Vita* but Mastroianni as he had appeared opposite the breathtaking young Sophia Loren years earlier, in *Too Bad She's Bad*.

But that would have taken a miracle. The resemblance was superficial. Carlo Pacinelli was just a pleasant, slightly stuffy academic, approaching middle age. A bachelor, presumably, visiting the home of a star pupil, meeting some foreign visitors, and getting a free meal out of it in the bargain.

Abramo Lazarini wore a black suit, a frayed white shirt, and a gray tie. A yarmulke clung to his sparse gray hair. In the light of the room, despite the difference in age, the family resemblance was even more striking.

Sara Amoroso was more generously proportioned than her husband, and obviously younger. Her thick, dark hair was graying. She wore a black dress with white trim, a small gold Star of David on a fine chain, a floral-printed apron. As a girl she might have been voluptuous; in early middle age, she looked comfortable with herself and her world. She carried an oversized wooden cooking spoon, her scepter.

Perfect.

Recorded music provided a background for conversation. Sara Lazarini said, "Signore Lindsey, Signore Berry, you like it? Schubert. Very late Schubert."

There was no sign of Mosé Lazarini.

Sara Lazarini retreated to her kitchen, nodding in time to the music. Her husband looked from Lindsey to Berry. He said, "You have been in Italy before? In Rome?"

Lindsey and Berry both said no.

"Ah. The lovely country. The beautiful city. You must see Rome. Everything is here. The museums, the statues, the paintings. I have traveled. Never to America, but to Francia, to Grecia, to Spagna. You must see the Europa. But the most beautiful is the Italia."

Berry said, "I've been to Okinawa."

Lazarini raised his hands. "*Scusi?*"

"Never mind. I'm sure it doesn't compare."

Lindsey said, "I'd love to visit Italy again to see the treasures. But Mr. Berry and I are not here for pleasure. Not this time."

Lazarini nodded solemnly. "Sì, I understand. So, you tell me why you come to Italia."

Berry flashed a look at Lindsey, then said, "We think some-one killed my brother because he knew where Caesar's Chariot is. Lindsey has been investigating the case since the day they found Cletus's body. I'm working with him."

Abramo nodded. He said something to Carlo Pacinelli in rapid Italian. While he spoke Sara returned. Cooking odors swept from the kitchen along with her. She had left her apron and spoon behind.

She said, "*Basta. Klops presso burik. Anche lokshen.* Abramo, *guiben mir a bissel vino, zei azoi gut.*"

Abramo served wine. He said, "*Bi'teh,* Sara, *inglese, inglese.*"

"*Bene, gueleebt, bene.* For dinner, you wait and see."

Pacinelli nodded to Abramo, answered him briefly and as rapidly as he had spoken, then said, "You know who killed your brother, Signore Berry? Some American gangster, American mafioso?"

Berry shook his head. "Lindsey knows more about that than I do."

Lindsey looked from Abramo Lazarini to Carlo Pacinelli. "Do you know of a man called Alcide Palmiro Castellini? Born in Italy, now living in America."

Both Lazarinis looked blank, but Pacinelli raised his hands in a gesture of surprise. He wore a gray tweed jacket, a white shirt, and a maroon knit tie. Lindsey hadn't seen a knit tie in years; he wondered whether Pacinelli was retro or avant garde, or just dressing his role as a professor. He wondered what Carlo Pacinelli and William Van Huysen would think of each other.

"Wait, I will fetch young Mosé, please. He knows everything I know, we are scholars together."

Pacinelli disappeared down a narrow corridor.

Sara Lazarini nodded after him. "He is, how you say, Abramo, in *inglese, eine yoi'sher goy, un giusto pagano,* yes?"

"The good gentile, righteous."

A boy appeared in the doorway followed by Carlo Pacinelli. They advanced into the room.

Sara wrapped her arms around the boy. "*Dammi un'abbraccio, meine liebling.*"

The boy looked at Lindsey and at Petrus Berry. He walked up to Berry and shook his hand. "I am Mosé Lazarini. You must be the uncle of my cousin, sir."

Lindsey heard an odd sound and saw that Petrus Berry had released the boy's hand and crushed him in a bear hug. Tears were rolling down Berry's face.

No one spoke.

When Berry released the boy he said, "I'm sorry." He pulled a handkerchief from his pocket and wiped his face. "I'm sorry. Since Cletus was"—he shook his head—"I thought I was finished crying. I—I don't know why now." As Lindsey watched, a shudder ran through Berry's body. Then Berry said, "I'm all right now. I'm okay." He shoved his handkerchief back into his pocket.

Still there was an embarrassed silence.

Berry said, "It just hit me. This young boy. My brother. I won't break down again."

Sara Lazarini patted Berry's shoulder. He turned and took her hand and held it to his face.

Mosé Lazarini stepped up to Lindsey and shook his hand. The boy did resemble his cousin Anna Maria. His hair was black and wavy and somehow shorter than Lindsey had expected. His skin was a Mediterranean olive, darker than Lindsey's but lighter than Anna Maria's.

"How do you do, sir," Mosé said. "You must be Signore Lindsey. I've heard about you from my cousin."

Lindsey nodded. "I know Anna Maria. You must be the other half of Professor Selvatica." Lindsey saw that Petrus Berry had recovered from his momentary breakdown. He had released Sara's hand and was directing his attention to the conversation.

Mosé laughed. "Yes, sir. Professor Blackberry at your service."

Sara Lazarini demanded the attention of the room. "*Andiamo a tavola, esen.*" She seemed to switch effortlessly between Italian and Yiddish—what little Yiddish Lindsey had heard in the home of Eric Coffman and his wife Miriam in Concord, near Lindsey's old home in Walnut Creek, California. Italian and Yiddish and an occasional bit of *inglese*.

They went to the table.

Klops presso burik, anche lokshen turned out to be meatloaf with hard-boiled egg, beets, and noodles. It was delicious. If only the Coffmans were here. Eric might have little in common with the quiet, austere Abramo Lazarini, but Miriam and Sara were sisters beneath the skin.

Carlo Pacinelli finally got his chance to respond to Lindsey's question about Alcide Castellini. He did so by prompting his prize pupil, Mosé. "You know of the Castellinis, *il padre ed anche il figlio*. You speak, Mosé."

The boy wiped his mouth with a napkin. This was his chance to show off his learning in the presence of his family and his professore. He cleared his throat.

"Professore Pacinelli and I, we study this. We have gone to La Spezia."

Everybody was going to La Spezia. First the old fascist Salvatore Castellini. Then, Lindsey guessed, Cletus Berry. Harry Scott, and now Professor Pacinelli and his pupil Mosé Lazarini. "It's still a port, then?"

"Very important. Venezia, Genova, Napoli, our famous ports. But La Spezia is very important, yes."

"And were you able to trace the silver chariot? Can you connect it to Salvatore Castellini and Alcide Castellini?"

"Sì," Mosé said proudly.

"Sì," Carlo Pacinelli echoed his pupil. "*Certamente.*"

And Abramo and Sara Lazarini, in unison, "*Gue'vis.*"

Lindsey and Berry exchanged a look. Lindsey leaned forward in his chair, Berry settled back in his. It was all a matter of style. They were both getting ready to hear Mosé's story.

There was no way the child could have learned this much on his own, but he was a bright student and his professore prompted him, calling him back from false trails and filling in omitted details. It was soon clear to Lindsey that Professor Blackberry was more than the fusion of Anna Maria Berry and Mosé Lazarini. Carlo Pacinelli, perhaps without knowing it, provided the biggest part of Blackberry's data bank.

Il dottore Mora Selvatica spoke with the words of two bright children, but with the thoughts and knowledge of a middle-aged scholar.

As young Mosé spoke, prompted by questions from both Lindsey and Berry and with his answers amplified by il professore Pacinelli, Lindsey jotted notes in his ragged pocket organizer. "Italy has an ugly past," Mosé asserted.

His father frowned but the boy continued.

"My people, we *Ebrei*, we Jews—we are part of Italy forever."

He was echoing words that Lindsey had heard in the Seventy-third Street apartment from Ester Lazarini. Lindsey tried to imagine being part of anything forever.

"We give Italy our love and what does Italy give us?" Abramo Lazarini had retreated to the sweet love of a man for his country. Sara Lazarini, to her home and her family.

Mosé, Lindsey thought, might once more lead his people against Pharaoh. Eric Coffman would love to meet Mosé Lazarini.

Later, Lindsey would amplify his notes into a report to Desmond Richelieu. But now he sat spellbound by the child's story.

Chapter Twenty-three

BENITO MUSSOLINI HAD the support of the majority of the Italian people (Lindsey paraphrased the boy in his long memorandum to Desmond Richelieu), at least in his early years in power. That included Italian Jewry. Mussolini was no racist, certainly no anti-Semite. Italy had been in a state of political confusion and economic turmoil in the years following the First World War, and Il Duce was seen as a unifying leader who would bring discipline and order to the nation.

In power for a full decade before Adolf Hitler became Chancellor of the Weimar Republic, Mussolini considered Hitler a petty upstart. The first time Hitler tried to grab Austria, Mussolini massed Italian troops and threatened war, and Hitler backed down. Il Duce was a hero to the British and French then. But the balance of power shifted. Hitler grew stronger. He and Mussolini became de facto allies in their support of Francisco Franco's Falangists in the Spanish Civil War, and once their alliance was formalized, Mussolini began to toe Hitler's racial line.

The first modern racial laws were not proclaimed in Italy until 1938, and even then they were never as severe as those in Germany. Jews were precluded from entering certain professions, for example, but even then exceptions were made for decorated soldiers of past wars and for other distinguished individuals.

As the situation worsened and the Second World War progressed, Italian racial laws grew more stringent. There were concentration camps, but even these, as severe as they were, came nowhere near the horrors of the Nazi death camps.

It was only with the fall of the Mussolini government, the surrender to the Western Allies, and the invasion of Italy by German armies that wholesale arrests and deportation of Jews to the extermination camps began.

There were attempts by some Italians to protect their Jewish brethren. Other Italians sold Jews to the Germans like so many cattle.

Flash back to 1937.

Salvatore Castellini, early supporter of Mussolini and later Fascist party hack, marries his childhood sweetheart. Blonde, blue-eyed, delicate featured, she looks neither Italian nor Jewish. Even her name, Anna Schoenberg, sounds more German than either Jewish or Italian. But in fact Anna is a Jew; she is a distant cousin of the composer Arnold Schoenberg.

A year later, Mussolini announces the first of his anti-Semitic laws.

Salvatore Castellini begins to worry. He is no beast, he is a sincere fascist. He believes in discipline, unity, nationalism. But part of that unity and nationalism is based on the conviction that all loyal Italians are potentially good citizens of the state. Now Jews are proclaimed aliens in their own land.

La Signora Castellini is in danger. So is her entire family, and, by association, so is Salvatore Castellini.

Italian Jews—and non-Jews who cast their lot with them—had better prepare for hard times.

Castellini finds himself assigned to the security apparatus of the Fascist party and state. He becomes a member of OVRA—the *Operazione di Vigilanza per la Repressione dell'Antifascismo*—and two years later his opportunity arrives.

World War II has broken out. The Italian Pavilion at the World's Fair in New York has been closed. The artifacts and treasures on display are returning to Italy aboard the *Fior di Rimini* and when word reaches Rome of suspicious doings aboard the freighter, OVRA springs into action.

Salvatore Castellini uses all of his considerable cunning to get the assignment for himself, and when the disappearance of the *coc-*

chio and the presence of the body of Massimo di Verolini are discovered, Castellini is the investigating official.

The small crate containing the *Cocchio di Cesare* is smuggled off the *Fior di Rimini* by the one man positioned to commit the crime . . . the official sent by Rome to prevent the commission of the crime . . . Salvatore Castellini.

Or was it?

The death of di Verolini, the disappearance of the chariot, the OVRA investigation under the care of Salvatore Castellini—these are all verifiable occurrences. These were duly recorded at the time, and the records survive. But did Castellini actually take the *cocchio?* This is not verifiable, only inferential. But the pieces all fit together; the evidence all points to Salvatore Castellini.

Lindsey finds himself thinking of Dorothy Yamura's memorable dictum about coincidences. If not a proven fact, then as a likely hypothesis, Salvatore Castellini had possession of that toy in the early days of 1940. But he was unlikely to lug it around with him; the chariot would be far too dangerous. He would have had to put it somewhere, or send it somewhere, deposit it somewhere.

Where does the fascist Castellini, the husband of Anna Schoenberg, this man torn between two loyalties . . . Where does Salvatore Castellini deposit the chariot?

In the hands of the Jewish antifascist underground in La Spezia, for as Mussolini had turned increasingly against the Jews of Italy, the Jews of Italy had turned increasingly against Mussolini, and the underground, itself a bizarre alliance of Jews, liberals, and Communists, is strong and well organized.

Italy is already involved in the war, and things at first go swimmingly, but as the tide of battle slowly turns, the chariot is moved from hiding place to hiding place. For a time it remains in La Spezia. The principle of "The Purloined Letter" applies. Then it is transported to Bologna, where it comes to rest in a storage room in the city hall. When bombs fall, it is moved, this time to Ravenna, where it is actually loaded onto a ship, the *Giovanni Acuto*, bound for Trieste, just across the Adriatic Sea.

The ship never leaves port. A stray artillery shell fired by a German garrison strikes the *Giovanni Acuto* and only the quick action of an anonymous crewman prevents the *cocchio* from disappearing into the murky harbor-bed.

The chariot makes its way as far south as Pescara, then across the width of Italy to Rome, where it falls into the hands of a group of Jewish antifascists, who hide it in—of all places—a catacomb beneath the subbasement of the Grand Temple, the splendid, extravagant synagogue that even the Nazis were too awed to destroy.

The Italian fascists, for all their ambivalence, never executed a full-scale pogrom against Italy's Jews. But once the Nazis took over, the full ferocity of a dying beast was unleashed. In Rome alone, more than two thousand Jews were rounded up and shipped to concentration camps. Two thousand, out of a tiny population. Not all of them died in the camps; records show that as many as fifteen individuals survived the camps and returned to Rome.

The insurance claim against New York Amalgamated Guarantee had been filed in timely fashion, as early as 1940, while Italy and the United States were still at peace, but it became obvious that it would not be paid while the nations were at war.

By the time the war ends, Italy is in ruins and in chaos. As for the chariot . . . no one knows where it is. No one knows whether it even exists any longer.

Lindsey and Berry had been on the edge of their chairs, resisting the urge to interrupt. It was Lindsey who yielded first.

"How do you know all this? Pardon me, Mosé, but for a boy of ten—how do you know so much of these events, going back fifty or sixty years?"

"I have studied, sir." The boy seemed sincere rather than smug. In any case, he seemed sure of himself. "Il professore and I, we study, we research. There are records. And there are stories. I swear you, sir, I tell you truth."

Lindsey nodded and settled back in an ordinary wooden chair that might have hosted a Jewish owner in the 1930s, an Italian fascist by 1942, a Nazi trooper in '43, a Communist partisan in '44, a GI in '45, and its Jewish owner again by 1946.

As a matter of fact (Mosé resumed his narrative and, later, Lindsey his paraphrase), the chariot was fifty feet beneath the Grand Temple, still in its packing crate.

Lindsey had his doubts. Through decades of clandestine searches, if the records existed and the chariot was indeed where Mosé claimed, would it not have been recovered long since?

Still . . .

What of Salvatore Castellini and his wife, Anna Schoenberg?

In the chaos of war and the internal strife that racked Italy even before Mussolini's downfall, Castellini had risen to the rank of major in OVRA and had been able to offer protection to his wife by passing her off as a German Catholic.

In 1945, with the struggle between Communist and anti-Communist forces beginning in Italy, Castellini offers his services to the American military. He knows the secrets of OVRA, he knows where the bodies are buried, he is a valuable man. The army refers him to G2, military intelligence, which refers him to the Office of Strategic Services.

Under the protection first of the Americans, then of the Italian Christian Democrats of Alcide de Gasperi, Salvatore and Anna live comfortably in a fashionable apartment on the Via delle Carrozze. Castellini's background—shadowy at best—should not bode well for him, but the Cold War is getting under way and both the Western and Eastern camps are known to hold their noses and put former Axis intelligence officers to use in their own burgeoning clandestine services.

In 1947 Anna gives birth to a son. Because Italy's political future is still in doubt, the proud parents name their baby after the leaders of the nation's two great political factions.

Little Alcide Palmiro Castellini grows up in the gray world of dubious undertakings, ambiguous characters, and black-bag operations. By the time he is twenty-five years old he has become friends with an American warrant officer named Cletus Berry and Berry's boss, a lieutenant colonel named Harry Scott.

Castellini has a reputation in the Italian shadow world. He has inherited his father's penchant for unsavory doings and dangerous associates, and his mother's unquestioned brilliance and artistic tastes. He is a man with no friends. He is also a man with few enemies, for those who interfere with his work are seldom seen for very long.

The Americans Cletus Berry and Harry Scott work with Castellini the younger in an illicit exporting business. When some army investigators start sniffing around the operation, Scott sacrifices Berry to save his own hindquarters.

The result: Berry winds up with a general discharge from the army. As far as I can tell (Lindsey interjected in his memorandum) Cletus never did find out who blew the whistle on him. And Berry winds up working for SPUDS. Harry Scott wins himself a commendation for betraying his partner and takes early retirement from the army. Alcide Castellini becomes an American citizen and buys a magnificent Stanford White townhouse on Gramercy Park.

And all three partners continue working together—until Cletus Berry is shot dead in an alley in Hell's Kitchen.

And where is the *Cocchio di Argento?*

Carlo Pacinelli looked at Lindsey and Berry.

They were seated facing each other at the dinner table. The meal was long since ended. Strong coffee had been drunk and lemon *babka* and honey *schnecken* consumed. The music had ceased to play, and the only sounds other than conversation were those of traffic in the Via del Portico d'Ottavia, and the occasional bark of a dog.

Where is the silver chariot?

Pacinelli said, "No one knows."

"Mosé said the chariot was beneath the Grand Temple."

Pacinelli smiled. "Perhaps. A legend. A myth. The Golden Fleece of Perseus, the Holy Grail, the *Cocchio di Argento.*"

The black bird.

"Then how do you know so much about it? The whole story—" Lindsey didn't know whether to be amazed at this windfall of information or furious that so much was known and nothing done about it. That is, if Mosé Lazarini and his mentor Carlo Pacinelli had any real basis for their story.

Professor Blackberry was a figment. Was he also a fraud?

Pacinelli said, "I have devoted my life to this research. My people—my nation—were guilty of terrible crimes. Too much we hide them, pretend evil things never happened. But I want to know everything. I want to expose everything. Only when everything is displayed in bright sunlight can Italy's conscience be clear."

He nodded as if to underline his words.

Lindsey saw that Pacinelli gripped the edge of the table, the white linen tablecloth that Sara Lazarini had laid on her table, with both hands. His fingers were as white as the cloth, from the pressure he placed on them.

"That still doesn't answer my question," Lindsey persisted.

"In the files of the Jewish community of Rome. In the records of the Grand Temple. The rabbis, the congregation, they let me in. They call me their *giusto pagano*. They are very kind to me, very helpful. When I was a student they gave me a job, I was the beadle, the *shabbas goy*. I would perform the little tasks that a Hebrew could not on the Sabbath." He grinned as if recalling a pleasant memory.

"And in the archives of the Memorial to the Jewish Martyrs. I searched there, too. They have records. And in the Ministry of Justice, where the OVRA files have gone. They were not so pleased in the ministry, when they learned what I wanted. There was still pressure, you know, from the Americans. But now the Americans are not so much afraid of Communists, so they do not press the ministry, and I have my degrees, my esteemed academic rank. *Dottore. Professore.* They think I am not interested in politics or in crime, just in history. So they let me search for facts."

This was exactly the kind of information that Lindsey needed to make sense of this case. But Pacinelli was so glib, so forthcoming, so genial. How had this information found its way into those archives?

Lindsey asked, and Pacinelli's forehead darkened.

"Anna Schoenberg wrote her memoirs and donated them to the memorial. In all the documents, she never refers to the chariot by name. She refers to it only by its crate number on the *Fior di Rimini* bill of lading, from 1940. It is only crate number 18 in all the documents. Only crate number 18."

"Her husband kept her safe all through the war?" Lindsey asked.

"No."

Lindsey waited for Pacinelli to elaborate. Instead, he remained silent. Somewhere a lonely dog howled. Finally, Lindsey said, "She was caught by the Nazis, then."

Pacinelli said, "Yes. She was sent to Dachau. She was one of the thousands rounded up and transported. She was one of the handful who returned." He leaned his elbows on the table, then pressed his forehead against the upraised palms of his hands. "When she came back, Salvatore Castellini welcomed her. They lived together. They had a son. All the while she was working with the archivists, documenting the horrors of the war."

Lindsey asked, "How did the Nazis capture her? You said she was married to a Gentile, she was passing as a German Catholic."

"Yes." Pacinelli paused. There were tears in his eyes. He hiccuped but it was not a comic moment. He gasped for breath, then dropped his fists to his lap. "The story. The Germans were suspicious. Salvatore Castellini, OVRA Major Castellini was afraid she would be found out and transported and he would share her fate, so he turned her in to the Germans. All the time she was in Dachau, she never knew her husband had betrayed her to save himself."

Just like Harry Scott and Cletus Berry, Lindsey thought, thirty years later.

"After Anna finished her memoir and turned it over to the memorial, an American officer came to see her. He had seen the records of OVRA that even Italians could not see then. He was doing a, what is it called, background check on Salvatore Castellini. He went to see Anna. He thought she knew. She was living with Castellini, she had borne his child, she must know, she must have forgiven him. But she did not know."

"Jesus!" Petrus Berry had sat quietly for a long time. Now he ground his teeth audibly. "Jesus save us. There is no end to it, is there? No end to the filth, no end to the betrayals."

Pacinelli stared, then said, "Please, signore, I beg you to not give up hope. Let me, at least, keep my hope."

Businesslike, Lindsey asked, "What did she do?"

Pacinelli whispered his reply. "She took her own life."

There was silence at the table, then Petrus Berry raised his face. To Lindsey it was as if a mask had descended over Berry's features. He said, "First place I'd look for the chariot would be in that catacomb."

Every head turned toward him.

"Simple police work," Berry said. "You're looking for something, you don't know where it is, you start with the last place you knew where it was and work from there." Just the way your mother would say, "Well, where did you have it last?" when you lose something.

A little later, as Lindsey and Berry were preparing to leave, Sara Lazarini excused herself for a few minutes. She returned carrying a cup full of coins. She doled them out to Lindsey and Berry, half to each. "You give these to *tsedokeh*," she told them. "*Per carita. Capite?*"

They both nodded.

Outside, in the Via del Portico d'Ottavia, waiting for a cab to carry them back to their hotel, they counted the money. The denominations were all small, and they didn't add up to any significant amount. As they were about to give up, Lindsey said, "Wait a minute. How many coins did she give you, Petrus? Not their value, how many actual coins?"

Even as he spoke, he was counting his own collection of Italian coins. There were eighteen of them.

Petrus Berry counted his and said, "Eighteen."

Lindsey was amazed at how quickly the Italians could act when they chose to. Or more likely it was the Italian Jewish community and not the Italian government.

Thirty-six hours after hearing Mosé Lazarini and Carlo Pacinelli's story in the house on the Via del Portico d'Ottavia, Lindsey and Berry were climbing down a wooden staircase beneath the subbasement of the Grand Temple on the Lungotevere de Cenci. With them was Carlo Pacinelli, temporarily resuming his long-outgrown role as beadle of the temple.

Lindsey had spent the day working on his report, transmitting it to Desmond Richelieu in Colorado, and, at Richelieu's urging, to Detective Marcie Sokolov at Midtown North in New York. He even purchased a handful of Villa del Parco postcards and a sheet of Italian postage stamps and dispatched greetings to the States. To Anna Maria Berry, to his mother and her new husband, Gordon Sloane, to the Coffman family, and to his old friend Mathilde Wilbur at her home in Oakland.

Then he turned another card, picture-side down, and held his pen poised over the message area. He could send a card to Marvia Plum. No, that was a bad idea. He settled for scribbling a generic greeting on the card and addressing it to Jamie Wilkerson. Marvia would see it, her new husband would see it; they would decide what to make of it.

Lindsey and Berry and Carlo Pacinelli were dressed in warm, quilted jackets, heavy shoes and thick socks, and woolen gloves. Unlike the catacombs of the early Christians, which had become religious shrines and tourist attractions for visitors to Rome, the Jewish catacombs—at least this one—were seldom visited.

The floor was hard-packed dirt. The ceiling was low. They were armed with a few simple tools: a crowbar, a hammer, a screwdriver, a roll of bubble wrap, a roll of duct tape. There was no installed lighting; instead two of them carried flashlights while the third carried the tools.

A claustrophobic chill ran through Lindsey. A shift of the earth, a minor cave-in, and they would be lost, buried like characters in a Poe story.

No holy relics here. The catacomb had become a storage room. Old records and files, abandoned equipment, broken furniture.

Why didn't they just throw it away? Far from being exotic, the catacomb could have been a storage vault beneath Midtown North or SPUDS Central in Denver.

Lindsey and Berry had taken breakfast at the Villa del Parco. Berry had become quieter since leaving New York, as if he had parted from his home territory and was uncomfortable, tentative in his new surroundings. Berry had acquired an education, Lindsey knew, and had traveled as far from home as Okinawa, but he was still the product of Pinopolis, South Carolina. He had seen the last years of the Old South and the first years of the New, but he hardly knew Rome.

And, Lindsey knew, he'd left his revolver in Zaffira Fornari's New York apartment. Desmond Richelieu's pull might get him a passport and a plane ticket in record time, but it would not get a firearm onto that jetliner.

They passed a pile of cracked pews, obviously long since replaced in the temple and abandoned beneath the earth. Somewhere nearby, Lindsey realized, the Tiber flowed. Some formation of rock and soil kept the catacombs dry despite the proximity of the river.

And there it was. A gray tarpaulin, a layer of dust, square corners protruding. It could have been a box of file folders, it could have been a case of wine bottles, but Lindsey knew. Somehow, they all knew.

"So many years," Pacinelli said.

None of them reached to pull back the tarp.

"I never looked for it. I did not—it is so strange—was I the only one who knew? And I never thought to search. I wanted to know, only to know. To learn and to teach. This is it, you think?"

Petrus Berry said, "I think."

Lindsey said, "You remove the tarpaulin, Petrus. He was your brother. You have the right to do it."

Berry lifted away the heavy gray canvas. Beneath it lay a simple wooden box. No fancy casket of polished wood and metal. Just an ordinary rough packing crate. Stenciled on the side, the figures faint and faded after more than fifty years, was only the number 18.

Berry held out his hand and Lindsey placed the crowbar in it. Berry slid the wedge-shaped end of the crowbar under the lid. He leaned on the other end and a half-century-old nail screamed and yielded.

He moved the wedge-end a few inches and pried again, then again, and then the top of the crate was upraised at an oblique angle.

Lindsey exhaled loudly. He realized he'd been holding his breath. Now it plumed from his mouth like smoke.

Berry dropped the crowbar. It landed at his feet with a soft thump. He grasped the edge of the crate with one gloved hand, the edge of the lid with the other, and pulled the lid upright.

The catacomb was sealed off from any natural light. Bright noon or pitch-black midnight made no difference here. The only light was provided by Lindsey's and Pacinelli's flashlights. Their feet had stirred up long-still dust particles, and their flashlight beams cast cones of reflected light.

Lindsey and Carlo Pacinelli both leaned forward, pointing their flashlights into the packing crate. All that was visible was a layer of sawdust. Berry plunged his hands into it and shoveled sawdust out of the crate, onto the dirt floor of the catacomb. He gestured with his head, to Lindsey, not speaking.

Lindsey understood. He handed his flashlight to Pacinelli and pitched in to the task. He felt an unidentifiable shape, worked his hands lower and felt a solid, squared-off corner.

Lindsey and Berry made eye contact. Simultaneously they lifted. It was peculiar; somehow, almost as if the chariot itself had lent them some previously unknown power, they worked in perfect synchronicity.

Pacinelli stepped back, playing both flashlights on the chariot as Lindsey and Berry lifted it. Lindsey ended his eye contact with Berry, looking down at the ancient toy. It was covered with a thin chamois sack. Lindsey and Berry worked it carefully out of its protective covering.

The black horse and the white, the silver work, the perfect miniature wheels with their spokes of ancient wood. What would William Van Huysen think of this!

The Hebrew letters, *chet yod*, were still visible, worked into the silver chariot. A dark stain marked one sharp corner of the dark marble base.

The explosion that echoed through the catacomb couldn't possibly be as loud as it sounded, but Carlo Pacinelli screamed and Hobart Lindsey and Petrus Berry turned to find the source of the sound. A second shot followed the first. Lindsey saw the muzzle flash and in that instant he was certain that he and Petrus Berry acted as a single organism controlled by a single nervous system.

They swung the chariot forward, released it, waited for what could only have been a fraction of a second but seemed like an endless, frozen moment in eternity, then heard the sickening crunch of bone as the chariot struck a human being directly in the face.

Carlo Pacinelli lay on the earth. He was moaning, so he must be alive. He had dropped both flashlights. One had gone out, its lens and bulb in all likelihood smashed beyond repair, but the other lay on the earth, still sending a beam of light through the stale, newly disturbed, dust-laden air.

Petrus Berry got to it first. He shined it on the gunman as Lindsey knelt beside him. The chariot base had crushed his face. The bland features, the whole nondescript, unremarkable face, was a hopeless, bloody ruin. There was a deep indentation, dead center on the pale forehead, precisely where the bullet had entered Cletus Berry's forehead in the alley in Hell's Kitchen. Lindsey laid his fingers on the side of the man's throat, searching for a pulse, knowing there would be none, then knowing he was right.

The chariot had landed right side up and apparently undamaged. Lindsey grinned at that, knowing how incongruous his reaction was. He said, "Look after Pacinelli, Petrus, this one is dead."

Berry turned away.

Lindsey followed him, followed the beam of light from his flashlight. They bent over Pacinelli. Lindsey looked at his wound. Apparently the first bullet had struck him in the shoulder. The second had missed altogether.

Berry said, "I don't think we should move him. We can't leave him here alone. One of us has to go for help, and there's only one flashlight working. Damn, damn. Okay, Hobart, you go. Take the light. Get back here fast with help. Fast, *capisci?*"

Lindsey couldn't repress another grin. He took the functioning flashlight from Berry and headed back toward the stairs and the subbasement of the Grand Temple. Before he reached the stairs, he heard Petrus Berry ask, "You recognize the shooter, Hobart?"

Recognize the shooter? "Yes," Lindsey replied. "Fellow named Morris Zissler. I didn't even know he was in Italy."

Chapter Twenty-four

ONE THING ABOUT flying on Christmas: it's the lightest travel day of the year. Especially on international flights. Nobody's going anyplace. Wherever people are, they're staying put. Hobart Lindsey and Petrus Berry were able to stretch out, take all the snacks they wanted, get all the attention they wanted from the flight attendants, act like a couple of big shots.

Lindsey was working on his report to Desmond Richelieu. Berry was reading a British edition of a Walter Mosley novel that he'd picked up at the terminal outside Rome. The sparse scattering of other passengers in the big jet seemed unanimously committed to ignoring the wholesome family movie that the airline had kindly provided for holiday viewing.

Outside the jet's windows—Lindsey's eyes were aching and he was relieved to drag them away from his laptop's monitor screen before they went on strike—he could see the Atlantic Ocean almost 40,000 feet below. The sound of a sixties song rang with perfect accuracy in Lindsey's mind's ear.

Eight miles high . . .

He pressed his forehead to the Plexiglas. The ocean was black.

Eight miles high . . . He could hear the guitars and the voices. His onetime schoolmate Artemis Janson would know whose song that was. Artie Janson had turned up at the wedding of Lindsey's mother and Gordon Sloane, the first time he'd seen her in a quarter century. There had been a momentary flash of energy between them, and then Artie was gone and Lindsey was gone and he wondered now if he would see her again, in another quarter century.

The black ocean rolled far beneath the jet. Three generations ago, in the era of the floating palaces, there would have been ships down there carrying elegantly dressed travelers between Europe and America. Bands would be playing, there might be a midnight service to honor the birth of the Christ Child, couples would exchange expensive gifts bought in the ship's own shops.

But the modern world didn't have time to cross the ocean in three graceful days. Not when it was possible to fly it in a few harried hours.

Lindsey drew a deep breath, then slowly released the air.

Petrus Berry marked his place in the Mosley book with his finger and looked at Lindsey. "You all right, Hobart?"

"I'm okay." Lindsey folded down the screen of his laptop. "Just tired. It's been a hell of a case, Petrus."

Berry nodded. "That it has." There was a silence, then he said, "How are you going to treat Cletus, Hobart?"

Lindsey stared at the black shell of his laptop. He didn't find any inspiration there. "I want to be as kind as I can."

"I know. He was your friend."

"He was your brother."

"But—"

Lindsey pursed his lips. "But, indeed. I have to tell the truth, Petrus."

"I'm thinking of Ester. And of Anna Maria."

"I don't think this will change anything. I don't see how International Surety could cancel Cletus's life policy."

"You don't?" Berry lifted his eyebrows. Lindsey didn't answer. "No line-of-duty clause there?" Berry asked. "No moral turpitude, no cancellation because he died in the act of committing a felony?"

Lindsey shook his head. "Cletus was never convicted of anything. And now he can't be. You know we don't conduct posthumous trials. Besides . . ." He let the sentence lapse and raised his eyes. Black ocean beneath, black sky above. But here where no city lights outshone them, a billion billion stars and galaxies filled the sky.

"Besides, we don't really know," Lindsey resumed. "Maybe Frankie Fulton was the intended victim, back in that alley. Maybe

Cletus tried to come to the rescue and—well, you know the drill."

"No, no." Petrus Berry's face was drawn. "You're trying to be charitable but I can't buy that. It's two plus two, Hobart. It makes four, we can't change it." He leaned forward and slipped the paperback book into the seat pocket in front of him. "I can't concentrate. Let the next person who sits here find it. Good writer. Good book." He shifted in his seat.

"You're right," he went on, "there's no way they can bring Cletus to trial and there's nothing really they can do to him. That life policy will be a big help for Ester and Anna Maria. I wouldn't be surprised, though, if the Feds don't slap a tax deficiency on the estate. Maybe even try and seize his bank account, IS stock, anything else he owned. What a mess. What a mess."

He looked away, gazed past Lindsey. "Cold and wet down there, eh?"

Lindsey grunted.

"It's still a blow, Hobart." Petrus Berry's forehead was furrowed. "My brother. I never thought he'd turn out to be dirty. My own brother."

"That hasn't been proved. We don't know for sure that he knew where the chariot was."

Berry smiled ruefully. "He knew. That's what Castellini was trying to get out of him. What a joke. Carlo Pacinelli could have turned it up for him. The whole thing went back to Castellini's own parents, back to the World's Fair and the *Fior di Rimini*. My guess is that Cletus and Castellini were playing a chess game over the chariot. Cletus overplayed his pieces. Castellini got little Frankie Fulton to bring Cletus to a showdown meeting and things got out of hand. I can't imagine Castellini wanting to kill Cletus. If he knew where the chariot was and Castellini killed him—stupid." He shook his head. "Just stupid."

Lindsey said, "I think it was Castellini who overplayed his pieces. He didn't pull the trigger. Johnny Thieu Ng was the triggerman. The way I figure it, Fulton was supposed to be an example. Castellini hired Ng to kill Fulton. Ng got carried away and killed Cletus, too. See what a productive worker I am, two hits for the price of one. Castellini got so angry that he had Ng killed, and Ng's buddy Bilbo Sax for good measure. And all the other people who've died for that damned toy. All the way back to Millicent Martin, who shouldn't have started hanging around with a reporter. All the way back to Massimo di Verolini."

He leaned his head on his hand.

Berry said, "It stinks, Hobart. It all just stinks."

On the in-flight movie screen, a couple of saccharine-sweet children were hugging a cuddly animal they had rescued from some fate worse than death. Somebody a couple of rows behind Lindsey was snoring. A flight attendant, looking as if she hadn't been off the airplane in a week, staggered past. Lindsey waved her down and asked if he could have a cup of coffee. Berry chimed in and asked for one, also. The flight attendant managed a ghastly smile and said she'd be just thrilled to accommodate them.

Berry said, "So the Italian government gets the toy back and it goes into a museum, I suppose."

Lindsey nodded. "I suppose."

"Professor Pacinelli gets to play the hero and your company—you think they'll get their money back?"

Lindsey managed his best grin in days, maybe weeks. "We'll ask for it, the Italians will date-stamp the claim, we won't hear for six months, we'll ask again, they'll date-stamp the request for a tracer. It'll be fun. You know how many years it took International Surety to pay the original claim? It'll take that long for the Italian government even to look at our request for reimbursement. They'll probably pay it, in current lira, which will be enough money to buy Desmond Richelieu a good Italian dinner at the best spaghetti house in Denver."

He latched up his laptop and slid it under the seat in front of him. He'd done all the work he was going to do on this flight. He could finish when he reached New York, or even Denver.

"What I want to see," he said, "is what's going to happen back in New York. I know that Richelieu talked to Corporate and got Harry Scott summoned back to headquarters for a face-to-face and Scott and his bella signora seem to have taken a disappearing powder."

"I like that," Berry smiled. "I haven't heard that expression in thirty years."

"Do I get in the old guys' club?" Lindsey asked.

"Don't ask me. I didn't even know I was old until"—he paused, and when he resumed his voice sounded different—"until my brother died. Then all of a sudden I felt old, Hobart."

Lindsey said, "I'm sorry. I didn't mean to joke."

"That's okay. I'm navigating all right. I've got to get back and do what I can for Cletus's women, that's all. But what *is* going to happen, that's what I want to know. If Giobbe were still alive, it would be different."

"Giobbe?"

"Zaffira's husband. I asked Cletus about him, once. I just thought it was such a peculiar name. Cletus said it was Italian for Job."

The flight attendant arrived with their coffee. They took the cups and thanked her. She headed for the back of the plane. Lindsey hoped that she would have some time off after they reached New York. If she had to fly again she'd be crawling up the aisle.

"I spoke with Marcie Sokolov while you were still packing at the Villa del Parco. She wants to talk to us when we get in. Mainly to me. But I think she has a kind of crush on you, Petrus, for the way you took out Merle Oates."

"I don't like to kill anyone. I don't like starting at my age, and I won't get over that soon. I don't care what kind of thug he was."

"Even so."

"What about Alcide Palmiro Castellini, Hobart? We keep coming back to him, and he keeps sliding away. We can't even have a conversation about him, he's so slippery."

"Sokolov wouldn't say much on the phone, but it looks as if she's after him. NYPD is trying to get the Feds involved. Try and make a John Gotti case out of it. Maybe even try and get up a RICO proceeding. If they can get Cele Johnston to help them, they might have a chance."

Berry grunted. He sipped his coffee, then lowered the cup to the folding tray in front of him. "You think she'll buy into that?"

Lindsey pondered for a while. He looked out the window again. The jet was skimming the top of a formation of clouds. He closed his eyes and leaned his head against the Plexiglas once more. At this rate he was going to leave a permanent forehead print there.

"Hobart?" Berry asked.

He opened his eyes and took a sip of coffee.

"Don't spill that on yourself," Berry warned.

Lindsey drank some more of the coffee. It wasn't too bad. Bad enough but not too bad. He put the cup down empty. "I don't think Cele Johnston will go for it. Not for a minute. Give up her fancy frou-frou antiques business on Fifty-seventh Street to take a cover job as an office manager for a restaurant supply company in Dubuque? Not a chance."

"But if she testifies openly and doesn't go into the program . . ." Berry left the sentence there. He didn't have to complete it.

"Funny thing is," Lindsey said, "Castellini tried to recruit me into his operation. He knew I was SPUDS, knew I'd worked with Cletus. He figured I knew where the chariot was, or at least that I'd find it. If he was in with Harry Scott and Moe Zissler—what a bunch, what a bunch! If I wouldn't find the toy and fetch it for him, he'd let me find it for myself, then have Scott or Zissler retrieve it for him. Scott funked it, Zissler screwed up, no chariot for Castellini."

"Are you sure Zissler was working for Castellini?" Berry asked. "Scott was involved, that's pretty obvious. But do you think Zissler was a freelance? You think he followed you around, Hobart, and decided he'd just make a preemptive strike and grab the chariot for himself?"

"I don't think so." Lindsey sighed. "I don't think he was smart enough for that. I think he was just another Castellini pawn. Maybe he was supposed to report in and take his orders from Harry Scott. I kind of think that was the plan. You know, Petrus, we became quite a team, didn't we?"

"That we did." Berry nodded. "That we did."

Lindsey toyed with his empty coffee cup, considered asking the attendant for a refill, decided it wasn't worth the trouble. He'd get something better when they reached New York. This time there would be no Morris Zissler to pick them up in his freshly washed white Buick, humming and blowing peppermint on them. This time Detective Marcie Sokolov had arranged a ride in a police cruiser from the airport into Manhattan.

Lindsey let out a long, deep breath. "I think they'll get Castellini, but it won't be fast and it won't be easy. It'll probably take as long to get Castellini as it will to get the insurance money back from the Italian government. And as for Castellini's pal Randolph Amoroso . . ."

Berry looked at him, waiting.

"If anything good comes out of this, at least Amoroso doesn't get his magic talisman. I don't know if that will stop him from getting into the Senate, but it just might. It just might. And Oliver Shea can go to Washington and try and do some good. Let him pretend to be Jimmy Stewart."

Petrus Berry said, "All politics is shit, Hobart."

Lindsey said, "You've said that before."

Berry said, "I'll say it again. We old guys say the same things again a lot. All politics—"

"Okay," Lindsey said, "I get the point."

The plane landed as dawn broke to the east. But once the jet dipped below the cloud layer, Lindsey saw that it was snowing again. They'd left Rome late in the afternoon of Christmas Day, and they were landing in New York early on the morning of the day after Christmas. In homes across the land presents had been opened, the happy tension had been released, and tens of millions of children and their elders were suffering from a kind of asexual postcoital *tristesse*.

Officer Gulbenkian met them at the mouth of the jetway, hustled them through customs, and got them back to Zaffira Fornari's brownstone flat. Gulbenkian said that Lieutenant Sokolov had told him to stay with them until they'd rested up, then escort them to Midtown North.

Petrus Berry said, "That's just fine with me. I'm headed for a shower and bed."

Lindsey nodded. They'd both dropped their flight bags in the vestibule and he realized that he didn't want that second cup of coffee or anything else to eat or drink. He felt tired and stale and desperately in need of hot soapy water. He rubbed his hand across his face. A shave, too. He badly needed a shave.

Petrus Berry had seized the bathroom. There was only one in the flat. Well, Zaffira Fornari would only need one.

Lindsey was afraid that if he sat down, even to untie his shoes, he would be unable to get up again. And Berry had the bathroom. Berry had the bathroom. Lindsey looked at Gulbenkian. He sat impassively near the door to the third-floor landing, his uniform cap and warm coat nearby, his holstered pistol on his hip.

Suddenly something grabbed inside Lindsey's chest. The robin—had the robin lost its way again, doubled back again, returned to the garden, the one place that it knew? If it had, Lindsey was certain, it was dead by now.

He crossed the living room to the French doors and opened them and stepped outside onto the tiny balcony. The morning was cold, but for once more bracing than chilling. He looked down into the garden. Even from here he could see that the snow was easily a foot deep. If the robin was there, it had died and been covered while Lindsey and Berry were in Rome. He couldn't shovel out the garden; he didn't even know whose garden it really was. The only way to know was to wait for the snow to melt and look for the robin.

He stepped back inside and closed the French doors behind him. Petrus Berry had finished his shower. Lindsey scrubbed and shaved and climbed into his makeshift bed on Zaffira Fornari's couch. He fell asleep even before the magic projector could begin showing a movie on the ceiling.

Lindsey knew that he and Petrus Berry weren't prisoners or even suspects. They'd been through that in Rome; the *poliziotti* and the *intendatore* and the *console americano* and the Italian *avvocato* that the *console* had got for them had dealt with that. Things had looked hairy for a little while. Harry Scott, of all people, had seemed more of an obstruction than an asset.

That was before the messages began zipping back and forth between the American consulate and the embassy in Rome, Marcie

Sokolov at the NYPD, the U.S. Customs Service, the Italian government, and last but not least International Surety. Not IS in the United States, not SPUDS, but International Surety/World Headquarters.

It was classic, Lindsey thought. It could have been an episode of the old "Four-Star Playhouse" series, with Dick Powell playing Dante the cabaret owner and sometimes, de facto private eye. Bring enough pressure on the weak underling and he'll betray his boss the big shot every time.

Desmond Richelieu hadn't gotten the right scoop on Harry Scott—or the complete scoop, anyway. Scott and his bella signora had disappeared, okay, but not before Scott gave up Alcide Castellini in exchange for a Get-out-of-jail-free card for himself and his gorgeous Italian wife. They weren't part of the U.S. Marshal's witness protection program, either. They were gone, living the good life in—Lindsey was never able to find out, through official channels.

But if you ask him if he got a little help from his friend Anna Maria Berry, he would probably change the subject before answering.

Lindsey and Petrus Berry were sitting opposite Marcie Sokolov now. Lindsey found himself staring at Sokolov's newest lapel decoration. Christmas was over, New Year's was coming, and she wore a lapel pin in the shape of a silk top hat and walking stick. The top hat and stick were shiny and black. The head of the stick was a miniature lightbulb that flashed on and off every half second.

The few wreaths and Christmas streamers that had brightened Manhattan North had disappeared into whatever black hole such decorations return to every winter.

Sokolov and Berry were talking and then there was a silence and Sokolov said something that ended with, "Don't you think, Lindsey?"

Lindsey shook his head and made an inarticulate noise.

"Don't zone out on me now." Sokolov frowned. "I know

you're tired. Jet-lagged. But you gotta hang in there just a little longer."

Lindsey inhaled deeply and rubbed his forehead hard. Maybe that would make the blood circulate to his brain. He said, "I'm sorry. Say again."

"Just a passing comment. Agatha Christie would have loved this. The old, least-likely-suspect theory. At first I really did think that Cletus Berry's murder was a random killing, or at most that he'd gotten mixed up with the wrong crowd and got killed for his trouble. After a while you convinced me that Alcide Castellini was involved."

"Have you arrested him?"

"The Feds have. They're doing the mambo over his art-smuggling racket."

"That's swell." Lindsey heard the bitterness in his own voice. "What about the killings?"

Sokolov chewed her lips. The tiny light on top of the miniature walking stick on her lapel flashed on and off. "We're working with the Feds. This is going to turn into the biggest thing since John Gotti finally went down. Castellini is standing in a pit right now, neck deep in pig shit, and the customs fellas and the DA's people are just throwing more and more of it at him, a bucket at a time. The only one who might have saved him was his buddy Randolph Amoroso, and he's running away from Castellini just as fast as his shapely little legs can carry him. Not that it's going to save him. The party bosses are scared now, and *they're* running away from *him*, and that makes it look like a free trip to Washington for Oliver Shea."

Petrus Berry said, "That's politics for you."

"I just can't understand Moe Zissler." Lindsey was coming awake again, rubbing the sides of his neck and then his cheeks.

Petrus Berry said, "Why not, Lindsey? Because he worked for your precious International Surety corporation?" He made an angry hissing sound. "So did Cletus."

"I know." Lindsey nodded sadly. "You just—I don't know— I should know better by this time. You just think that a crook is some guy wearing a black shirt and a yellow tie."

"I saw the same flick," Sokolov put in. "He's got a scar on his cheek, and he likes to slap women and kick puppies."

"Not so." Petrus Berry sighed. "Well, maybe he is. Sometimes. Castellini sounds like a classic."

"Good old Alcide." Sokolov toyed with her top-hat pin. "And sometimes a decent guy like Benjamino Bermudez just gets in the way."

"You think that's what happened?" Lindsey asked.

"I'd bet a pair of Knicks tickets on it," Sokolov said. "My partner Roland Roscoe took that question on while you fellers were out of town. He went right along with your theory, Lindsey. Castellini was getting panicky after Cletus Berry's death. That was supposed to be a quiet little misfortune. There was too much fuss being raised. Largely by you, I should add."

She tapped Lindsey's sleeve with a startling, scarlet-painted fingernail.

"He had to get up to Berry's nest and vacuum the files. He was familiar enough in the Torrington to get in at night, but he couldn't have poor Mino telling us he was there. So—" She made a toy gun of her hand and pointed it at Lindsey and said, "Pow!"

She grinned. "For once he pulled the trigger himself. It's going to be a bitch to prove it, but that's the one that will make Miss Marcie a happy little she-dick."

"Pinning a Castellini to the wall is almost fun, isn't it," Petrus Berry asked.

Sokolov said, "You bet it is."

"But what if the nasty isn't a Castellini?" Berry resumed. "What if he's just another guy. Loves his wife and kids and roots for the Knicks and he brings home a big tree at Christmas and trims it all up for Santa. But he smuggles things or robs banks or he kills people for a living. He's your next-door neighbor. What if he's a decent man who just—what if he's your brother?"

Lindsey asked, "Why would—?" He felt like a fool. The moment the words were out of his mouth he wished he could call them back but it was too late.

Petrus Berry said, "I was a cop for thirty years and I can't tell you that. What about you, Detective Sokolov, do you know?"

Sokolov said, "Christ, Petrus, ask me a hard one, why don't you?" Her telephone made a peculiar sound and she picked it up and murmured into it. She put it down and said, "Look, this is going to take months to clean up. Maybe years. We have a permanent address for both of you?" Without waiting for an answer she opened a manila folder, nodded, then laid it down. She looked from Lindsey to Berry and back. "Pinopolis, South Carolina? Denver?"

Berry said, "I may stay in New York. I've got my pension and my Social Security. Anna Maria's my only kin. If Zaffira moves in with Ester and Anna Maria maybe I can get her place. Permanently. I want to be near that little girl. I can't replace her daddy but at least she'll have an uncle."

"Okay. Good. Lindsey?"

"I'm headed back. If you don't need me, I'll be on the first flight I can."

"Long as we can reach you."

Lindsey got halfway out of his chair, then slid back down. "One thing I don't understand."

Sokolov raised her eyebrows.

"Castellini and his, ah, associates—"

Sokolov nodded encouragingly.

"They didn't mind killing people. I've worked on murder cases before, even cases where there was more than one murder. But I've never been involved in one where they just keep killing and killing."

Sokolov and Petrus Berry waited.

"Why," Lindsey asked, "didn't Castellini have me killed before I ever left for Italy? I was getting into his plans, I was stirring things up and making trouble for him. And he didn't mind having people killed."

Sokolov and Berry exchanged glances.

Lindsey waited. Sokolov's walking stick blinked on, off, on. Finally she said, "I'm sorry, Lindsey, if this hurts your ego."

Lindsey widened his eyes. "Go ahead."

"You were a pimple. Alcide Castellini could have popped you anytime but then you might have got infected. You understand what I'm saying? This case only blew up on him to start with because he took Cletus Berry out. Or had him taken out. Then your company sent you in. I know who your boss is. I know about Desmond Richelieu. And so does Alcide Castellini. Castellini might not have been afraid of the NYPD, but he didn't want to take on Desmond Richelieu. If Castellini took you out he'd have Richelieu himself to contend with. He figured it was easier to leave you in place than to deal with somebody tougher."

Lindsey stood up. Petrus Berry hesitated, then did the same. Lindsey shook hands with Marcie Sokolov, waited while Berry did so, then turned and started away from Sokolov's desk.

Then he turned back. He waited, for some reason, for her walking stick to blink a couple of times. Then he said, "That's what Castellini thought, is it?"

Sokolov said, "That's my guess."

Lindsey said, "That doesn't hurt my ego. Castellini's going to get his, sooner or later. He's—how did you put it so elegantly?—neck deep in pig shit and they're throwing more of it at him. And I am going home."

Chapter Twenty-five

LINDSEY BOOKED HIS own flight back to Denver. He didn't have much packing to do. Some paperwork at Midtown North and some more at the U.S. Attorney's office. He was starting to feel as if he and Petrus Berry were the Hardy Boys.

He had walked into a family smashed by grief, and helped them to find a degree of peace and hope of justice. But that was tempered by the dawning realization that Cletus Berry, paterfamilias, had been dirty for most of the past two decades.

Faithful husband, loving father, dear brother, criminal.

It was strange, Lindsey thought, how he had taken to New York. As apprehensive as he'd been before his arrival, he'd found its astonishing dynamism a challenge and then a pleasure. And the great city had lived up to its promise as a town with a heart. Trouble was, to find it, you had to peel away the layers of anger and filth.

He'd succeeded, but now he was going home.

Petrus Berry proposed a farewell dinner. Hobart Lindsey agreed, and suggested that Ester and Zaffira and Anna Maria be included in the invitation. International Surety would pick up the tab.

They were assembled in the Seventy-third Street apartment. Lindsey and Petrus Berry announced the plan. Anna Maria wore a Rangers jersey and jeans. She held little Ezio Pinza on her lap. Ester and Zaffira, still in black, the mirrors and pictures on their walls still covered, declined.

"But Anna Maria should go," Ester urged. "She needs to live."

"You, too, *Sorella, Shvester.*" Zaffira touched her sister's cheek. "Live. Live!"

Ester shivered visibly. "Anna Maria, go. With your uncle and Mr. Lindsey. Try to enjoy your dinner."

Anna Maria put her dog on the floor. "Can I bring Shoshana?" Ester looked to Lindsey. He said, "Of course." Anna Maria headed for her room. Almost at once Lindsey heard the squeal of a questing modem and the clicking of her computer keyboard.

Anna Maria emerged from her room. She had worked a magic trick and changed her clothing in an instant, to a pale button-down shirt, plaid woolen skirt, and black tights. She had metamorphosed into a slim, vibrant woman of twenty. The brilliant mind that shone from her eyes was equaled only by her olive beauty.

She crossed the living room to Ester's side. She pressed her face against her mother's shoulder. Ester folded her black-clad arms around her. "Shoshana says she can come but her mom says we have to eat at her dad's restaurant. She'll meet us downstairs."

She turned those dark eyes on Lindsey, those deep eyes. To the two men she said, "You'll like it. It's a real New York place."

Lindsey blinked and she was a little girl again. She had reached inside of him and grasped his heart in her small hands. He realized that he had fallen in father-love with this child. That was the story of his life. Whom he loved, he lost.

Shoshana was a lighter-skinned version of Anna Maria. Another pair of sisters beneath the skin. Lindsey and Petrus Berry and the girls caught a cab on Lexington Avenue and headed downtown through slush-filled streets to Pete's Tavern.

As the neighborhoods changed, so did Anna Maria's air. By the time they reached the low fifties she put her hand on Lindsey's sleeve.

"Tell me about my cousin."

Lindsey had been staring at the city's lights, his eyes and his mind out of focus. "Your cousin?"

"Mosé. And Abramo and Sara, too. They're my aunt and uncle, I'm entitled to know. But mainly I want to know about Mosé."

Lindsey looked at Cletus Berry. Berry nodded. Lindsey said, "Abramo and Sara. They're from the old school. They seem much older than your mother or your Aunt Zaffira. Sara"—he smiled at the recollection—"she speaks this wonderful language all her own. Yiddish and Italian and Hebrew and English all mixed together. And your uncle—Abramo is a quiet man. Serious. They were very kind to Cletus and me. I don't know what else to tell you. I'm sorry. That's not much, is it?"

"What about Mosé?" They passed a window illuminated with green neon and the reflection flashed from her eyes like a double laser beam. "What about my cousin?"

"He's a lot like you, I think. He even looks a little bit like you. Smart. He's interested in history."

"I know that."

"But I think he's more interested in the future. He cares about the past but—he's just a little boy, Anna Maria."

"I know that."

"Well, then." Lindsey didn't know what else to say.

"Girls mature faster than boys," Anna Maria said. Her friend Shoshana nodded in agreement. Lindsey thought, *You bet they do.* "I want to visit him," Anna Maria resumed. "My cousin and my other relatives. I want to go to Italy and to Israel and to Africa. I'm African too and I want to find where my black ancestors came from, too."

Lindsey inhaled. "I think that would be a very good idea."

The cab pulled up at the restaurant. Lindsey paid the fare and made a note for his expense account. They picked their way over a soot-blackened berm and pushed their way into the warm, noisy restaurant.

The girls ran into the kitchen to visit Shoshana's dad.

The black-jacketed manager treated them like royalty. The place was dark and felt old. Polished wood and polished brass. Well-heeled, comfortable clientele. No sign of the uptown, Broadway crowd, and not a tourist among them, that was for sure.

Had Victor Hopkins and Millicent Martinelli shared a romantic dinner here before she wound up with duct tape over her mouth and nose? Perhaps. Had Cele Johnston dined here with the anonymous customer who later backed out of her big-buck purchase and sent Johnston into a seething, silent rage? That seemed less likely.

Lindsey and Berry settled at a white linen-topped table. They ordered only ice water. Before long the two girls strode back from the kitchen, not squealing children but young princesses, aware of the power they were coming into and reveling in it.

Petrus Berry signaled the waiter and asked for menus for four but the waiter said it was taken care of.

Soon the food arrived. A steak for Lindsey, just this side of rare, and another for Berry. Lindsey had largely abandoned red meat, yielding to the mood of the times, but somehow this was right. The girls had pasta with seafood. Not kosher—Lindsey knew that, thanks to Eric Coffman—but if Shoshana's father was the chef here then the families must have reached an accommodation with the world.

Shoshana said, "My dad is one of the top chefs in the whole city. There was an article about him in *New York*."

Lindsey said, "We have some pretty good restaurants in Denver, too. And in San Francisco."

Shoshana smiled condescendingly.

"Maybe I'll take you girls to see Pinopolis some time." Petrus Berry tore the corner off a roll and dipped it into the juice of his steak. "Bad manners," he said. Then, "Shoshana, I think you're right about your dad."

Something made Lindsey look up. He was facing the street entrance of the restaurant, his back to the kitchen. Sitting in a hard bentwood chair, he could scan the length of the dining room. Between him and the street door, dining with their heads close together, sat Alcide Palmiro Castellini, his flunky Campana, and the nameless woman who had greeted Lindsey at the Stanford White house.

Lindsey froze. Had they been there all along? Had he and Berry and the two girls walked past their table and never noticed them? Or had Castellini and company arrived after Lindsey and Berry were seated at their own table, while the girls were visiting in the kitchen?

Whichever it was, he should have known. Or at least been on the alert. The restaurant was within whistling distance of Gramercy Park. Somehow Lindsey had expected that Castellini would dine at home, especially under the circumstances, but obviously he'd been wrong on that count.

Castellini wore another of his elegantly tailored suits. His perfectly groomed hair caught the soft light of the old-fashioned fixtures. His teeth shone. He lifted a glass of red wine and sipped cautiously. Across the rim of his glass he made eye contact with Lindsey. Then he reached across his table with his free hand and took the hands of his two companions, like a fond elder benignly playing Cupid for the shy younger couple. He turned his eye from Lindsey, not pausing first to wink.

Lindsey turned back to his own party. Anna Maria was alternately animated and subdued. Shoshana followed her best friend's moods. The girls demanded a recounting of Lindsey and Berry's adventure in Rome. Lindsey had answered Anna Maria's questions in the cab, but she pressed him for details.

"What did my Aunt Sara make for dinner? What does the Via del Portico d'Ottavia look like? What kind of cabs do they drive in Rome? Do they have a subway? Did you go shopping?"

She could have asked her cousin the same questions but there must still be a place in the world for people to sit face-to-face and talk without the help of a computer. Lindsey did his best. He handed off half the questions to Petrus Berry. Anna Maria couldn't hear enough about her cousin Mosé and his parents. She wanted to learn everything about Professore Pacinelli. She was fascinated by the Jewish catacombs beneath the Grand Temple.

Lindsey glanced up, checking the Castellini table often. Castellini sat at a right angle to the front door. He could swivel his head ninety degrees and see the entrance to the restaurant or Lindsey and his companions. Lindsey hoped that the two girls would leave the table again, and finally they did, just before dessert was served, to visit Shoshana's father.

As soon as they were out of sight, Lindsey leaned forward and told Berry that Castellini and associates were a few tables away.

Berry nodded and answered in a low rumble, "Of course. They got here same time as the breadsticks."

Lindsey had another glimpse of Castellini, then looked beyond him.

The glass and brass front doors of the tavern were steamed against the cold Manhattan night. Even so, Lindsey could see the telltale police cruiser flashers outside. The steamed doors swung open to admit a party of men and women, some in uniform. Two uniformed New York City cops stationed themselves in the doorway.

As the newcomers in civilian clothes moved into the restaurant Lindsey recognized Marcie Sokolov and her partner, Detective Roland Roscoe. Roscoe had cleaned up his act—shaved and combed his hair and climbed into a clean jacket and slacks. He was barely recognizable. Sokolov was dressed for success, but the cane-and-top-hat pin was winking steadily on her lapel. There was a look of almost sexual excitement on her face.

Campana started from his chair. One hand moved toward his shoulder. At the same moment Lindsey sensed Petrus Berry tensing, reaching toward his own shoulder. But Castellini grabbed Campana's wrist and pulled him back into his seat.

Castellini shot a look of cold fury at Campana. They made a frozen tableau. Lindsey counted the beats silently. *One, two.* Campana lowered his hands slowly to the white tablecloth. Castellini and their young woman companion did the same. Lindsey could see Castellini nod slightly and mouth something that looked like, "All right, then."

Cletus Berry nodded and smiled. "I liked that," he said.

Lindsey shook his head. "You liked it," he echoed.

Under Marcie Sokolov's direction, uniformed officers brought Castellini's party to their feet. They removed weapons from all three. The woman even had a small revolver in her purse. When he saw that Lindsey wished he had a camcorder with him.

"Could have been very difficult," Petrus Berry said. "Very dangerous. You have to make the suspect aware that resistance is futile before he does something foolish and nasty. You don't want a shoot-out. Especially in a crowd."

"We went through one together, Petrus."

"Sometimes you can't help it. But if Mr. Castellini or either of his helpers thought they could blast their way out of here—wouldn't have made much sense, where would they go, how could they hide—but if one of them panicked and drew a weapon, the police might have fired first. And look—there must be seventy-five, hundred people in here. All crowded in together. Cop could get shot. Civilians could get shot. It could have been nasty. Bloody. Very, very bad." He picked up the remnant of his crisp dinner roll and crunched it between his teeth.

In minutes Sokolov and the cops and Castellini and his pals were gone. At a table near Lindsey's, an attractive dark-haired woman was complaining to her husband that her food was slow in coming. Her husband was a lanky, worried-looking man. Behind thick glasses he blinked, then he said, "It's all right, just share mine until yours arrives."

Anna Maria and Shoshana returned from the kitchen. They'd missed the excitement. The room full of blasé New Yorkers went on eating and drinking.

Dessert was cream puffs with chocolate sauce and whipped cream. Berry pitched into the confection but Lindsey stared at his, unable to touch it, wishing he could preserve it as a memento. Instead, Anna Maria and Shoshana split it.

"One divides," Shoshana began.

"And one decides," Anna Maria concluded.

Desmond Richelieu said, "This is a hell of a thing, Lindsey." The sunlight glinted off his gold-rimmed glasses.

For some reason Rome seemed very near to Lindsey; his experiences there, very real. By contrast, his time in New York was more like a vivid dream or a visit to a virtual reality parlor. Every color and sound, every meal and every walk through slush-edged streets, was vivid in his memory; vivid but unreal.

"We found the chariot," Lindsey said, "and the company is entitled to get its money back." He paused. "If we're not in any hurry."

Richelieu swung around in his swivel chair and gazed up at the portrait of J. Edgar Hoover. When he swung back his head drooped. "The chief in a dress," he whispered. "In a dress."

To Lindsey he said, "You've done it again, buster. I send you on a straightforward assignment and you wind up, up to your neck in crazy complications."

Lindsey spread his hands. "You want me to go back to paying for fender benders? Why did you shanghai me into SPUDS? You knew what you were getting."

"New York SPUDS is in trouble," Richelieu said. "*We're* in trouble. Harry Scott was a shock, but that's IS International's problem. And Morris Zissler—who'd have thought it?"

"Not me," Lindsey admitted. "I didn't think he had the brains to brown-bag a lunch and claim a fancy meal on his expense account."

Richelieu smiled ruefully and snorted softly at that.

"But Cletus Berry. God damn. Cletus Berry. He was one of my own. We were family. I sent you to nail the bastard who killed a member of my family, Lindsey, and you discovered that he was dirty. I can't get over it."

He stood and strode to the window, gazed down at the stream and the grassy park outside IS's suite in the Denver high-rise. There was a January thaw in the air. The ice clogging the stream had broken up and the fresh water was flowing again. The snow had melted enough to show patches of green against the white.

One thing about Denver snow, it stayed a lot cleaner than New York snow.

Richelieu spun on his heel.

"Lindsey," he barked. "Lindsey, how would you like to go put New York back together for me?"

Petrus Berry was in New York. Anna Maria Berry was in New York. It was something to think about. Marcie Sokolov was in New York.

Lindsey did not feel compelled to answer at once.

Author's Note

WHEN THE INITIAL volume in this series, *The Comic Book Killer*, was first published, a number of readers wrote to me to inquire whether the "MacGuffin" of that story actually existed. The MacGuffin was a 1953 comic book, *Gangsters at War #27*, and it actually did (and still does) exist, although the metaphysics and epistemology by which its existence could be determined were more than slightly ambiguous, and not unconvoluted.

Later volumes involved other MacGuffins—a 1928 Duesenberg Phaeton; a 1931 film called *The Werewolf of Harlem*; a World War II–era bomber named *Bessie Blue*; and a 1951 paperback novel titled *Death in the Ditch*. Questions arose in each case as to whether the object written about was real or fictitious. Once more, the question is simple but the answer is not.

And even before *The Silver Chariot Killer* was completed, fans and followers of the International Surety novels were inquiring, *Is the chariot real? Or are you just making this up?* And the answer is, *Maybe a little of each.*

Stay with me for a few paragraphs, please.

Over the course of my long writing career I have uncounted times received the compliment, "You have such a wonderful imagination." Alas, while kind, these words are not accurate. The truth is, I have one of the world's most impoverished imaginations. Sometimes I'm not sure that I have one at all.

My main writing tools are observation and description. That which I have not personally experienced, or witnessed, I base on vicarious experience that I obtain through research. When time and my budget permit, I visit the locales of my books. I try to interview participants in events about which I write. Failing this, I ask authorities on the subject, look at artifacts in museums, or study books, periodicals, photographs, films, and audio and video recordings.

In preparing to write *The Silver Chariot Killer* I received invaluable assistance from many friends and associates. These included Professor Patrick Egan of San Francisco State University and my colleagues Steven Saylor and Colleen McCullough, all of whom know far more about the classical world than I could ever hope to learn.

My wife, Patricia E. Lupoff, shared with me her experiences exploring the catacombs beneath Rome.

For information on topics of Judaica I turned, as ever, to my dear friend Ira Steingroot, and for guidance to information on events in Italy before and during World War II, Ms. Elissa Mondschein. Information on conditions in Italy in the years following World War II was provided with wondrous graphic detail by Ms. Dori Gores.

Information concerning the New York World's Fair of 1939/1940 came from several sources, but chiefly from my own recollections, colorful and vivid after fifty-six years. My gratitude to the shades of those dear family members, all of them now deceased, who made for me this mitzvah.

Assistance in colloquializing my crude and stumbling Italian and Yiddish was provided by Ms. Eve Buckner.

And details to refresh my decades-old recollections of Manhattan geography were provided by Messrs. Larry Block and Gordon Van Gelder.

All in all, *The Silver Chariot Killer* is based with as much accuracy as I could muster on real places and events. On the other hand, it *is* a novel. By definition, it is a work of fiction. As for the silver chariot itself—it would be presumptuous to suggest that it is as real as that so-famous black bird, the stuff that dreams are made of—but I would hope someday that it would achieve a similar, if lesser, degree of reality.

Finally, a message for the staff of Pete's Tavern: Keep that spaghetti hot; the dark-haired lady is coming back for her dinner!

Richard A. Lupoff
Near the Pacific Ocean, 1996